Mme. Proust and the Kosher Kitchen

MME. PROUST and the KOSHER KITCHEN

KATE TAYLOR

DOUBLEDAY CANADA

Doubleday Canada and colophon are trademarks.

NATIONAL LIBRARY OF CANADA CATALOGUING IN PUBLICATION DATA

Taylor, Kate, 1962–
Mme. Proust and the kosher kitchen

ISBN 0-385-65834-6

I. Title.

PS8589.A896M34 2002   C811'.6   C2002-900513-2
PR9199.4.T39M34 2002

Jacket images: Kara Kosaka
Jacket and text design: CS Richardson
Printed and bound in the USA

Published in Canada by
Doubleday Canada, a division of
Random House of Canada Limited

Visit Random House of Canada Limited's website: www.randomhouse.ca

RRD   10   9   8   7   6   5   4   3   2   1

for the companions of childhood:
Andrew, Sarah, Pegatha, and James

"Life is very nice, but it has no shape.
The object of art is actually to give it some . . ."

—Jean Anouilh, *The Rehearsal*

S OPHIE NEEDED SOME STONES, but could not think where she might find any in the midst of the city. She wasn't looking for a great boulder, but neither would she be satisfied with the few scrapings of gravel she could surreptitiously remove from the tiny, urbanized garden that jutted but a metre onto the pavement in front of the ground-floor flat in the building three doors down from her own. Wondering where she could get more sizable specimens, she remembered now with fondness and regret the tin bucket of pebbles and seashells that the child had kept in her bedroom for many years, souvenirs of their holidays that the little one had gathered on the beach and then refused to part with when it came time to get on the train and return home. And Sophie recalled too their regular walks in the nearby woods where there must surely be some stray rocks lying about beneath the trees. But the child was older and far away now, the tin bucket long since discarded. The family had not taken a trip to the Norman coast since the war began, and although the entrance to the Bois de Boulogne was but ten minutes on foot from the apartment, Sophie was increasingly cautious about venturing any further than the baker's shop at the corner and did not want to risk an extra outing on top of today's mission. She would just have to rely on finding stones at her destination.

She noted with relief that Philippe had also gone out earlier that morning, so that she did not need to explain her own departure.

Communication was increasingly strained between them and she lacked the energy to think of a lie that might cover her as she pulled open the apartment's heavy oak door. As long as the child was still with them, they had been united in their plans and resolute in their execution. Their daughter was to find safety, even if it cost Sophie and Philippe their life savings. But once word had got back, nine long weeks after the night they had parted, that her group had made it through the checkpoint at Hendaye and safely crossed into Spain, then their focus dissolved and their unity fractured.

At first, Philippe had sought Sophie's permission before he sold anything. From the start they had agreed that the silverware, their wedding gift from her mother, each piece so delicately etched with a tracery of vines, was sacrosanct, and then they had agonized together over what was more dispensable. But now she realized what he took only when she noticed it missing. Sitting reading in the salon, she would look up to the marble mantel to check the time and find that the gilded clock with figures of wood nymphs holding up its white-and-black face was not there. Reaching into the china cupboard for a plate onto which she could arrange a meagre meal of boiled potatoes and white beans, she would sense that it seemed less crowded than before and realize that the Sèvres was gone.

These losses were unspoken and Philippe no longer told her of his plans, but she knew that he was probably visiting another dealer that morning. These days that was the only reason he had to leave the apartment. When they first imposed the quotas and he lost his practice, he was out every day, hurrying down to the Cité on the Métro because Maître Richelieu gave him work clerking in his office. But Philippe could no longer take the risk of the daily trip any more than his former colleague could take the risk of hiring him. He spent his days reading the newspaper and sorting uselessly through his old files. Suspended between their former life and some uncertain future, they seemed for the moment to have abandoned time. Increasingly, Sophie longed for something to disrupt this condition and had begun to think that when a knock came on the door, it would be nothing but a relief.

She just had this last task to complete. She belted her drab-coloured trench coat firmly around her—she would need its strong, deep pockets to carry any stones she did find—and slipped quietly onto the landing. She peered over the wrought-iron banisters down four floors to the hallway, checking that Mme. Delisle was not about, sweeping the carpet or polishing the brass newel posts. The hall was empty for the moment and Sophie walked swiftly but silently downstairs. She moved without sound down the last flight, glided across the empty hallway like a ghost, and stepped out into the street.

She walked towards the Métro quickly, attempting to set a pace that was rapid enough to suggest legitimate business but not so hurried as to hint at flight. The day was pleasant, still hot although it was now mid-October, and despite herself, she warmed to the light on her face. From La Muette, the stop where she had safely and thoughtlessly boarded a train so many times before, she took the Métro eastward, keeping her head down so as not to catch anyone's eye, anxiously scanning not the faces of the other passengers but their equally revealing footwear. She was fearfully looking for the well-polished leather boots that would belong to either a gendarme or a German officer, but she saw none and forty minutes later arrived without incident at her stop, Père Lachaise.

This is the most famous cemetery in Paris. As she entered the gates, Sophie heard herself saying these words in her head like some sort of tour guide, and she realized that she was talking to her daughter. This is the most famous cemetery in Paris, she continued as she started up one of the beaten dirt paths, home to Sarah Bernhardt, Oscar Wilde, and Marcel Proust. Look, dear, there is the grave of Alfred de Musset, there with the little willow tree. He's the man our street is named for, a great writer. Privately, she had always thought the tree was ridiculous. The poet had requested that he be buried beneath a willow, and instead of finding some suitable riverbank, his family had put him in Père Lachaise and planted this pathetic specimen above the grave. But Sophie would not share this criticism with her daughter.

This is where France's great artists are laid to rest, she would continue, the writer Alphonse Daudet is here, so are the painters Géricault and Delacroix, the playwright Beaumarchais, the poetess Anna de Noailles, and Georges Bizet, the composer who created *Carmen*. This is where the Faubourg Saint-Germain comes to a bitter end. That monument holds the bones of the de Guiches. The de Brancovans are here somewhere, the Rothschilds, all the great families. There's the Comte de Montesquiou, a famous dandy in his day. And look, that's the grave of Félix Faure, president of the Republic. Died in his mistress's arms at the height of the Dreyfus affair. Not that you would tell such a thing to a girl not yet twelve, any more than you could explain how the English writer Oscar Wilde came to be buried in Paris, exiled and disgraced.

As she spotted the Faure monument, Sophie also noticed a rough patch of clear ground beyond it, where there was space for some future grave. She approached and started kicking through dried leaves and half-dead grass with the toe of her shoe. Soon she found what she was looking for, a round pebble about double the size of a one-franc coin. By dint of more kicking, she amassed half a dozen such stones, putting them in her pockets, before moving up the hill towards the top of the cemetery.

As she arrived at her own graves, Sophie realized why she was talking to her daughter. She should have brought the child here before she left. The thought had not occurred to Sophie then, there had been so little time, only a day to pack a bag small enough that a little girl might carry it by herself, to make promises, to cherish her for a moment, a moment cut short when a lady and a gentleman arrived to pick her up ten minutes before the appointed hour. Well, Sophie would make up for it now, and she continued the guided tour in her head.

This is my family, she would say as she turned to the black marble monument inscribed with the name WEIL. Originally, they came from Metz, in Lorraine. We went there once, when you were little, well, you won't remember, you were very small. Anyway, it doesn't matter, we have all lived here in Paris for years and years. The men in my family were always business people. My great-grandfather made his fortune in buttons. Well, dear, everybody needs buttons, you know, and somebody has to make them. He had a whole factory where all they did was make buttons.

And my father, your *grand-père*, was a soldier, my dear, fought in the war. Not this war, the Great War, 1914. They awarded him the Croix de Guerre, a medal, for being brave at Verdun. He lived too, survived the trenches, but when he came home he caught the influenza. It killed many people in those days. Now they have all kinds of medicines, but back then it was different. You just got sick and died. I was only a little girl, I barely knew my own papa, but your grandfather was a hero, my dear. Don't forget that in the new place. Tell them your grandfather fought for France.

And there's *Grand-mère*. The summer before last, remember? Better that way, she was old, best that she should not have seen . . . well, better that way.

Sophie turned her head from her mother's name and looked down the path towards the grey stone that marked the grave of her in-laws. BENSIMON.

This is your father's family. They are unique, the only Bensimons in Paris. They were merchants once in Tangier and Amsterdam, but they have lived in France since the Revolution. They are grand Parisians now, and lawyers each and every one of them. Just like Papa.

Our people belong here, my dear. Oh yes, the Rothschilds, they were Napoleon's bankers, and Sarah Bernhardt, the most wonderful actress France has ever produced. She is over there somewhere, to your right. Henri Bergson is here, a philosopher, an old man. He died last year. It was his lungs, I think. And Marcel Proust, the famous writer, just over here. He too. Jewish. On his mother's side. She was a distant cousin of my father's, in fact. Yes, we are buried right alongside all the high and the mighty.

We belong here, my dear, in Paris. And here in Père Lachaise, all Paris is at our feet.

Sophie took some stones from her pocket, and balanced them carefully on the flat top of the Bensimon monument, before walking back to her own family's grave. Here, the upright grave marker was arched at the top, so she could find no safe place for her stones except on the ground. She dug them in a bit, calculating they would stay put longer that away. As she arranged them, it occurred to her that it would have been easier if she practised her neighbours' religion. She wouldn't have had to go grubbing for stones. The florists' shops had been all but empty that winter, but with summer their stock had improved and there were still pretty bouquets to be bought on the boulevards, little clusters of chrysanthemums one could bring to a grave. But if she practised her neighbours' religion . . . She brushed the thought away, stood back, and surveyed the effect. This was her remembrance, with stones, as was the tradition. The task was complete. Perhaps the knock would come that very night. Sophie was ready now for the next chapter.

The doctor is furiously angry with the English. He received a letter this morning from the ineffectual Dr. Thompson, filled with doubts and excuses, and citing all sorts of medical reasons why the plan cannot go ahead, which is all nonsense, of course. Just the British playing politics as usual. He got quite incensed about it at dinner yesterday, and when I asked how Dr. Thompson could possibly make any medical objections to the *cordon sanitaire,* Adrien exploded at me: "Of course, he cannot, he is just inventing them to satisfy some petty-minded officials at Whitehall." He was so violent about it that I permitted myself a gentle remonstrance. It is not my fault if the English are determined to thwart him and he really should keep his temper in front of the servants.

He calmed down enough to explain it has all got mixed up with Egypt—apparently the English are suspicious of our imperial ambitions in that direction! It would be risible if it were not sad. Adrien concluded by saying he did not give a damn who owned Egypt, he just wanted to save all Europeans from cholera, and I felt quite sorry for him. He truly means that and cares so much for the project, it has turned his head quite white in the last few years.

And he has put on several kilos already this autumn, yet we are almost two months from New Year's Day. All those holiday meals to get through. I have suggested to Félicie that we always have fruit or a jelly for dessert rather than a pâtisserie, although it does not seem fair to Dick to deprive him of his sweets just because his father does tend to overeat. At any rate, Félicie and I agreed we can try to keep our menus frugal at home, but neither of us can do anything about all the dinners. Even if I were to accompany Adrien more often, I could not stop those menus. There were both lobster and salmon before the beef and the veal when we dined at the Faures' last week, and five different cakes for dessert! The table did look beautiful and Madame was so soliticious, but I found the whole outing a strain.

Just eight more days.

PARIS. SATURDAY, NOVEMBER 8, 1890.
I put on grey this morning for the first time. I suppose I could have done so a month ago, but I have become accustomed to the colours of my grief. Adrien, who just stuck his head in the door before going into his office to see a patient, was very sweet about it, and said how well I looked. I imagine Marie-Marguerite will have something stronger to say when she arrives for tea this afternoon. While she is utterly sympathetic and kind, acknowledging fully the depth of my grief over the loss of Maman, she is always frank about death and feels we make too much of a show of mourning. She has already advised me several times that I must start receiving again as soon as the year is up. She says it is odd that just when we need our friends most, to comfort us in our bereavement, we invent rules to keep them apart from us. Not that I was ever one to be holding a salon. My day at home was never more than a few ladies enjoying a cup of tea and a little gossip. But I will venture out to others' houses more in the new year. I must remember to tell Marie-Marguerite I did attend the Faure dinner, even if I found it an intimidating debut.

I spent yesterday evening with Dick going over his philosophy essay very carefully, so there would be no repetition of last month's little tragedy. It is well written enough, and makes a strong argument for the triumph of the sciences (his father would be in complete agreement!), but we had to work very hard to eliminate all awkward constructions, which was what let him down last time. He certainly does not have his brother's fine style.

Seven days, only a week.

PARIS. SUNDAY, NOVEMBER 9, 1890.

We had a congenial family evening with a good rabbit stew. Marie-Marguerite was very tactful about the grey at tea time, so after she had left and I was changing for dinner, I tried a violet collar in place of my usual black and Georges paid me a compliment. He was in fine form last night. It is not that he misses Maman less than I do, but he manages to forget his loss once he is in good company or has launched into an amusing tale from the courts. Dick was delighted with a story his uncle says has been going around his colleagues about a judge who is notorious for retreating to his chambers to nap. The courtroom lawyers all claim they can hear his snoring out in the halls.

Georges was teasing Dick about medicine, telling him he would make a fine doctor, just like his father, and asking him about the science exam, calling him Robert all the time. (He says Dick is no name for a grown man and we must drop our pet name lest Robert be thought a baby when he gets to medical school.)

The men then had a great debate about pasteurization. They are all in favour, naturally, but Adrien says it cannot be used effectively until people understand its purpose. To illustrate his point, he had Jean fetch Félicie in from the kitchen to ask her opinion. She played her role admirably, saying she has never heard of such a thing and that it would ruin the taste of the milk, much to Adrien's amusement.

Six days.

PARIS. MONDAY, NOVEMBER 10, 1890.

Sometimes one's griefs get confused. I was just leaving my room after lunch yesterday afternoon, preparing to go out for my walk, when I caught sight of that photograph of Marcel taken a few years ago, just before he went up to the lycée. I found myself overcome with pain at the sight of those deep, dark eyes, and, alone in the room, started to weep. I retreated to the little sofa, struggling to keep my tears under control—I know how Adrien tires of such demonstrations and argues that much prolonged they can be only bad for the health—when I came to wonder at myself and ask why I was crying. Marcel, for all that his constitution worries me, is alive and well, and ready to return to us in five short days.

I think I was crying for Maman, or perhaps just the march of time, the children growing up, but mainly for Maman, I believe. Yet, sometimes, despite her death, it is Marcel I miss the most, feeling his absence throughout the apartment. My yearning for him is not a reasoned thing, retreating into the distance steadily as his return approaches, but rather varies wildly from one day to the next. One time it is a faint tinge one can easily ignore to get on with the day's business, another it is a great broad boulevard of pain that there is no avoiding. So, it all gets muddled.

"There is not a nook or corner in this house which does not wound me to the heart. Your room kills me." So wrote our dear de Sévigné after her daughter's departure.

PARIS. TUESDAY, NOVEMBER, 11, 1890.

Adrien says there is increasing doubt about whether this tuberculosis vaccine the Germans have invented is actually efficacious against the disease. He goes this afternoon to a meeting of the Permanent Commission at the Ministry and says de Fleury will tell him more, but he is afraid false hopes have been raised. I do admire the breadth of his concerns. Some of his colleagues become quite obsessed with their particular speciality and just reserve a little corner to themselves, never venturing out beyond it. Adrien would never ask why there is not a standing commission for the defence against cholera, rather he hurries over to help with tuberculosis. He still has such energy. Dick inherits that. I only wish Marcel did. I had hoped the year away from us would strengthen him, teach him some measure of control, but often I fear the reverse will be true and he will return to us with his digestion ruined and his temperament yet more prone to extravagance.

I went to Marie-Marguerite's yesterday afternoon and enjoyed a really fruitful tête-à-tête, one of those conversations that remind you why you are such great friends. Not that you need reminding—my affection for Marie-Marguerite never wavers—but sometimes you have these flashes of insight into a friendship. I was discussing how muddled I feel at times, and unable to distinguish between grief for Maman and missing Marcel, and she understood perfectly.

She was recalling an episode from the weeks before her wedding, on a day when she was supposed to see the dentist. Her mother decided that this was the time to impart to her some discreet details about what she might expect in the marriage bed. She said that in the carriage that afternoon, she had to keep reminding herself she was going to have a tooth examined—a nerve-racking experience in itself—not preparing for her wedding night. "Not that I wish to denigrate your tender feelings for Marcel and your late mother by comparing them to either toothache or nuptial bliss, but you know what I mean," she concluded, and we both had quite a good laugh over the odd mélange of life's trials we had somehow brought together in one conversation.

PARIS. WEDNESDAY, NOVEMBER 12, 1890.
I received a letter from Marcel this morning. It will be his last, of course, and annoyingly it had crossed with the one I had posted last week. As Mme. de Sévigné aptly noted: "The trouble with corresponding over long distances is that all the answers deal with the wrong cards."

If I recall correctly, however, she continued by saying that one must accept the gap as natural, for the stifling of one's thoughts would be altogether too constraining. Unfortunately, I wish I had stifled my thoughts about Marcel's diet, for now he reports that his bowels are loose again—if anything, tending too much that way—and I fear it would have been wiser to counsel him to eat a great deal of bread rather than avoid milk. My hope is that his return to Paris will enable us to control his diet more effectively and ensure that he gets enough sleep, so that he can conquer his tendency to infirmity once and for all. The poor boy has had a hard year of it, despite the visits home now and again. The idea of making a soldier of him is, in the end, a little bizarre. Never mind, the waiting is almost over and on Saturday he will be with me.

THE MANUSCRIPT ROOM in the old Bibliothèque Nationale smells of leather and dust. The buttery scent of literature wafts out from shelves of thick, calfskin-bound volumes arranged all the way down one long wall. A sharp whiff of history blows up from behind the decorative grilles that hide creaking iron radiators from both the eye and the broom. The one lush, the other acrid, the two odours meet and mingle, filling the narrow space with a single elusive perfume. A reader, lifting his nose to the air, might savour the scent and puzzle, for a fleeting moment, over its origins. But none does. Here, heads are bowed to their reading, bodies hunched over the long tables, minds occupied, and senses inattentive. Smells go unsmelled and the sunlight is not missed in the odd half-darkness of this room. On the wall facing the bookshelves, high windows would let in the poignant sunshine of a September day to bathe the scholars' tasks in a pure bright glow were there not canvas blinds hanging down from each frame. Precious documents are thus protected from rays that would fade them, while the readers themselves turn delicate pages with white-gloved hands.

In fact, the leather books that surround them are something of a fraud, or at least an irrelevancy, row upon row of out-of-date catalogues, and seldom-consulted nineteenth-century annuals stored here for want of other space: the heart of the *salle des manuscrits* lies elsewhere. Its pages are unpublished and unbound, yet all the more closely guarded for that, secured in the stacks hidden behind this room. I imagine a vault filled with a scaffolding of metal shelves on which cardboard containers the size of big shoeboxes and portfolios as large as kitchen tabletops are balanced. Secreted in this storehouse, watched over by dutiful librarians who will expose their precious charges only to those who can show good reason why they should be permitted to behold them, are tons and tons of paper, parchment and vellum—diaries, notes, letters, recipes, typescripts, illuminations, Bibles, psalters, account books, chapbooks, books of hours, books of days.

These are the literary treasures of France. It is these manuscripts that the scholars have come to consult and admire. It was from this collection that a precious copy of Froissart's *Chronicle*, a manuscript scrupulously copied out by some anonymous hand more than six hundred years ago, was carefully removed to be placed in front of

Voltaire, waiting somewhere in this same building, working in what was then a rather new library. It was from here that Voltaire's original notes for his eighteenth-century histories of Charles XII and Louis XIV were brought forward to be shown to Michelet, who was seated in this very room, then just recently constructed. It was here that Zola, who used to position himself at that far table, waited to consult Michelet's manuscript for his *Introduction to Universal History* (1831). You can imagine the great novelist over there, his coat tidily folded on the chair beside him, and his head bent so low to decipher Michelet's scrawl that his beard almost touches the table. And it is here that you, in turn, if your credentials pass muster, can examine Zola's manuscript for his 1885 novel, *Germinal*.

But mind that you arrive at the library early. The regulars snag the best spots, and if you tarry, you may be placed near the reserve counter, where the comings and goings will disturb your concentration. Soon, the Bibliothèque Nationale will move to giant new premises over on the Quai François Mauriac, where four book-shaped glass towers will be stuffed with computers and the manuscript room will be a windowless vault with low light and strict humidity controls. But for now, this is the place.

I do not belong here. My white shirt is crisp, my grey flannels freshly pressed. A cashmere sweater thrown over the shoulders with a deceptive casualness and a few well-chosen pieces of jewellery soften the plain clothes, while on my feet I wear the Italian leather loafers favoured by generations of well-dressed Parisians. My accent is impeccable, without trace of the Canadianisms that so incense the French. My letter of introduction, quickly faxed across the Atlantic by an obliging friend at the University of Quebec, manages to suggest that I am a student of literature without actually lying about my profession. Down in the ground-floor reception area, they have read it casually, issued me with a reader's card, and waved me encouragingly upstairs to the second floor. I approach the glass cage framed in ornate wooden carving that blocks the entrance to the manuscipt room and exchange the library card for a small disc of green plastic. It assigns me a seat at one of the long tables where I settle my belongings before proceeding to the reserve desk at the far end of the room. There, I exchange the green disc for an orange one that I must finally surrender before a manuscript may be brought out. I fill out my first request form but the clerk will not take my little orange token and sends me back to my seat.

Twenty minutes later, I am summoned to the desk of the assistant manuscript librarian back at the end of the room. He also reads my letter, more carefully this time, inquiring about my interests. M. Richaud—that's the name engraved into the little sign sitting in front of him—seems unhappy and faintly annoyed by my presence, asking in a high quavering voice how long I plan to stay. A day or two, a week perhaps. Who knows what I might find here? How can I really say what I am looking for? After much negotiation, he finally grants me cautious permission, wiping a pasty brow with a pale hand before correcting the call number on my request form and appending his signature. Within a few days, M. Richaud clearly regrets his decision. From time to time, he rises nervously from his place at the end of the room and ventures forward to spy on all the scholars, his scrawny body hovering awkwardly near the central information desk, his damp eye peering at me with particular distrust. He must suspect that I am only a tourist in the halls of scholarship, a dilettante, the kind who probably harbours a forbidden ballpoint somewhere on her person. He worries that he was wrong to let me pursue my quest. I have been here several days. I do not seem to be going away.

Certainly, his confident underling, the assistant assistant librarian, a tall, chestnut-haired man all too aware of his own good looks, knows that I am only an interloper. Every day, as I arrive in the morning but minutes after nine, eager to exchange my green disc for the orange one, and settle at a desk that is comfortably removed from M. Richaud's line of sight, the assistant's assistant spots me and salutes me with an ironic *"Bonjour, mademoiselle,"* as if to say, "My pitiable boss may not have the stamina to challenge you, but I see right through your scholarly pretensions." He smiles knowingly and moves on. Standing guard at the counter of the reserve desk, the clerks, in their turn, eye me warily as I pass over my request and return to my place. Ten minutes later, one of them rolls up to the table with a metal cart, the top of which is fitted with a bin lined in yellow felt. The clerk removes a document box and places it in front of me. I don my white gloves, lift off the lid of File 263, and take out the first notebook: 1890–1891. Here, at least, is a kind of home.

PARIS. SUNDAY, NOVEMBER 16, 1890.
Ah, but he's handsome, my soldier. I met him alone at the station yesterday afternoon—Adrien and Dick were both busy—and I was quite surprised when he stepped off the train. He looked so grown-up. I have seen him often enough in his uniform, on weekends and at his dear grandmother's funeral last winter, but yesterday for some reason he looked so full of authority and health. To think that he did not have a single attack in Orléans since his summer break—or at least no serious ones, just some laboured breathing. If growing up means being free of that horrible ailment, it will be a blessing, even if I will miss my little wolf.

The doctor was home for dinner, anxious to see Marcel, and, of course, he wanted to launch into a discussion of studies and careers right away. I had to hold him back so that our first evening together would remain a lighthearted affair. The boy needs time to settle in and let his lovely dark hair grow again!

After all his loneliness (and mine), he told us that he

quite enjoyed the military life in the end. I wonder what happened to the twelve tablets of chocolate that I instructed him to set aside. He probably gobbled them all up in one go last autumn and by summer had utterly forgotten our scheme to get him through his exile!

He even asked the Colonel to extend another six months. The man quite rightly rejected such a request. It was nonsense, just one of my Marcel's little fantasies. Anyone can see he will not be a military man or, for that matter, a doctor like his father, but there will be no shortage of careers open to him once he completes his studies. There is the question of willpower; he has always lacked his father's and his brother's stamina, but his intelligence will find a suitable place for itself, of that I have no doubt. His great sensitivity should be of use in diplomacy at least, if not in law. And as long as he can count on his health, he will work hard, I am sure of it.

Well, there, the cake is eaten, all twelve pieces gone. The year flew by, just as I told him it would, and he is home again. I have let him sleep late on his first morning home, but it is now almost ten and I have finished my correspondence. I will go and see if he is stirring.

Paris. Monday, November 17, 1890.
Marcel went over and saw Jacques Bizet yesterday afternoon and came home very excited. He says Mme. Straus seems ready to admit him into her salon, so he has well and truly grown up. I know that she and Jacques's stepfather have not always considered Marcel suitable company for the boy, but they seem to have changed their opinion, and are now very welcoming. (Such nonsense it all was, Marcel can be extravagant in his emotions, but the idea that he was actually a bad influence on

Jacques was too ridiculous. All those two ever do is discuss literature. At any rate, Marcel has never taken any offence, and has always held Mme. Straus in the highest regard.)

Finally began my reading of Pierre Loti's book last night. His description of his mother, drawn on his earliest memories, is deeply touching.

PARIS. TUESDAY, NOVEMBER 18, 1890.
Papa and Uncle Louis are to dine with us this evening. I thought lamb would be good for a change. Marcel will find his grandfather much changed, I fear. How differently people react to death. I never doubted that Uncle Louis loved his wife, but he has always been a joyful widower, liberated from domestic cares, happy to play with his coquettes. (Georges would be just the same, I imagine.) Papa, on the other hand, seems so shrunken since Maman's death, and I find it difficult to reach him in his grief.

Marcel wants to attend Mme. Arman de Caillavet's salon this Sunday (or whatever it is she now calls herself. That family adds names at a rate one can hardly keep up with—de this, de that.) He had visited once or twice before his military service, and has made friends with both her son Gaston and his friend, the Poquet girl. He says Mme. Arman de C. will be delighted to have him back. He greatly hopes for further conversation with her most regular guest (and, they say, her lover), Anatole France. I said I would ask his father whether he may go.

PARIS. WEDNESDAY, NOVEMBER 19, 1890.
Much discussion about Marcel's career prospects at dinner and Adrien told him he may visit Mme. de Caillavet's on Sunday, if

on Monday he goes down to the Sorbonne to register for law. His father also wants him to give more thought to the political science program at the Ecole Libre, saying that is the best preparation should he chose diplomacy. Marcel still says he would prefer a literary career, but will follow his father's wishes. And really, it is only sensible, although I cannot quite imagine Marcel as a lawyer and the separations that diplomacy would entail quite frighten me. At least, his health continues strong, even if I had to issue a gentle reminder yesterday about the number of pâtisseries it is wise to consume in one afternoon. His presence almost consoles me for his grandmother's absence.

Paris. Thursday, November 20, 1890.
My joy over Marcel's apparent good health was premature. A horrible attack yesterday evening—one of his worst kind with that awful wheezing and gulping that makes you think he is going to expire at that very moment.

It happened after dinner. His father and Dick had been in high spirits during the meal. It was their usual banter, but particularly joyous because Dick has announced he is definite about medicine once he finishes at the lycée. It was no surprise, of course, but Adrien did make a huge show of congratulating him. They were laughing about it all through dinner with Adrien regaling him with tales of all the pranks they played at the Faculty in his student days. Marcel joined in at first, but became quieter and quieter. We had just moved into the salon when he started that little wheezing sound of his. It is such a small noise, but I swear it is so horrible it could summon me from the other side of the Boulevard Malesherbes. His father told him to sit down and breathe calmly, but it only got worse and worse. We helped him to his room and tried to prop him up on pillows, but by this time he was panicking. Finally Adrien gave him some morphine—Marcel's never liked the stuff and we hardly ever use it, but there seemed no choice. He quieted down, but still it was several hours before his breathing was regular again. I sat with him and read to him from Loti, which he has just started himself, while Adrien and Dick went back to their coffee.

THESE ARE MY own translations. You will excuse me if they are not as elegant as they might be, if I seem unable to purge a certain Gallic extravagance from her prose, perhaps making her appear pretentious where she is, in fact, highly sensitive. The syntax is slippery; her constructions a trifle formal by contemporary standards. How shall I deliver her voice to you?

This is not, you understand, my regular line of work. I am a certified conference interpreter. A simultaneous translator. Academic papers, political speeches, that kind of thing. Like an old-fashioned typist, I pride myself on speed, accuracy, and a certain sixth sense about language, a premonition of what lies ahead—or perhaps merely an ability to reproduce correctly what has been only briefly glimpsed. A good interpreter will anticipate what direction a speaker's sentence is taking him and form a construction that will fit it, so that she finishes up at the same spot that he does only seconds after him without recasting, repeating, or pausing. She will recognize a particular idiom or a piece of slang he tosses in and instantly find the equivalent in the other language. She will mimic his tone and his thoughts. She will talk and listen at the same time. It's a narrow skill performed under exacting circumstances. Like an air-traffic controller, the interpreter is well rewarded for the stress involved.

The literary translator is not as well paid, of course, but the calling is loftier. There is no need for speed here, and accuracy is taken for granted. The talent lies in nuance, in recognizing the layers of meaning in a word or a phrase, and finding some stylish version in the other tongue that will render not only the pretty surface but also hint at the yawning depths. I must confess these subtleties are often beyond me. Well, it is not professional ambition that has brought me here.

PARIS. WEDNESDAY, DECEMBER 31, 1890—TOWARDS MIDNIGHT.

The first anniversary of Maman's death is but three days away. I could not write this morning and finally tried to distract myself from my grief this afternoon with a much-delayed outing to the shops for a few New Year's gifts. I had already picked an Anglo-Saxon theme for Marcel, George Eliot and Dickens, and I ventured down to Calmann Lévy where I bought *Middlemarch*—they have finally got the translation in. I look forward to discussing it with him, sharing Dorothea and Casaubon and all the rest. I also so want him to read Dickens and finally decided on *Great Expectations*.

I was looking for a wallet for Dick and had the carriage drop me on the Boulevard Haussmann. The crowds were such that the cabman could not get near the doors of the Galeries Lafayette let alone wait for me, so I paid him off there, and eventually walked home despite the cold. The store windows were full of bright lights and colourful displays, elegant gowns, silk scarves, and holiday baskets; the air smelt of roasting chestnuts and fresh waffles, and people bustled everywhere, the whole parade accompanied by music provided by an accordion player on the corner. The street vendors cried out with what seemed to me even more vigour than usual, perhaps desperate that there were only a few hours left to make their sales. The crowd pressed in on me, forcing me towards one of the vendors who stepped into my path and held some trinket out for my inspection. Even when I tried to brush him aside, he persisted: "*Mais regardez, madame.* Look at these beauties . . ." But he saw his answer in my unsmiling face, and I pushed past him into the store. It was not much quieter there, and it was all I could do to stand such a crush of humanity, make my purchase and find my way back to the Boulevard Malesherbes.

As I write the men are out at the midnight mass at Saint-Augustin, now leaving their Jewess safely at home. I sent Marcel off with three scarves, one under his waistcoat, one under his greatcoat, and the third overtop, I am so afraid this chill weather might trigger another attack. He has been well enough the last few weeks—thankfully we have not had a repetition of November's horrible scene. Since then, he has suffered only a touch of indigestion from time to time. I would not let him go out to Mme. de Caillavet's Sunday, the weather was so cold, and wanted to keep him at home tonight, but knowing how he loves the pageantry of a good mass, I did not stop him.

We will see in the new year very quietly when they get home. Georges and Emilie had another invitation, and Uncle Louis said he would see to Papa. I was just as glad only to have the four of us. Next year will be a better time for a proper *réveillon*.

Paris. Monday, January 5, 1891.
I have pulled myself out of mourning for the sake of my little wolves, and have promised Dick, who must return to school next week, a walk in the Bois this afternoon followed by treats in the tea room. The weather is so much warmer, which does make one more enthusiastic about the idea of stepping out. I

must continue to follow Maman's great example of fortitude and grace, and learn to be brave in grief. Marcel especially needs my strength, even if he is becoming such a grand socialite.

There were a flood of New Year's invitations. Mme. Hayman has suggested he start visiting her salon now, and he can be seen at Mme. Straus's every week. He is chattering away with the big people as much as he is visiting with Jacques Bizet these days. Jacques' mother is a great wit, to be sure, and his stepfather is a lovely man. Marcel says that last week some new guest, an elderly lady acquainted with M. Straus but not apparently with his wife, asked whether Mme. Straus liked music. She paused and replied, much to the amusement of those around her, "Oh, in my first family it was quite the rage."

I don't suppose the poor old thing knew she was talking to Bizet's widow! Or perhaps she knew but had forgotten in her eagerness to make conversation.

Paris. Thursday, February 5, 1891.
That is over, thank heaven, and I think it went well enough, the doctor's grand dinner. Félicie had Geneviève's help and managed the lobster nicely, while you can always count on her truffle sauce for the chicken. And the Nesselrode pudding looking spectacular standing on the sideboard. It is so hard to tell with these occasions, but the men stayed a long time talking in the dining room after we ladies had withdrawn, which is usually a sign some serious business is getting done. Adrien said he was very pleased, and feels things are progressing well enough on the planned conference that he can get back to his essay about neurasthenia on which he really has not managed any work since the new year.

Marcel is becoming quite the ladies' man, it seems. Adrien saw Mme. Hayman at a dinner the other day, and she was full of his praises, saying soon no lady of the Faubourg Saint-Germain will be safe from those eyes. He seems particularly smitten by Jeanne Pouquet, who has been giving little receptions for her girlfriends that he attends.

I just hope he manages his affections with a little more tact than he has in the past. All ladies want to be admired, to be sure, but Marcel gets himself in such a stew, I believe it frightens people—or worse yet, amuses them. That fuss over the de Benardaky girl back while he was still at school. Kicking about all day just waiting to go and play Prisoner's Base with her and her comrades on the Champs-Elysées. Her parents were perfectly pleasant people, if a bit exotic, but really, Marie herself was all of fourteen or fifteen. They were far too young to be talking of love, and Marcel was making himself sick over the whole thing. Adrien agreed with me completely that it had to stop before the child lost all control over his emotions. Still, I often wonder if I was right to forbid him seeing her any more. As soon as I did he had the most dreadful attacks, as if to punish me for my firmness. At least, he is old enough now to take a more sensible attitude towards a pretty girl.

PARIS. WEDNESDAY, FEBRUARY 18, 1891.
Marcel is making an utter fool of himself over Jeanne Pouquet. And apparently the girl is engaged to Gaston Arman de Caillavet. What her parents must think, I cannot imagine. Marcel thinks he can hide it all from me, but it is obvious to any fool he is in love. Mooning about all day just like he did with Marie de B., just waiting until the next tea or

outing. Jacques Bizet did nothing to calm my fears by telling me a little story yesterday, when he dropped by to fetch Marcel and was waiting in the salon while he dressed. Jacques says that last year in Orléans, during his military service, Marcel was always writing to the Pouquets, and proposed mother and daughter should come for a visit. If you please, the young prince was going to rent a nearby château, just a little one, of course, in which to entertain his new friends. Sometimes I wonder if the boy can distinguish between his dreams and reality. Jacques found the story screamingly funny, but I could think it only sad. I will not tell Adrien, it would just make him angry. He is increasingly worried that Marcel is not paying enough attention to his studies.

PARIS. THURSDAY, MARCH 5, 1891.
I took tea with Uncle Louis yesterday and in the foyer of his building crossed paths with his friend Mme. Hayman. I know Adrien sees her at various dinners from time to time, but it has been several years since I have laid eyes on her. Her beauty certainly is not diminishing with age and she does not wear a speck of rouge, unlike most coquettes over thirty these days.

She may be a demimondaine but she dotes on Uncle Louis more than his late wife ever did, and I am hardly a blushing bride any more to take some high moral line, so I acknowledged her politely, and we wound up having quite a chat. She was telling me of all Marcel's social conquests. Indeed, he regularly attends her Tuesdays—where he will meet all sorts of dukes and princes, if not perhaps duchesses and princesses. I spoke quite earnestly of his need to study and find the right career, but she only laughed and said, "Madame, that one, the salon will be his career."

I told Uncle Louis that I had spoken with her, just in case she mentioned it to him, I would not want him to think there was any difficulty on my part. He is very eager to open the house at Auteuil as soon as possible, and was urging me to come with Adrien and stay around Easter or longer.

PARIS. WEDNESDAY, APRIL 8, 1891.
Well, the Proust household is to be torn asunder over the question of chrysanthemums. Not small French ones, of course. There would be no point destroying a family over those scant blooms. No, it is the large Japanese ones that were all the rage this winter and sought after by every lady from the demimondaine to the duchess, if not perhaps the doctor's wife. It is those towering bronze flowers that we are fighting over.

To be brief: Adrien has seen Marcel's bill for the florist. I am not entirely sure to whom these bouquets were sent, besides Mme. Hayman, who recently informed the doctor that Marcel had offered her a most extravagant bouquet with a little billet attached filled with allusions to Primavera. She thought we should know, bless her. Meanwhile, I believe Mme. Straus had made it clear that she did not wish to receive such offerings, and Robert de Billy's mother even mentioned to me at tea last week chez Faure that she was rather shocked that Marcel had sent that young man flowers. Of course, the family is Protestant, so they are apt to be more surprised by demonstrations of this sort. I hope that those at least were some small package of daisies.

I did point out to Adrien that Marcel may spend his allowance as he pleases, but there is no arguing with the doctor. The cost of these flowers, the emotionalism of these assaults on the human heart, and the persons to whom those hearts belong, are all out of order. I finally got the doctor, who had happened to find the bill in this morning's mail and opened it without noting it was "Monsieur M. Proust," not "Monsieur A. Proust," to agree that I would speak to Marcel first, before he broached the subject with his son. It does Marcel's health no good at all for him to see his father angry, even if Adrien always argues that it is by pampering him that I make him ill.

Another few weeks, and we will be the first of May. Vendors will be hawking lilies of the valley on every street corner. Charming and cheap!

Paris. Saturday, April 11, 1891.
M. Barrère came for dinner yesterday, a family dinner, although he did want to see Marcel, and that one had escaped to a party after our difficult encounter in the afternoon. Dick was able to entertain him instead. We had a long talk about the progress the Germans are making—they have developed an antitoxin for tetanus, Adrien reports. He and M. Barrère were debating which would be more significant in stopping disease, the possibility of antitoxins or simply improved hygiene itself. Adrien was betting on hygiene, of course, and Dick got very involved in their talk, arguing the future lay in the antitoxins. The men were cautioning him not to believe in miracles (already the idealistic young medical student!). M. Barrère was complaining that his political masters never pay any attention to these matters until an epidemic is right on top of them, and then they want the doctors to have developed a cure the day before yesterday.

The interview over the chrysanthemums was not a pleasant one. I took Marcel aside after lunch and tried gently to explain that it embarrassed people to receive excessively large gifts and that the cost was out of proportion to his allowance. He said it was only because I lacked finer feelings that I would consider such gifts overwhelming, and that in the households of the Faubourg Saint-Germain, large vases of fresh flowers were considered indispensable. He got very angry and insulted all the potted ferns in the salon before bursting into tears. I rushed to the defence of my ferns, announced, "We do not live on the Faubourg Saint-Germain," turned on heel, and made a sweeping exit. Both mother and son should be ashamed of such dramatics, worthy of Bernhardt herself!

OUR DIARIST WRITES DAILY, every morning, without fail, covering these pages with entry upon entry. I can imagine her after breakfast, clothed in a morning dress that we would mistake for a ball gown, in a little study off her bedroom, or perhaps at a writing desk in the spacious salon, carefully recording yesterday's events in her notebooks in a small, precise hand. Outside her window, carriages roll up and down the Boulevard Malesherbes, and she can faintly hear the clop of horses' hooves through the glass. Inside, there would be only the sound of a clock ticking in an overfurnished room, with heavy curtains, dark wood, chairs upholstered in red velvet or damask, and ferns filling every corner not already stuffed with large porcelain vases, small statuettes, and Oriental curios that the doctor brought back from his voyages. Then Marcel, rising late, interrupts, looking for his gloves, or Jean enters discreetly, seeking instructions on the dinner menu.

She is faithful, regular, and consistent, but I cannot keep up. So, I have started picking and choosing now, selecting the more telling entries and leaving out the more mundane. I have begun to give her life shape.

Do you think it wrong of me? Unscholarly. Unscientific, perhaps? Like the hovering M. Richaud, you must suspect me of some ulterior motive and read a guilty tension in my white-gloved hand or a less-than-innocent angle to my pencil. I confess that I have started to look for a pattern here. May not a translator aspire to storytelling? Or do you detect an act of hubris? A fledgling literary translator, already testing the limits of her little wings, eyes the far-off treetops where the editors and novelists nest, and stupidly thinks that with a bit of flapping she might join them. Max used to say I was a better listener than speaker, always putting the pieces in the wrong order or neglecting the context needed to understand a tale, like a child so anxious to relay a joke, she babbles out the punchline with none of the necessary wind-up. He suspected it was the fault of bilingualism: a precocious talent for languages may clutter as much as it clarifies. Not that Max proved much of a teller in the end. But this is not his story nor mine. Let me prove my fluency with someone else's words.

TROUVILLE. HÔTEL DES ROCHES NOIRES. THURSDAY, JULY 9, 1891.

I wrote Marcel a much longer letter than usual yesterday and sent it to Jean's attention, so that he will make sure it is on the table when Marcel arises tomorrow morning. That way the boy is sure to be greeted with birthday wishes from his dear mother at breakfast. How silly that we are not together today, but he will be here with me at the seaside before the month is out.

And sometimes it is easier to tell a son how much one loves him in a letter. I have recalled for him July 10, 1871. The instability of those times seems so far away now, the Republic so solid. To think Adrien was almost hit by a bullet in the middle of a Paris street, it just seems unimaginable today! I do not forget the worry though. I think I have carried that with me ever since Marcel's birth, although that is not how I put it in my letter. Besides, that is a mother's privilege: to watch over a child every day.

Trouville. Hôtel des Roches Noires. Monday, July 13, 1891.

Marcel has sent me the most beautiful letter responding to my birthday wishes, which I have just finished reading and to which I immediately replied. That boy is so sensitive, he always sees right to the heart of any emotional question. He started by thanking me for the little history lesson—how ridiculous of me, of course, it is not as though the student of political science does not know all about the Commune and the Germans attacking Paris, and the siege, but, as Marcel goes on to say, one likes to tell children the same family stories again and again. It is a way of reassuring oneself that the bonds are still strongly tied, I suppose.

How many times I must have said to him, "Marcel, when your little mother was carrying you in her belly, all Paris was hungry but I had you to keep me full . . ." His father had to send me to Auteuil for safety, and when I did deliver him, he was so sickly the doctor who attended me did not think he would live. I do not imagine I mentioned that part to him when he was little, nor the stray bullet that almost killed his father—it does not do to frighten children with tales of sickness and death, after all.

In his letter, Marcel describes my face to me, and tells me how dear it is, and quotes Loti: "I would like to greet her with special words, words made specially for her." He admits that he feels so sad sometimes because he knows he causes me pain, what with his ill health and his lack of willpower. I hurried to write him back to reassure him on that score, that I rejoice to see him apply himself in his studies, that he has never caused me pain that it was not a mother's privilege to suffer. In closing, I turned to Mme. de Sévigné's letters to her daughter: "How well you justify that excessive love that everyone knows I feel for you."

PARIS. TUESDAY, OCTOBER 27, 1891.
Things have not begun auspiciously in this our autumn of academic seriousness. Marcel has effected a rapprochement with Mme. Straus.

Indeed, M. Straus himself dropped by last week to tell Marcel that all is forgiven and he may return to the lady's salon every week as before. It is tacitly understood there are to be no more inappropriate bouquets or extravagant compliments, which I suspect were more annoying to Monsieur than to Madame, but the young man's presence is eagerly awaited.

Marcel is overjoyed, and burst out with the news the moment M. Straus had left (after the gentleman had very kindly paid his compliments to me on his way out). Well, they are charming people, the Straus. Jewish, of course, but very cultivated, and Madame's salon is, I am sure, full of the most erudite and literary people. Yet really, the child does not need social distractions, he needs to study. I warned him not to go yelling this news to his father, or there will be trouble.

Meanwhile, the season is starting up again at Mme. Baignères's and at Mme. Arman de Caillavet's, where Marcel is hoping to pursue his friendship with the great M. France himself, no doubt to further his own literary ambitions. Yesterday, I finally insisted that Marcel draw up a timetable, with a set number of hours for reading each week, and pointed out that if he insists on coming home in the small hours of the morning, nine o'clock study periods were not very realistic.

PARIS. FRIDAY, NOVEMBER 27, 1891.
With the weather still so warm, Mme. Faure and I slipped out for a walk yesterday before seasonal preparations make such things impossible. What a round of dinners and balls she must attend next month—the lot of a political wife. I felt I was actually doing her great benefit, just providing a little tête-à-tête with a good woman friend for a change. We talked long of conjugal duty, and asked each other to what extent one should close one's eyes. I had not realized M. Faure is quite so active outside the home. Poor thing, these matters are such a trial, as I have reason to know.

Marcel is very excited because he met the Princesse Mathilde at Mme. Straus's. I had heard that she styles herself as a simple woman, and does not hesitate to mention the Bonapartes' humble origins. When Marcel took her hand and made to kiss it, she abruptly turned it over and shook his instead. Adrien was quite impressed, and said, "Imagine the grandson of Louis Proust shaking hands with Napoleon's niece!" I had to gently remind the doctor that he professes to be a republican.

PARIS. FRIDAY, JANUARY 8, 1892.
We are recovering from the Neuburger-Bergson wedding. Marcel and Dick looked very smart standing beside the bride and groom under the canopy. (So kind of them to honour them so—I was a little surprised since they did not feel Maman was a close enough relation that the proximity of the

anniversary of her death needed to be avoided when they were setting the date.) That new suit from Eppler is very well cut in the end, with a nice line across the shoulders. Perhaps I should tell Dick to get the shirts he wanted done up there instead of next door.

Marcel is very taken with his new cousin. They had a long discussion of M. Bergson's work at one of the receptions before the new year, and Marcel was trying to explain his theories to me. It is about the way we experience our memories of the past, but I was not sure I was grasping it at all. Louise looked lovely, her dress had the most exquisite beading.

M. Blanche is really pressing Marcel on this issue of the portrait. He is a youngish man, yet already he has something of a reputation as a painter, so I urged Marcel to go ahead and agree to sittings. It is a distraction from his studies, this is true, but it would be regrettable to pass up such an opportunity. M. Blanche would undertake the portrait of his own volition—apparently, he likes Marcel's Italian eyes, so a mother must surely feel he is a man of discernment—but I suggested to Adrien that if the portrait is a success, we might even buy it. This summer, my little wolf will be twenty-one, and what a present it would make!

Paris. Monday, March 7, 1892.
We had a great family debate about the merits of the telephone at dinner last night. Dick is all for it, and says one day every house will have one. He was even trying to convince Adrien it would be very useful for his practice, pointing out that in America doctors are now all on the line. Marcel is skeptical and was arguing strongly for the pneumatic, saying there was nothing a telephone could do that a *petit bleu* could not achieve just as

fast. Dick replied that if you were sending an invitation, and the other person could reply just as soon as the question is put to him, it could actually speed things up. Marcel cleverly pointed out that often you do not want to reply right away, but want to delay a few days and consider your social schedule and the other invitations you have received. I have never much taken to sending messages by the pneumatic, always preferring a letter, but perhaps it really will be as Dick says and we will get used to the telephone.

Now that he's chez Straus so often, Marcel is very much back in with Jacques Bizet and Daniel Halévy. The old Lycée Condorcet set apparently wants to launch a literary journal, and Marcel is now busy at inaugural meetings and the like. He also wants to have a dinner for his friends this season and now I have only to convince the doctor that he should be allowed it. After all, he is young, it is natural to want to go into society when one is young, and one cannot be always visiting without ever opening one's own doors.

Auteuil. Monday, April 25, 1892.
Will we never be free of this demon asthma? It was not a bad attack, just wheezing and gasping and it passed quickly enough, but the anxiety it causes my poor little Marcel is almost unbearable for me to watch. It will be monstrously unfair if he is still held back by his health even as he grows up.

Ever since that day in the Bois, we have lived under this cloud. I realize it must be exactly eleven years ago now, for we were spending the Easter holidays at Uncle Louis's when it happened and he was nine at the time. There we all were, a perfectly lovely spring day in the Bois de Boulogne, and suddenly he was gasping and choking and writhing about on the ground, clutching at his chest. The image will always remain with me, the way a perfectly innocent, sunny day can suddenly, in one moment, become a nightmare. You look up expecting somehow the weather will have changed to account for such sorrow, and now the blue sky mocks you and the clarity of the air seems almost evil.

I suppose it is the trees—they are just coming into full leaf this week, late after that hard winter. I was set to return to Paris at the end of the week, but told Uncle Louis I will return right away, in the hopes Marcel will be more comfortable if he stays indoors in the apartment. How funny that we think of the country air at Auteuil as being healthy, yet for him it is the cause of disease.

PARIS. FRIDAY, MAY 27, 1892.
I went to the Louvre alone yesterday afternoon and spent most of it lost in contemplation of Caravaggio's *Fortune Teller*. I must have seen the canvas often enough before, but perhaps the keepers have moved it to a new location or cleaned it and that is why it caught my eye in particular today. The fortune teller is a common peasant woman with a ruddy round face, but her client, who extends his hand and eyes her a little warily, is clearly a nobleman, with fancy clothes and fine features.

I had never noticed before how much he looks like Marcel. The nose is long and straight, with the slightest bump or arching just below the bridge. The eyes are deeply set, with a pronounced line across the middle of the lid that separates the flesh of the lid proper from the flesh of the brow, as though the skin itself was carved from stone. The cheeks are flushed and the lips full and red. Well, people often remark that Marcel's look is Italian. His darkness is actually Semitic—he inherits it from his grandfather Weil—but to be sure, there is something of the young and noble Florentine about him. Apart from the hair—the fortune teller's client has the most lovely curly locks—and the skin—Marcel's is less olive in shade—they are very close. Oh, but he is beautiful.

I will not bore Marcel with a mother's indulgent comparisons. He is already all puffed up with his hostesses fawning over him.

I saw max in the library today. He was behind the reserve desk, where the clerks load returned manuscripts onto their carts and wheel them back into the stacks. He had his back to me and was pushing a cart in the opposite direction, towards the glass door that leads to the unseen vaults, but surely it was him. I recognized the way his curls cling to the back of his head, and his gait, light, springy, and tentative somehow, as though he did not entirely belong to this earth. Only the cart seemed to anchor him to the floor. The library overalls, a one-piece affair in faded blue, looked too large on his small frame, and I can imagine he complains that they don't fit properly and make him look shrunken or insignificant.

He was always a bit vain. In the old days, walking along St. Catherine Street together, I would sometimes catch him spying on his own reflection in the shop windows, checking that he was really as beautiful as he wanted to be. This morning, I want to rise from my desk to follow him, to catch up with him and see his face, but a certain lightness in my stomach gives me pause.

Fear and desire have begun a swift little ballet in my gut. Five years since he left Montreal, left for good, and his image still unsettles me, the idea of being in his presence, even a great room's length away, fills me with fluttering hopes, all false, I know, and impossible little dreams. Can one call it love, this attenuated longing stretched over months and months until they become years? I both yearn for him and dread him, wondering sometimes if it is not simply the habit of heartache that has ensnared me. In moments of reason, I see that I am miles away from the real Max and wonder if I could actually love whoever it is he is now. And yet here he stands, all too familiar and infinitely desirable. I see him clearly, if at a distance, hovering at the end of the room. I am unable to rise and go to greet him; I am too certain this apparition will prove to be only a chimera.

I return my eyes to the desk. I am allowing some fantasy to distract me from the task at hand. Mme. Proust is tireless and I must work faster if I am ever going to get through the notebooks. I'll just skip ahead a few months here: I am determined to finish this one today, and move on to 1893.

Paris. Thursday, September 8, 1892.
Great excitement yesterday because Marcel went off for his first sitting with M. Blanche. He returned in good form, filled with awe at the spectacle of the studio, with its huge north-facing windows and a young model who was hurriedly reclothing herself when he entered! Well, that sounds odd, but I do believe this M. Blanche is really perfectly respectable. He seemed very pleasant when we met him at Trouville last year, and after all, his father is a doctor too.

Marcel is to wear his dinner jacket—he hid it under his greatcoat and several scarves in the cab on the way up—and was explaining to me how difficult it is to stand perfectly still. About every twenty minutes or so he is allowed a little break, but M. Blanche marks on the studio floor in chalk the outline of his feet so that he can take up the exact same pose when they begin again. Marcel says he chews on the end of his brush and sighs a lot as he paints, and absolutely forbids the boy to talk. I worry that Marcel is not taking his courses at the Sorbonne seriously enough, but at least the sessions with M. Blanche will be a distraction from his silly pursuit of Mme. de Chevigné. I believe he is waiting in the street outside her house to catch a glimpse of her, because he is up and out suspiciously early in the morning these days.

Paris. Tuesday, November 22, 1892.
Eh bien. We are to have a visit from the famous Mr. Wilde. Marcel met him at one of his soirées and was enchanted. He says he is so witty that he makes Mme. Straus herself seem dull, and he wears the most colourful waistcoats. Marcel has invited him here for dinner Thursday, before his Paris tour comes to a close and he must return to England. The boy insists that his father and I should be present, saying that even though Mr. Wilde speaks beautiful French, my English must be ready in the wings just in case the gentleman should prefer that language. Reading is one thing, and talking quite another, but I imagine I can muster enough to show Mr. Wilde we French are not without sympathy for the English people and the English language. (Although, I have just recalled that he is, in fact, Irish. Does it make a difference? I wonder.)

Paris. Wednesday, November 23, 1892.
Great preparations for tomorrow. Have decided on the *blanquette.*

Paris. Friday, November 25, 1892.

We have received a visit from the great Mr. Wilde and I did not even lay eyes on the man! He was to dine yesterday evening. Adrien made great efforts to come home from the hospital in lots of time, despite an afternoon meeting of the board, and he and I were all ready in the salon at seven o'clock. Marcel was late—he is getting impossible on that score; I wonder that he ever gets to his parties before they are over—and had yet to arrive when the bell rang and Jean went to open the door. No one ever appeared in the salon, but Jean told me later than Mr. Wilde peeped into the room, and then asked for the facilities. Marcel arrived a few moments later, there was some hurried conversation in the hall, and then Mr. Wilde disappeared again, all without even so much as a "*Mes hommages, madame.*" What extraordinary behaviour!

Marcel was mortified, and clearly took it very personally. Apparently there was some misunderstanding about it being a dinner invitation *en famille*. Mr. Wilde had perhaps been expecting a tête-à-tête and was unprepared for a larger gathering. Not that we are so intimidating, after all. At any rate, there was a great deal of injured pride all round, and I spent the evening soothing both Marcel and Félicie ("a perfectly good *blanquette de veau* gone to waste, and all that work on the seafood sauce for the sole . . ."). Adrien, on the other hand, was very cheerful about the whole affair and said he was just as happy to spend the evening working on his papers. At least he tucked into Félicie's veal with appetite, so she was somewhat assuaged, but Marcel refused to eat a thing and departed to his room in tears.

Were it not for my great affection for Mr. Dickens, Mr. Wilde might drive me to quote Montesquieu himself: "The English are busy; they don't have time to be polite."

Marcel came home from M. Blanche's studio all breathless and excited this Saturday, not sure whether to be upset or delighted with the turn of events. Apparently, the portrait has not been going well since they resumed work after Marcel's recent illness, and yesterday M. Blanche announced he was giving up and would destroy his work. Marcel was appalled and pleaded with him, but the artist snatched up his big easel. Marcel then tore the still-wet painting from his hands; M. Blanche snatched it back, saying it was his work and he would do with it what he pleased. After all, Marcel had not commissioned the portrait. Marcel responded that it was his likeness and surely he could buy it from the artist if he wanted to. M. Blanche refused, saying it was not for sale and Marcel finally ripped the canvas from him, but got away with only the top half, running into the street with it in his hands.

He had quite the time trying to get it home in a cab without disturbing the paint. Luckily, the top of the work was largely dry, for it was the legs M. Blanche had been working on most recently. That is where he seemed to get stuck. (Marcel said he complained he just could not get the pose to seem natural.)

Anyway, what remains looks fine to me—we are left with a nice bust portrait rather than a full-length one, but it is a grand likeness. Blanche has made his skin very white, but the long, straight nose, the cupid-bow lips, and the heavy-lidded, dark eyes are all there. Marcel is wearing evening dress and sports an orchid in his buttonhole. A portrait of a young dandy—perhaps M. Blanche felt he had failed to capture some of Marcel's intelligence and sensibility. He certainly has captured his beauty.

PERHAPS YOU NEED SOME context for my translation, some sort of introduction. I should explain myself at least. When it comes to the hovering librarians, I'm the reader with a reserve on File 263 and I don't elaborate. Why should I justify myself to them? But you won't share their narrow, academic prejudices. You'll appreciate the personal note.

When I was a girl I lived here . . . but no, this story begins later. It is experienced as a memory, a very first adult memory, a recollection of childhood as something now past.

Let me describe to you then a fifteen-year-old girl, standing on the steps of the Royal Ontario Museum in Toronto. She is not yet a woman. Scrawny and flat-chested, she has long black braids, a heart-shaped face, white skin, pink cheeks, and the unformed features of a child. I am she.

I am dressed in the tight, straight-legged blue jeans that I always wear. They are a European fashion, just now replacing bell-bottoms, and perhaps in this way I can be seen as a trendsetter, one who leads rather than follows in the fierce social hierarchy that marks every adolescence. But these jeans are my single eccentricity. Otherwise, I am shy, silent, unnotable, and unnoted, preparing myself to pass through life as an observer.

I have come here from my home in Montreal, on a school trip, and have spent the afternoon in the company of dinosaurs, potsherds, and other fifteen-year-olds. As the 1980s begin, Toronto is outstripping its historic rival to become the pre-eminent Canadian city, or at least a place certain of its own importance if not yet self-confident enough to be sure that others agree. So, it urges its achievements at you, boasting, displaying. The museum is world renowned; the telecommunications tower the tallest anywhere; an Olympic bid is a definite possibility. Clustered together on the steps of the museum, we schoolgirls are convinced, sensing that the city is a more weighty thing than any fifteen year old and so, more impressive than any place she might come from. We want to touch the city, to belong here, but hide our awe and our desire behind embarrassed giggling and inconsequential conversations that we conduct in unnecessarily loud voices just to prove to anyone who might overhear us that we speak the language.

We are Montrealers, but we can speak English. We do speak English. In the street, to a neighbour, to anglophone friends, and even to some of our relatives. No problem there. And yet Toronto's flat and self-sufficient tongue intimidates us as much as the museum's echoing hallways. The city seems simply not to need French, not to even know it exists. Happily unaware of what it is missing, it never has to choose between languages. There is no awkwardness or difficulty, there are no hesitations, false starts, or left turns. Toronto just keeps on speaking English as though there were no alternatives. The idea is novel, and yet as we twist our minds around it, we can't help but realize that if you lived in this place, you would have half the homework. This thoughtless unilingualism is so different from our ever-questioning bilingual reality, our linguistic jostling, our Montreal—and what is different from us is better.

I share my classmates' excitement; I am convinced of this envious world view, although it is quite new to me. Two years ago, I had never heard of such civic pride and geographic comparisons. I had not yet learned how to yearn. Until my thirteenth birthday, I had lived at the centre of the universe and never conceived that any other place in the world might be worth living, nor that any citizen of the planet who lived elsewhere counted for much at all. I had lived in Paris.

On a chilly November day at four, as the light dies in the streets, I am standing outside the elegant grey-limestone building that houses my school. I am dressed in the grey skirt, white blouse, powder-blue cardigan, and navy blazer that are the required uniform, but they are not enough to keep me warm. There is a good four-inch gap between the top of my wool knee socks and the bottom of my pleated skirt, and a breeze blows up my legs. School is out and I am waiting for my mother.

Set amongst the gracious streets laid out one hundred years before by the Baron Haussmann, the school is at the end of an affluent cul-de-sac and backs onto a large park made up, like all French parks, of walking paths of buff-yellow dirt and large expanses of grass fenced off with green-painted railings so that no one can enter them. Uncomfortable metal chairs, painted the same colour as the railings, are dotted about, unused. At the edge of the park, strategically placed so that the smell from his brazier wafts towards the uniformed children now tumbling from the school's large, wrought-iron doorway, is a chestnut vendor.

I unstrap the hard, leather satchel from my back and carefully take a one-franc coin from the pink plastic pencil case that I keep in the front pocket.

"*Des marrons pour mademoiselle?*" He speaks in the exaggerated tones of all Parisian street vendors, punching his consonants hard and cocking an eyebrow at me. I hold out my coin and in exchange he hands me a paper cone twisted shut at the top.

The roasted chestnuts must be peeled, and with my satchel back in place, I hold the warming cone between my knees so that I have both hands free. There are shells lying on the hard ground of the park where other children have discarded them, but I carefully tuck mine into my blazer pocket, and sample the first chestnut. Its hot flesh almost burns me, and I toss it about inside my mouth, puffing out my cheeks and rolling my tongue. When it becomes cool enough to taste, I can savour the sweet, pasty pulp with its subtle flavour.

A slight, black-haired woman hurries towards the school. She is wearing a trim little Chanel suit from which emerge slim legs and delicate feet that carry her trippingly forward. With small features and bright eyes, she possesses the kind of dainty prettiness that will fade and shrivel with age. But her fragile charm must still be discernible now, in her forties, just barely, hidden as it is behind anxiety and haste. This is my mother and she is late.

She is always nervous, my mother, always worried about something, always loudly insisting on English when I need her to speak French, always launching into her accented French when her proper English would do. My big, French-Canadian father dotes on her, calling her his English rose, and laughing indulgently when she reminds him that her family was Irish once. But she and I are forever bumping into each other and hurriedly retreating, like two little animals who have both startled the other by appearing unexpectedly.

She leads me away from the chestnut vendor's brazier to the car she has parked at an outrageous angle in the cul-de-sac, worrying as she walks. Has she got a ticket? Have I caught cold waiting? Have I spoilt my appetite? Are chestnuts not too oily to be good for me? As I hurry behind her, skipping to keep pace with her skittish gate, a boy calls my name. "Marie, Marie."

He is standing on the other side of the narrow street, cheerful, affectionate, grinning like mad. He has blond, curly hair and shines with health. His skin is so gold it looks tanned, but perhaps this is only a trick of light, an unseasonable ray of sun having just now emerged dramatically from behind the November clouds. This is David. He is American, or at least his father is, and the son has inherited that particularly American brand of self-confidence. Although his mother is French, he has moved here only recently and is not fully aware yet that Paris is the centre of the universe. He is even so assured that he might not believe it once this fact is pointed out to him. He appeared in our midst only last year and is unperturbed by his slow progress in French class. I am infuriated by his refusal to accept our standards—and was once moved, with an uncharacteristic lack of control that I instantly regretted, to kick him beneath the desk when he laughed off a mistake in conjugating his subjunctive—but I envy him his easy charm and lust after his blond curls. Outside class we chat together in English, happy to have this in common and delighting in our schoolmates' incomprehension. They, in turn, mock us.

"Doo uu speek Inglish?" they squeal as they dart up to us and then dash away.

Perhaps because I am his ally in this new place, because we are both foreigners, David, despite the swift kick, confesses to a crush on me. I find it hard to believe my remarkable luck in this regard, but it is true. We have passed notes on the bus during school outings, admitting to a love that, measured by a grading system borrowed from our teachers, reaches a full 19½ out of 20. This declaration made, we are unsure what comes next, and excitedly circle each other without ever taking any action.

Improbably, David is Jewish. I say improbably because, in these Parisian days, I know few Jews personally, and David's blond hair and happy manner are utterly unlike the other Jews I do know, the ones in the pictures they show us at school. They are emaciated, living skeletons in striped pyjamas, indistinguishable one from the other.

"Have you seen Delvaux's horror show?"

"Has Delvaux showed you his dirty pictures yet?"

Every year in September, as the younger students are still nervously assessing their new teachers, the older ones sneeringly ask these questions. It is Monsieur Delvaux, our history teacher, who early in the fall term will set up the school's single, wheezing slide projector, draw the dusty roller blinds down over the windows, issue a warning to the weak of stomach that they should leave the room and devote a class to the lesson of the Holocaust. In the dim light created by the projector's bulb and the few rays leaking through the blinds, he dwells on the atrocities at length, and watches our faces closely, hoping to shock his charges as much as he wants to educate them. Men and women rounded up into cattle cars. Gas chambers disguised as showers. Lampshades made of human skin. He longs to disturb the bland surfaces of our unmarked faces, to add some small measure of horror, fear, or perhaps simply doubt to our cossetted lives. M. Delvaux was born at the end of the war— he seems to regret that he was not personally present for its events—but his father, he says, was in the Resistance. The older children have heard his stories many times, and hoot with laughter when we younger ones earnestly inform them that M. Delvaux's father fought the Nazis.

These stories are not new to me either. Indeed, I cannot remember ever not knowing the fate of six million European Jews. Her brief words clipped by embarrassment, my mother has told me that I will bleed every month, that babies are made by the union of an egg and a sperm, and that there are other things I will learn when I am older, but she has dwelt with firm patience on the lessons of history. She and my father were teenagers when the war ended and the unspeakable news came out of Europe. In the sixties, as the world did begin, slowly at first but with increasing desperation, to discuss the stories of Bergen-Belsen and Auschwitz, they were new parents doting on their new baby, their first and only child. My mother expresses her daily anxieties— what if the gas leaks? what if you catch cold? what if your father is late? what if the franc falls? what if the Socialists win the election?—with cramped tones and furrowed brow. Only when giving voice to the greatest fear of all does she become large and gracious: "It must never happen again."

At the dinner table, my parents are instantly, unspokenly alarmed when I tell them of the slide show in Delvaux's history class. They can catch a whiff of prurience a mile away, for it is the very odour they are most anxious should not attach itself to their gentle attempts to share the greatest horror of the adult world with their twelve-year-old daughter. There is a lengthy pause, and I sense, too late, that I have stumbled across taboo. My father speaks.

"Were you frightened by the pictures?"

"Oh, no, Papa. I wasn't frightened."

No, I am not frightened, but rather awed by the great weight of history that has carried these people away. I feel small and inadequate in my security, and sure no such powerful event could ever mark my life. These suffering skeletons in their striped pyjamas seem to me as noble and as distant as the bleeding Christ and weeping Virgin whose image hangs on the wall of the small classroom where we dully receive instruction in our catechism every Wednesday afternoon.

David, of course, is exempt from catechism class, and may spend his Wednesdays as he pleases. This freedom only enhances the aura of easy good fortune that seems to surround him. I long for David; I long to be David, to be that lucky, that blond.

Yet, for all his happiness and health, David too makes some claim to the special status of historic victim. He has told a circle of breathless French schoolgirls that David Smith—that bland, Anglo-Saxon label he bears—is not his real name. His real name is David Aaron Goldberg, but his parents changed it when they moved here, to his mother's homeland, fearing that anti-Semitism would impede his father's progress in the world of European business. The other girls are deeply impressed. An exotic name change beats Philippe's recent holiday in Martinique and Bernard's dark eyes. "People are stupid, you know," David says, and they all nod wisely. "Oh yes. Your father was right to be careful," says one. But I am not sure whether to believe David.

Certainly, he has a mischievous streak, and often urges me to cut catechism class to join him on a Wednesday afternoon. When I do so, it is within the safety of the group. Our ringleader Sylvie has decided we shall all skip class and head for the Métro.

At the top of the Champs-Elysées, underneath the triumphal arch at the Place Charles de Gaulle, three lines of the Paris Métro intersect. The result is a labyrinth of connecting corridors that schoolchildren have discovered is ideally suited to tag. As you tear down the hallway leading towards the platform *Direction Porte Dauphine,* you can vaguely hear pounding feet and joyful cries below you in some other corridor. On the orange-tiled platform *Direction Nation,* where the train reaches a terminus before starting back down towards the Left Bank, it disgorges passengers onto the right track before opening doors to receive new ones from the left. If you time your arrival carefully enough, you can elude a pursuer by running right through a car during the few moments when the doors are open on both sides. Even better if he manages to get onto the train only to have the exit doors across from him slam in his face. Turning to go back the way he has come, he will find those doors closing too, and while his prey laughs delightedly in the background, he will be carried down the line to the next stop, Kléber.

I have pulled off that trick on at least one occasion, but David is no fool and times his quick passage through the doors correctly, catching up with me on the other side. He tags me with a hand on my arm and keeps hold of me, panting heavily with the exertion of the game and unsure what to do with his prize.

Sylvie, the instigator of the afternoon's activities, rounds a corner from the other direction, calling my name in French: "*Marie, Marie.*"

I am Marie, after my grandmothers—Mary, a shrunken little Englishwoman hidden away in an old-age home in Liverpool, and Marie, an elegant Quebec dowager retired to a cottage on the shores of a Laurentide lake. Marie is just French for Mary, the Virgin's name, a plain enough label in English, slightly prettified

by its rendition in French as *ma-rie*. But say it in English—mu-ree—
and it's a silly, pretentious little name that makes me think of the
tunes from American musicals that my father whistles, or of a bleach-
blonde hairdresser in a Liverpool beauty shop I once visited, under
protest, with my mother. I am *Marie*, but would rather not be Marie.

My father's family sailed to Canada from Normandy in 1690, at
least that is what *Grand-mère* says. My father reversed the voyage in
1960, making a young Quebecker's pilgrimage to the motherland
and stopping in Paris. He met my mother in a gallery of medieval
ivories at the Louvre, and fell in love with a hesitant young
Englishwoman who spoke bad French and worked as a nanny for a
Parisian family. They were married within a year, and stayed in
Paris, partly out of romanticism and partly as the first of my father's
many concessions to my mother's desires. She wanted to remain
close to her family in England, and so they compromised on France:
his language, her side of the Atlantic.

At home, the three of us speak together in English. My mother
trips along in the proper middle-class accent she was taught in her
Catholic day school; my father offers a flawless version of the flat
North American tones he learned from *les Anglais* of his youth in
Montreal. My accent hovers in between. My mother calls it mid-
Atlantic and I have an image of a rocky island somewhere west of
Britain filled with people who speak English the way I do. In French
there is no choice. The soft, sweet drawl of my father's Canadian
tongue is an impossibility. I speak as my Parisian classmates do, with
unctuous *u*'s, rolled *r*'s and *t*'s spat out like orange pits.

We live in France like permanent tourists, forever visiting, noting and distinguishing, savouring the culture yet holding ourselves
aloof. "In England . . ." my mother will begin, as she remarks on a
difference in custom or habit—the hour at which people eat or the
age at which they marry. "Now, there's something you'd never see
in Canada," my father will pronounce at the sight of everything

from a Gothic cathedral to a boy pissing in the street. Our weekends and holidays are filled with museums, churches, and castles, as though perhaps our stay in this fascinating place would not last forever. My father sells antiques; my mother practises self-improvement; all three of us, we believe in art.

And so it is that a hundred French villages will live forever in my mind's eye. Shaded avenues, stone facades, winding streets, giddy spires, northern walls, southern roofs. The wind blows across a beach in Brittany; the sun warms a roof garden in Provence. Some I can name—Etretat, Bergerac, Vaucluse—but others bear the faintest identities, hardly distinguishable from dreams. There is a place along a riverbank, a few urban streets quickly giving way to small country houses with gardens opening onto the towpath. Men fish, my parents walk ahead of me along the river. Have I visited this place or dreamt it? Was it the destination of a weekend outing or has my imagination given three-dimensional life to a scene painted by Seurat or Monet that I must have seen in a museum? I cannot tell, but cherish its vague outlines, knowing there must be some reason they dwell with me.

A hundred French villages live in my mind's eye, but I know only one place in Canada: the cottage. Every other summer, my mother packs huge suitcases, fussing about swimsuits, rain gear, and warm sweaters, while my father struts about the apartment beaming, showing me plane tickets and passports, checking the progress of our preparations. We fly to Montreal, a city that flickers large and sprawling beneath the descending plane but on the ground never proves to be anything more than an airport and circling highways. We soon leave it behind because, despite the long flight, my father is impatient to keep going. He rents a car and drives us northward.

It is always dark when we arrive, alighting in a deep blackness that silences you so thoroughly you can hear the rustle of trees and the sound of waves. I would pause to savour this new yet familiar place where the scent of pine, air, and water hints at a great wildness that might yet be glimpsed if I could wait long enough for my eyes to grow accustomed to the night.

But my parents have no reason to dally. They hustle forward, anxious to announce their appearance, seeking the warmth and babble of the cottage kitchen with its big stone hearth. The generous room smells of woodsmoke and is filled with the kissing and chattering of uncles, aunts, and cousins. We exchange greetings, unpack gifts, relate our travels, and made hungry by the excitement of arrival, we eat bread and cheese washed down with black tea, talking until exhaustion overtakes us. A long night ends on a narrow bunk in the dormitory behind the kitchen, warmed by the backside of the same stone hearth, and there begins a languorous summer of breakfast in blue jeans before the dew has evaporated, warm swims at noon under big, blue skies, berry picking on scorching afternoons when the heat bugs sing, and gentle evening canoe rides past the large, lurching pine that marks the edge of our bay.

My cousins laugh at my French vocabulary—*cuisinière* for *poêle*, *shopping* for *magasiner*—and when it comes to English, mimic my trans-Atlantic accent, but they are happy to include me in their games. They speak largely in French, with English, the language of the schoolyard and the street, thrown in for bravado. We devote a whole summer to paper dolls, a swimming contest—who can make it into the lake every day no matter how cold the water—tag, kick the can, or skipping rope. We teach each other our rhymes.

"*Am stram gram, pic et pic et colégram, bourre et bourre et ratatam, am stram gram pic dam.*"

"Engine, engine number nine, going down Chicago line . . . And you are not it."

"*Ne pleure pas, Jeannette, Alazim boum boum, alazim boum boum, ne pleure pas, Jeannette, nous te marierons . . . avec le fils d'un prince ou celui d'un baron . . .*"

"Tinker, tailor, soldier, sailor, rich man, poor man, beggar man, thief, doctor, lawyer, Indian chief."

Jocelyne, the eldest of my cousins, always treads on the bright-pink rubber rope on "rich man" or, failing that, "doctor" or "lawyer." She already knows these are the professions of wealth, and slow moving with a burgeoning plumpness, she will purposely let the boys catch up with her when we play tag with the neighbours. I love Lisette, her younger sister, better. Wiry but awkward, she will step on the rope unpredictably.

"A tinker, Lisette, a tinker. You're going to marry a tinker." We have no idea what a tinker might be, but sense the small, cramped English word promises little.

I am long-legged and strong-limbed and can skip rope forever, never missing a beat, exhausting my cousins' arms.

"Tinker, tailor, soldier, sailor, rich man, poor man, beggar man, thief, doctor, lawyer, Indian chief, tinker, tailor, soldier, sailor, rich man, poor man, beggar man, thief, doctor, lawyer, Indian chief, tin-kertailorsoldiersailor . . . *Tu ne te marieras pas, Marie.* You won't have a husband, you won't have a husband." I just laugh, secure in my strong legs that can always evade the rope and carry me out of reach of the boys next door.

David is calling to me in English from across the street— "Marie, see you tomorrow"—as my mother hurries ahead. I wave and then run after her to the car parked at an outrageous angle in the cul-de-sac.

Outside the Royal Ontario Museum, there are vending carts covered in pink and silver balloons, inflated toy animals, and striped pinwheels. Beneath this gaudy and bobbing array, the cart is anchored by a glass case of yellow popcorn at the front and includes a bicycle seat and double wheels to propel the whole contraption from the back. In the middle, there is a brazier, tended by a withered little Mediterranean man who roasts European chestnuts over his coals. On a November day, the smell of bitter smoke and sweet pulp wafts on the chill breeze and a fifteen-year-old girl breathes in and remembers a childhood in Paris.

R ACHEL PLOT TURNED FROM the cabbage borscht she was stirring, wiped her hands on the wide expanse of her floral apron, and took the mail from Sarah's hands.

"There will not be any more letters."

She said the words gently but with certainty, stating a fact rather than a prohibition.

Every day since Sarah had started school that fall, she had stopped on the Plots' front porch on her way back into the house at four o'clock and checked the battered red-tin mailbox that hung underneath the number plate. Today, she had come into the kitchen clutching the Canadian Tire catalogue, the electricity bill, and a postcard of Quebec City sent by Rachel's flighty Montreal cousin Leah who had just spent a weekend there with her husband.

At first, when the Plots had noticed Sarah's anxious stops at the mailbox, the couple had merely caught each other's eye and then looked away, saying nothing. In October, they had briefly discussed the matter, and after that Rachel made sure she cleared the box herself after the postman's afternoon rounds. But it was now December, and she had dropped this practice, soon tiring of Sarah's shy but resolute daily question: "Were there any letters for me?"

There had been a letter for her once—just once. It had arrived in September when she had been staying with the Plots for two months. Smuggled out of Paris by means the Plots could only guess at, the letter bore a Spanish postmark and was addressed to Sarah Bensimon, c/o the Jewish Immigrant Aid Society, 4145 Boulevard Saint-Laurent, Montreal, Quebec, Canada. It did not arrive in the red-tin mailbox—Rabbi Cohn brought it himself after Sarah had left for school one morning, and Rachel had presented it to her that afternoon, hovering by her to hear what it contained.

For all the circuitous and improbable route their missive had taken to reach Sarah, her parents had little to say. They were well, they hoped she was well. Papa was still finding some work in M. Richelieu's office, and they would stay in Paris for the time being. Oncle Henri sent his love, as did they, knowing she would study hard and keep healthy until they could be reunited. With their kindest regards to her Canadian hosts, they ended their one-page letter.

Sarah kept it carefully folded inside its original envelope in a cigar box at the back of her underwear drawer, along with a few French francs and the pearls her mother had hung around her neck the day before she left. In years to come, she was to pull it out from its envelope so often the paper eventually disintegrated. She would read its sentences until she knew them like a prayer, but most of all she would simply stare at the words, "Your loving parents," as tangible proof that Philippe and Sophie Bensimon had existed. Indeed, it was her proof that she herself had existed before the day, four months before her twelfth birthday, when she arrived in Canada and became Sarah Simon, the prefix of her last name lopped off by a Halifax immigration officer who just wanted to make her adjustment—and his paperwork—that much easier.

In Paris, where her family practised little of their distant ancestors' religion but knew which neighbours were Jews and which were Christians as part of an unspoken hierarchy they seldom pondered, Sarah Bensimon's name instantly—and dangerously, as things were to turn out—identified her race. In Toronto, where Rachel and Sam Plot lit the Shabbat candles with affectionate pride every Friday night just as their parents had done in the Russian and Polish villages from which they had emigrated, Sarah Simon bore a name that allowed her to pass as part of the Anglo-Saxon majority. She had always spoken English well, for Sophie had been vigilant in her supervision of Sarah's schooling. Within a year in Canada, the girl's accent had all but disappeared and Sarah, with her light-brown hair and small features, had become invisible.

Rachel sometimes wondered, when Sarah first arrived in their home or later, after the war had ended, with what sort of foresight the Bensimons had been blessed. While their neighbours debated whether they should comply with the orders to register with the French police, some arguing it would all blow over if one just laid low, others believing it was safest to comply with the letter of the new law, were the Bensimons somehow immune to the optimism to which lesser souls still clung? Did they know from what fate exactly they had rescued Sarah? How could they not know, Rachel wondered, for what mother would send her child across the ocean to a family she had never met unless she believed it was the one way to save her life.

If Rachel pondered the situation, trying to imagine what Sarah's mother felt, it was because, while she could never know for certain what had moved Sophie to give up her daughter, she suspected exactly why she, Rachel, had been chosen to receive the girl. She had been chosen by Rabbi Cohn because he pitied her. She was certain of it and felt ashamed. Well, perhaps he respected her too, she might hope, believing that she would provide for the girl a good Jewish home—even if she and Sam did seem a bit isolated, all the way out here in the west end of town. But mainly she saw that he felt sorry for her and, giving precedence to the wrong needs, thought that the young Sarah would provide for Rachel.

Rabbi Cohn had met Rachel two years before Sarah arrived, in 1940, or rather he had met Sam, at a meeting of the Workers'

Benevolent Association in a hall down on Spadina. Since he himself had arrived in Toronto from Cleveland in '38 to lead a small Conservative congregation on Berkeley Street, the rabbi had never set foot in such a place, but tonight he needed the members of the Workers' Benevolent Association. He was there to talk about events in Europe and to ask the men to volunteer their homes: Canada had agreed to accept five hundred European orphans who were to arrive from France in less than a month's time. Committees in Montreal, Toronto, and Winnipeg had been established to find the families who would board them. Uptown, at Holy Blossom, his Reform colleagues were beating the drum, making speeches and raising money, but maybe they hadn't found so many people who really wanted a stranger's child underfoot. At any rate, they were looking downtown now, and had called him. His congregation, in turn, was puzzled that the children were being sent to Canada not Palestine, and, finding few volunteers there, he had agreed to help further by speaking at a meeting called by the Benevolent Association. At the end of the evening, the Zionists were still protesting that greater efforts were not being made to settle the orphans in Palestine, while others said the matter would require further debate. Only one person had come forward to volunteer.

"I'm Sam Plot. I will talk to my wife and call you."

And, after one long, agonizing week of talking to Rachel, he did call. They had discussed it for hours, the wrongs and the rights of it, had finally agreed this would not solve their problem, that they must not even hope it could solve their problem, but yes, they would be happy to provide a home for an orphan. "We will take a child," Sam told the rabbi.

As Ottawa dragged its heels on issuing visas and debated what numbers could be accommodated, Rabbi Cohn found he had plenty of time to visit the homes that would receive the children, and Sam got off the phone again one evening to tell Rachel to expect a caller.

"A rabbi? What's he going to think of us?" she wanted to know. "I had better start cleaning."

But when he entered the house on Gladstone Avenue, Rabbi Cohn did not sense Rachel's nervousness that her house and housekeeping were about to be judged. Instead, he saw the quiet, uncomplaining facade she presented to the world, appreciated its gentleness, and quickly guessed at the greater sorrow that lay beneath. When he asked, Rachel revealed she was thirty-five. There were no children in the house.

The Toronto committee, not to be outdone by Winnipeg's eager response, eventually found its quota of Jewish homes, but in the end the five hundred orphans never came. There was this problem, there was that problem. Rabbi Cohn lost track of them all, and sent out a form letter to most of the volunteers, but he went to tell Rachel the news himself.

"So you wouldn't need us after all?"

"No."

"Well, perhaps this too is God's will . . ."

She sound gracious rather than defeated.

The rabbi, on the other hand, did not accept God's will with the equanimity that one perhaps might expect of a religious man. He was righteous and, by 1941, he was furiously angry. He did not think Rachel Plot deserved to be barren, he did not think one could stand idly by while the Nazis in occupied Europe sent Jewish parents off to work camps and then declared their children orphans, and he did not think it was necessary to be polite to the bureaucrats. In guilty moments, he gave into this wrath and designed horrible tortures or imagined just fates for the intractable Mr. Blair, director of the immigration branch in Ottawa. His contacts at the Jewish Immigrant Aid Society, who had once accepted his help eagerly, no longer permitted him to attend their increasingly desperate meetings, still believing that gentle words would sway Canadian officials where the rabbi urged threats and demonstrations. In fact, he had not heard from the society in almost a year, when an official called to say that a dozen refugees on special permits had somehow made it to Halifax and they needed a home for one child. He called Rachel that afternoon. Since 1935, from the hundreds of thousands of Jews who had applied to leave Europe for resettlement in North or South America, Canada had accepted 3,273. Sarah Bensimon was one of the lucky ones.

But Sarah did not feel very lucky. Rather she felt small. On the red streetcar that clanged along Bloor Street, leading her from the Plots' home on Gladstone Avenue east to the shops and lights of Yonge Street, she would catch herself staring at strangers, trying to fathom their Canadian lives. Where were they all hurrying to? What did their parcels and bags contain? Did they like it here? Perhaps they did since they knew nowhere else. Once a man got angry with her, and barked out, "Have I got something on my nose, then?" She flushed and looked at her shoes, belatedly reminded that other people could actually see her.

At Yonge Street, Sarah would change cars to head south, towards the vast lake that lies at the bottom of the city. In winter, it was cold and barren, abandoned by all but a few rugged ferry boats, still crossing to and from the Toronto Islands. By June, its beaches were filled with pale-skinned people drunken on the strong sunlight of the brief Canadian summer. Sam Plot had taken Sarah there, to go swimming, a week after she arrived. The day was sweltering, the kind of heat that hits you like a wall when you walk out of the darkened house, but Sarah found the huge lake surprisingly cold and stayed only a few minutes in the water.

By fall, as fierce winds blew off the lake and the city shrank northwards towards its brick houses and small parks, Sarah stopped venturing this far south any more, but knew to get off the Yonge car at Queen Street. There she would trip up the steps to the cavernous Eaton's department store to explore the wonders that lay inside its marble halls. Hats, scarves, bangles, lipsticks, Sarah pondered them all.

Rachel had introduced her to the delights of Eaton's in October, when the first cold snap came and the air acquired an edge Sarah had never felt before. She had survived thus far on the few clothes she had brought from France, and the many donations of the Immigrant Aid Society, but Rachel pronounced that her good wool school coat, navy blue with a velveteen collar, would not do. So, she and Sarah took the streetcar to Eaton's, and spent a full hour discussing with a massively fat saleslady the competing merits of two coats—one powder blue with something the lady called a princess skirt that flared out in a way that Sarah worried might look babyish, the other dark green with straight lines that Rachel called sensible and Sarah considered dull. Both were made of solid, tightly woven wool and, to Sarah's eye, looked much like the coat she already wore. When she tried them on, however, she felt the difference. They weighed on her shoulders as heavily as any bookbag, and she wondered whether she would not exhaust herself walking under such a garment. The saleslady expertly flipped up the hem and showed Rachel the heavy felt lining. "That's what will keep you warm, Sarah," Rachel said, and in the end they agreed the green was more grown-up.

It was important to look grown-up, for if Sarah had yet to parse the fashion code of her Canadian classmates, had yet to fully grasp their subtle distinctions between types of pleated skirts or wool knee socks, she had quickly understood that to be babyish was to be instantly dismissed. Shoes with a strap and buckle rather than laces were babyish; two pigtails were babyish while a single braid was permissible; hopscotch was babyish, although skipping was still possible, especially if one were able to jump two ropes at once, what the girls called double dutch.

Sarah learned these things slowly, in the schoolyard between classes, watching and listening to the others, although not yet invited to participate in their games. On the first day at school, they had surrounded the new girl and asked her questions. Where had she come from? Why did she speak funny? What did her parents do? Well, if her parents weren't here, who was looking after her, then? But after a day or two, they left the French girl, as they called her, well alone, and Sarah sat on the school steps and watched and listened.

"Tinker, tailor, soldier, sailor, rich man, poor man, beggar man, thief . . ." The rhymes were new to Sarah's ears, and she waited, wondering whether she would be ever be able to clear the rope with the same leisurely ease as her classmates.

"In nineteen hundred and forty-two, Columbus sailed the ocean blue, and the waves went higher, and higher, and ooooover they went . . ."

"In nineteen hundred and forty-two . . ."

"Stupid. It's fourteen hundred and ninety-two . . . Nineteen forty-two, that's now."

"Yeah, that's this year. If Columbus sailed the ocean, Hitler would blow him up."

"Yeah, the Nazis would get him . . ."

For these girls, whose fathers were too young to have fought in the Great War and too old to fight in the current war, events in Europe seemed vague and distant. They whispered occasionally about Jane, whose father was over in London and had to go underground at night to avoid the bombs, or about this new girl sent to Canada for safety's sake. When they spoke of these things, they adopted a hushed air of matronly solicitousness that did little to disguise the thrill of pity that coursed through them when they considered those less fortunate, less secure, than themselves. But these were rare moments, soon forgotten when compared to more immediate excitements—Frances had been chosen to play Mary in the Christmas pageant; Bob Lamberts had told Shirley that he liked her.

Their fathers muttered over the evening papers, grumbling at the slow progress of the war. Their mothers knitted socks and saved the fat from the Sunday roast in a jar that sat on the kitchen windowsill, the contents of which were regularly donated to the people who made guns and bombs. At school, Mrs. Heathgate gave the boys and girls an occasional update on events by pointing to places on the big map of Europe at the front of the classroom. But talk at home was largely devoted to the upcoming church social and whether or not the roof would last another winter, while in history class, Mrs. Heathgate spent more time explaining that, in 1492, Christopher Columbus set off in the *Santa Maria* to discover the New World than she did on current events. In 1603, Samuel de Champlain sailed up the St. Lawrence to Quebec. In 1917, thirty-five hundred brave Canadian soldiers lost their lives at Vimy Ridge.

The girls were proud to be Canadian, loyal subjects of the British King. They were certain that the Allies would soon win the war, but had little sense who it was they were fighting. To be sure, Martha had called Sandra Newberger a Kraut last week, and had been forced to apologize by Mrs. Heathgate. And the girls knew they were to hate Germans, pity subject Europeans, and claim their place alongside just nations like Britain. Most of the time, however, they could not conceive of a world that operated differently from their own.

This was a safe and simple place governed by rules on which they could all agree. You were to sing "God Save the King" with gusto every morning and then close your eyes to intone the Lord's Prayer. And if a Jewish girl did not like that, it was certainly better to put up with it than to draw attention to yourself by leaving the classroom.

You were to complete your homework neatly and hand it in promptly, but never boast about what mark you received. Any girl not wearing a wool vest under her blouse by Canadian Thanksgiving—a Monday early in October—was probably a slut and any girl still wearing one after Queen Victoria's birthday was only to be pitied.

It was at that time of year, in May, as their vests and sweaters were put away, leaving only their cotton blouses to cover their torsos, that the girls watched carefully for the appearance of brassieres. Sitting in class on a sunny day, you could see through their shirts the telltale strap across the backs of the bigger girls. Clearly, they already needed what Mrs. Heathgate referred to delicately as "a little support."

"You might want to consider a little support, dear," she would say quietly after class to any girl whom she felt needed the advice—once she had carefully ensured that no boys were within earshot.

On this subject, if on few others, Rachel Plot had anticipated the embarrassment a new girl in a new school might feel, and that spring, spotting the burgeoning flesh on Sarah's chest, broached the idea of a bra. In this regard, Rachel was determined to do her duty. Soon after Sarah's arrival in Toronto, she had raised the subject of her monthlies, noting to herself that the child was small but worrying that the unexpected arrival of blood would add another burden for one who already carried more than her fair share. She found Sarah confused on the subject, unsure whether she was to bleed for one day every week, or one week every month, and she carefully clarified the issue, placing a box of Kotex napkins and an elasticated belt in Sarah's underwear drawer, reckoning that way she would get used to idea before the time came. She even showed Sarah how to secure the belt and pad, demonstrating as best she could over the top of her skirt, and tried valiantly to place the spectre of the monthly visitor in a larger picture. Sitting on the white chenille spread that covered Sarah's narrow bed, she delivered the speech that begins: "When a man and a woman love each other very much . . . they marry . . ."

Sarah, who had heard whisperings about blood and babies before, was still not entirely aware that what was being described to her was a conscious act. She considered what Rachel said about eggs and seeds, and wondered, since it was clear from their small glances and light laughs that Rachel and Sam loved each other very much, why there were no babies in the house on Gladstone Avenue. She did not ask, however, but took this, along with information about school coats, skipping rhymes, and Samuel de Champlain, into her heart to ponder.

So, whether it was time or not, that first spring, Rachel again took Sarah to Eaton's, for a quiet, almost furtive discussion with the lady in the lingerie department. And it was there, standing amongst the stockings and panties, that Sarah saw her mother.

Sophie Bensimon was wearing a drab-coloured belted raincoat and was busy examining a stocking. Her head was turned away from Sarah, so the girl could only catch the faintest corner of her mother's profile. Yet she knew that this dark, svelte woman was her. There was something in the way she wore the coat, its waist tightly cinched, its shoulders squarely aligned with her own, something even in the way she held the stocking, as though she were interested but unconvinced by it, that summarized for Sarah the wisdom and elegance of her own mother. Sophie radiated a quiet grace without appearing arrogant, the poise of a woman who could tell the salesgirl that the stocking was certainly not ten denier without giving the least offence. Beside her, Rachel Plot looked stout and poorly dressed.

Sarah's heart rose. Her stomach felt empty, her head light, her throat dry. She lurched forward, ready to fling herself at the svelte and dark woman and cry, "Maman, here I am." And yet, at twelve,

Sarah's experiences had already lodged inside her something hard and adult, a measure of what some call realism and others hopelessness. Whatever it was, that thing held her back, silenced the words in her throat, quieted the movement in her limbs, left her standing at Rachel's side as a stranger rejected a stocking that she had been considering and walked towards the exit.

Sarah was to see her mother again and again over the next years—a woman across the street, a woman boarding a bus, a woman seven rows ahead at the movie theatre, a woman pushing a baby carriage through a park, a woman turning the next corner and hurrying out of sight. Sometimes Sarah even gave chase, following small, dark women until she lost them in crowds; sometimes, she simply stared until the woman, sensing her gaze, turned her head. And then Sarah would see the beloved profile of her mother with its little nose gently tilting up and away from its brief yet full lips dissolve into the pudgy featureless face of someone else. Sometimes, her mistake was ridiculous—why this woman was Chinese; that one old enough to be her grandmother. Other times she seized on one single feature, a sparkling eye, a rouged cheek, and stared only at it, measuring how close a match it was with her mother's.

At night, alone in her room, Sarah would rail at these ghosts, anger fighting sorrow for a place in her heart, and momentarily conquering it. "Why did you send me here?" "Why do you get to stay home with Papa?"

And so, as Sarah made friends in the schoolyard and learned to skip double dutch, as she memorized the name of every prime minister since Confederation and sat the Senior Matriculation Examinations, as she joined a Zionist youth group at the urging of a classmate, as she rode the roller coaster and ate cotton candy at the Canadian National Exhibition, as she enrolled in honours French at the

University of Toronto, as she took a part-time job shelving books at the University College library, as she kissed a boy she had met at a picnic, and as she laughed with the girls in her class, she remembered that there was something that kept her apart from these events. It was a distance less tangible than the absence of her mother tongue, yet simpler too: Some day, she would go home.

She told Sam and Rachel of her intentions not long before the end of her second year at university. She had saved money from her job at the library, and once classes finished in the first week of May, she would take a trip to Europe. She would spend some time in Paris. She had found an inexpensive pension, where she had booked a room for a month, but could stay longer if necessary. Professor Manfred in the French department had recommended it as clean and quiet, suitable for a North American girl. She hesitated on the words, and finally said simply to Rachel, "I want to know."

Rachel lowered her head and said nothing. It was Sam who exploded into speech: "You will learn in Europe one word, one word you will learn—Auschwitz."

Embarrassed by the tears now flowing from his eyes, he left the room, barging out the front door and hurrying off down Gladstone Avenue towards College Street. Sam was slow to anger, more likely to shake his head over the griefs and offences of his life than to raise his voice or his fist. It was not for his own sake that he had yelled at Sarah, but for Rachel's. He had accepted their childlessness as the will of nature, of God perhaps, if you believed in such things; he had volunteered to take in a refugee child from Europe because this was clearly where duty lay. He had quite consciously tried to be kind, friendly, and sympathetic to Sarah, hugging her in his arms on the way through the door or handing her a package of the honey cake he had brought home from a bakery near the factory where he worked. He had liked the child, she was quiet, she gave no trouble, but he had never hoped nor wished that she were his own. Rachel, he knew, had sometimes had such dreams. More before, back in those futile weeks in 1940 when they had first said yes to Rabbi Cohn, and then again, the second time, in the few days that had separated another phone call from the actual trip to Union Station to greet Sarah. In those times, Rachel had permitted herself a fantasy or two, he could tell by the little vacant smile he would find on her face when he came into the kitchen in the morning or the nervous way in which she pleated her fingers as they rode the streetcar south to the train station.

Not that Rachel had ever presumed, once Sarah had arrived. You couldn't possibly with that child—her formal manners, her silence, her seriousness kept you at a distance. If your gesture was tentative, if your laugh was the least bit forced, her intelligent gaze would stop you cold, seeming to say, "That's not love, that's pity." And yet to love her properly was also impossible, for this silence stood between you and her as a gap that could never be fully crossed. And so, over these nine years, as Sarah had grown, there remained this small resentment in the Plot household, this little piece of bitterness, because Sarah Simon somehow refused to become Sarah Plot. Rachel would never speak of it that way, she would never say a word against Sarah, for Sarah's burden was already too great, Sarah's pain already unimaginable, yet still, Rachel no longer truly tried to love Sarah.

The subject of Europe was taboo in the house on Gladstone Avenue. When Sarah had arrived in 1942, she had been "sent on ahead" by wealthy Parisian parents "eager to emigrate to Canada or indeed any British protectorate that would afford them entry." That was how her case was described in the letters received by the Immigrant Aid Society. In 1943, she was a refugee child, saved from the war in Europe, sent to Canada by parents whose "situation surely must be desperate." That was how the principal at Sarah's school described her to Miss Laddersmith, who was to be her teacher for her second year in Canada. In 1944, all was silence. As those around her became increasingly aware what must be the fate of Sarah's parents, they grew too uncomfortable to even whisper about it amongst themselves. Rachel and Sam did not speak of the war, had not seen Rabbi Cohn for over a year now, and quickly turned the page of the newspaper if their eyes lighted on a story of atrocities in Europe. In 1945, British, American, and Soviet soldiers liberated camps where the living looked like the dead and the dead lay in tangled piles that did not look like anything the world had ever seen.

And still in the house on Gladstone Avenue, Rachel and Sam did not speak of the war and Sarah did not tell them that she had started scanning the posted lists of displaced persons before she had even turned fifteen. In the end, she sought out Rabbi Cohn and, with a defeated maturity that he could barely stomach, asked if inquiries might not be made in Europe to ascertain the fate of her parents.

"I've looked on the DP lists. They aren't there."

Rachel and Sam eventually knew that Sarah was in correspondence with the Red Cross, for the letters arrived in the old red-tin mailbox that hung underneath the number plate beside the front door. Once Rachel even found it within herself to ask: "Any news?"

"No news," Sarah replied.

In her first year in their house, Rachel had sometimes caught herself secretly hoping for a letter from Europe that would announce the death of the Bensimons. She guiltily withdrew the thought the moment it entered her head, but never fully repented it. With Sarah's parents dead, the girl could mourn, and the Plots adopt. She and Sam had believed an adopted child was never really your own, they had talked it over long and hard that week in 1940 after the meeting of the Workers' Benevolent Association and reached that conclusion, but still, once Sarah was in their midst, Rachel was not so sure. She thought somehow a legal bond might make them closer, happier. But no news ever came and Sarah was twenty now. Despite Sam's anger on her behalf, Rachel recognized that it was too late. Sarah would never be Rachel's daughter, and so, as Sam stormed down the street, she lifted her head to the girl and said, "We have done what we can for you. Go to Paris."

PARIS. WEDNESDAY, AUGUST 9, 1893.

It is not often I am still in Paris at this time of year, and I do not believe it is healthy. It has been stifling hot. One cannot think of anything one really wants to do, except lie still and, at best, read a book. Thank goodness Marcel has left. This weather would be sure to incapacitate him. Dick barely notices, and keeps studying in his room. I have told him he must take a break soon, but he insists that it is necessary to be well prepared for the autumn term.

Adrien made Marcel promise before he left for Saint-Moritz that he would give serious consideration to the issue of his career, and start studying to resit his law exams. It must be resolved by autumn. Marcel has suggested the Ecole des Chartes might be a possibility. His father is unsure, and does not think he has the patience and endurance required for museum work. I had to point out to Adrien that his position is not entirely consistent: one cannot urge the boy to apply himself more resolutely on the one hand, and then tell him he is unfit for careers that require such application on the other. Adrien still thinks Marcel should do law despite last term's fiasco, but I feel a museum would perhaps be a good compromise, as it might answer some of Marcel's artistic tendencies.

I have been trying to make my way through Monsieur Zola's latest. It is supposed to be the last in the *Rougon-Macquart* series, a summary of all its themes. Marie-Marguerite was teasing me that I have chosen it as my summer reading only so that I do not have to bother with all the preceding volumes, which is true enough. I gave up on *Germinal* halfway through, and it seems to me there have been several more since then. This new one is hardly edifying at all. I have just got to a bit where the Docteur Pascal has relations with his niece. I do find M. Zola's insistence on such details unnecessary in the end.

TROUVILLE. HÔTEL DES ROCHES NOIRES. MONDAY, AUGUST 21, 1893.

There is good company at the hotel this year, less of the Semitic element that troubled us last summer, and amongst the people with whom we are already acquainted in Paris, we find the Hanotaux. Adrien had a long conversation with Monsieur yesterday from which he emerged quite buoyed. He had been tactfully discussing our concerns over Marcel's future career and M. Hanotaux was very encouraging about the possibilities of combining a serious employment with some literary interests, which he always managed. The key is to get the career on track, and he said that in our place he would urge Marcel to take his licence in law, arguing it did not necessarily mean one would work as a lawyer, but was a good basis for public service. I told Adrien I would speak of the suggestion to Marcel in today's letter.

TROUVILLE. HÔTEL DES ROCHES NOIRES. THURSDAY, AUGUST 24, 1893.

Letter from Marcel today replying one cannot combine two things as Gabriel Hanotaux has done. Indeed, he was quite rude about it and said M. Hanotaux has not successfully combined the two, for if his political career may be deemed fruitful, his histories are only boring. (Adrien said that was just spite, but silently I had to agree with Marcel. I have always found the books unreadable.)

I have started *La Rôtisserie de la Reine Pédauque,* and am quite captivated by the Abbé Coignard and all his troubles. Such a relief from Zola. I must tell Marcel to pass on my compliments to Monsieur France when next he meets him at Mme. A. de C.'s.

I am always slightly amazed by that household. Marcel says M. A. de C. is quite open about the relationship between M. France and his wife, and makes bitter little jokes about it whenever he sticks his head in to see her guests. Once someone not quite in the current introduced himself, saying how happy he was to meet the master of the house, and Monsieur replied no, he was quite mistaken, that was the master over there, indicating M. France. I have always thought that if one is to tolerate these things—and after all, one tolerates them, what choice is there—it is best to do so with grace. But I suppose it is much different for the men.

No news from Dick, always such a negligent correspondent.

TROUVILLE. HÔTEL DES ROCHES NOIRES. SATURDAY, SEPTEMBER 2, 1893.

Adrien returns to Paris tomorrow and I fear the last days of his holiday have not been as restful as they should have been. He really needed a proper month—two weeks is not a vacation. He and Marcel just upset each other with their exchange of letters, and yesterday we got a final response from Marcel that did not please him. Marcel said he would resit the law exams next month and has reapplied himself to his studies with that in view, which should have pleased his father. But I think what really angered Adrien was that he spoke of bowing to our wishes, as though they were not reasonable plans, and also repeated his affirmation that a career outside of philosophy or literature would just be so much lost time for him.

I only wish he would be more realistic about this. To make one's bread from literature alone seems unlikely. I have nothing but admiration for M. France, for example, but if M. Hanotaux is rare in combining literature and politics, M. France is rarer still in making a good living from his pen alone. It is such an unstable and unpredictable career.

It is not, I suppose, that Marcel will need that much money. One does not like to speculate on these things, but in the fullness of time his share of his grandfather's and his great-uncle's fortunes will pass to him, of course. But inherited wealth should never be used as an excuse for frittering away one's life or avoiding one's duty. I am composing a stiff letter to Marcel, although Adrien's last words on the subject were affectionate enough—"Tell the boy to cut back on cream cheese," he advised me, because Marcel has been complaining of his digestion too.

TROUVILLE. HÔTEL DES ROCHES NOIRES. MONDAY, SEPTEMBER 4, 1893.

Saw the doctor safely onto the train yesterday. I bumped into the Faures in the dining room at lunch. They had just arrived, late in the season, but some business had kept him in Paris and she was staying with her relations in the interim. Pleasant to see them again. Her devotion to her girls is quite touching to witness—she talks of nothing but her love for them. Lucie is a mother now, but Antoinette has yet to marry and we agreed she and Marcel must get reacquainted in Paris this autumn.

Sometimes, I really feel lucky I do not have daughters. Sons may need a bit of prodding, but imagine having to round up candidates for a daughter every season. It would be exhausting work. If the girl was not married by twenty-two, a mother might drop dead from the sheer effort of it!

Anyway, an introduction between Marcel and Antoinette

must surely be arranged. How quickly they grow up—certainly the last time I saw here she was only a little girl. Her mother showed me her photograph: she now has the most lovely dark hair, rather like the little de Benardaky girl with whom Marcel was once so taken.

TROUVILLE. HÔTEL DES ROCHES NOIRES. THURSDAY, SEPTEMBER 7, 1893.
Marcel has arrived and retreated to his room, saying the journey had utterly exhausted him and that he can smell pollen in the air. I protested that we are several miles away from any fields, but he just smiled that patient and sorry smile he gives me sometimes and said, "Really, Maman, I do apologize, but there is pollen in the air." He was not best pleased either when I told him he must meet up with Antoinette Faure when we return to Paris, and just said, "Well, Maman, for the moment I'm not fit to meet anyone, let alone a young lady." I had so looked forward to his arriving, but now that he is here we seem to have started off on the wrong foot.

Adrien writes in this morning's letter that old Dr. Charcot has died. The lunatics will surely miss their guardian but his work lives on. Adrien says his Austrian follower, Dr. Fruden, is now pursuing his teacher's research into hysteria, so that Dr. Charcot will not soon be forgotten. I feel guilty that we had not seen him nor Madame in several years, and must write her a little note of condolences.

TROUVILLE. HÔTEL DES ROCHES NOIRES. SATURDAY, SEPTEMBER 9, 1893.
Marcel is fearfully ill. The poor little boy was just recovering

from his voyage yesterday, and had moved into the bathroom when the maid came in not realizing he was still in the room and, despite my strict instructions to the manager on the subject, opened the window to air the place. Marcel came in from the bathroom, horrified first that there was this young servant in his presence and he still in his pyjamas and then appalled at the sight of the open window. His breathing became instantly laboured, he got right back into bed and sent the maid off to find me. I hurried up from breakfast and there he was in the throes of a ferocious attack.

It is all so stupid. The sea air is supposed to do him good and here he is suffering from his asthma as badly as if we were in Auteuil. I had to go around the hotel with the manager, inspecting other rooms in the hopes of finding one that had not recently been aired, and did finally find an awfully small one up on the fourth floor that seemed all right.

I looked in on him just now and he was fast asleep, with that regular breathing, the sound of which floods me with relief after any attack, but which most of us take for granted every day. I wonder if there has been a month of that child's life when I have not worried. It is a mother's job in the end. I am not sure how I would fill my days if I did not have Marcel and Dick to care for.

It was Ruskin who told us: "Give a little love to a child and you get a great deal back."

TROUVILLE. HÔTEL DES ROCHES NOIRES. THURSDAY, SEPTEMBER 14, 1893.
Marcel and his father have reprised their correspondence on the career question with a long letter from Adrien about the Cour

des Comptes if Marcel does not wish to pursue law. I have told Marcel that his father and I wish him only to be happy and that there is no dishonour in keeping France's account books for her, but I cannot help but secretly agree with him when he says such employment would not suit him. His father, however, is much taken with the idea and seems to have been seeking advice all over Paris.

I had a drive with M. and Mme. Faure yesterday afternoon, followed by tea on the veranda. She has recently discovered Dickens so we had a long talk about his books. Mme. Faure says her favourite so far is *The Old Curiosity Shop,* which I always found a little sentimental but clearly reflects the lady's tender sensibilities. She demanded I pronounce a favourite, and without really giving the matter much thought, I said *Great Expectations,* just because the idea of the jilted Miss Havesham still sitting in her wedding dress after so many years is such a wonderful image of lost love. Mme. Faure said she would get to it next so we might discuss it too, but warned me it might be some time as all Dickens's novels are so very long. She is right, although I never mind a long novel myself as long as the author has a strong moral.

Trouville. Hôtel des Roches Noires. Wednesday, September 20, 1893.
Adrien seems to have abandoned the idea of the Cour des Comptes and I think it is best left forgotten. I will not ask why he has changed his mind, better just to let the whole thing drop. Instead, he and Marcel are now arguing about the law and the possibility of the Ecole des Chartes. Marcel had received a reply from Monsieur Grandjean about that—three years of study to become an archivist, but the Ecole du Louvre is only two

years. He is very worried that a museum job really would leave him no time to write, which seems once again to be his foremost concern. I suggested he write again to M. Grandjean and discreetly inquire how many days a week the keepers are expected to attend the museum.

I really cannot bear the idea of the alternative, which will have to be diplomacy, but there may be nothing for it. I cannot tell Adrien how much I dread the idea, for he would criticize me for being too soft on the boy and I cannot tell Marcel for fear of discouraging him from any path that might be open to him. All I can do at the moment is advise him to give the Ecole du Louvre serious consideration. What a privilege it would be, after all, to dwell every day amongst the beauties of the museum.

I am reminded of a truthful phrase of George Eliot's— there is something in *Middlemarch* about youth being the season of hope only because our elders are hopeful about us.

Trouville. Hôtel des Roches Noires, Friday, September 22, 1893.
Marcel has written a final letter to his father saying he is ready to sit the exams on his return, and enter a law office as soon as he passes. We seem to have arrived at this decision simply so as to arrive at a decision. Marcel is resigned rather than relieved, but I hope that once past these technical hurdles he will warm to the work itself. He leaves on Monday, and I have suggested that he have lunch with his uncle Georges immediately. I shall return at the end of the week, and this morning gave the manager our notice.

A pass. Marcel seems a little unsure what to do with his success, and has still not decided that law is the right route, but Georges will give him advice about how to find a situation. Papa dropped by yesterday afternoon to get word as soon as the results were posted. He was delighted and told him so most heartily. "You are coming along nicely, Marcel, no more silliness, eh?"

Marcel speaks no more of the idea of a novel, thank goodness. These projects are only a waste of time.

WHAT LOVELY IRONY there is in these entries from the summer of 1893—indeed, I have selected these passages to underline both the poignancy and the ridiculousness of the situation. No, Marcel would never become a lawyer and his parents' interventions in his career would prove fruitless in that regard.

You will have gathered that I call Marcel Proust friend. Of course, I never met the man. He died in 1922, forty-four years before I was born. Yet I like to think of him as a friend, a comrade in pursuit of memory, and I have come to the Bibliothèque Nationale to visit him, transported back one hundred years thanks simply to Air Canada.

Certainly, I appreciate his literary achievement. I have read the novel with careful attention, studied the biographies, sought out some critical commentary, yet my affection extends beyond that of an appreciative reader. I feel personal gratitude for what he wrote and sense some human bond. Yes, I know the link is one-sided; I am not delusional. But I don't think my fondness is merely artistic idolatry, that tedious elevation of a distant genius by the dilettante who would aggrandize herself with this connection to a greatness she will never achieve. Proust himself struggled with that demon when he was translating Ruskin: he placed the Englishman on a pedestal and devoted years of his life to Ruskinian pilgrimages, following the critic's footsteps to Venice and Amiens with his art books for guides. In the end, Proust produced some lovely translations of Ruskin's essays, but they merely delayed his own artistic maturity. Another case of getting distracted from the task at hand. My own translations will be less beautiful, of course, yet I hope they are more than a distant tribute. I offer here a real vote of thanks for the novel and some attempt at understanding the man.

Let me explain. I was about fifteen—indeed it was not long after the school trip to Toronto—when I encountered the great French novelist Marcel Proust, or rather a small reproduction of his portrait by Jacques Emile Blanche, staring out from the pages of my high school reader. He is a fragile figure with unnaturally pale skin punctuated by large dark eyes, like pools of balsamic vinegar sitting in white porcelain saucers. His lips are small but gracefully shaped, promising a gentle sensuality. His black hair is parted emphatically down the middle and slicked into place like the Sunday coiffe of a docile schoolboy. He wears evening dress and a white flower in his lapel. He appears as a gentle dandy, romantic, exotic, more intriguing, more desirable than the heroic masculinity of Balzac, Hugo, and Zola whose portraits I have encountered on the preceding pages.

Proust's novel, *A la Recherche du Temps Perdu* or *Remembrance of Things Past,* published in seven books between 1913 and 1927, is more than three thousand pages long—more than a million words devoted to minute description of the narrator's emotional states, aesthetic observations, and social relations in Paris during the *belle époque.* The prose is labyrinthine, the sentences huge puzzles of interlocking clauses that often create whole paragraphs each, sometimes whole pages. The inattentive reader can easily lose her way in this maze, thinking herself all cosily tucked into bed with the narrator as he describes his somnolent state halfway to sleep only to foggily realize that they have somehow been transported downstairs and are now in the hallway tapping on the barometer before setting on a pre-lunch walk, their move quite surprising to her, for in some clause or another she has allowed her attention to wander and so has lost the thread of his story.

Some readers try the first volume, in which the narrator recounts his cossetted childhood, his pubescent pining for his aristocratic playmate Gilberte Swann and the story of her father, a family neighbour in the country and Parisian man-about-town who has an obsessive affair with the courtesan Odette. Few proceed into the next six parts to follow the narrator's rapid rise into the great salons of the Faubourg Saint-Germain; his witty and trenchant observation of their inhabitants like the agate-eyed Duchesse de Guermantes or the arrogant Baron de Charlus; his bourgeois parents' despair that this young socialite will ever make anything of his life, and his dissection of his own obsessive love for a girl called Albertine. Fewer still make it to the very end of the novel to experience the narrator's poignant summation of time recaptured through physical memory, nor to witness the dissipated Baron begging to be whipped by a male prostitute.

Our middle-aged French teacher, her hair wrapped into a tight bun, her owl's-eyes glasses firmly in place, certainly does not want her teenage charges to read such things, nor expects them to venture into such an intimidating text. Yet, it is great literature, which she considers it her duty to teach. We have struggled through the full length of Balzac's *Eugénie Grandet,* we have read Racine and Corneille aloud in class, each of us taking different roles and rendering the classic French alexandrines as nothing more than a monotonous singsong. For Proust, however, we must rely entirely on our reader, which offers a truncated biography, the pale-faced portrait, and a few brief excerpts from the novel.

My best friend Justine and I, girls filled with cultural pretensions despite our inability to grasp much of what we are taught about art and literature, do admit to a certain amused fondness for this man. We giggle over his preciousness, reading in the biographical notes that at age fourteen, in a parlour game, he revealed that his worst fear was to be separated from Maman, and that he spent his later years in bed in a room lined with cork to keep the noise out as he wrote. We know there is something unusual, slightly contemptible about this sick and sensitive creature. On our second day devoted to these excerpts, when Mme. Desjardins steps out briefly to confer with the school principal in hushed whispers in the echoing hallways about some piece of mysterious administrative business, Justine snatches my reader from my hands and, tittering, takes her pencil to the Blanche portrait reproduced there. To exaggerate his unhealthy air, she darkens the circles under Proust's eyes with her lead and erases what little colour there is in his cheeks. Laughing, I pull my property back across the desk to admire her handiwork.

Despite our patronizing delight and giggling vandalism, we have, whether we admit it or not, discovered in our brief taste of his novel a sensitive child in whom we recognize ourselves. A shy waif, he hovers on the staircase while the grown-ups are all at dinner, hoping finally to catch his mother on her way up to bed and secure from her the good-night kiss denied him when his less patient father dismissed him abruptly from the salon as the guests were called to the table. We find there too, more easily admitted, a wealth of detail that inspires our awe and a life dedicated to art that we would emulate. But in the first excerpt that we are required to read, I find more than that—I find a friend's voice speaking to me across time.

This passage is, unbeknownst to our young selves reading drowsily in an overheated Canadian classroom on a grey winter afternoon with the smell of warm, wet wool rising from our clothing, the most famous moment in twentieth-century French literature.

On a cold and dreary day, the adult narrator returns home to his mother who offers him a cup of herbal tea, thinking to warm his body and cheer his spirits. Dipping into his tea that soft, shell-shaped French sponge cake called a madeleine, the narrator is suddenly transported back to his childhood, to the pre-lunch walks, the grey stone church, the eccentric aunts and uncles of his holiday visits to his relatives in Combray. There, he recalls, his bedridden Aunt Léonie would dip a biscuit in her tea before passing it to him, feeding him a mouthful of the soft, sweet crumb thus created. Analyzing his sudden warm and delightful return to childhood, the narrator realizes that the taste of the madeleine contains within it the key to unconscious memory.

Reading this in the classroom, my grey day is equally enlightened. I have encountered in literature, for the first time, an experience I recognize.

That summer, after school is out, exam papers marked and progress to our next grade assured, I go to the public library and select the first volume of *A la Recherche du Temps Perdu*. Little knowing what she was doing, Mme. Desjardins has handed me the key to literature, locked away, so impenetrably it seemed, behind the author's complex language and the child's inability to imagine the adult world. The massive gates swing open, and I begin to read.

ENEDICT, BENDIX, BENJAMIN, Bernard, Bernard, Bernard . . . Bernheim . . . That's all."

"So . . ."

"So? There's no record, mademoiselle."

"No record?"

"No, mademoiselle." The young man was barely polite.

"Is there nowhere else to look?"

"Well, I can see if we have a file." He shrugged his shoulders and disappeared around a metal filing cabinet almost as tall as he was. Sarah stood at the counter waiting, her eyes taking in the cabinets that stretched to the back of the high-ceilinged room and the small window above them, set so high it required a great long crank to open it, as it was now. From somewhere outside she could hear the faintest sound of children's voices, calling while at play, and a little puff of warm air floated down towards her.

She had spent the first days in Paris arranging her few belongings in her small room, visiting museums, buying gifts for the Plots and her Toronto girlfriends, and looking up addresses in the street directories at a nearby post office, the way a writer sharpens pencils to avoid the moment when she must put one to paper. A week passed in that manner before she had the courage to secrete a small piece of paper bearing the address of the Red Cross into the zipper section of her pocketbook and set out by Métro to come here. At the front door, she asked where she might inquire about displaced persons and was directed to the second floor. The young man, thin, small, and dressed in a black suit, was sitting behind the counter, reading a book when she entered and asked her question. He reappeared now, carrying a pale-blue manila folder.

"There's a file," he said. "Inquiries have been made."

Sarah felt fear and hope churning in her stomach, rising up and forcing the air out of her lungs. He handed her the folder, but she found only her own letters inside.

Cher Monsieur. Je vous écris . . .

The young man looked over the countertop, turning his head at a steep angle to read the papers that lay facing Sarah.

"There's a daughter, in Canada . . ."

"These are my letters . . ."

The man looked puzzled.

"But then, you already know, mademoiselle. We have written you." The young man pulled the copy of a reply from the Red Cross towards him and followed the words with his finger as he read them out rapidly, barely bothering to enunciate as he went. "We have noted the registration of both your parents' births in the records of the Mairie of the Eighth Arrondissement and located a copy of your father's professional licence from 1923, but we can find no later record of his address or activities. Specifically, we can find no record of his or his wife's whereabouts after May, 1942, as per your request . . . etc. . . . etc." His voice trailed off as the letter proceeded with its final formalities.

"Can we not look somewhere else?"

He sighed.

"We can look again on the German lists, but if there was any death registered there, we would have transferred it over onto our files," he said. "Still, if you want, we can take another look. It will take a day or two. Someone has to go and get them out of storage, and that's over at the Quai Malaquais."

"I will come back tomorrow," Sarah said firmly.

She returned the next afternoon to find the young man still reading his book.

"Yes." He looked up more promptly this time. "Yes, you were looking for information." He pulled a piece of paper towards him to remind himself of the names. "Philippe and Sophie Bensimon, formerly of 22 Rue de Musset. . . . Their names do not appear in the German records."

Sarah paused and swallowed, then spoke.

"What does that mean?"

"The Germans did not have a record of them living in Paris . . ."

"But they did live here . . ."

"Mademoiselle, these lists . . . During the Occupation, the Germans asked all Jews to register, arrondissement by arrondissement. Your parents weren't registered."

"They didn't register . . ."

"They didn't, they couldn't, they were missed somehow, they chose not to . . . We don't know."

They chose not to. Sarah seized on the words. "They hid?"

"Mademoiselle . . ." the man paused, stopped, and chose not to speak. Then he repeated, "We have no record."

Sarah returned every week to the young man in the Tracing Bureau. She knew that to return every day would be unreasonable, would somehow cross a line that separated her quest, the natural anxiousness of a child to ascertain the whereabouts of her parents, from a mad grief from which there was no recovery. She held herself straight, clasped her pocketbook firmly at her side, and asked her questions with quiet resolution. Every week, the young man told her that there had been no further news, and that the Red Cross would send letters to either her Paris hotel or the Canadian address, whichever she preferred, both if she wanted, as soon as any other information became available.

"You know, mademoiselle . . ." He tried for a moment to sympathize and managed to phrase the words gently. "The war has been over for six years. Little new information is emerging. Most people who were displaced have now registered with the authorities."

On one of her visits, he explained the filing system to her.

"This is the list of everyone on whom we have information," he said, indicating the ledger on the table. "It records their status and points me to a file. Those are the active files, like those of your parents—whereabouts unknown, inquiries being made, immigration recorded . . . and those—" he nodded towards a second bank of filing cabinets—"that's the book of the dead."

"What do you have to do," Sarah asked "to get a name registered there?"

"One witness," he replied. "One witness's account, it doesn't even have to be first-hand. Someone was with someone else in a camp, on a train . . . One witness and we record the name as deceased."

He looked up at her. "It's important, you know, if there's money, an estate . . ."

Sarah nodded.

She had not yet gone to look for her parents in the one place where she might expect to find them—in the spacious fourth-floor apartment on the Rue de Musset that she had left nine years before. It might reasonably have been the first place where she went, and indeed, she anticipated bypassing the concierge on the ground floor, riding up the small iron elevator, knocking on the right-hand section of the impressive double doors that would greet her as she alighted, and walking back into her parents' flat. Simone would step aside to let her in, bobbing politely as she did so, and Maman would emerge from the salon wreathed in smiles. Papa could be seen in his study, tidying up some papers before lunch, and would rise from his desk to join them.

"Sarah, you're back . . ."

"We were just going to write . . ."

"We've just got back ourselves . . ."

"We just haven't had time, things have been so chaotic since the war ended . . ."

"We were just about to send for you . . ."

"We were in hiding, but now everything's back in place . . ."

"We were in a camp but we escaped . . ."

"We were in a camp but we were liberated . . ."

"We hid . . ."

"We ran . . ."

"We survived . . ."

"There's asparagus for lunch—and a good piece of beefsteak."

Like some jilted lover planning every detail of a reunion that would never take place, Sarah would find herself arguing over the logistics of such scenarios in her own mind. It might not be Simone who opened the door; she had left several months before Sarah did, escaping to a family who lived in the unoccupied zone. Would she have returned to the same employer after the war? Could they afford steak for lunch? And surely her parents would have traced her to Toronto long before Papa went back to work or Maman set about tidying up the apartment. "But it's my dream." Sarah would argue back, "We can do whatever we like in my dream . . . What's the point of having a fantasy if you are going to be realistic about it?" And at that point the whole construction would come tumbling down.

On another visit to the Red Cross, the young man confided in Sarah: he expected the Tracing Bureau to be shut down soon.

"They are going to consolidate all the files in Germany, ship them up to Arolsen. I heard that they are already packing boxes at the Quai Malaquais. We're running out of real work, anyway. There used to be ten ladies here who spent hours poring over bits of paper, trying to match names, all enthusiastic. But there's a limit. Let the Germans poke through the stuff. We have done all we can."

Sarah began slowly circling the Rue de Musset, retracing old walks, rediscovering nearby streets she had forgotten existed. She followed the route to her old school, a few streets from the apartment. The Bensimons had moved to the neighbourhood when Sarah was five, so that she could walk to this school: it was a private secular institution, reputedly as good as any of the Catholic schools. She watched the children go in every morning and come out again at the end of the day, laden with the heavy bookbags they carried on their backs, their faces pale in the late-spring sunshine, their limbs thin. They looked undernourished yet happy enough, the stragglers running to catch the bell, a big one looking out for a younger sibling, a clown sending his audience into fits of giggles, a bossy one lecturing the others. One day she was standing outside the school at five-thirty, long after the students had gone home, when an older pupil, a girl almost Sarah's age, emerged from the front door and saw her standing on the sidewalk.

"Anne-Marie's just coming," the girl said, and then stopped, realizing there was an error. "Were you looking for someone?" she tried instead, politely.

Sarah shook her head and moved on.

Eventually, Sarah investigated the Rue de Musset. There was still a bakery on the corner. There was still a church further along—

the spire could be glimpsed but the apse was now hidden by a new building erected at a slight bend in the street. And, directly in front of her, the apartment building stood unchanged. She remembered the great wrought-iron and glass front door and the red carpet she could see on the other side of it, running down the middle of the marble stairs that led towards the elevator and secured with a brass rod across the back of each step. Once, the Bensimons name had been tidily written on a slip of white paper secured inside a small panel that hung beside the door, listing the tenants and their floor numbers. The panel and the names were gone; in their place was a new doorbell. On Sarah's third visit to the street, she rang it.

An elderly woman in a flowered pinafore and brown carpet slippers emerged from behind a set of curtained French doors to one side of the lobby and shuffled her way forward. She examined Sarah suspiciously and opened the massive door a crack, struggling to hold its weight back.

"*Pour qui?*"

"Who do you want?" she asked.

"Madame, I was looking for some people who used to live here, the Bensimons. Perhaps you could tell me . . ."

"I know nothing," the woman replied, and made as if to close the door.

A name suddenly entered Sarah's head.

"Madame Delisle. You don't recognize me, I am older. I am Sarah Bensimon. I used to live here with my parents."

"They are long gone. Everyone left. The war, you know."

"Do you know where they went?"

"I regret I know nothing," she said and closed the door.

On subsequent visits, no one answered when Sarah rang the bell, although once she saw the white curtain on the French doors twitch. She went into the bakery at the corner and asked after her parents. The woman behind the counter said she would go and fetch her mother. The lady herself soon appeared. She looked familiar to Sarah, and said she remembered the Bensimons, but had no idea when they had left the neighbourhood.

"You know, with the Occupation, it was . . . well . . . disorganized." She looked sorrowfully at Sarah, presuming what sad reality lay behind her questions. "Have you tried at the Commissariat?"

Sarah did and the police sent her back to the Red Cross.

Now that she had found the courage to walk her old street, she did it daily, buying bread and cheese at shops along the way and making herself a sandwich to eat in a nearby park. Small and barren, it was not a park she remembered clearly. She had always been taken to play further afield, in the Bois de Boulogne which was just a few more streets over. Perhaps because the Bois was a larger and healthier place for anyone whose legs would take them that far, this little square of dirt with its green benches, metal chairs, and manicured lime trees seemed to be the preserve of the elderly. Two old men played chess together on one bench while a shrunken lady muttered to herself on another.

One day in July, as the weather grew unpleasantly hot and the city quieter, Sarah recognized an old man sitting on a chair across from her. She observed him for a while, then screwed up her courage and approached him, standing awkwardly over him to speak.

"Monsieur, excuse me, but I believe I recognize you. I used to live in this neighbourhood. My name is Sarah Bensimon."

"Leave me alone." He closed his eyes.

"Please, monsieur, I believe you knew my parents. I am anxious to know what happened to them."

He remained silent, his eyes still shut.

Sarah crouched down so that she could bring herself to his level in the chair, trying to make the gesture seem deferential rather than condescending. She tried again.

"Monsieur, I recognize you. Surely, it wouldn't harm you just to tell me if you know where they went."

He opened his eyes and when he spoke he spat the words at her. "*Va demander aux Boches . . .*"

"Go ask the Krauts what happened to your parents. Go ask that bitch across the street," he said, gesturing with his head towards the front door of the apartment building. "That bitch, she's still sitting there, she hasn't sacrificed anything."

He gulped and sank back into bitter silence.

For the first time since her arrival in Paris, Sarah felt herself close to tears.

"I have a right to know . . ."

But the man would not speak and waved her away with his hand.

From then on, Sarah came to the grim little park every day, but the man was never there. She would spend all day on a chair or bench, arriving early with her lunch ready packed, not leaving until the dinner hour approached. She would read a book while she waited or simply sit and think. She found her face and hands became sunburned so long was her vigil, and she bought some expensive cream at the local pharmacy to smear on the exposed skin. The regulars started to recognize her, and would nod their heads at her as they arrived or left. She returned their glances briefly, not wishing to appear rude yet wanting to avoid conversation, especially with the shrunken lady who wore an old and dirty wool coat more suited to December than July and whose muttering occasionally rose to an angry pitch.

It was another one, a friendlier sort, who simply plopped herself down on the same bench one afternoon on Sarah's sixth day in the park and struck up a conversation. She was working away on a tiny sweater (in a purple so lurid that Sarah wondered if the baby for whom it was intended might not take fright at the colour), and she timed her questions to the click of her needles.

"You're a student, are you?" she asked, and began to probe Sarah's life, while offering up details about her own along the way: her poor sister, so ill with the cancer, now deceased, the apartment, her daughter in Lyon, her son-in-law's smart job, the baby that was due next month. Sarah was reticent about her reasons for being in Paris, not wanting to show her hand lest she scare off this woman the way she had the old man. It soon became apparent that the woman had not been long in the neighbourhood, having moved to Paris from Lyon to nurse her ailing sister whose apartment she had subsequently inherited. She needed to decide whether or not to sell it, and was debating this issue at length, when Sarah seized the opportunity of a brief pause in the woman's deliberations to tentatively asked about a man she had seen in the park a few days before. He seemed nondescript, indistinguishable from the other old men who sat there, but she did her best to find some detail the lady would recognize, describing his wispy bits of white hair and sunken face with increasing bluntness.

"Oh, that might be M. Letsky," the woman finally offered. "What did you want him for?"

Sarah tried a lie she had been rehearsing in her head since the lady first struck up conversation, saying she had a found a book in the park that she believed he must have left behind.

"A Jewish book, eh?" asked the knitter, with a nasty emphasis that suggested something distasteful or nefarious, yet made no point that was discernible to Sarah. She fought down her own distaste, ignored the question, and asked where she might find this M. Letsky.

"He'll be in the café," the knitter replied, incuriously enough, indicating a darkened establishment across the street, in the opposite direction from the clean, well-lit place where Sarah had taken to using the facilities, always being careful to purchase a quick coffee or a postcard first.

At four o'clock, the knitter finally packaged up her wool and needles and left, suggesting she might see Sarah the next day. Before her courage failed her, Sarah hurried down the street to the café. It was an unpleasant little place, dusty and sour-smelling, and peopled only by a few crumpled old men, the indoor equivalent of the park. The bartender stared at her laconically as she entered and stood on his threshold, unsure of what she planned to do.

It was M. Letsky who saved her.

"Got tired of sitting in the park, did you?" His sarcastic voice carried across the silent café. She turned to the sound, and walked across the room to his table, her stomach churning in fear.

"I'm sorry," she began, but he waved her to a seat and called to the bartender.

"*Pour mademoiselle . . .*"

Neither bothered to ask what she might drink and the bartender simply produced another tumbler of the rough red wine all his patrons were drinking. Sarah, who had barely touched alcohol in Toronto, sipped and repressed a shudder.

She looked up at M. Letsky and the odd pair stared at each other for a moment without knowing what to say, while the other patrons and the bartender stared at them. Then, perhaps sensing some business needed to be transacted, the bartender turned up the radio loud enough that it would cover their conversation, and the other drinkers turned back to their tumblers.

"So, information about the war . . ." M. Letsky spoke gruffly, angrily, but his mood was apparently more charitable now. "When did you leave?"

"It was a good time after Paris fell, the spring of 1942, my parents sent me to Canada. I don't know how they arranged it. I spent a month at an orphanage in the south, and then took a boat from Lisbon to England and from there to Halifax."

"Yes, by then the smart ones had got out—or were trying to.

Your parents were smart. I didn't know them well, your parents. I was just the little Pole at the stationery shop, yet you recognized me nonetheless."

Suddenly the image of his shop came back to Sarah. It had been an impossibly narrow little place down the street across from the church. Every September, during the first week of school, she would make a trip there, staring up at the high wooden shelves packed with brown-paper packages and cardboard boxes that looked as though they hadn't been touched in years while her mother and M. Letsky went through the long list of her teachers' requirements for the new term. Pens, a bottle of ink, a new diary, a ruler for geometry class, loose-leaf paper, notebooks: M. Letsky would pull them all out from the lower and more accessible corners of his inventory and pile the items up on the counter, adding them up as they went along, and then deferentially present her mother with a bill. Sometimes, she would venture there herself in mid-term when the ink had run out or a notebook was filled, and she remembered now that she had always been a little afraid of M. Letsky.

"Yes, M. Letksy. I remember now, I remember your shop."

"I was the stationer," he nodded, "but your father, he was some fancy lawyer. Well, yes, the camps were great levellers." He ejected the words in a bitter laugh.

"We had all been told to register with the Germans that winter, that must have been before you left. There were stories of roundups, people disappearing in the night or volunteering for work camps. I didn't bother to give them my name, but they found me anyway. Your father too. First, they concentrated on the Eleventh Arrondissement, but they got to us eventually. They rounded up many in this neighbourhood the next autumn and winter. Bad luck your father was a lawyer. They were obsessed with lawyers. 'Too many dirty Jewish lawyers.' We were sent to Drancy. You've heard of it? Outside Paris."

Sarah nodded. It was the transit camp, not twelve kilometres from Paris, more than twelve hundred from Auschwitz. She had heard of it in Canada when she started making inquiries.

M. Letsky continued, speaking in short, staccato sentences as though his own words might soil him if they were to linger one moment longer than necessary on his tongue and lips.

"The conditions were foul. Pee-pee and ca-ca everywhere. Not enough food. Maybe it weakened your mother. We were sent to Auschwitz. She must have died soon after we arrived there. I don't know when. Your father never spoke of it. I could just tell she was gone. The men and women were kept separately, but sometimes messages got through. Someone must have told him. Or maybe he just realized what happened to the weak ones.

"He never mentioned her name. He spoke of you sometimes, though. 'My daughter in Canada.' Kanada. It was our name for the lucky bastards who sorted through all the stuff that was confiscated every time a new transport arrived, piles of coats, ladies' purses. Sometimes they could smuggle things out into the camp, little things, and trade them for a bit of extra food or something, a kind of black market. Kanada," he snorted. "Wealth beyond our dreams. Sometimes we would imagine what you were eating there. Your father was a man who liked his food, I think. A nice *blanquette de veau* for lunch; a sole, a sole *meunière* . . .

You could say he survived. He died the day after liberation."

"He died. How did he . . . ?"

"The hunger. Malnutrition. I don't know."

"But . . ."

"He died, mademoiselle."

Sarah looked at the old man's face and saw his speech had exhausted him. She wanted to pay for the drink, but felt later that she must have badly botched her offer, for he rebuffed her rudely. She tried another gesture, asking politely, "Do you still have your shop?" before realizing her mistake.

"I lost the shop," he said briefly. "I have my pension now."

She put all the gratitude she could into her final attempt: "Thank you. You have been so kind."

He shrugged his shoulders and she left the café.

She went the next day to the Red Cross office but the young man behind the counter was not there. In his place was a motherly figure in her fifties who greeted Sarah with a friendly smile.

"Can I help you?"

"The man who works here . . ."

"Michel? You are looking for Michel? He has moved back downstairs, to Blood Services. You can find him there."

"Oh." Sarah paused, feeling bereft somehow. "Why did he leave?"

"Well, I suppose he is better suited to work in Blood Services." The woman smiled tactfully. Sarah swallowed.

"But I have a file here . . ."

"Oh. I thought you wanted Michel. I can help you with a file. Are you Mademoiselle Simon? Michel told me you might come by."

"Yes. I have found information about my parents. He said I needed only one witness."

She had her witness. The woman listened to M. Letsky's information, opened the huge ledger that still lay on the trestle table, and inscribed the words: "Sophie Alice Weil Bensimon. Born April 30, 1908. Died winter 1942–43 at Auschwitz, exact date and cause unknown."

Then she turned to another register, looked up the date of liberation, and added one day. "Philippe Jean-Jacques Simon Bensimon. Born March 27, 1900. Died as the result of malnutrition at Auschwitz, January 28, 1945." She proceeded to copy the information onto a piece of foolscap, a few black lines at the top of the long white sheet, and then went round to the filing cabinets to tuck the paper away. She returned to the counter, opened another ledger, and made a few notes in its pages.

She looked up and smiled at Sarah.

"It's a relief, information." She smiled again. "We can contact your witness and arrange to have an affidavit signed. I've just made a note here. Then you can get copies of the file whenever you require them."

"Yes, I'll come back," Sarah said, anxious now to be gone. She left and went downstairs, wondering what to do next. She lingered in the hall for a while. There was a sign clearly pointing the direction to Blood Services, so eventually she followed it, pushing through a great swinging door with a window of frosted glass. She entered a pristine white room that seemed entirely empty, with no clerk serving at its shining stainless-steel countertop and no file in sight. She stood there for a while, unsure what to do. Just when she was debating whether she had the courage to cough loudly or would simply leave, a figure in a white lab coat emerged through another swinging door, behind the counter. It was the young man from the Tracing Bureau, Michel.

"So, you found me."

"Yes." Sarah felt embarrassed, but persisted. "Why did you leave?"

"Some people just aren't suited for Tracing." He said the words archly, as though mimicking an officious but friendly superior. Then in his own natural voice, he added, "You have to have hope to work in Tracing, a bit of hope."

"I found a witness."

"Yes. Did Madame record it for you?"

"Yes."

He looked at Sarah, still standing there, and felt both pity and annoyance rising within him. He was tired of these Americans, with their belief in justice and knowledge, as though knowing would make any difference. He had lost both parents and two brothers to the camps, while he hid with a Catholic family in the unoccupied zone. He saw also that she wanted to tell him. Trying to keep all exasperation from his voice, he asked, "What did you find?"

Sarah hesitated. It was her first test. She knew that she must now learn how to tell this story.

"My parents were sent to Auschwitz. My mother died soon after they arrived, we don't know exactly how, but my father survived. He died the day after liberation." She paused. "The man, the man I found, he had been there with my father, he said it was malnutrition." She stopped again, uncertain. "But they had been liberated. They must have had food by then."

Michel looked at her, and with something that was almost cruelty, but perhaps it was a certain kind of generosity, who can say, he gave Sarah one further piece of information.

"The Soviets liberated Auschwitz from the East. It was one of the first camps they encountered. The only prisoners left were sick and dying. The Nazis had cleared out anyone who could move. The Russians did not know what to expect, how to treat the diseases. When you are famished, your stomach shrinks. They gave the liberated prisoners full rations . . ."

The next week Sarah took the train to Le Havre and sailed for home.

PARIS. FRIDAY, APRIL 13, 1894.

Paris has erupted into the most spectacular spring, perhaps made more intense by the cold winter. There is a green haze along the boulevards as the chestnut trees come into leaf. I took a carriage into the Bois yesterday afternoon, and from its windows I could smell the soft breezes and hear the cries of the children. I had forgotten the feeling of anticipation that accompanies the spring, an intensity filled to bursting with the sense that something is about to happen. You have to shake your head to remind yourself that life is the same, and unlikely to suddenly become any different. Husbands are unfaithful, children get sick, parents die, and there is little to look forward to except a nice piece of beef for dinner—and the sight of the leaves on the trees after a long winter.

PARIS. WEDNESDAY, APRIL 18, 1894.

Marcel is all agog for he has met the famous Comte de Montesquiou at Mme. Lemaire's. He joined me at breakfast this morning, an unusual event, but I gather he had been so excited by the musical evening at Mme. Lemaire's that he could not sleep and was just waiting for dawn. He described the Count in such detail, I could almost see the man, and could not help laughing—both at Marcel's enthusiasm and at the description itself. Apparently, the Count lives up to all the little stories one hears society ladies telling about him: he is both fabulously handsome and fabulously rude. To think, yesterday evening he asked his hostess why her guests were particularly ugly this evening and was this to continue next season too!

Marcel said even the ever-garrulous Madeleine Lemaire seemed at a loss as to how she should reply and just said, "Oh

Count, you're so witty." Marcel and I agreed that was quite inadequate as a response and amused ourselves thinking up alternatives, arguing how much moral disapproval one could risk expressing without fear of losing the great man from one's guest list! "Why, M. le Comte, beauty is quite out of fashion these days," was our best effort. Naughty Marcel repeated to me a remark of Mme. Straus that he felt was appropriate for the occasion. Last year, she defended the literary tone of her salon to some great lover of women by saying, "I provide brains, not bosoms." More seriously, I warned Marcel that there is some great hurt inside a man who would take such a perverse pleasure in shocking others, but he would not hear a word against the Count and is quite captivated.

We would do well to remember our Montesquieu—only one letter different, but how much more wise: "Running after wit, one catches only foolishness."

PARIS. SATURDAY, MAY 5, 1894.
Surprising news from India, good news, I should say. The cholera epidemics have been fierce and Adrien has been following reports with grave concern. Without a source of drinking water uncontaminated by their own filth, pilgrims at Mecca have been dying in the thousands, and it seemed India was just as bad, but one of the Germans has cut the death rate in half by using a vaccine he had tested on himself. Adrien is considering a trip. He is getting too old for such things, but there is no point my trying to dissuade him if he decides to go.

Marcel remains very busy with his parties, and is quite enchanted with the company he meets at Mme. Lemaire's, including this week a pianist and a poet.

PARIS. MONDAY, MAY 21, 1894.

Marcel is being pursued by the Comte de Montesquiou no less. I gather the Count is to be seen not only chez Mme. Lemaire on Tuesdays but also at the Princesse Mathilde's Wednesdays, where Marcel is now regularly invited, and the great man has taken an interest in Marcel's idea of a literary career. This all came out yesterday when I was arguing with Marcel about his future, urging him to heed his father's advice and reserve what strength he has for pursuing an occupation. He replied that not everyone agreed with us, and indeed the Count himself had urged him to consider literature as a profession. Marcel has agreed to dine with him soon. I don't trust the man: from all I hear he is decidedly odd despite his breeding.

PARIS. FRIDAY, JUNE 8, 1894.

Marie-Marguerite is having terrible problems with her ankle. She sprained it last week in the Bois, wearing solid shoes but a stone tripped her up nonetheless, and now the swelling just will not go down. When her servant told me she could not see me yesterday, I sent a message saying I would visit today or tomorrow. She would not hear of it at first, but really she does not need to stand on ceremony with me, and we can have a good talk while she rests. I suggested Adrien attend to her, but he says Dr. Pozzi will give her excellent care. He is such a flirt I wonder that M. Catusse would want him at his wife's bedside, but Adrien says his medical skills are never in doubt, even if his fidelity to his wife always is!

Marcel's new friend, the young pianist M. Hahn, dropped by yesterday to pick him up to go out for the evening. The hour was late, but he very politely came into the salon to meet us. He is a fabulously handsome young man, darker than Marcel, with a lovely nose, strong but very straight, and black, curly hair, much thicker than Marcel's or Dick's. Apparently his family is from Venezuela, but have lived in Paris since he was a boy. Jewish on his father's side, but quite literary and integrated from Marcel's description. His manners are very pleasant, and I told him he must come to tea with his mother one day soon. (She knows the Neubergers apparently, so we have that connection.) He said that he would, and would be honoured if he could play for me too.

PARIS. MONDAY, JUNE 18, 1894.
Marcel is full of high spirits these days, and when not racing out to some dinner or party with Reynaldo Hahn, he is busy writing in his room. I am not sure these literary ambitions are wise, but one does not like to question him when he is so obviously happy. He is already weighing his many invitations for summer house parties.

I may well spend my holidays alone this year. The doctor expects to be very busy in the next few months getting research out of the way, so he can really concentrate on the plans for the *cordon* next autumn, and does not expect to get much time away. And Dick will want to spend as much of the summer as possible with his comrades before he has to start his dreaded service. They are not soldiers, my little wolves! I am debating the merits of Trouville versus Cabourg, and wondering if I might convince Marie-Marguerite to accompany me for a bit. I might even luxuriate in some time away from family after all.

It certainly has been a relief in these years, although I would never tell Adrien this, not to have to make the annual trek to Illiers. It is a lovely little town, to be sure, and the walks we did there were so beautiful. Elisabeth was very kind, but I never did feel completely comfortable in that little house. Marcel loved it dearly and was so sad when his asthma just made it impossible to keep going, but I always wondered what the Amiots really thought of us. When the boys were babies it was easy enough, little children always build a natural bond between their elders, but as they grew it had been increasingly difficult to find ready subjects of conversation. Well, the differences between the families were starting to show, that was all. Adrien really did travel a long journey from Illiers to the Hôtel Dieu and the Faculty of Medicine. Perhaps it would have been easier had I been Catholic, although, of course, the Prousts and the Amiots were always open-minded about my religion, I have no complaint there. But I was never one of them.

Paris. Wednesday, June 20, 1894.
Félicie is making a fuss about wanting July rather than August for some reason, but I have told her it is quite impossible since the doctor will definitely still be here. I suppose he could go out to Auteuil or stay with a friend, but it is not particularly convenient. I suggested to her that if she really must, Geneviève could do all the cooking in July for the doctor. It was naughty of me as I knew her professional jealousy would never let her accept such an arrangement. Meanwhile, Marcel announces that he and Reynaldo H. are invited to Mme. Lemaire's château in the Marne for as many weeks as they choose to honour her with their company.

This affair of the Jewish captain is very worrying. They have charged him with treason, the papers say. So, there is an onslaught of denunciations and calls for vengeance. It makes me feel sick to read them. I fear all Jews will pay for this betrayal. Don't such people know they owe rights and liberties all to France?

THERE'S A SOFT SHUFFLING sound behind me. The library clerk is padding by my desk. He wears socks and simple sandals attached to his foot with nothing more than a single broad strap of brown vinyl. To keep them from flapping loudly, he drags his feet as though he had barely the energy to walk. I can't think why I mistook him for Max. He is about the same height, and has dark curly hair, so they look a bit similar from the back, but the clerk is North African, with black skin and a dramatic beak where Max has a smaller nose and fairer complexion. The man in blue overalls does not float above the ground at all, I was quite wrong about that: he plods quietly and looks visibly depressed, worn down by the burden of tending the manuscripts and keeping order in the library—or perhaps, more likely, by his own cares. If Max had cares, it seemed as though they must be glamorous secrets. There was always a whiff of exoticism about him, a tiny hint of poetic suffering. He hovered above the mundane somehow, suggesting a certain distance from life yet exuding an intense gaiety too. That was his irresistible charm. The very first time I spoke to him, I remember, he posed a mystery that drew me in.

He enters the doorway of the classroom, slinging a black knapsack full of books off his back to position it under his arm while hailing a friend in the hallway behind him.

"Are you going to be there Friday? Oh, you have to come. Yes, you will come." His pleading is jovial; his energy infectious, his attention focused, and the flattery irresistible. The woman will surely agree. But instead she mumbles something unclear, and rushes off to catch her lecture.

Max turns and enters class—Renaissance Painting 202—happily aware he is holding up the proceedings.

Except he is not Max. Not yet. At first, he is just this man, this boy, who usually sits a few rows ahead of me. He seems to know everyone, bemoaning a fierce biology assignment with one acquaintance while planning a surprise birthday party with another. I would like to dismiss him as just another of the Varsity men with slender brains and significant means who prowl the hallways looking for sex before a liberal education. But his question about iconography last week was deft—and he does not look like them. He is neither tall nor fair, but rather slight and dark. His hair is black and curly and long, his skin olive yet his colour high, his features small with a perfect little half pyramid of a nose delicately inserted into the middle of his face. His beard is light, but a few stray and thicker hairs sit up on his cheekbones. There, the skin is so often flushed pink that he has a permanent air of discomposure that makes his ebullient self-consciousness easier to forgive.

I have made quite a study of him, but only become convinced that we are destined to be friends when I hear him speaking French after class one day. McGill is the university of English-speaking Montreal, a bastion of the old and fading anglophone hegemony, but by the 1980s, you do occasionally hear the language of contemporary Quebec spoken even here. A newly hired mathematics professor gives some instructions to the departmental secretary. A pair of bilingual students switch into their mother tongue. They speak fast and flowing Canadian French, flattening their vowels and adding extra consonants between words, offering a little taste of the rawer, yet more vibrant voices you can hear just outside the university gates, down McGill College Avenue as the Métro driver calls out the names of the stops or the cashier at the *dépanneur,* the corner store, hands over the change. What makes this boy's French remarkable is that it contains a totally different set of mannerisms—he dwells on his vowels, but rounding them or spreading them with an *ouu* or an *ahh* rather than twisting and pulling them. Consonants he pronounces only when unavoidable, and flings from his mouth as if they were burning pebbles. He speaks the swift French of Paris, the sharp yet rich language of the glittering metropolis, and in those few sentences overheard as I pass by in the hallway, I hear the comforting language of childhood, as though he were not a stranger, but an old playmate newly rediscovered.

One Monday he is not in class, but on Wednesday, as I look about for him, pretending to myself I have no special need to see this curly haired boy but am merely an observer of types, he returns and sits down only a row ahead. He is early for once, and the class is not yet full. Apparently seeing no one he knows in the row beside him, he turns to look behind and meets my eye.

"Were you here on Monday?"

I nod.

"Can I borrow your notes? I couldn't make it, I had to go home for the weekend."

I turn back a few pages in my binder, spring open its metal clasps, and as I start to release the appropriate pages from their snare and so have an excuse to look downwards, away from his friendly gaze, I muster the courage to ask, "Where's home?"

"Toronto."

"Toronto?" I repeat with doubt.

"Toronto," he replies, laughing with lightly passing bemusement at my response.

"I'll get them back to you next week," he says as he takes the pages with elegant, long-fingered hands that seem too big for his small person. And then, as if to seal the transaction, he offers me his name. "I'm Max. Max Segal."

I say my name carefully, stressing that it is French: "*Marie Prévost.*"

"*Bonjour, Marie,*" he says, raising an amused eyebrow, and turns back to face the front.

He is now more intriguing than ever, a mythical beast, the Toronto francophone.

In Montreal, the word Toronto means two things: money and the English language.

"They don't speak French in Toronto," says my *grand-mère* uncomprehendingly, as though to live outside her language was to have abandoned civilization altogether.

"They don't speak French in Toronto," says my aunt Carole with breathless indignation, as though instead they ate their own children and danced naked in the moonlight.

"They don't speak French in Toronto," says my father, who has not crossed the Ottawa River into Ontario since our return from Europe. He utters it as a single, dismissive sentence that is quickly over.

"They don't speak French in Toronto," says my mother, lingering with a trace of sadness over the words, as though it might be rather relaxing to live in a place where only one language was in operation.

Max Segal now has a name, and a puzzle attached to it.

In the *salle des manuscrits*, the library clerk moves on, pushing his cart before him, and I return to my task. In September 1894, it was, for once, Mme. Proust's younger son who required her attention.

RUEIL. WEDNESDAY, SEPTEMBER 12, 1894.
It does really seem that Dick will be all right. Today, the horrible little emptiness that had lodged itself at the bottom

of my stomach on Saturday has disappeared. I feel as if I have not quite breathed properly for four days and can finally fill my lungs again. Adrien arrived Monday night and discussed his situation with Dr. Guinard yesterday. He says the bone has set well and should mend without leaving any permanent weakness. To think that on Sunday I wondered if the boy would ever walk without a crutch!

Adrien has met the driver of the wagon who was very apologetic, but I suppose since Dick fell directly in his path he can hardly be blamed for not managing to stop his horse in time. Adrien says the tandem cannot have been balanced properly with only one person on it, but imagine if the girl had been with him and been hurt. That might have proved horribly awkward at the very least, if not downright disastrous. Who knows what type of family one might have found at her bedside! As it is, she is installed at Dick's.

I have tried to be polite and discreet, which I think is necessary since she does seems rather sweet and caring. Dick looks rather amused by the situation, which is a sign, I suppose, that he is recovering well. As soon as we can move him, he shall go to Auteuil. Uncle Louis says he will be glad to have him. It has been so inconvenient having him out at this provincial hospital, but Adrien pointed out there is so much traffic in the streets these days that if he had fallen in front of a carriage in Paris, instead of a wagon at Rueil, the accident might have been far worse.

AUTEUIL. WEDNESDAY, SEPTEMBER 26, 1894.
Dick is making excellent progress, and has started to hobble about the house with a stick. The colour has come back to his face. I had not realized that was why he looked so very ill until

I saw him yesterday sitting in the sunlight in the garden with rosy cheeks and knew he was really and truly on the mend. I feel a bit guilty about it all, since he had followed my advice to work less hard this summer and bought that silly bicycle. But he is full of jokes about it and is as always a hardy soul. One never has to worry about him too much. The authorities have agreed he is to postpone the commencement of his military service for at least six months.

Uncle Louis seems rather pleased to be useful, and has been fussing away over Dick like an old nursemaid. Papa came to visit yesterday too, and the pair of them fiddled with Dick's pillows until I had to laugh. Papa is in fine form. The summer seems to have restored his spirits.

PARIS. SATURDAY, SEPTEMBER 29, 1894.
Marcel is finally sleeping, his breathing regular if rather laboured. It was a horrible attack, he was still fighting for breath when I arrived from Auteuil, wheezing with such ferocity I thought he was about to breathe his last. Uncle Louis had called a cab and I had come as quickly as I could, but still it means he must have remained some two or even three hours in that condition. He had taken Trional the night before but to no avail, and things had just gone from bad to worse in the morning. Thank goodness he finally insisted that Jean send for me. It is the pollen that triggered it. It is a bad summer for it, so much rain that everything is wonderfully green. Marie-Marguerite was complaining to me the other day that she is sniffling because of it, which she has never experienced before. So for Marcel, it must be torture, poor boy. I gave him a second dose of Trional and sat up most of the night with him before it finally seemed to have some effect.

Adrien and I had a disagreement this morning about Marcel's continuing attacks. The doctor says the pollen season must surely be over by now, and that if Marcel is still in bed, it is because I allow him to fancy himself ill. We have had the same discussion a hundred times, but really, when Marcel is about to collapse from his asthma, I do not know what I am supposed to do. Adrien is worried about Trional and says he will consult a colleague about its use. I argued that many doctors prescribe it, but he replied, "Only in moderation, and that boy doesn't know the word." He suggested that we might try burning some medicinal powders instead, that they sometimes have some positive effects on asthmatics, and he would ask his colleague about that. I have always hoped that as Marcel's twenties advanced his breathing would improve—Adrien says these attacks are often a passing phase in young men who will settle into normal life as they grow older—but we see no respite.

My poor little wolf has missed several parties and not been able to receive any visitors except Hahn, of course, who is so very kind and devoted. If Marcel is not up when he arrives, he just sits and chats with me very pleasantly or, if I am busy, reads in the salon until Marcel wakes up. His season has started up again and is filled with engagements, but he is here every afternoon without fail. He and Marcel have been invited to Madeleine Lemaire's château next month—she is so fashionable she does not re-enter Paris to begin the season until December's parties beckon—and they hope to visit her if Marcel's health permits.

PARIS. WEDNESDAY, OCTOBER 17, 1894.

Adrien is increasingly disheartened by the slow progress of
negotiations with the Germans and says he has abandoned all
hope of ever bringing the English on side at all. He came in to
dinner yesterday angered by a letter he had received in the
afternoon post and made quite a speech about it while we ate.
He may be frustrated by others' recalcitrance but at least he
never loses confidence in his project. He was angry enough that
I suggested he might just take a break from it for a while and
leave it to others, and he instantly was his usual self, and said
that was nonsense, he would go on and attend the German
conferences as planned. He does look careworn these days, and
it was not an easy autumn with Dick's accident. Although it is
more Marcel about whom he worries.

PARIS. THURSDAY, NOVEMBER 15, 1894.

I received the most touching letter from Marcel this morning.
Although it rains without ceasing at Réveillon, he and Hahn
are warm in their rooms where the one devotes himself to
writing, the other to composition. Marcel is working on his
story, which he has now given the title "La Mort de Baldassare
Silvande," after its hero. He is convinced that he will write a
novel next and has Reynaldo's encouragement. He writes that
his only goal is to live a life devoted to the arts, surrounded by
those he loves.

My cousin Mathilde said she would drop by this afternoon
with Nuna, and the Cottins are here for dinner, so we are busy
with our engagements. Unfashionably so, by the standards of
Mme. Lemaire!

Marcel has had some kind of falling out with Reynaldo but
will not tell me what it is all about. He is quite turned over
with anxiety and will not sit still for a minute, but prowls
about the apartment fiddling with the *objets d'art*. I suggested
I write to the boy urging reconciliation, but Marcel will not
hear of it.

His father insists we must address the career question once
and for all, and it is all I can do to fend him off. I told him
that Marcel was far too upset over his dispute with Reynaldo to
give serious consideration to other issues at the moment, and
he accused me only of indulging the child's emotions. If this
continues, I wonder that Marcel's health will bear up.

What news about M. Faure. No one expected it. Just
yesterday morning Adrien was saying that Brisson was sure to
win. I wonder how Madame feels about it. I imagine she will
be quite pleased, for she has always valued her husband's
achievements despite the difficulties of their relations. She
deserves it, poor thing, for there are many joys that man never
gives her. Social standing can be some compensation for a
lack of tenderness, and if one is to put up with the duties of
the political life, one might as well do it in return for the
largest prize, I suppose. I do not imagine I will be seeing
much of her for a while. Her new functions will surely prove
too onerous to take time out for walks.

Paris. Sunday, February 3, 1895.
As I had feared, Marcel has collapsed—a ghastly attack finally
quieted with Trional at three in the morning. I write
because I cannot sleep, but brought my diary here to the
antechamber to Marcel's room. I listen for his breathing,

timing each stroke of the pen to the rise and fall of his lungs. Would that we were free of this demon.

I rehearse the events of my pregnancy, his birth, and his childhood again and again in my mind, wondering at what moment I could have prevented this route. Was I wrong to indulge a sickly infant? Should we have paid less heed to the attacks once they started? Did all my ministrations, my fears, the words whispered in his room when he was a little boy who could not sleep, the hand stroking his brow, did they all lead inevitably to that horrible day in the Bois, when he lay choking on the ground?

His father has high ambitions for him, for all that he says he only wants the boy to choose any career he pleases, no matter how undistinguished. Me, I would give my life just that Marcel's could be normal.

Paris. Thursday, February 7, 1895.
After several unpleasant days of rasping breath and a second albeit milder attack, Marcel has recovered. Nonetheless, I will not let him leave the apartment as it is bitterly cold these past few days. His illness has had one welcome effect: a reconciliation with Hahn, who found out about his illness from some friends with whom Marcel was supposed to be dining on Tuesday. He rushed over here and was tenderly received. Jean showed him into the salon at first, since Marcel had left instructions he was not to be woken, but I was sure he would make an exception for Reynaldo, and tiptoed into his room to announce his visitor. I left the two alone and did not see Reynaldo when he left, but Marcel looked decidedly better and took dinner with us for once, so I gather all is forgiven, whatever it was they had quarrelled over.

I seem to be behind on all my domestic tasks since Adrien's return from his latest German trip, but I cannot say that I have had any particular obligations to keep me so busy. It has been a pleasure to have him around more, and less distracted than he has been. I had feared that I was to become a total stranger to the pleasures of conjugal life at what is not, after all, such an advanced age. He has returned from Berlin more gentle and sensitive than I have seen him in some years and I have revelled in his attentions. Every real marriage has its joys and its sorrows, its peaks and its valleys, and then, just when we think the landscape is entirely familiar and holds no surprises, a new summit emerges.

I finally found time to write a little note to Mme. Faure, which I had been putting off. How does one congratulate a friend on her husband's elevation to the presidency? I was not quite sure but managed a few sentences of well wishes. I feel for them both as they embark on such an arduous journey, but Adrien laughed at me at breakfast when I said so. "Jeanne, only you could be so soft-hearted as to worry yourself about a president," he said, and declared I would worry about the Deity himself, if I could only get news of him.

It is typical of Adrien not to see the toll that hard work can take on one's health and happiness, and to think that social or political elevation is necessarily to be desired. I suppose that he shares that with Marcel in a way, for all that he doubts the wisdom of the boy's dallying with duchesses. Secretly, I think he is sometimes proud that his son moves in such circles. Certainly, he listened with great interest to Marcel's account of dinner at the Marquise de Brantes's last week.

And I am not so sure that I am soft-hearted, although Marcel and Dick always say so too. Perhaps I am just better at hiding my harsher judgements than some.

Adrien dined with Uncle Louis in Auteuil last night and says he is worried by his heart, noting that he puffs horribly at the slightest exertion. They had a grand old time nonetheless, for Adrien was not home when I feel asleep at eleven, and told me at breakfast it had been after midnight that he returned. Uncle does not have energy for his lady loves any more, but it must do him good to have the occasional entertainment.

What odd news from London about Mr. Wilde's trial. The man has been sentenced to two years hard labour in an English jail and one hears the conditions in these places are horrific, worse yet than any French prison or even Devil's Island. The courts clearly had no choice but to find him guilty, but one really wonders what the man can have been thinking. These relationships happen, many suspect they do, but to have advertised it to the world so unashamedly. He was asking for trouble, and now he has got it.

Mme. Dauvergne, who is a very silly woman at the best of times, was at Marie-Marguerite's yesterday afternoon, and clearly dying to gossip about the case. Really, I have no interest at all in the affair, and she kept pressing me, saying she sought my opinion as an anglophile, and was it true to say the English were more reserved in their public manners, but less upright in their private morals than the French. I could not silence her, and finally it dawned on me that she must have heard from Marie-Marguerite—who really tolerates her only because of the family connection—of that odd occasion two or three years ago when Mr. Wilde was supposed to have dined with us. So, finally, I said to her, "Really, madame, I know nothing of M. Wilde and his morals. I have never met the man, although I believe my son did shake his hand once at a reception." And then I gave her a very firm look that closed the conversation at last.

Had I the wit of a Mme. Straus—and her conversational courage—I would have reminded the good lady of a passage from Tartuffe: "Those whose own conduct gives room for talk are always the first to attack their neighbours."

MME. PROUST WAS TO spend years struggling to help her son establish what she called a normal life, and yet, through her anxious love for him, somehow preventing it too. His health would never improve.

The librarians have rung the warning bell: it is time to return files to the reserve desk, for the *salle des manuscrits* shuts promptly at six o'clock and leaving the room takes some time. I take my box back up to the desk, retrieve my orange disk and exchange it for the green one, and then stop by the information desk to get a chit signed by the assistant assistant librarian once he has inspected my bag to ascertain I am not removing precious documents. I hand that paper and the green disk in at the entrance booth and may now leave the library, but I plan to squeeze in one further piece of research before I head home for the evening.

In Paris, the Proustian pilgrim is an impoverished soul. Apart from this archive, there are few physical remains of the great writer in the city where he lived his whole life. No museum is dedicated to his memory; no house or apartment carefully preserved. The Musée Carnavalet, an old *hôtel* full of displays about Parisian social history, has recently acquired a few relics, including the writer's bed, bookcase, desk, inkwell, and hairbrush. These pieces were donated in 1989 by one Mme. Odile Geraudon in memory of her mother, Céleste Albaret, the writer's servant at the time of his death. With these artifacts, the museum has recreated Proust's room at 102 Boulevard Haussmann, where he lived from December 1906 to June 1919, and where, on the advice of his friend, the poet Anna de Noailles, the walls were lined with cork to keep out the noise.

There is something pathetic about this little shrine, a small cramped bedroom of dark wood and faded furnishings squashed in amongst the society portraits and art nouveau café fittings that make up the museum's testament to *la belle époque*. Crowded with reminders of the past, the place seems empty of memory. I visited it one afternoon in my first week here in Paris and left disappointed.

But today, armed with a list of addresses, I pursue my pilgrimage a few blocks north from the Bibliothèque Nationale to the Boulevard Haussmann, named for the great urban planner whose broad avenues, limestone facades, and blue-slate roofs made his the most beautiful city in the world. It is rush hour now and I work my way upstream against the flow of people emerging from the offices in the heart of the financial district and heading for home. I hurry along the street, past the big department stores that have stood there since Proust's day, where vendors hawk vegetable choppers and hair bows with cries of *"Regardez, mesdames . . ."* I imagine myself belonging to this crowd, a well-dressed Parisian with a schoolboy in freshly pressed blue jeans and a husband who favours colourful ties waiting for her at home. Perhaps my heels are not quiet high enough nor my figure chic enough to pass, but I walk forcefully on, knowing that determination can compensate for many lacks.

Number 102 is now a bank. I hesitate outside, looking up. A man in a suit leaving the bank glances at me, wondering perhaps if I need directions, but as he follows my gaze, he smiles to himself and moves on. Above our heads is a discreet marble plaque with gold lettering of the type used to mark historic sites all over Paris: "Marcel Proust, writer, lived in this building from 1906–1919." It is the apartment of the cork-lined room.

I go also to 44 Rue Hamelin, the building where Proust lived from 1919 to 1922. To reach this street, I get on the Métro and ride a few stops westwards into the heart of the Sixteenth Arrondissement and emerge in the Place d'Iéna. It is growing dark now and the street lamps reflect off the cobblestones. Forty-four Rue Hamelin is now a small hotel, and I stand across the street from it, beside a laundromat, scanning the facade for some sign of the event that occurred there in 1922, but I fail to find any acknowledgment of the building's most famous occupant. Puzzled, I check the address again and then, about to give up, I notice what the glare of the spotlights that illuminate the hotel's striped canopy had obscured. Just above them hangs another plaque: "Marcel Proust, writer, died in this building November 18, 1922."

These are the sites where Proust wrote his great novel, but the places of childhood and youth, the years with his doting mother, are not so well remembered. At 9 Boulevard Malesherbes, an elegant facade goes unmarked. It is a classic Parisian building of grey-limestone with wrought-iron balconies and a mansard roof. Translucent lace curtains obscure any clear view into the apartment on the third floor, but a hazy yellow lamplight shines warmly into the street and a figure is just discernible, sitting in a large armchair by the window, a head bent over, sewing perhaps, or reading. It was in these rooms that Mme. Proust wrote in her notebooks.

PARIS. SATURDAY, SEPTEMBER 21, 1895.
Adrien is quite excited about a new prospect he has discovered for Marcel. He was dining with M. Hanotaux the other night, whom he has not seen in a while—the man's public duties keep

him horribly busy—and was again discussing the possibility of Marcel entering the diplomatic service. Of course, some discretion is required there, for Marcel would have to sit the exam and pass through the regular channels like any other candidate, even if the minister is a friend of his father's. Adrien was carefully asking M. Hanotaux how difficult the exam might be, and worrying that Marcel would never really be healthy enough to do foreign postings, certainly not in a difficult climate. M. Hanotaux suggested that a post at one of the libraries might be more in order, and said they are always looking for librarians.

From what Adrien gathered, a man of Marcel's education would not take any of the paid positions, but the voluntary attachments are respectable occupations for one of a literary nature. It sounded to me an ideal solution. It is not as if Marcel really needs to earn a living; his allowance is perfectly sufficient for any reasonable wants at the moment. It is only because he is so extravagant that it seems anything less than generous. And, in time, his inheritance would allow him to establish a household without need of other income.

It would be good to see the boy with paid employment— it teaches the value of money, of that there is no doubt—but it is not strictly necessary. And work at a library would suit his literary interests and provide some discipline in his life. I agreed with Adrien we would wait a few days, think it over, and then approach Marcel together when he returns from Brittany. It is always better to show him that his parents are united in their ideas on the subject of his career.

PARIS. FRIDAY, OCTOBER 4, 1895.

Adrien has just set off for Pasteur's funeral, very melancholy. He is of the party that will follow the casket all the way to the Panthéon. I hope it will not tire him overly. He says the great doctor's work on infectious diseases will eventually overshadow the renown of his discoveries on heat and bacteria, and that we owe the idea of inoculations as much to him as to the Germans. Adrien is so admirably free of envy, and sees no threat in other men entering his field, only the advancement of the cause of science. Still, we seem to hear nothing but talk of inoculations these days, and not so much of the *cordon sanitaire.*

I will ask Félicie to make a peach tart for dinner with the last of the summer's fruit, which should cheer us. Marcel will be back with us Sunday.

PARIS. MONDAY, OCTOBER 14, 1895.

Lucien Daudet came to visit yesterday. What a charming young man he is. He had been eagerly awaiting Marcel's return to consult him about some literary project that is afoot—I lose track of all their schemes, these days—and came in to have tea with me. Marcel was in fine form and had us both laughing with an imitation of the Comte de Montesquiou, for he had dined there last night. I am not sure if it is altogether ethical to accept the great man's invitations and then mock him behind his back, but he is an easy target for satire, of that there is no doubt, and Marcel has always had a theatrical side and a talent for mimicry. He has mastered both the Count's mincing ways and his great literary pretensions: "My poetry, monsieur, is not just for any man's delectation, but must be savoured only by those endowed with the ears to hear it."—this to a guest chez Mme. Straus, who dared to ask if he might be treated to a reading. Lucien was beside himself with joy at the imitation.

When he left, I was praising the Daudet family to Marcel, saying such fine boys as Lucien and Léon are a testament to their parents' intelligence and breeding. Marcel grew suddenly quite serious and said, "Maman, do not be so sure of what kind of people they are just because their sons are so fine. Old M. Daudet is so frightfully bourgeois, and Madame is anti-Semitic." I was saddened by his words, that people so full of ideas could also find place in their souls for prejudice.

PARIS. THURSDAY, OCTOBER 17,1895.

I worry about these medications on which Marcel relies so much. He is back on his feet today, but only after dosing himself repeatedly with Trional. It is saddening since he returned from Brittany in excellent health. But with the return to Parisian air and that whirlwind of activity—checking final proofs for the story that is to be published next month and getting in touch with all the friends he had not seen over the summer—it was only to be expected that he would fall ill within a matter of days. I am so disappointed that all the good work the summer had achieved is so quickly demolished by his unwillingness to work on things at a measured pace. I gave him a stern talk on the subject yesterday, but he was quite sharp with me and pointed out that one minute the doctor and I complain he does not work hard enough and the next we insist he slow down. I was angry enough to push a little further on the issue, and said exactly, what I was arguing for was the need for balance. He writes to me so lovingly when away, and then can be so short with me when at home. I suggested Reynaldo and his mother come for tea some day soon, but he just dismissed the idea.

Marcel is impossible. His hours are increasingly erratic—but perhaps I should not say erratic, for they are in fact increasingly predictable. If he goes out it is not before eleven at night. He comes home in the small hours of the morning and writes then or all night through, but is seldom in bed before seven or eight and rises only in mid-afternoon. I sometimes see him for tea then, but he usually takes dinner out. All this is throwing the household into disarray. I have given up waiting up for him when he goes out. I cannot stay awake until two or three in the morning (sometimes these days I suspect it is dawn) and then be breakfasting with Adrien at eight. Félicie complains bitterly that she never knows who will be home for meals or what time they might want them. I have told her that a cold chop is all she need leave out for Marcel, but in truth I think she resents his absence from lunch and dinner more than she objects to the extra work.

He tells me he is not taking any Trional now that the flowers have died away, but his odd hours can hardly be good for his health. We argued fiercely about it yesterday, but he finally won me over, pleading that he has to write and might as well do it at night since he can never sleep then.

Paris. Friday, October 25, 1895.

I have ordered Jean not to bring Marcel a breakfast tray when he rings—at two or three in the afternoon, for the love of heaven. He cannot live under our roof but refuse to live by our schedule, without any consideration for the servants. I barely speak with him these days, unless he deigns to join me in the salon when I am taking tea, so I left him a note saying henceforth he would have to find his own bread and coffee. Jean must be allowed to take some time off after lunch if he is to serve dinner, and I cannot run a household according to the whims of a child.

PARIS. WEDNESDAY, OCTOBER 30, 1895.
Too angry to speak, let alone write. Maman's Venetian glass. How could he?

PARIS. WEDNESDAY, OCTOBER 30, 1895—AT 3 P.M.
Have sat closeted here all day, and must surely do something to end this horrible silence between us and rise above our dispute. Just as surely as we are enlarged by art and music, we are diminished by our petty jealousies, trivial domestic complaints, small hurts, and minor lapses until the largest souls are no better than the most common fishwife bawling in the marketplace.

PARIS. THURSDAY, OCTOBER 31, 1895.
Like a storm exploding the pressure built up in the air, leaving the world damp and calm, the affair of the Venetian glass seems to have exhausted our anger. After skipping lunch and pondering the situation all afternoon, I finally wrote Marcel a little note at five o'clock and slipped it under his door. I reminded him of the wedding ceremony in which the broken glass stands not for rupture but rather for union, and told him we would regard my vase this way, as a marriage of our souls. He came out of his room soon after and kissed me in the old way. All is forgiven, although the sight of Marcel spitefully flinging the glass to the ground will remain with me forever. And I only wish I could forget the words we exchanged before that. To think we were arguing over a pair of

gloves, grey when he wanted me to buy him yellow.

As always in difficult times, I have been thinking of
Maman, but now with shame, that I should have fallen so far
from the model of tender solicitude and maternal devotion
that she set. Sometimes I hear her voice in my head, repeating
some inconsequential phrase, calling to me from the landing,
before she was through the door—"Jeanne, you must read M.
Hugo's new book, I have it from Delorme's . . ." "See how
delightful Marcel looks in his sailor suit." "What a fine day.
Shall we not have a walk?" "What did you think of the opera?"
The generosity of her spirit never failed. I was daily moved by
my love for her and gratitude for her affection.

"Long habit never accustomed me to her worth, the taste
was always keen and new," writes Mme. de Sévigné. So too is
the loss, always keen and new.

PARIS. TUESDAY, NOVEMBER 19, 1895.
Marcel came home from his interview yesterday rather subdued.
He was one of three candidates for three posts, he learned, and
his interviewer placed him last. This means he has been
offered what is considered the least agreeable of the three
positions, one shelving books at the Mazarine. He is to start
right away, but since there is no salary attached to the position
there are generous provisions for leave, and he hopes to
defer his debut until January. That way, he can enjoy the
holiday parties and spend some time working on his novel.
Not that the library should prove too onerous once he does
begin, since they require only a minimum of five hours
twice a week, helping to tidy the books. I do hope the air
does not trouble Marcel too much. But perhaps I am simply
being romantic, imagining some dusty old place where the

books have not been looked at in years. No doubt it is all very modern and clean.

I was gladdened by Marcel following his father's proposal in this regard, and I spoke warmly to him of the importance of the work he will be doing, no matter how small a role he plays in guarding the great treasures of literature for the French nation.

"VOUS ÊTES PROUSTIENNE? You are a fan of Proust?" The assistant assistant librarian is standing near the counter and, smiling and curious, engages me in talk as I return my box at the end of a day's work.

"Have you visited Illiers? You would be interested. It's not far to go . . ."

"Oh, yes. I have been to Illiers. Of course. Good night."

I hurry away, avoiding his smile.

Oh, yes, I've been to Illiers, or Combray, if you will. Of course. It is the one Proustian site that has the makings of a cult. I went there before I came here to the library. It was one of the first places I could think of to go.

On the great plain south of Paris, the mismatched towers of the Gothic cathedral at Chartres rise out of the landscape several miles before the train that left the Gare d'Austerlitz an hour before actually pulls into the station. At Chartres, I cross the platform and board a local that heads out across fields of sunflowers towards the Loir River. In August their leonine heads would lift towards the light, but now, in September, with heads drooping and some stalks collapsed altogether, they look like a defeated army. As I alight at my destination and start down the Rue de Chartres, a cool wind rustles the sparse foliage of the lime trees.

I have been in France less than a week, staying in a little studio I have rented in a working-class neighbourhood in northern Paris.

The next-door neighbour is deaf and apologizes for playing his television at a ferocious volume, but it matters little to me. I have completed my tour of the Musée Carnavalet and now spend my days at the Louvre, or wandering the streets retracing childhood routes, and fall into bed each night too weary to care. After four days with nothing but paintings and cobblestones for company, I finally call the railway from a pay phone and copy down information about schedules. I am not entirely sure why I have come to France; I have difficulty defining what I'm looking for, but at least I can start with a pilgrimage to Illiers-Combray.

For years, Illiers, a small town of some five hundred souls sitting on the Loir, a sluggish little river that should not be confused with the sparkling Loire, was just Illiers. Its most famous son was surely Adrien Proust, the child of the local grocer and candle manufacturer who grew far beyond those roots, studied at the University of Paris and became a leading French doctor and authority on infectious diseases. In the early years of his marriage, he and his young Parisian wife, Jeanne, the daughter of a wealthy Jewish stockbroker, would bring their two sons to visit Dr. Proust's sister, Elisabeth Amiot, who lived in a small provincial house not far from Illiers' main square. It was these visits from the age of six to nine, when his asthma made holidays in the country increasingly difficult, that inspired Marcel Proust, almost thirty years later, to create the village of Combray, the town of his memory conjured up from a cup of tea. Decades after the publication of *Remembrance of Things Past*, the town of Illiers voted to add the name of its more famous, fictional version to its own, creating the hyphenated fusion of literature and fact: Illiers-Combray.

Illiers-Combray exploits the memory of its famous visitor with discretion and good taste. Walking into town from the station along the Rue de Chartres, you pass the Lycée Marcel-Proust. The park where the young Proust brothers once walked is marked with a plaque; the house of Tante Léonie, as Proust renamed his aunt, is a small museum resolutely closed for lunch; the bakery next door boasts that it is the place where she bought her madeleines; the local postcards include the writer's portrait; and the best restaurant in town, Le Florent on the main square, offers a *Menu Proustien* that includes monkfish and plum tart.

The waitress hands me the menu with the page deliberately turned to this offering and I feel suddenly and guiltily exposed, as though she has seen through my disguise. But, looking down at my khaki pants and stout walking shoes, I realize I can easily be identified as one who might wish to order the *Menu Proustien*. One or two other literary tourists wander the empty streets of Illiers-Combray during the lunchtime hush while the restaurant, where I have retreated until the museum opens, is filled with prosperous business people in suits or sports jackets. Still, I won't be pigeonholed and deem the waitress's suggestion too coy. I choose instead a cheaper yet more luxurious menu, eating a terrine of leaks followed by saddle of hare cooked with prunes. Tasting the buttery slice of hare, I realize that the restaurant's rather urban-looking clientele has probably made the twenty-minute trip from Chartres to eat at this excellent table.

Down the street from the restaurant, just off the main square, the front of the museum is marked with the medallion of Dr. Proust that the English artist Marie Nordlinger originally created for his grave in Paris. The entrance is round the back, through the garden. There, I join a few other solitary visitors to tour the house that was the source of Proust's memories. The guide takes us through the dining room where the narrator of *A la Recherche* indulged in a quiet pre-lunch read with only a wall of earthenware plates for company, before we move upstairs to the bedroom overlooking the garden to which the sulking child retreated, waiting for a mother's kiss, and the front room from which an invalid aunt could watch the comings and goings of neighbours.

But our pleasant guide is scrupulously honest about the connection between fact and fiction: in his novel, Proust fused his Jewish relatives who lived very comfortably in the Parisian suburb of Auteuil with his father's simpler, Catholic connections in Illiers to create one single, idyllic, and exclusively Gentile childhood, just as he would also eliminate an unnecessary sibling and make his narrator an only child. In reality, the two families, separated by class, religion, and geography, never met and many of the scenes that the writer set in Combray would have been based on events that actually took place at his great-uncle's country house in Auteuil. That house was demolished before the turn of the century.

Deflated, I leave the museum to follow a riverside walk marked with a functional signpost but without any indication of how it corresponds to the fictional *Swann's Way*. In the gardens, the pink hydrangeas are fading with the fall. In the byways and fields, there are still poppies, and blackberries sweet enough to eat. I return to the station by way of the bakery. One biographer has suggested that Proust's most famous epiphany was in real life triggered by the taste of a hard rusk dipped in tea, not the soft, plump cake he described in fiction. It makes more sense when you think of it, for sponge cakes dissolve into pulp if you dip them in liquid while the hard, twice-baked biscuit would soften to a manageable tenderness. The local bakery seems unaware of this historical detail and offers its madeleines proudly at double the price of the most elegant Parisian pastry shop.

Instead, I buy the after-school snack of my own childhood, a flaky pastry with a bar of dark chocolate squirrelled away inside, and sit amongst the end-of-day commuters at the little station, chewing slowly on my *pain au chocolat*. When the clanking local train arrives, I board it and ride the short, noisy distance to Chartres. Looking out the window as I ride backwards across the plain, the fields of drooping sunflowers now retreating away from me,

I consider what it is I should do, where it is I might find what I am looking for. I know there's some kind of archive in the Bibliothèque Nationale, and I remember the talents of my girlhood friend Justine, now a professor of French literature at the University of Quebec at Montreal. Her masterful control of the idiom of academic business got me a reader's card at the UQAM library last spring. I spent some of the summer there, before I bought my plane ticket for France, poking through all twenty-one volumes of Proust's collected correspondence. Perhaps Justine's letter-writing skills can work the same magic in Paris as they did at home.

I change trains at Chartres, and on the smooth ride northwards, I relax into my seat, satisfied with my decision. Tomorrow, I will begin looking for Marcel Proust in earnest.

PARIS. TUESDAY, JANUARY 21, 1896.
Marcel is forging ahead with his collection of writings, and says it should be published in the spring. After much pressing, Mme. Lemaire has finally delivered her illustrations, and he is also still hard at work on the novel. He has decided it is impossible to do any more work at the Mazarine in the meantime, and has been granted a year's leave of absence from his library duties. His energy seems high and his health stable, but I worry that this current degree of control depends increasingly on drugs. The Trional is a blessing, to be sure, but I have warned Marcel he must not become utterly dependent on it. The doctor agrees and says it is a phenomenon often observed in the medical literature that the more accustomed one becomes to a drug or medicine, the less effective it is in controlling the disease, so what started out as a cure becomes nothing more than a crutch. "Nearly all men die of their remedies and not of their illnesses." It is Molière who told us so.

Meaning to discuss Marcel's health with him, I wound up having a long conversation about his literary ambitions. He is still not out of bed, but was well enough this morning to be sitting up and I went to him when he rang for his breakfast just now. I tried to tell him how worried his father and I are about his health, and especially his reliance on Trional, but he, unusually, seemed loath to discuss his symptoms and turned the conversation towards his career, a topic he normally avoids. He has great hopes for *Les Plaisirs et les Jours*—that is the title he and Mme. Lemaire seemed to have agreed on for their collection—and says it will launch him as a serious writer, paving the way for his novel. Anatole France himself has agreed to write a preface. Literature—that will be his career, he announced. I told him how glad I was to see him committed to a project, and spoke of the need for willpower in all things in life, whether it is one's good health or the task of writing. He may mingle with aristocrats, but he surely does not want to be one of those young men who spend their days entertaining their friends and their mistresses and have nothing to show for their lives at the end of them. I spoke to him of his grandfather and his uncle Louis; selling stocks, let alone selling buttons, may not seem like a prestigious career, but as they grow old, they have achievements to look back on, businesses, factories, houses, and families they built themselves, not ones they were simply handed by the previous generation. As for Marcel's father, well, I think how many lives Adrien must have saved, and that is what encourages him forward, that sense that some things have been achieved in the past and more must be done in the future.

PARIS. SUNDAY, MAY 10, 1896.

It is pneumonia. I sat with Uncle Louis until the early hours of
the morning until Georges finally sent me home. The doctors
are doing all they can, but he is barely conscious and Adrien
clearly fears the worse. Marcel has volunteered to come with me
this afternoon, and Dick says he will join us this evening. I am
supposed to sleep now but find it impossible. Instead, I went to
see Papa first thing this morning with the news. He seemed
almost angry and grumbled, "Oh, that one always did make a
fuss about the slightest sniffle." I had to laugh, and bite back my
tongue. It would have seemed so ridiculous to argue with him
about whether or not his brother was truly dying! Instead, I
pointed out that Uncle Louis was usually the robust one.

PARIS. TUESDAY, MAY 12, 1896.

The funeral was quite touching, beautifully simple but with
dozens of mourners. As Uncle Louis grew older, one had tended
to forget just how many business acquaintances he had. There
were men and women there I had not seen in years. Old M.
Fuch, who I would have thought was long dead and I do not
believe I have seen since my marriage, came up to me and did
not say a word, just placed his hand on my cheek. Mme.
Hayman did not come, which was discreet of her, although I am
sure she loved Uncle well, right until his last year. Marcel has
spoken with her and she sends her condolences. She has a large
soul that woman, even if it is not perhaps what some would
consider a pure one! Nuna is beside herself with grief and Papa
is quite despondent, more silent than usual, if that is possible,
but he did manage to the walk behind the coffin, which I feared
would just be too much to ask. The sight of him walking with
Adrien, Georges, Marcel, and Dick did my heart good. The

boys look so tall and young in their black suits and I felt somehow comforted by the sight of those five male backs, one small
and shrunken, two broad in middle age, and the final pair slim
and straight.

I realize Papa's anger in recent days was at the prospect of
being abandoned. With both Maman and Uncle Louis gone,
he has lost those of his own age to whom he was closest, and
he has never been particularly good at making friends with
those younger than himself. Death of a loved one is sad
enough, but to feel that it conspires to leave one increasingly
alone in the world is harder still. Louis was always the leader
of the two.

PARIS. THURSDAY, MAY 21, 1896.
Adrien has been so sweet through this time, more tender
somehow than when Maman died. He has been home more
lately but is quiet in the house, and very solicitous of my health.
Perhaps it is because he was closest to Uncle Louis of all my
family and will miss him truly. Uncle was always more warm to
Adrien than Papa was, I suspect that has been part of it. It is
funny how one chance word or encounter can follow you
through life. I remember years ago as I was putting on my wedding
dress with Maman helping me, and Papa came into the room to
watch the final preparations. "Well, he's very lucky, the
Christian." he said. Adrien was not Jewish, it was only the truth,
but it was the one moment where Papa showed a slight resentment
that I had married an outsider. He never mentioned it before or
after that day, and yet I always suspected that Adrien felt he was
not entirely welcome in their house and found an ally in Louis.

PARIS. SATURDAY, JUNE 13, 1896.

I did not think we would get through yesterday. The books have been sitting in boxes at Calmann Lévy's since Wednesday, but were officially delivered to the shops and the literary editors today. Marcel went over to pick up his copies and came home with his arms full, just bursting with excitement, like a little boy again. Adrien had already gone out when he came in, so Dick and I had to congratulate him over his achievement. Dick has not been in the house much lately, he is growing up so fast and so involved in his work at the university that he cares less and less about family affairs, but he was very sweet about the whole thing and made a great fuss over Marcel, and ran his hand over the book's cover the same way he caresses that new canoe of his. Reynaldo came over too this morning. Goodness, it has been ages since I have seen him and I was wondering if he and Marcel had had some kind of falling out, but they looked as pleased as ever to be with each other this afternoon, with Hahn fairly cooing over the book. After lunch, I shall have to sit down and read it, such a pleasant change from illness and sorrow.

PARIS. SUNDAY, JUNE 28, 1896.

We are still awaiting reviews, and aside from a pleasant but inconsequential mention in *Le Temps,* the papers seem to be ignoring it, which will not help with sales. Marcel says Calmann Lévy feels the price is very high and some of the papers will thus judge it to be a speciality publication and not a priority for their literary pages. It was the cover and those beautiful endpapers on which Marcel insisted that drove the price up—that and the paper, but there was not much point having Mme. Lemaire contribute her art if it was not printed on the best stock. I dissuaded Marcel from going across the street to Cerisier's yesterday so he could telephone editors himself, saying surely established writers did not do such a thing, but pretended reviews were nothing to them. I consoled him by teasing him about the difficulties of the literary life and could see he was no end pleased to have his desired profession mentioned in that way. The whole thing has had the most deleterious effect on his bowels, forcing his father to finally prescribe a laxative.

PARIS. THURSDAY, JULY 2, 1896.
The funeral was quiet compared to Uncle Louis's, but I think it was what Papa would have wanted. It was difficult to see so many of the same faces in such a short span of time, and people kept telling me that he really could not have enjoyed life much without his dear brother, which is true but not what one wants to hear over and over again. Adrien says it is a blessing, and certainly he was tired of life. Better a sudden seizure, I suppose, than a lingering illness.

The last few days just seem a blur. I was frantic when they called me and rushed to his side, as though one's own haste and anxiety can ever help the dying. I fairly tripped over Jean racing to get to the carriage and then spent hours sitting doing nothing, just watching him. He never really regained consciousness. His eyes fluttered once or twice but he did not say anything. Adrien says it is a painless way to go, that we should all wish to be thus blessed.

PARIS. FRIDAY, JULY 10, 1896.
I was doing quite well this week, getting on with things around the house despite this ache inside, when suddenly,

yesterday, the thought occurred to me that I am now well and truly an orphan. I do not know why I had not thought that before but somehow the very word seem to strike at me, and I collapsed weeping. It is silly. A woman of forty-seven does not need her maman and papa like a little girl. Marcel is twenty-five, Dick twenty-three; they are adults themselves and Dick certainly has little need for his parents these days. It is different perhaps with Marcel, his health is such that he will always need his mother. He is still anxious about the criticism, and hopes that something should be out shortly in the *Revue Blanche*.

He was telling us yesterday at dinner about Reynaldo's cousin Marie, whom he met last week. He says she is what the British call a bluestocking and wants to make her living with her sculpture. She sounds quite horrible, I thought.

PARIS. TUESDAY, OCTOBER 6, 1896.
There is discussion again about that Jewish spy who was court-martialled a year or two ago. His family have always protested his innocence, but I suppose the mother or father of the most brutal murderer would find it impossible to believe that their child were guilty of such a thing. But others are coming out in their support, and Marie-Marguerite told me yesterday that she believes the man to be innocent. One can hardly believe that the army could make such a mistake. I said so to Marie-Marguerite and she laughed at my naïveté, saying the officers are no wiser or stupider than any other group of men after all, and if I was capable of believing Adrien might occasionally make a mistake—give a patient the wrong prescription, for example—then surely I could see that an army officer might seize on a man without checking very

carefully, just because they needed to find someone guilty. She pointed out there was indeed firm evidence of spying, so somebody must have sold the papers to the Germans, but perhaps they have the wrong man.

Dreadful to think of him shut away on Devil's Island, it must be almost two years now, if he is innocent all that time. What must go through his head as he sits there, one wonders. Does he despair of justice ever being done? Or perhaps he is the spy they sought and he just sits there cursing himself for having got caught. I do not suppose that the truly hardened criminal feels much remorse for his crime, more anger that he did not manage to get away with it.

The news from Calmann Lévy is not encouraging. We expected slow sales over the summer, but there were simply no sales at all. And there are no signs of any particular revival since the beginning of the month. It is disappointing for Marcel. He does not really need the money, but it would certainly lift him up if the book were not only a *succès d'estime* but a good seller too, and it would help him convince his father that literature can indeed be a profession. He is still very wheezy, and the pollen also leaves his eyes horribly itchy. Nonetheless, he keeps working away on the novel, increasingly at night, saying he cannot sleep then anyway, so why not work?

Paris. Wednesday, October 14, 1896.
All we ever hear about is Lucien Daudet these days—it is always Lucien this and Lucien that. Marcel has even, I believe, shown him some of his novel. I would be surprised if he is capable of forming much of a judgment, that one. For all his literary antecedents, he is more a beautiful man than

an intellect. I do not suppose the friendship can do Marcel's literary ambitions any harm, on the other hand. Perhaps his father can even help with the publication of Marcel's novel when the time comes.

It is the Comtesse de Martel's day, and I think I will drop by for once.

PARIS. TUESDAY, OCTOBER 20, 1896.
I had the most alarming conversation with Marie-Marguerite yesterday afternoon. She is always so honest, which I value, but sometimes her news is painful to hear. She is never fully impressed by Marcel, and I know she thinks I dote on him too much, but nonetheless her literary and social instincts are strong ones. She says *Les Plaisirs et les Jours* can only give him the reputation of a dilettante and socialite; that however beautifully written the contents, Mme. Lemaire's illustrations and that expensive cover have guaranteed the book will not be taken seriously by the critics. It is a harsh judgment. She would have been more discreet had I not leapt to Marcel's defence the moment she voiced hesitations about the book, but my protestations encouraged her to become harder and harder with her words. She was quite apologetic by the end of our walk, for I am sure I was looking upset by her verdict. It is the last thing that his father would want, any suggestion he approaches his projects with a lack of seriousness. I am sure she overstates the case.

Glorious good weather. Dick, at least, is happy, since the boating still continues.

PARIS. FRIDAY, JANUARY 8, 1897.

Much to his father's sadness, Marcel has sought yet another year's extension on the leave of absence from the library. He has barely set foot in the Mazarine since he was assigned there. Adrien wonders what will become of a boy—a man, who has no profession and spends so much time in his bed. He says my dreams of his literary prominence are only that and that the novel will not amount to anything. I argued with him long and hard at breakfast just now—at least since Marcel is not around at that hour to hear us, we can be perfectly frank with each other about our fears. I said that if we are to be consistent with our stated desire for Marcel to find a career and pursue it, we must give him encouragement in his writing, while Adrien argued that anyone with such a disastrous lack of willpower could not hope to become an artist. He pointed out that great artists are invariably those who burn with a creative energy from an early age, and found many fine examples to support his case. I fear he is right. If nothing else, Marcel's health will preclude him from pursuing a literary career with the diligence and hard work required to make a success of an endeavour in which the ranks of those who fail are so much larger than those of the laureates.

PARIS. THURSDAY, FEBRUARY 4, 1897.

This article in *Le Journal* is a disaster. It is so ridiculous. It is months after the book came out. To what good is publishing a bad review after such a long time has lapsed? And this piece by this Jean Lorrain is so vicious, so personal in its attack. It insinuates I do not know what about Marcel. It is utterly unfair. Marcel is furious, and is threatening to challenge the man. I have pleaded with him to do nothing rash, and wonder whether I should consult the Daudets myself since their good name is at stake too. It is vile, this kind of insinuation, just vile.

PARIS. FRIDAY, FEBRUARY 5, 1897.
I am done begging and pleading. God knows I tried to stop this ridiculous and painful affair from continuing any further. The suggestion that Marcel could fight is ridiculous. His health is far too delicate, yet nonetheless he goes ahead tomorrow at dawn. Well, they will play at musketeers, the boys; it is just silly. I am sitting here with knots in my stomach and know I will not sleep tonight. Everyone keeps telling me that no one ever gets hurt, the pistols are simply discharged into the air, but really, with loaded guns about, what might happen? Who can say? It is so dangerous. If Marcel were to be hurt, I would never forgive myself for not having stepped in. His father is ignoring the whole thing, refuses to intervene, and simply does not want to hear about it, pretending it is not going on. So it is me who sits here worrying. I will go mad with the fear. It is so ridiculous, to expose oneself to such a risk.

Marie-Marguerite came for tea the day before yesterday and we discussed where we might spend the summer. It seems like a million years ago, in a different country altogether.

Voltaire said: "Man was born to live either in convulsions of worry or in the lethargy of boredom."

PARIS. SUNDAY, FEBRUARY 7, 1897.
After a good night's sleep I finally feel a little more in form. Of course, I did not sleep at all the night before last. Marcel forbade me from sitting with him, but I could hear him moving

about in his room until Hahn and Robert de Flers called for him before dawn. They all returned three hours later—they must have been the three longest of my life. I greeted Marcel in the hall and kissed him, assured myself he was unharmed but did not make a fuss, not wishing to embarrass him in front of his friends. He accuses me of making a show of my affections, but little does he know how I suffer.

For his part, he was quite pleased with himself, and bragged that Lorrain would know better next time, stick to sneering at the Comte de Montesquiou and keep his insinuations off M. Proust. Reynaldo was giggling away about the whole thing, a release of nerves, no doubt.

Jean brought me my breakfast in my room, and I tried to sleep again, but the anticlimax was such, I could not. I was exhausted all day and then fell into a deep sleep at five. I was quite disoriented when I awoke at seven, and full of relief at something, but it took me a moment or two to remember what it was. Adrien and I did not discuss the matter at dinner—he is still pretending all this nonsense simply did not happen—but he must have noticed at least that I was eating like a horse. Again, a release of tension, I suppose. I have not spoken with Marcel since he came in yesterday morning. Little can he know how bottomless my fears become when his health or security is at stake.

How often I recall Mme. de Sévigné's words to her dear daughter: "A whole other friendship could be made, my child, of the emotions I hide from you."

THE MANUSCRIPT ROOM is shut on Sundays, so I have taken the opportunity to visit Drancy. It's a mere fifteen-minute ride from the centre of Paris on a suburban train that glides out of the Gare du Nord every eleven minutes and deposits you in another world, far away from Haussmann's gleaming metropolis. Drancy is part of the so-called Red Belt of Parisian suburbs that traditionally vote communist and have suffered economically for their choice. You would recognize the sort of place, a grim half city where post-war utopianism has given way to aging concrete, sparse grass, graffiti, and blowing litter.

As I ride bus 148 from the station to the town centre, I spot a few substantial houses covered in cream-coloured stucco and topped with red-tile roofs. They offer a small reminder of provincial France but they are far outnumbered by the high-rise housing developments with their ill-kept grounds, the office blocks surrounded by unused plazas, and the long streets of low bunkers that house an odd assortment of grocers, bars, garages, and beauty parlours. I get off the bus at city hall, seek directions, and walk the last few blocks to the Square de la Libération.

There, the original buildings still stand. They were constructed to house policemen in the 1930s and their unadorned facades have weathered well. Four-storeys high, they form a squared-off U around a central courtyard that serves both as park and parking lot. The upper floors overhang the ground floor, creating a barren little arcade with a few clubs and social services as its tenants. Numbered doorways dotted at regular intervals along the way lead to the interior staircases by which the apartments above can be reached. On one side of the complex, some painting is in progress and a pale, dirtied pink is giving way to a fresh coat of institutional green. On the other, giant blue plastic recycling bins all but block one's path along the arcade.

This place is plain and poor, but clean enough. It would be wrong to call it a slum; untruthful to say it was pleasant. The buildings look like what they now are, social housing, barely distinguishable from the more recent apartment blocks that surround them. Housing was in short supply after the war. Why tear these apartments down? At the front of the site, there's a small memorial made up of a modernist sculpture in rough-hewn stone and a single cattle car. To its right, there's a low stone plinth topped by a metal plaque bearing a text in which the French Republic remembers "crimes against humanity committed under a de facto authority known as 'the government of the French state.'"

This was the gateway to death for 65,000 French Jews. You can read all about it in the little museum tucked into one of the ground-floor offices. When the Germans first invaded France in 1940, some Jews fled into the unoccupied zone in the south, run by the collaborationist government based at Vichy. It was, in theory, possible to emigrate from there, if you could find a country that would take you in. Some made it to Spain and Portugal and from there to the Americas, but most stayed put. Emigration was difficult and this was their home. And so they remained, in Paris and in the rest of occupied France. Registering with the French police, observing a curfew and quotas on the number of Jews who could serve in the professions—these requirements were uncomfortable but not life threatening. Besides, to the assimilated Jews who had lived in France for generations, the "Jewish problem" referred to the influx of refugees from Eastern Europe who had been arriving since the mid-1930s.

The first roundup took place in August 1941, when four thousand Jews from the Eleventh Arrondissement were transported here to a camp run by the French police under German authority. The camp was not ready to receive them, there was neither food nor sanitary provisions, and many died at Drancy before eight hundred feeble survivors were released that November. Internments continued, however, focusing on the Eastern refugees, Paris lawyers, and anyone who fell foul of the anti-Semitic regulations.

Then, in the summer of 1942, the Nazis, unimpressed by the French administration, took over the camp. They began to impose the Final Solution on France in earnest now, systematically rounding up all French Jews and shipping them eastward via Drancy. Sixty-four transports left here between 1942 and 1944, carrying nearly 65,000 people. Most of them were headed for Auschwitz and died there. By the end of the war a Jewish community that had numbered as many as 350,000 had lost 77,320. About a third of those were French-born; the rest were Eastern Europeans who had immigrated to France after the First World War or who had fled there in the thirties—but had not run far enough.

If you look up the survival rates in the *Encyclopedia of the Holocaust*—the UQAM library has a copy, I discovered, along with the twenty-one volumes of the Proust correspondence—you'll find that the Jews of France fared better than those of Belgium and Holland, let alone Poland. Paradoxically, both the collaborationist regime in the south and a strong resistance in both zones made France a leaky conquest for the Nazis, and many French Jews escaped, hid, or even managed to live quietly until liberation. Their Catholic and Protestant compatriots had a mixed record in their regard. France is full of stories of the cousins hidden in the barn or the child whose hair was dyed blond, but there were also multiple betrayals. It was the Paris police, after all, who compiled the lists, arrondissement by arrondissement, and it was the people on those lists who were brought here to begin the journey east.

Jeanne Proust died before the First World War and both her sons died before the Second. I wondered what happened to Mme. Proust's relations, the Weils and the Neubergers? What happened to Reynaldo Hahn, to all his sisters and brothers, and to Jacques Bizet? Did France sit by as writers and artists were loaded onto the trucks and buses headed for Drancy? Would she have finally spoken up had her greatest novelist still been living and threatened with a sentence of death? Perhaps the question is futile: the lives of merchants and mechanics must count for just as much. A lawyer and his wife, no less disposable than a writer and his mother.

Yet, still I ponder the deportees of Drancy. What do we owe the unjustly dead, we who shared neither their faith nor their fate? Can we offer an act of memory, or are our tears hypocritical and our stories presumptuous? Do we honour their history with our *Sophie's Choice* and our *Schindler's List*, or merely dramatize it for our own pleasure? Will our remembrance guard against repetition or is it only self-congratulation?

How can I be so sure that I would have been the woman with a child stowed in her attic and not the one who was counting her neighbour's silver? Where would you have been as people are herded onto the crowded vehicles that will take them here? Is that us shepherding a friend to the basement? Or peeping out from behind a blind? Or ticking a name from a list? On the bus, it is dark, you can see nothing out the window, can't follow the road, but trust the driver knows the route even if you fear your unknown destination. Around you there are whispered conversations, a loud question quickly hushed, some silence, even the snore of a man who has managed to fall asleep.

The bus gently shakes its way through the night. The city has dropped away, and the dark highway seems endless. Most of the passengers doze, occasionally jostled awake by the motion before dropping off again. Max and I use the odd jolt as an excuse to rub shoulders, and then leave them there, sleeve delicately brushing against sleeve, transmitting a degree of comfort to the flesh beneath.

Our friendship is fresh and flirtatious. Max has cajoled me into the art history department's annual trip to New York when I should be finishing an English essay and he studying for a mid-term exam in chemistry. He dangles the delights of the museums we intend to visit, the paintings we will see, but I am tempted simply by his company. We are still greedy for information about the other, and have found some conversational excuse to empty the contents of our wallets into our laps. We laugh at the photos on each other's student cards, and pick through memberships for the independent cinema, library chits with due dates stamped in red ink, and drivers' licences encased in plastic.

"What's the *B* for?" I ask, gesturing at his middle initial.

"Oh, nothing." He pulls the plastic card away.

"Come on." I start to wheedle for the information, like a child seeking candy.

"It's my mother's maiden name . . ." He seems embarrassed by it.

"So, what is it?"

"Bensimon."

"Bensimon?"

"Well, *Bensimon*," he concedes, pronouncing the name in French.

"She's French?"

"Yeah, that's why I speak French. She came here from Paris."

"When was that?"

"During the war. Her parents sent her over. My grandfather was a lawyer. I guess they could afford to get her out."

"Get her out? Without them?"

"Yeah, well. They couldn't leave."

I want to ask what happened, but find the question too intrusive to pose, slightly shamed now by my persistence about what the *B* stood for.

"Did she ever go back?"

"Yeah, she goes back from time to time," he replies, ignoring my real question.

"And your grandparents?"

He pauses, as though summoning the courage or perhaps evaluating the risks in discussing his family history with me. Eventually, having started down the road, he continues.

"Her parents died at Auschwitz. We don't know exactly what happened to her mother, but she must have died early on." His tone is matter-of-fact. "My grandfather survived, and was liberated, but he died of malnutrition anyway."

"Malnutrition?" I persist, realizing that I have gone too far, yet seeing no way to retreat. Max is now annoyed at my curiosity.

"The soldiers who liberated the camps fed the prisoners. Their stomachs couldn't handle the food. His gut exploded."

We lapse into silence. I am appalled most of all by the nonchalance with which, once decided to tell the story, he relates it. We speak as though his grandparents were characters in a novel, rather than his own family. Perhaps they are, for he must know them only through his mother's stories.

"That's horrible." I try some conventional motion of sympathy. He shrugs.

There is only a cattle car at Drancy; a cattle car, a one-room museum, a stone sculpture, and a few plaques commemorating deportees, resisters, Allied prisoners of war, and the French poet Max Jacob who died here before he ever made it east. These attempts at memorial seem pale to me somehow; they are dwarfed both by the enormity of what has gone before and the banality of what has followed. The ghosts do not walk at Drancy. There are no answers here.

I retrace my steps to the station, and manage to catch the 4:43 train back to Paris, dashing through the automatic doors just as they are closing. The car is half full, with tired families returning from visits to grandmother's house and expectant suburbanites preparing for an evening in town. I find a pair of seats in the corner, putting my bag down on the empty one beside me. The Bibliothèque Nationale will reopen at nine tomorrow morning. I pull out my notebook and begin to review my translations.

R ACHEL WAS DECORATING a cake when Sam answered the door and called out an unnecessary warning: Clara Segal paraded into the kitchen carrying a huge tray covered in wax paper that she lowered with ostentatious care onto the table. Rachel was in the midst of the tricky part, coaxing the icing to cling vertically to the sides, when the bell had rung and her knife had slipped leaving a splotch of white froth on the pristine glass cake plate. She bit back her annoyance at the interruption, moved away from the counter, and came over to the table to dutifully admire the cookies and pastries Clara proudly unveiled.

"Beautiful, beautiful, and so much," said Rachel, noticing all the while that Clara had included a large sponge cake amongst the petits fours, meringues, and cookies, even though they had agreed that she, Rachel, would take care of that. After all, everyone acknowledged it was her speciality, a sponge cake that was simultaneously richer yet higher and lighter than any baker's dry offering, a sponge cake made according to a method handed down from her grandmother. Her mother had even kept the old notebook in which the recipe was carefully copied in Yiddish, the letters formed with thin strokes in a spidery hand that Sam had deciphered for her when it was passed on to Rachel in her turn. Not that the secret was actually written there: no, that part was oral history. Her mother had shown her the proper technique for beating all twelve eggs when

Rachel was still a girl. The results were infallible and delicious enough to be eaten plain—or with a little fruit compote overtop. Still, for this occasion, admiring the grand concoctions she saw pictured in magazines, Rachel had decided she would ice the cake, and the task was proving a little more difficult than she had expected. And now here was Clara, with her own sponge cake. Oh well, you could never have too much food at a wedding.

In truth, the preparations had proved difficult from the start, as soon as the first joyous news of the engagement had given way to practical realities. The date was agreed on easily enough, but Clara and Lionel, having recently abandoned the cramped little Orthodox *shul* of their youth and transferred their allegiance to the brand-new synagogue up on Bathurst Street where Rabbi Cohn and his congregation had moved the previous year, simply assumed that the wedding would be held there. It seemed fortuitous. The rabbi would preside, and afterwards they would hold the reception in the social hall. That was settled. But to Rachel, trying to run her household on a strict budget so that her husband could pay down the debt on the hardware store he had opened after the war, and to Sam, who only stuck his head in at a little Polish synagogue a few times a year and didn't care much for parties, this plan sounded alarmingly elaborate. To the bride herself, it sounded alarmingly large.

"All those people I don't know . . ." Sarah had complained faintly to Rachel as the numbers on Clara's guest list climbed higher and higher with each passing day. Rachel tried to block Clara's plans with a little string of protests and concerns, gentle at first but growing louder and firmer as she met with resistance. Finally, Sam stepped in and put his foot down: the wedding would be held at home. That was his decision.

"It's natural, under the circumstances," he told Clara and Lionel. "I wouldn't mind the expense at all, that's not the problem, business is good, but the girl . . . well, let's think of her feelings. She doesn't want a big fuss. You can understand."

Coaxed into acquiesence by her own son's pleading and pacified somewhat by the idea of planning a large party for the opening lunch that month, Clara magnanimously conceded this territory—because she had little choice. She was going to have a lot of explaining to do to her cousins and her friends; she would complain to any sympathetic ear she could find that she was being required to keep her guest list to twenty-eight, but if the Plots chose to hold the thing in their own home, she could hardly stop them: the bride's family organized a wedding, after all. With the Segals' consent thus secured, Rachel and Sam got to work: Rabbi Cohn would perform the ceremony in the living room; the caterer would bring in enough chafing dishes and warming ovens to make the meal in the kitchen, and if all the furniture was moved upstairs, they would squeeze thirty-six guests into the dining room at four round tables rented for the occasion. There would be no room for a band, but Sarah said she didn't care much for dancing. And the food would be kosher, of course. The Segals had recommended the caterer. Rachel knew their family to be more observant than hers; it was only reasonable that their requirements be respected. All seemed in order. But then the caterer presented his quote.

"It's a monopoly," Sam complained to Rachel as he sat at the dining-room table, scratching his head over this fantastical bill. "They're in league with the butchers." Rachel nodded but said nothing. Her mouth felt dry. This was the disaster she had feared from the start. From the day that she first met the Segals, she had suffered from a persistent anxiety that the discrepancy in wealth between the two families would prove deeply embarrassing. The Segals were uptown types, a doctor and his wife; Clara was wearing a fur coat that first day although it was only November and drizzling outside. She and Sam, meanwhile, had not only the store to worry about, but still owed monthly payments on the Chevy, even if the car itself was starting to show signs of rust, and they wouldn't have any money for extras after they had paid for the china tea service that Rachel had already picked as their gift to the bride. They had carefully budgeted for the photographer, the flowers, the tables and the chairs, the waiters, and the catering too, but they could not cover this alarming amount. Nor could they expect any help from the Segals, since they had rebuffed all their offers when insisting on the small wedding in the first place. Just imagine what the meal might have cost if they had given into Clara's initial plans, Rachel thought, but even with the reduced guest list, this bill was impossible. The anxiety was real fear now, rising from her stomach into her throat and mouth, where it deposited an unpleasant and slightly metallic taste on her tongue.

"You'd think religious people would have a little more respect for each other, not try to make money like that," Sam continued. Rachel recognized the warning signs of one of his infrequent but impassioned speeches. "But that's capitalism for you . . ."

She swallowed, refrained from pointing out that he too was now a businessman, and forced some words out of her mouth to stop him before he could get fully launched.

"It's a lot of work to make food for a crowd, and there's all the extra work for kosher," she said, pulling the bill from his hands to get another good look. "This salad course—we don't need salad. And the desserts. Look how expensive they are. I can do them myself."

"Rachel, you aren't going to cook a whole . . ."

"Yes, yes. It'll be fun."

And so began the battle of the dessert table.

"And I'm going to make the desserts myself," Rachel said lightly, trying to slip the item through as the two couples gathered in the Plots' living room one evening to discuss a long list of arrangements.

"But they won't be kosher," Clara had promptly replied. "We are going to have meat for dinner?"

"Of course, of course. I'll only use Crisco, no dairy, I promise," Rachel answered.

"Still, your kitchen . . ."

"Surely, it would be easier to let the caterer do the desserts," Lionel interrupted his wife with a more tactful approach. "Less work for you."

"No, I want to do them. I'll make sure they're kosher," Rachel insisted.

"They won't be kosher if they're cooked in your kitchen," Clara retorted, hardening her position because she felt she had lost so much ground on the question of the synagogue and the guest list.

"It really will be much easier if the caterer . . ." Lionel continued, trying to pacify Clara.

"Sure, sure," Sam agreed, now desperate to avoid embarrassment. "We'll get the caterer to do the desserts."

"No." Rachel, equally desperate about the cost, was now adamant. "No, I'm making the desserts."

"No," Clara replied. "I'm not eating *trayf*."

The meeting ended sooner than expected.

Privately, each woman thought the other was being unreasonable and had complained to her husband.

"Why haven't they taught the girl the rules?" Clara asked Lionel. "Surely, that was their duty."

Lionel, reasoning that people could not be expected to adopt extra religious practices along with a child, demurred.

"It is not as though she would have kept kosher in France," he said. "I mean, the French . . ." He wasn't sure what he meant, but had some image of Parisian decadence in mind that didn't include kosher cooking.

Rachel, meanwhile, wondered whether God really cared if the kid happened to be cooked in its mother's milk. She was perfectly familiar with the prescriptions of her parents' religion, but her partial observance of the dietary laws was more a matter of cultural habit than religious fervour. She would instinctively never serve pork, shellfish, butter on the potatoes or a milk pudding hard on the heels of the roast, and had separate dishes for Passover, which she took carefully out of tissue-stuffed boxes every year. But she and Sam had always considered their more Orthodox acquaintances overly observant and couldn't help thinking there was something unsophisticated and a little embarrassing about these enthusiasts with their double sets of dishes.

"Surely, in this day and age, with fridges and everything, it doesn't matter as much," she said to Sam the next day.

"We still don't eat pork," Sam replied. "You can't ask people to abandon their traditions."

"I am not asking them to abandon their traditions, just to be a little bit more flexible for one day," Rachel said, feeling an unusual anger that made her heart beat a little faster. "I've promised I wouldn't use any dairy."

In the end, the two women hammered out a compromise between themselves. Rachel would clean her kitchen under Clara's supervision and borrow Clara's mixing bowls and utensils. She would use no butter or milk in her baking; no animal fat in her pastry. Her desserts would be pareveh, or neutral, and so could safely be eaten after the caterer's kosher meat.

"It's not as though I ever bake with lard," Rachel muttered to herself as she closed the door on Clara after that meeting, hurt at the mere suggestion that she might be in the habit of using tallow of unknown origins. She swallowed her disgruntlement and started leafing through her recipe books and planning her menu.

Clara was also unhappy with their arrangement, suspicious that Rachel, even once her kitchen had been cleaned, would not be as diligent in the preparation of her baking as she, Clara, would have been. And while she doubted whether Rachel could be trusted not to pull out one of her own mixing spoons or muddle up the dishtowels, she could certainly be counted on for an impressive spread that might even rival the fancy sweets the caterer would have provided. Rachel had served some very pretty cakes at their recent encounters, delicacies that Clara had sampled out of politeness before it became apparent she was going to have to take a stand on the issue of Rachel's baking. Folks do love their sweets and Rachel was going to get a lot of compliments on the big day. Everyone would be amazed she had managed the desserts herself. Rather than a disaster, the dessert table might actually prove a triumph. Somehow that annoyed Clara although she wouldn't have been able to say why. She too had noticed the economic gap between the families, and was resigned to the Plots and whatever wedding they could muster. Her son had been uncharacteristically fierce in his final insistence that their wishes were to be respected, had eventually pointed out to his mother that when Sarah had no real family of her own it would be tactless to overwhelm her few connections with the Segals' many friends and relations. So, Clara had accepted Sarah, the Plots, and the small wedding, but Rachel's dubious dessert table didn't fit within her notion of their place.

As the weeks went by and she felt more and more aggravated by the whole plan, she decided she had better make some of the desserts herself. She hadn't wanted to, had not volunteered at the outset, because now that her vision of the wedding had been rebuffed, she felt clear in her mind that the whole thing was the responsibility of the bride's parents and she refused to be manipulated into extra work by Rachel's ridiculous insistence that the dessert table not be catered. Still, Rachel was going ahead anyway and now Clara itched to step in. She called Rachel and suggested she would provide some cookies.

"Oh, no, don't trouble yourself."

"No, really, it's no bother at all. I'd like to."

"No, but you're already doing so much, lending me all the utensils . . ."

"Oh, that's nothing. Really, I'll just make a few cookies. It'll be fun."

As the wedding drew nearer and Clara's family heard of her plight, the few cookies multiplied again and again. In her own carefully segregated kitchen, her sister Rose could make an apple strudel with a paper-thin pastry that required nothing but flour, water, and a little oil so that it could be safely eaten at the end of any meal, while their cousin Lily could, also without resorting to either diary or meat, create the most exquisite petits fours, those little squares of white cake iced so smoothly in pink they almost look too perfect to be edible. And as for Clara's contribution, of course, her luscious-looking, oversized meringues, round things about as big as an onion and sharing the same pointed top, as well as her fluffy little coconut macaroons, would be very acceptable, for eggs are considered to be *pareveh*. She might even make a sponge cake too. Rachel could hardly take offence at their generosity.

So, on the eve of the wedding, Clara arranged all these sweets on two of the largest trays in her kitchen and asked Lionel to drive her to the Plots' house where Rachel was assembling the desserts in plenty of time for the next day.

Putting the wax paper back in place over one tray, Clara moved away from the kitchen table, where five cakes and three large plates of cookies were also assembled, and turned to the counter to inspect the last of Rachel's work.

"Not a butter icing?" she asked anxiously, as she peered at the frothy blob now disfiguring the edge of the cake plate.

Sarah sensed there was tension between her surrogate mother and her future mother-in-law. She guessed that Rachel, always kind and uncomplaining, was not receiving the consideration she deserved and wanted to speak to her, to thank her for her generosity and her patience, to express her great relief that the Plots had managed to keep the wedding small, but she was too nervous and distracted to find the words or the moment. If Sarah had, in her twenty-five years, shown both a good measure of quiet courage and the occasional flash of initiative, she increasingly relied on Daniel to direct her through life. He had found her, singled her out from all the other girls at the university, asked her to dances and picnics, proposed marriage, bought a ring, and now even found an apartment. She marvelled at his ease with all practical arrangements and, like many a bride-to-be, was living the days leading up to her wedding in something of a haze. And when it came to areas in which a young man could not be expected to have any knowledge or authority, that is, when it came to the food and the dress, Sarah was entirely in the hands of the women and simply did as she was told. Rachel and Clara saw to the dessert table while her friend Lisa, an old classmate from the university who would stand at the ceremony as her matron of honour, took her to Eaton's bridal salon to pick out her dress.

It was a large gown if not a long one. The bodice was tight, with long fitted sleeves and a neckline that traced two arcs above Sarah's small breasts before dipping to a sharp point in between them. From its narrow waist, a big bold skirt shot outwards rather than downwards and required a crinoline to keep it in place. This petticoat was an extra expense Sarah had anticipated, but she had not properly budgeted for the gloves, the shoes, and the little pillbox hat that would secure her large veil. Lisa enthusiastically pointed to pictures in magazines, telling Sarah that everyone in Europe was wearing this look. Indeed they were, for rationing had ended, and with fabric no longer scarce, the Parisian designers were celebrating by using as much as they could. The women in the pictures were taller than Sarah, and leant slightly backwards as they stood in a very ladylike way with their ankles crossed, a pose that exaggerated their height. They also had long, swanlike necks and held their heads so high that their pillbox hats crowned their smooth hairdos with glory. In this big dress with its large veil awkwardly secured by the little hat, Sarah, who was barely five feet tall, looked pretty, but she did not look beautiful. She was a woman who should have been married in lace, a dress of a simple shape made from threads as delicate as her own small body. No matter. If Sarah sensed that all was not right with the preparations for the dessert table, she was perfectly happy with Lisa's choice of dress, even if she had to dip into her savings to afford it. On the afternoon of her wedding, she marvelled at her own reflection in the mirror as she hung Sophie Bensimon's pearls about her neck.

Sarah had not expected to marry. Not that marriage was unlooked for or unwanted. On the contrary, she longed for it, dreaming of the man who would make everything whole, happy, and real. Rachel and Sam were also fervently hoping for a nice boy, inquiring tactfully but regularly about her dates. During her years at the university, she still lodged with the Plots while a small scholarship covered her tuition and her part-time job at the library paid for a few clothes, books, and the occasional evening at the movies. Neither Sam nor Rachel had asked her how she intended to support herself after that, but without any profession on the horizon, they saw marriage as the obvious solution. Sarah, meanwhile, was too proud to acknowledge the question, to confess to them that she too wanted something for the future, but she knew exactly what lay behind their little inquiries about Saturday night or Sunday afternoon. No, Sarah knew full well what was expected of girls, and what girls could expect, after university.

It was just that if her whole life in Canada seemed unreal to her, a temporary state that would somehow end one day when school was finished or girlhood complete and she would pass into the adulthood she might have dreamt of in the years before 1942, then marriage here in Toronto seemed impossibly concrete.

For Sarah, men appeared as distant albeit prosaic creatures, and she was always a bit surprised when one took a romantic interest. Usually, when a boy in one of her classes or the brother of a friend, attracted by her dainty looks and intrigued by her shy dignity, bothered to chat and question, he gave up soon enough without proffering any invitation to a dance or movie. He had quickly discovered that what he had taken for a ladylike docility was actually a kind of quiet hardness the like of which he had never encountered amongst the simpler and friendlier girls to whom he was accustomed. He did not dislike Sarah, but he was puzzled, stymied even, by a demeanour that seemed so gentle yet a character behind it that seemed so closed to him, so free of need. Indeed, it was just this kind of misunderstanding that was underway the night that Sarah met Daniel.

Coaxed to a dance by Lisa, who was eager to enjoy one last hurrah before the girls began studying for their final exams, Sarah sat at a table by herself while her friend was busy on the dance floor. Well, she was not entirely alone, for Lisa had made sure to leave her some companionship in the form of Boxer Walker before she hurried joyously off on the arm of his friend Michael Smithson, a young man whom she had secretly hoped would be there. It was uphill work for Boxer, struggling against both Sarah's reticence and the volume of music played by a jazz band at the front of the room. He was getting a bit desperate at the situation and a bit annoyed at this resolutely serious young woman, and found himself starting to babble. He stopped firmly but blurted out:

"Aren't you having fun? Smile, smile!"

Sarah had few ideas of how to live life, but she was intelligent enough that she could not oblige the brash young men who offered her instructions on what to do with it. She secretly detested what she saw as the Canadian habit of happiness, an insistence that everyone be always enjoying themselves as though seriousness, let alone sorrow, were an admission of failure. Her face, until now a mask of quiet grace, was looking increasingly stony. It was Daniel who rescued her.

"Boxer, hello." A short man with broad shoulders, an open face, and a head full of black curls, who had been watching Sarah from the other side of the room, had spotted his chance, and was cheerfully greeting an old classmate of his cousin's whom he had met only a few times before.

"Daniel, right?"

"That's right. How are you?"

"Fine, fine. I'd like you to meet, this is . . ."

"Sarah," she said firmly, and extended her hand without smiling. "My name is Sarah Simon."

Daniel grinned at her with such genuine warmth that her encroaching sullenness fell away, and she smiled gently back.

"I am Daniel Segal."

"Refills? Refills? Another Coke, Sarah?" Boxer hurried away to get soft drinks. By the time he returned, Sarah and Daniel were deep in conversation and he was glad to put the glasses on the table and melt back into the crowd with some mumbled excuse about finding Michael.

Daniel had seen something in Sarah. Like a scene from one of the romantic movies to which the girls would sometimes treat themselves, he had looked across a crowded room and recognized a total stranger. That quality he had perceived in Sarah, a mix of frailty and resilience, fine intelligence and stupid pride, that he would never fully define for himself in fifty-five years of marriage, was somehow telegraphed to him that night through the chatter, the cigarette smoke, and the jazz. His reaction was immediate and urgent: excited and nervous, trying to dampen his own ridiculously premature hopes but not succeeding in the slightest, he had made his way to her side.

He spent the rest of the evening there, chatting about nothing at all, until the band stopped playing, someone threw a switch, and the sudden, hard light recalled the dancers to themselves. Lisa, only now guiltily remembering Sarah, came back to the table with Michael's offer to drive them both home. Her face flushed with the delight of her own conquest and the surprise of finding Sarah so intensely occupied, she garbled some introductions and explanations. For a brief moment the four stood in an embarrassed silence as they wondered how they should part, and then Daniel said a quiet good night and left, knowing that Boxer would surely be able to secure for him Sarah's telephone number by calling Michael.

One evening in June, after exams were well over, he arrived at the house on Gladstone Avenue. It was one of the plainer dwellings on the street, an elongated Victorian row house, attached to neighbours on both sides, with two full storeys marked by slim bay windows and a narrow attic squeezed behind a peaked dormer. Daniel puzzled over the neighbourhood, sized up the red-brick facade— middle-class but just barely—and mounted the wooden steps onto the front porch. That was how it was done: you did not meet a woman at a restaurant or downtown at the movie house, but went to her home in plenty of time for her father to inspect you while the girl and her mother, safely hidden away in some pink bedroom upstairs, put the finishing touches on the hairdo. At least, it was a scenario of that kind Daniel was expecting. In reality, Sarah's back bedroom on the second floor had always been painted a fresh shade of yellow, it had been several years since Rachel had ventured into it, and on the night Daniel called, Sam was out visiting, so when he rang the bell Rachel was sitting alone in the living room, pretending to read a book. Sarah opened the door and invited him in to meet her.

"This is Daniel Segal," she announced and fell silent.

"Mrs. Simon, nice to meet you," Daniel boomed with his habitual self-confidence, moving forward with an outstretched hand. There was a small but painful silence before Rachel corrected him.

"It's Rachel Plot." She rallied and tried something friendlier: "You must call me Rachel. Everyone does. That's what Sarah calls me." It was true, as Sarah's stay with the Plots had lengthened, "Mr. and Mrs. Plot" seemed increasingly odd while "Mother" and "Father" had never been possible, so she called Sam and Rachel just that.

"Nice to meet you," Daniel repeated, while Sarah still said nothing.

"Sarah tells me you are going to be a doctor," Rachel continued. "Your parents must be very proud."

By the time he and Sarah reached the door to leave, Daniel had already pieced things together. Certainly, Sarah had never said, "Pick me up at my parents' place," nor "My parents would love to meet you," but had, he now recalled, talked vaguely of "the house." Her slightly formal, even foreign, way of speaking, her quietness, her resolution, Daniel now thought he understood them.

He said nothing that night, nor on their second date. It was on their third, on a warm evening towards the end of that summer, that he quietly asked, "How long have you lived with the Plots?" They were dining in a Yonge Street restaurant, which he had chosen because he couldn't picture Sarah eating in some kosher deli at College and Spadina, but where he was spending two weeks' allowance on a meal they both merely picked at. The weather was muggy, dampening the appetite; she was nervous; he had already eaten at home because he did not want to confess his stupid plan to his mother.

Sarah pushed a boiled potato to one side of her plate, and replied in an unemotional voice, "Since I was about twelve."

"And before that?" Daniel was cautious, but felt that after his mistake at the Plots' and this expensive dinner he had some rights to the knowledge. "In Europe," he prompted.

Sarah avoided telling people her life history. Cheerful questioners tended to be embarrassed when she explained her loss and fell silent or, worse yet, made a fuss over her the way you might pet a married woman who has just revealed that she is pregnant or a bright student who announces she has won a big scholarship, a kind of attention that in turn deeply embarrassed Sarah. Her friends, and there were few who considered themselves close ones, accepted the long frontier Sarah seemed to extend before herself and knew that their friendship did not include a passport with which to cross it. Of course, she had told the story sometimes. Other students, their parents, colleagues at the library, people would ask, "Where do you come from?" "Who is your family?" And Sarah had learned how to explain her antecedents as neutrally as possible. It was that quiet, unembellished version she now delivered.

"I grew up in Paris. My father was a lawyer there. When the Germans invaded France, my parents sent me here. I am not related to the Plots, they just gave me a place to live."

Sarah dreaded the question that usually followed this recital. In the two years since her trip to Paris, the shame of admitting the truth seemed not significantly less than the shame she had used to feel when she could say only, "I don't know." Once, in her second year shortly before the trip to France, a particularly dense girl from Lisa's history class had pushed further, exploding in comic outrage, "How can you not know?" and only ceded the point when Lisa squelched her with a fierce look.

But Daniel knew better than to ask these questions. As Sarah finished her brief tale, he reached a hand across the table and covered hers, saying, "We will try to find better things to speak of."

Sarah never liked it when people took the liberty of touching her and withdrew her hand from underneath his.

Even in the best of times, Sarah hated September. It was a month of lost hope, of sorrowful realism, of back-to-school, knee socks, and notebooks. It was the time when the summer light, after the long hazy afternoons of August, achieved such a clarity and intensity you knew this had to be its last days. It seemed that things could happen in the summertime, that life might change, that lightness might prevail, then September arrived, bringing with it an aching disappointment and mute sense of loss.

It had been the month, in 1942, when Sarah had been forced to recognize that her visit to Toronto was not some exotic summer holiday: she was not going home this year. Starting school that autumn, not long before the October of her twelfth birthday, had seemed so wrong to her, at best an unpleasant compromise demanded by the circumstances and at worst a betrayal of her parents. For eleven years now, it had proved impossible for her to fully enter into this other life as though it might be a natural one. Each September marked another year between her and her past, yet no change of feeling, no progress in her life. The gap quietly appalled her: to cross it was to abandon her parents; to stay on this side was to forgo the adult cares and pleasures that must of necessity fill the future if she was to have any future at all.

This particular September was the month she had to recognize that it was more than three weeks since Daniel had telephoned, and that he probably would not call again. As she wept silently one afternoon in her room, she simultaneously indulged her heartbreak and questioned it. Had she really fallen in love with Daniel Segal, or was it simply that his silence echoed with other losses? Her griefs seemed confused and indistinguishable from each other, all melting into the aching passage of September sunlight that passed clearly through the window and filled the room.

There was a hesitant knock at the door. Sarah sniffled, wiped her face, and swallowed.

"Yes . . ." To her ears, her voice sounded firm enough.

"Sarah, I am just having a cup of tea, dear. Come down to the kitchen and join me, won't you?"

"Oh, no thank you, Rachel. I'm fine just now."

"You're sure? No harm in a cup of tea."

Sarah felt anger rising within her. No harm in a cup of tea, but no cure, either. Why could Rachel not leave her alone, always hovering, worrying, plying her with cake and cookies, stuffing her with kasha and kugel. Not that Rachel ever voiced her anxiety, no, that wasn't her way, just the silence of a martyr. It was so unjust. She was a silly woman, she didn't understand.

"No. Thank you." As Sarah said the words harshly, guilt flooded in to mix with her anger. She was unfair to Rachel, always unfair.

"Thank you," she tried again, more gently. "I just want to be alone for a bit."

Rachel's footsteps retreated.

At dinner that night, Sarah, although she had barely considered the idea until that moment, tried an announcement: "Lisa and I might get an apartment."

Stung, Rachel looked up from her food and began to protest— "But this is your . . ."—when a fierce glance from Sam silenced her. She stopped, swallowed, thought for a moment, and then said firmly, "You are welcome here as long as you like." Sam concentrated on cutting the gristle away from his meat and said nothing.

All that summer and autumn, the crews were still digging a great trench east of Yonge Street, desperate to finish before the frost arrived, praying they would not run into rock. Three years before they had encountered a wall of limestone between Front Street and Queen and been forced to use explosives, warning the citizens beforehand but startling the unprepared birds, who turned the sky above into a chaotic mass of squawking and swirling whenever a charge exploded. Now, the men were working well north of Carlton Street, and the progress was slow, safe, and steady, with steam shovels and jackhammers where they could but often by hand with shovel and pickaxe where the drawings showed they would find some hidden wire or pipe. Inch by inch of asphalt and stone, yard by yard of rubble and soil, they cleared it all, shovelling it into trucks which then dumped their loads into the lake at the east end of the harbour, creating acres of land where one day new streets and buildings would rise. By Remembrance Day, the engineers were breathing down their necks, demanding of the foremen when the work would be done, and on their long shifts the cold and the damp seemed almost unbearable to the men who dug. But once all the wires and pipes were safely exposed, the planking laid over their heads, and the streets reopened to traffic, the diggers discovered that the wind that now whipped down Yonge Street did not blow underground. They felt secure in their newly created cave, and pitied the chaps working north of them in the open cuts up to Eglinton. They were happy with their progress. They had reached Bloor Street before Christmas, right on schedule, and could soon invite the concrete finishers and the electricians to join them underground. By March, the track gangs, who had been working their way up and down the line for almost a year now, were panting to lay the last rails. In May, the new Toronto subway opened.

It ran from Union Station at the southern edge of downtown, not far from the lakeshore, uphill all the way to Eglinton Avenue.

It would replace the clanging and shunting of the Yonge streetcar with a smoother and softer vibration, whisking the bankers and stockbrokers home to the tree-lined streets and imposing houses of Rosedale while the secretaries travelled a few stops further north, to the six-storey red-brick apartment buildings on the side streets off Eglinton. It was a huge source of pride to Toronto, for its rival Montreal, long acknowledged as the more important Canadian city, the seat of finance and culture, the port of entry for immigrants, did not have a subway yet. Paris, London, New York—real cities—teemed with underground life and could move millions of inhabitants from place to place without ever coming up for air. Toronto was growing, pushing forward, the war was ancient history, almost ten years now since it had finished, and the future beckoned.

For Sarah, the opening of the subway was a distraction, an event to which she could look forward. It seemed to her right that it should open in May, for if September were her least favourite month, May was her most. She felt unaccustomedly lighthearted in those days before the subway opened, debating with Rachel whether they should try to join the crowds for the ribbon cutting at Union Station on the Friday, or wait until Saturday, the first official day of business, to take a ride. Would Sam be willing to leave the store for a half-hour and drive them over to Yonge Street, or would they have to take the Bloor streetcar eastward from Gladstone Avenue to reach the new subway line? "It will be there again the next day, and the day after that," Sam told Rachel as she pondered the best hour to enter the subway that first day, but unlike her husband, most people embraced this new thing with fervour. Even Lisa, who had got engaged at Christmas, could be distracted from her wedding preparations to join them. The women had agreed they would enter the subway at Bloor Street, ride south to Union Station, turn around, and retrace their route, riding all the way northwards to Eglinton and then south again to Bloor. It would be like a game, a fairground ride, this trip to nowhere in particular, and Sarah felt as excited as a child who has been promised a great treat.

She slept badly that night, unable to settle into unconsciousness, and she awoke feeling groggy with that annoying tickle at the back of the throat that precedes a bad head cold. She felt no better after breakfast, but was determined not to miss the fun, and set off in the car with Sam, Rachel, and Lisa, who had arrived at the house all breathless with excitement at the crowds she had seen on the street, the balloons, the children dressed in their Sunday best. The day was warm for May, as though nature knew that pleasant weather was required for the event. Sitting with Lisa in the back seat as Sam inched his way through the Saturday traffic, Sarah grew uncomfortably hot. By the time Sam dropped them at Yonge Street, she was feeling decidedly feverish and looked with dismay at the long queue that had formed outside the subway entrance.

"Oh, dear, perhaps Sam was right. We'll have to wait for hours," Rachel said, looking back towards the car.

But by now Sam had pulled away from the curb and turned southwards away from them, so there seemed no choice but to join the line. Certainly, Lisa was not to be disappointed and pushed her way through the crowd to question the uniformed officials supervising the queue. She returned to tell them it would only be a quarter-hour before they would board a train, her optimistic assumption that this was a reasonable wait stilling any opposition they might have expressed.

They joined what seemed to be an immobile crowd of people backed up Bloor Street and soon found dozens more had arrived behind them. The waiting made Sarah feel hotter still and the scratch in her throat was becoming painful, but it was also making her listless and reluctant to speak, so she did not find the energy to protest and insist they turn back. Half an hour later, with feet aching from standing on the pavement, they were only beginning to file down the new subway steps to the fare collector's glass booth, but once through the turnstile, the crowd finally began to move, pressing towards the platform. There it seemed less crowded than out on the street—Lisa reasoned that the collector's booth had created a bottleneck—and now the women stood near the front of the platform with room around them to breathe in the peculiar air of the underground. It was warm and not unpleasant, slightly dusty but slightly sweet, and as a current quivered lightly, then picked up speed and rushed towards them through the tunnel heralding an approaching train, there was added to it an almost yeasty smell as though someone were baking bread further down the line.

Sarah, cooler now, breathed in deeply.

She was standing on the platform, a platform punctuated with green wooden benches, looking down at the dirty concrete under her feet which were laced into black leather school shoes, collapsing her girlish body inwards to match the slope of the white-tiled wall against which she was leaning, the wall that curved up towards the exuberantly floral lettering announcing the stop "La Muette," and warm air rushed into the station, bringing with it a pleasant odour that somehow simultaneously reminded one of coal dust and fresh pastries, and her mother was standing beside her, holding her hand as the train approached, with its file of green cars, and its one red car for the first-class passengers, and Sophie Bensimon warned, "*Attention, Sarah,*" as the Paris Métro came nearer and nearer.

As the new Yonge Street subway pulled into Bloor Street station, Sarah fainted.

"Counting the days?"

"Oh, yeah."

Daniel grinned in agreement as he fell in beside a classmate and walked up towards the hospital. It was housed in a looming red-brick

Victorian mansion perched on the far bank of the Don River, next door to the city jail. Its aging facade was covered by the desiccated brown vines of an ivy that never seemed to bud nor bloom, but did succeed in obscuring the old stone nameplate carved over the door so one could no longer read the words, The Toronto Hospital for the Isolation and Treatment of Contagious Diseases. The hospital had been established to house cholera patients in the 1830s, purposely located at some remove from the original city; then it had treated diphtheria, scarlet fever, smallpox, chicken pox, and eventually polio. Now it mostly specialized in chronic care and had been renamed the Don Hospital some years ago, but the medical students still insisted on its old nickname, the Contagion.

Daniel studied medicine well west of here, at the University of Toronto, as his father had before him, attending lectures in the same Gothic pile, laughing with his classmates on the same green campus. Medicine was the choice dictated by respect for family, by acknowledgement of what had been sacrificed and achieved since 1891 when Daniel's grandfather had arrived in Montreal from Poland by way of Hamburg, with no English, no French, and no money. Barely more than a teenager, he had walked the streets with a pushcart collecting rags and bones, eventually building up a garment business that he soon moved to Toronto along with his new wife, two young sons, and baby daughter. There, Grandfather Segal grew so rich that his third son could choose whatever career pleased him and so had enrolled at the university. In just two generations, the Segals had gained such peace of mind and prosperity that they now could afford altruism: medicine was the hallmark of their social achievement and their family was to produce factory owners and doctors in equal measures for years to come.

But for Daniel, medicine was also a vocation. Since his boyhood in a doctor's home, he had felt a gentle thrill as he watched his father splint the injured paw of a stray dog and as he himself took charge of his younger brothers when they sledged down a snowy hill or sought summertime frogs in the muddy bottom of a ravine. Now, he knew the joy of benevolent power when nature obeyed his commands and a wound healed or a fever dropped, the swelling pride when a patient rallied and a mother smiled her gratitude. Daniel was both a realist and an optimist, a man who saw the world as a place that could be fixed.

Perhaps that was why he so hated, from the moment he boarded the streetcar and rode out across the Bloor Street viaduct, each day that he had clerked in infectious diseases at the Contagion, a place where little healing seemed to be going on. The halls were long and narrow, their floors covered with a cold and echoing tile, their high ceilings dimly lit. The wards were only worse. Open one of the solid oak doors, beautiful pieces of Victorian carpentry into which windows had been hastily and badly carved at some later date so that doctors could look in on their patients, and you found stark quarters where the cracked plaster was painted an unappealing shade of green while the windows were so grimy you could not see the grounds outside. At least the first and second floors were full of bustling nurses tending to a full house, but up on the third floor in the remnants of the isolations wards, the patients looked abandoned in their bleak accommodations, a few frail figures propped up in iron beds, only three or four to a room, as though anyone so obstinately unfashionable as to catch an infectious disease in the age of vaccines and antibiotics could hardly warrant a great deal of medical attention. Indeed, the worst cases were on the remaining polio ward, where a weeping Mediterranean mother, withered with worry despite her youth, would watch and pray as a child fought the fever. Daniel felt angered by these women. The vaccine had been available for a full year now, but they had been frightened of these new medicines, or slow to take the child to the doctor for immunization, or had not understood enough English to read the letter that came in the mail, or had immigrated here only a few months ago. The sad reason would be noted somewhere on the chart. The doctors would reassure her—"He'll live, he'll live"—but could not say whether the infection had spread to the spinal column where it might cripple and maim for life. The answer would be revealed only in the weeks to come as a slow recovery, exhaustion that never seemed to clear, and muscles that would not obey commands would mean the worst.

So, this day in May towards the end of the academic year, it was with relief that Daniel and his classmate heard Dr. Sanderson call over his shoulder, "I've got a measles case for you this morning," as he hurried through the hallway at the head of a group that included residents, interns, nurses, and the two lowly student clerks. The pair were undertaking clinical rounds with lassitude that morning, knowing the term would soon be over and they would leave the Contagion for good. They were glad of the diversion that a measles patient might offer. Today, perhaps, they would be spared the polio ward.

Summer had already arrived in the city, making the hospital hot and airless. An electric fan had been placed in the lobby, its vibrations painfully shaking the elongated pole on which it was mounted but producing cool currents nonetheless. But on the wards themselves, no such provisions had been made for the sick. Lecturing on the virulence of what are known as childhood diseases when contracted in adulthood, Dr. Sanderson opened an oak door and led his group from the close air of the hallway into an atmosphere that seemed to be made more stifling still by the body temperature of a fevered patient.

At first, Daniel did not recognize Sarah. Her hair had disappeared, the long strands pulled back from her face by an efficient nurse and the soft curls plastered against her head with sweat. Her eyes were shut, her face was gaunt, and her small, crisp nose now protruded so sharply from it that her gracious profile had turned to a blank mask sliced down the middle by a hawk-like beak. It was only when he saw the name on the chart he was passed that he suddenly realized who this patient was.

He started forward, about to speak, but bit the words back.

"Segal?" Dr. Sanderson turned to him.

"Nothing, sir." Daniel handed the chart to the other clerk.

"Most cases can be treated at home, in children and adults, unless the fever becomes dangerously high in the later stage of the illness. That's what happened here. A week with sore throat, and spots, then the rising fever. Brought in last night with 105. Semi-delirious. Not surprising at that temperature." As if to illustrate these remarks, the patient shifted on her bed and, without opening her eyes, started to mumble anxiously for a moment before subsiding back into stillness.

"Unclear how the patient caught it. She has no contact with children, and there are no current reports of measles in the schools. She's European originally. Did not move here until age twelve, or thereabouts. That may explain why she was not exposed to measles in childhood. Infection patterns vary."

He turned to a particularly eager intern.

"Dr. Smythe, for the benefit of our clerks here, describe Koplik's spots and tell us how the fever should now be treated."

Daniel, who had been concentrating fiercely on the doctor's words both to steady himself and in hopes of discovering Sarah's actual condition, now drifted into his own thoughts.

"It's measles, only measles, just measles. She'll be okay, fine, okay."

The doctors agreed that the temperature in the room was no aid to recovery and moved on, instructing one of the nurses to find a fan for the patient, but Daniel lingered a moment, wanting to do something immediately, uncertain how to leave. It was then that Rachel Plot entered the room, carrying some flowers and a small suitcase.

"Daniel!" She looked at him in delight. "How did you . . . ?"

"I was just . . . They are doing rounds, the students . . . it's a teaching hospital. Maybe they didn't tell you that at the desk. The students . . . um, we follow along."

"Oh, I see," Rachel replied. She was wearing a little suit of beige cotton, the material was thin, but the jacket tight, and she shifted uncomfortably in the heat, putting down the suitcase to wipe her brow with her one free hand, then walking towards the bedside to set the flowers on a small table.

As Rachel moved, Sarah, perhaps sensing a presence even if she had not wakened to the doctors, stirred again and began mumbling. A single white sheet covered the bed, its folds clinging to her fevered body like drapery on classical statuary, and as she grew more agitated, her hands grasped the edge of this shroud, wringing it to and fro. Rachel hovered at her side, worried but unsure what to do. Sarah's anxious but unintelligible chatter grew louder now, firmer, until its sounds finally coalesced into a single, discernible word, and as she suddenly ripped back the sheet from her body with her right hand, she cried out, "*Maman!*" and then stilled.

Alarmed, Daniel moved rapidly towards the bed, but stopped as Rachel rushed to pull the sheet back into place. She covered Sarah and her short, blue hospital gown with a firmness that tainted him with a hint of voyeurism, so emphatic were her smoothing hands over the thin fabric. He took a breath and continued forward, taking up a place near Sarah, on the opposite side of the bed. He looked across at Rachel. She averted her eyes, looking down at the sheet. They did not speak, both wanting to act as though they had not heard the cry but not quite able to manage the pretence. If Daniel now felt a trespasser in the room, as though he had been caught spying on a family's pain, Rachel was no less embarrassed, sensing Sarah's cry as both a humiliating condemnation of her years as the girl's caregiver and all-too-naked revelation of how much they now needed Daniel to take over the job.

"She'll be fine," Daniel eventually assured Rachel, finding some words to fill the silence. "Some delirium is to be expected with the fever, and her temperature is falling. I know it doesn't feel like it."

He gestured around the room, as if to indicate the heat, but it annoyed him that he felt a need to defend the hospital.

"One of the nurses is going to bring a fan, so it will get a bit cooler in here."

He moved awkwardly away from the bed, and turned to leave the room, indicating with a half-hearted extension of a limp hand that he needed to catch up with rounds.

"I'll call," he said, and hurried away.

He did call. If he had not done so earlier, if he had never lifted the phone in the ten months since their expensive dinner, it was not because he had made a mistake, not that he found himself, on further acquaintance, unawakened and unmoved by Sarah. Rather, he had encountered a dead end, a wall he did not fully understand and so did not know how to begin to climb. And, of course, his pride had been hurt. Sarah had said good night and thank you very prettily that evening, but the moment when she had withdrawn her hand rankled. He heard himself justifying his behaviour— "I was only trying to help"—in a tone that sounded cringingly petulant even inside his head. But he was a man who lived in the present. The months had dulled his shame, and now confronted with her transfigured form on the hospital bed, he felt again the kind of desire he could simply act on, whatever the embarrassments of his encounter with Rachel. He did not tell Sarah of the scene in the hospital and did not ask if Rachel had ever told her, but simply called a month later to see if she might care for a movie next Saturday night.

Catching up with each other's news as they sat waiting for the lights in the cinema to dim, he said only that he had been very busy with school, preparing for graduation from medical school that spring, trying to find a hospital that would take him as an intern. She had been busy too, she lied, still working part-time at the library even though she had finished her degree. She and Lisa had talked about getting an apartment together, and looking for proper jobs, but Lisa was to be married. She and Michael, next month. So, Sarah was still lodging with the Plots. And she had been ill recently, she confessed, the measles, funny she had thought only children got it, anyway, it took a while to recover, longer than you'd think.

At the end of a summer of picnics, movies, and walks, on a sunny day towards the end of October, Daniel proposed an outing. He had borrowed his father's car and arrived in great style at the Plots' that Sunday afternoon, his own sense of occasion somehow making him nervous. She opened the door herself, wearing a light dress and cardigan that would prove too flimsy the minute the sun began to set, and sling-back shoes that would make walking in the woods difficult, but she wanted to ignore the approach of winter and had dressed as though summer were still with them. She too felt this was an occasion, and seemed to move more slowly, even more tidily than usual, as she walked down the front steps, stood quietly as Daniel carefully opened the car door for her, and slid into the passenger seat. On their drive out into the countryside, their conversation seemed happy yet newly brittle as though they were moving backwards through their acquaintance rather than forward.

"What a beautiful day . . ."

"The colours should be perfect . . ."

It was a Canadian ritual this, the October drive out to the woods to admire the sharp reds, mellow oranges, and brilliant yellows of the autumn leaves, colours whose intensity was unknown in Europe's gentler climate, produced here by the sudden change of hot to cold when summer days gave way to frosty mornings in the space of a few weeks. As they drove westwards, great swathes of red and yellow appeared in the green of the landscape, and they fell into a comfortable silence. At a park about an hour from the city, Daniel brought the car to a stop in a gravel lot, turned off the engine, and sat staring at his knees. Now that he had stopped concentrating on his driving, he somehow could not find the motivation to move. It was as though some extreme energy would be required for the next stage of their outing, and instead he was filled only with a warm, lazy heaviness. Sarah shifted slightly in her seat and the rustle of her skirt roused him from his odd lassitude: he looked up, smiled at her, and then got out of the car and went around to open her door. He had brought a picnic—some salmon sandwiches his mother had made, soda pop, and the crisp new apples that had still been hanging on a tree two weeks before—and he spread it out before them on a plaid blanket they had first laid on the grass, grasping a corner each as they wafted it to the ground.

"My father used to bring us to this place when we were kids."

"I've never been here before . . . It's pretty."

Afterwards they walked along a trail that climbed through the woods towards a hilltop, and talked—or at least Daniel talked, of how the Toronto teaching hospitals still had no place for Jewish interns or residents, of how the door of the club was shut in your face, of how his father, one of the original forty Jewish doctors who had founded Mount Sinai on Yorkville Avenue, had finished his studies in Philadelphia back in the 1920s, of how Daniel had delayed looking in the States, hoping that things had changed. They would have to change, they would change, soon, but in the meantime Daniel had finally found a spot down in Rochester where he would begin work in January. Just another a year, a year away, twelve months of living on a student's stipend, and then he could come back to Toronto and start a family practice. His father could lend him the capital he would need. He would be ready to settle down. Sarah, who knew these things already, said nothing, not even offering a murmured "yes" or "I see" of encouragement, but Daniel had come to understand her reluctance to please and to admire her pride.

When they reached the top of their climb, they stopped and looked out over the coloured hills. The valley before them was bathed in the clear, pure light of autumn, the sunshine in its turn made golden by the reflection of the flaming leaves. Around them the trees hummed and glowed in this last burst of the season, and they held their faces towards the warmth. The sun, already sinking lower in the sky, was now at a level that blinded them as they looked towards it. Sarah closed her eyes, saw exploding yellow fill her head, and dwelt there for a little while. Daniel, sensing the setting sun, spoke: "Time to be getting home."

On the hilltop all was still bright and warm, but there was dark and dampness back in the woods, dewy spots that the increasingly shortened daylight had not reached in weeks. Sarah felt chill now and, in unspoken agreement, she and Daniel set a quicker pace. As they climbed back down the steepest section of the path, her attention fixed on negotiating the stones at her feet, she stepped on a collection of wet leaves, all plastered to each other so that they created a single slippery page of the most beautiful deep purple. Unable to find purchase on this slick surface, Sarah's right foot shot out from underneath her. Gasping as she fought hard not to fall backwards, the adrenalin flooding her body as though this were some mortal danger, she flung herself awkwardly upwards from this potential fall only to catch her shoe on a rock. Now she pitched straight forward. In front of her, close enough that there was barely room for her to fall without hitting him, Daniel heard her cry out, sensed her sudden movement, and turning rapidly, caught and held her. She hung on for a moment, relying on him to steady her until she found her footing again, and then stepped back.

"All right?"

"Fine. I just slipped on a leaf or something."

As they started out again he took her hand, holding it firmly as he lead her back downwards the rest of their walk.

Under the *chuppah*, the bride looked as small as a child. At her side, Daniel seemed to tower over her, as though nervousness was enlarging his body whereas it was shrinking hers. He stood slightly apart from her, kept at bay by her protruding skirt, and they looked, on this day, a rather lopsided pair. Rabbi Cohn smiled encouragingly at Sarah, not the warm, straightforward grin he offered all the brides and grooms in his care, but a more meaningful and loving look. The rabbi very much wanted a happy ending for the girl he had helped settle in Canada fourteen years before. The war was over, it was time to move on, to leave the past in its place.

"You are happy, Sarah," he had told rather than asked her during his first interview with the newly engaged couple. He had been impressed then with Daniel, and remained so during the wedding preparations—an upright young man and a doctor too. Sarah, he suspected, was in need of healing. He extended his loving look towards Daniel now, bringing them both into his encouraging ambit as behind him the cantor began to sing the blessings.

Daniel's voice shook and cracked with emotion when it came time to repeat the rabbi's words—"You are consecrated to me . . . "— while Sarah, with no words to speak in the ceremony, kept her eyes on her feet. On his first attempt, the glass, carefully packaged up in a dishtowel so that it would not spread shards when it shattered, just popped out from under the slippery leather sole of Daniel's brand-new shoe, and the guests laughed tightly. On his second try, he succeeded. There was a muffled splintering, Sarah shuddered slightly at the sound, and so, they were married.

Seated side by side at one of the four round tables sandwiched into the Plots' dining room, Daniel and Sarah barely spoke. They were too busy eating the wedding dinner—the chicken fricassee, so full of subtle flavours and rich titbits you couldn't begin to distinguish them from each other; the brisket, juicy enough if not quite as tender as what Rachel or Clara might have prepared in their own kitchens; the carrots and onions that had roasted with the meat until they were sweet and soft; the beans, fresh and crisp; the comforting solidity of the potato kugel—huge helpings because Rachel had instructed the caterer to feed the newlyweds well and now leaned across the table with exhortations to eat. Observing tradition and his mother's suggestions, Daniel had spent the day fasting, a purification before a new life, while Sarah might as well have been fasting too, she had eaten so little that day. Rachel worried about her health: although her engagement seemed to agree with her, she still had not regained her strength from that grim winter of unspoken loneliness and the springtime bout of measles that had preceded a year and a half of planning and gaiety. Rachel had visions of the bride fainting under the *chuppah* and had urged both breakfast and lunch on her that day, but Sarah felt so nervous all morning and afternoon that she could manage nothing at all. Finally, at Rachel's insistence, she took a cup of broth only minutes before the rabbi was due to arrive at the house for the signing of the *ketubah*, the contract that would bind her husband to her. She was already dressed by then, so Lisa held a large towel over her to protect her gown from mishap and reapplied Sarah's lipstick once she had finished. At dinner that evening, Sarah and Daniel were both famished, and happily accepted when the waiter came round to their table with seconds.

As the other guests were cleaning their plates, Sam rose to his feet, cleared his throat, and brought the room to attention. The toasts and speeches began. Sarah tried to relax, to listen to the jokes, the kindness, the expressions of hope and goodwill; she tried to concentrate on Daniel's words, to remember for years to come that moment when he spoke of his love with naked truthfulness in front of this whole room of people, but the talk seemed distant, a quiet chatter out somewhere beyond the roaring inside her own head. As the voices rose and fell, the applause and laughter echoed, the unreality of the last few months threatened to engulf her utterly.

Speeches finished, she and Daniel were called on to cut the large white cake that was sitting in one corner of the room. A great high affair with three tiers supported by little plastic columns and decorated with sugar roses, it had been provided by the caterer and was whisked away to the kitchen as soon as the newlyweds had put their knife into it, never to reappear. This formality dispensed with, the guests pushed back their chairs and got up from the tables to chat with each other. Sarah and Daniel found themselves swarmed with well-wishers again, each one demanding a few moments of attention, stopping long enough to offer a *mazel tov* or compliment Sarah on her dress before being elbowed aside to be replaced by the next one. And so it went, seemingly for hours, no proper conversation ever established in the din. Alternately excited and exhausted by more talk, more people, and more attention directed at her than she had ever before experienced, Sarah felt her smile might crack her face.

It had just dawned on her that the crowd seemed thinner now, that there was finally some room to breathe, when Daniel drew her away by the arm. One of his brothers had brought a record player and an extension cord: people were dancing in the backyard. Daniel pulled her through the kitchen, down the back stoop, and out onto the grass where the younger guests had formed a large, laughing circle. Delighted by their own spontaneity and by the appearance of the bride and groom in their midst, they cheered and applauded while someone rushed back into the kitchen for a pair of chairs. Soon, Sarah found herself hoisted into the air on the shoulders of the groomsmen who had held the little makeshift *chuppah* unwavering that afternoon. Across from her, Daniel was similarly elevated, and as she watched him bobbing about in front of her while she too heaved and rolled, she feared that the muzzy feeling in her head would turn to dizziness. "Let me down," she pleaded, putting a hand onto one of the shoulders that held her, but she could barely hear her own voice, let alone make a sound that would rise above the music and the laughter.

As the youngsters danced, Rachel and Clara busied themselves in the dining room and kitchen, overseeing the waiters as they cleared away the meal and set up a trestle table in the hallway that ran the length of the ground floor. Clara was checking that it was good and secure when Rachel brought forth a lace tablecloth and, with help from the eager women who now crowded around, laid it out and smoothed it down with a proud hand.

"My grandmother's . . . all the way from Russia."

It had always seemed a miraculous thing to her, this one precious heirloom that her late mother had somehow managed to bring across continents and oceans. "Look at the handiwork," her cousin Leah cooed, sensing Rachel needed the cloth to be admired.

Pleased, Rachel surveyed the cloth and then beckoned to a waiter to start loading the stacks of plain white china plates onto the table. They were rentals, not as fine as the lace on which they would sit, but she hadn't enough of her own good dishes to serve this many. Down in the basement, where Rachel had resorted to storing the desserts, Clara was gingerly removing wax paper from trays, readying each one for Rachel, knowing better than to bring anything out to the table herself. Delicately, gently, with care not to disturb a single cookie, Rachel started to make the little trips up and down the basement steps, bringing out a perfectly iced cake, a lush-looking strudel, or big dish of sliced fruit, placing it on the table, standing back to survey the effect, then returning for another. At ten o'clock, she gave Sam the signal. He went round the guests now scattered about the living room and dining room before heading out to the yard to shepherd the dancers inside. It was time. The dessert table was ready.

Suddenly, Sarah found herself alone under the silent night sky. Through the ceremony, the dinner, and the impromptu dancing, she had felt uncomfortably hot, but now a spring breeze was blowing and she shivered. Wearing a fiercesome girdle and clinging stockings underneath a dress that exposed her chest and shoulders, she could feel both the perspiration running down the inside of her thighs and cool chills passing across her back. All day she had longed to be alone, to be rid of Rachel's fussing, of the cantor's singing, of the eager guests pressing to congratulate her, of the wild dancers who lifted up her chair. But now that she was here, she just wanted Daniel. She had not spoken to him all day and, indeed, had barely looked at him, for she had not found the courage to meet his eyes as he had signed the *ketubah* and helped lower the veil over her head, nor the words to share with him as they had sat together at dinner. She started up in awareness that all the rest were gone and hurried back into the house to find him, through the kitchen and the dining room, but she could not see him anywhere. The lights were dim, and to Sarah, hot, cold, exhausted, and still dizzy, the people in these rooms looked increasingly indistinguishable. The more she looked for Daniel, the more impossible it became to recognize any face at all, the longer she did not see him, the more panicked she became. The bride, queen for the day, had suddenly become a lost child, and as she pushed her way from room to room, excusing herself as she slipped between people who barely seemed to notice her now, there were no more well-wishers or dancing partners, just a mass of bodies amongst which she did not belong.

For the second time in her rush through the house, she reached the dessert table in the hall, and standing there, fought down panic only to find it replaced by awkwardness. To whom should she speak? Where should she move? To cover her uneasiness, to suggest some purpose for this desperate push to the table, for she was no longer hungry in the least but rather felt unpleasantly full, she reached across to the stack of white plates, took one, placed it down on the table in front of her, and began to help herself to the dessert nearest at hand. It was as she sliced into Rachel's sponge cake, drawing the knife through the delicate waves of white icing, that she saw a shining figure amongst all the grey forms. He was standing down at the other end of the table, squashed out almost to the vestibule by the length of the table, and was looking right back at her, his face transformed by two simultaneous expressions, the one a deep tenderness, the other a wry amusement at their predicament.

And as she looked at him, it was as though Sarah was recognizing Daniel for the first time. During their courtship she had noted his gentleness, appreciated his tact, and felt that he did not demand her to be other than she was, most of all that he did not insist that she be happier than she was. Yet, if she had said yes when he had proposed on that day at the end of their autumn walk, she embraced him more with gratitude than passion, regarding him most of all as a solution. He was what you might call a compromise, although Rachel and Rabbi Cohn would call him a good husband. Now, alone with his face, Sarah knew the depths of his emotion and felt her own love rise to meet it. He would embrace their partnership as joyous work and expect her to do the same. It would be a union of equals, free of pity and pride, and it would raise her up to the serene place she secretly knew she deserved.

For the first time that day, Sarah could feel the solid ground beneath the tight little satin pumps that, she now realized, were pinching her toes. She put down the knife, leaving a smear of white icing on the pristine glass cake plate, and extended a hand down the long table, reaching towards her husband as she said his name:

"Daniel."

Max suffers.

It is not a physical pain that nags his body but rather some gentle anguish disturbing his soul. Every day, he wraps himself in a glittering social garment of lively conversation, bright charm, and excited flattery, yet beneath it you can sometimes glimpse the soiled rag of sorrow in the heave of his sigh or a brief vacancy in his eyes. His only willing display of this emotion is as some kind of juvenile ennui: he is reading Goethe, *The Sorrows of Young Werther*, the book that made suicide fashionable amongst eighteenth-century boys. Perhaps this is why at first I dismiss his hurt too easily, underestimate it as so much undergraduate pretension, long talks in dark coffee houses about the existence of God and why the camps ever happened.

"The world is shit."

"Is it?" I am hesitant, as though trying to pacify him.

"Yeah, look around. Shit. I don't know how anyone could think there was some god presiding over this."

"Well, it's about faith, I believe, or at least I think I do."

I don't understand his alienation, can't glimpse its source, and sense that his cynicism could one day form a wall between us. Yet he trusts me to listen, seems to value some intelligence in me that I don't myself recognize.

"Marie," he will say, fixing me with an earnest gaze, "do you believe the world is good, or is it rather fundamentally evil?"

It is all I can do to keep from laughing, they are so self-consciously philosophical these questions. Max lugs around consciousness like a small child trying to drag a big chair, while I have learned that it is a burden best laid aside. Without a word, my family has taught me that well: In moments of extremity, my mother goes out shopping and my father pours another drink. From time to time, they put on good clothes and seek some unthinking solace in the mass.

Yet, Max and I are both at an age where we believe in solutions, and think we are better than our parents, so for the sake of our friendship I puzzle hard and try to offer him answers. Besides, this way I can distinguish myself from amongst his many friends. I am not one of his set, rarely go to the university parties and worry that I must be less desirable to him than the other girls he meets. So I have decided that our companionship is something higher, some kind of intellectual bond, and I use his anxiety as the occasion for intimacy.

"There is good, there is love, you have to believe that . . . What worries you so much? We live in nice houses, our clothes are warm, we always have food."

Over our university years, Max's questions grow more subtle, my responses less banal, but his kernel of suffering always endures. As both our friendship and we ourselves mature, I have to acknowledge that this anguish is no pose, but somehow fundamental to Max.

Of course, I have identified the obvious culprit from the first, and try tactfully to initiate discussions of his family's past, but I find his answers curt and almost callous.

"Do you ever think of going there?"

"Paris, sure, I went there last summer."

"No, I mean Auschwitz. Do you ever think, well, of visiting Auschwitz?"

"Why bother? Probably just some field and a bunch of huts."

"You might find out . . . well, you might find out something."

"What difference does it make?"

"I don't know." I have no answer so instead I say, "I read somewhere that the barracks . . . there was this storehouse, where they put all clothes and stuff that they collected from people, as they arrived . . . and the storehouse, the prisoners called it Canada . . . because it was a place of wealth, I guess. "

"Yeah, I've read that too." He is silent again, and I change tack.

"It must be hard for your mother."

"I don't know. She can probably barely remember."

"Max. She was ten? twelve?"

"Yeah, about that, twelve or so."

"You can remember everything from that age. I was thirteen when we left Paris and I remember everything about it. Does she ever talk about what happened?"

"A bit, when I was younger. You know the speech. It must never happen again, and all that."

"Imagine what it must feel like though, for her. I mean, imagine losing your parents when you were twelve years old."

"Yeah."

I try to bring Max around on this, to lead him gently towards some sympathy for a loss that must be felt lifelong, but he will not discuss it further. I am forced to recognize that for him she is merely the familiar, domestic figure of his own mother, and so he cannot impart to her the nobility that I do without ever having met her.

On the rare occasions when Max voluntarily mentions his mother, he talks not about her history but about her present incarnation, hinting at persistent demands and outrageous anxieties.

"My mother phoned . . ."

"I just have to go call my mother . . ."

His tone suggests saintly forbearance.

"She worries, Max, what's wrong with that?"

"Yeah, well, I wish she wouldn't."

Now, there's annoyance, even contempt in his voice.

"My mother wants me to apply for med school."

"I'm not sure about med school, but my mother . . ."

He sounds exhausted.

"She wants you to get a good job, Max. It's only natural."

"It's not natural."

"What do you mean?"

Cornered, he finds an example for me. After much parental pressure, he has indeed applied to the McGill medical school and has been accepted. He is to begin the program the next fall. When he phoned his mother to tell her, she announced that this was the happiest day of her life.

"The happiest day of her life?"

"Yeah. The . . . happiest . . . day . . . of . . . her . . . life." He stresses each word separately with bitter sarcasm.

"Why?"

"I don't know. Now, I wouldn't starve or something."

It seems to me an odd choice—was her own wedding day not happier? Or the day Max was born? What will she say if Max some day presents her with a grandchild? Her priorities are strange to me, and I puzzle over her statement, only concluding again that she must be haunted by her past.

Max refuses that past, will not mourn his grandparents or even admit to regret that he never met them. Yet still he carries some larger wound and seems to live under a shadow of what has gone before. Whatever his feelings for his mother's losses, he says he is "coming to terms with his Judaism." I am Catholic and unsure what that might mean.

In the *salle des manuscrits*, the North African clerk shuffles by my desk, sighing over some hidden trouble as he passes. He pauses to check that there is no forbidden ballpoint in sight, and moves slowly on, frowning now as he goes. I watch him leave and then dip back to File 263. In September 1897, Mme. Proust returned to Paris from a holiday with Marcel in the German spa town of Kreuznach, and took up a fresh notebook. Proust was working on an autobiographical novel in those years, an immature work he would later abandon, but it is surely the case of "that Jewish spy" that will preoccupy our diarist and her son in the months to come.

PARIS. WEDNESDAY, SEPTEMBER 29, 1897.

Dick has convinced Marcel of Dreyfus's innocence, and
Marie-Marguerite agrees with them. They argue it is nothing
but blind prejudice that led to his arrest in the first place.
Marcel confides in me that he finds the salons difficult this
season as there is much talk of Dreyfus and, in some, repeated
denunciations of the Jews. Dick says some students have
started to whisper behind the back of one of the professors who
is also Jewish. The boys have not raised the issue with their
father, for it is clear to all of us that his sentiments lie in the
opposite direction. He cannot believe that the army would allow
a miscarriage of justice to take place. I only wish I could agree
with him, but more and more I think of that poor soul on
Devil's Island and wonder how he suffers.

Marcel's pollenosis is not nearly as bad as it was in the
spring, but still he sniffles and rubs his eyes ferociously. It is
funny to long for colder weather but so we do.

PARIS. THURSDAY, OCTOBER 21, 1897.

Marcel had a most difficult dinner out in Passy Tuesday
evening. He had gone with Lucien to visit the Comte de
Montesquiou and they were enjoying themselves thoroughly
until conversation turned to the subject of Dreyfus. The Count
is certain of his guilt and made some sort of remark about the
Jews—Marcel wished to spare my feelings and would not repeat
just what was said. Whatever it was, he felt he could not let such
words stand, and reminded the Count of my ancestry. The
Count, always so eager to stress his great aristocratic antecedents
and perhaps hoping to change the subject, replied by listing his
own ancestors, but then, warming to his subject, concluded that
he was proud to assert there was not a Jew among them. Marcel

was further hurt by this and stayed only as long as was strictly necessary before excusing himself. Poor Lucien did not know what to do and did not wish to appear impolite to his host, so Marcel left him behind.

Adrien is very pleased—one of the medical publications that came in this morning's mail contained a glowing review of his book, and also praised in more general terms his work against disease. History will vindicate his efforts and remember his name.

PARIS. FRIDAY, OCTOBER 29, 1897.
I have been reading sections of *Jean Santeuil!* Marcel writes such a beautiful French, I cannot but believe this novel will make a literary reputation for him one day. There are the most exquisite passages inspired by our summers in Illiers— Marcel describes with loving detail how to mix the strawberries into the cream cheese, measuring the colour as you go along. Perhaps I shall be remembered in the annals of literature as Mme. Santeuil!

I confess I approached my reading with some trepidation, as I know Marcel did, since the novel is largely autobiographical, but the portrait is not unflattering after all. (Or perhaps Marcel is just not showing me the bits he feels might offend me. What a thought!) The one part where the mother looks a bit barbaric is about the girl with whom Jean is infatuated.

According to Marcel's account, the mother insists he stop visiting the girl, because she believes his passion is making him ill, but succeeds only in making him more sick in the end.

Perhaps I was wrong to put a stop to his love for the Benardaky girl. It seemed so unhealthy at the time, but certainly my censoring it has not cured him of infatuations. Indeed, his lady loves are never more than that. Marcel has made the girl's family very wealthy, but if I remember correctly, the Benardakys were perfectly ordinary folk, if a bit exotic with their Russian name and all that—were, probably still are. I imagine they still live in that poky little apartment over on the Rue de Chaillot.

But I indulge myself. Posterity will judge a great novel, not the writer's mother, to be sure. I returned the pages to Marcel this afternoon and could find almost nothing to say, he makes my heart swell with so much emotion. I only told him that one day he would make his father very proud.

Paris. Tuesday, November 30, 1897.
After yesterday's revelation, the papers are all scrambling to deny the remarkable news. The *Figaro* has had a real coup even if the others will not admit it. Marcel was up unusually early—I suspect he did not sleep at all with the excitement—and he and Dick and I have spent the morning poring over the *Figaro*. Fortunately, the doctor was not in the house, although I wonder now whether he will be able to maintain that the army has done everything for the best. Esterhazy's letter is remarkable—imagine such contempt for France in a military officer. And while none of us are handwriting experts, it seems clear that it is he who also wrote the note to the Germans in the first place. Apparently, there was indeed a spy in the ranks, but the army has the wrong man. Surely now it will not be long before Dreyfus is brought home. His poor wife must be so relieved.

Georges was here for Sunday dinner, and says they are to extend the Avenue Mozart right where Uncle's house stands, so that it must be torn down. Such a shame for that garden to be lost, but they call this sort of thing progress.

PARIS. FRIDAY, DECEMBER 17, 1897.

Adrien caught Marcel outside the house tipping a handsome young cab driver a whole ten francs and was furious at him. They came into the apartment arguing away about it. Marcel was contrite, but his father asked what good do his apologies do when he repeats the same acts over and over. Adrien was particularly alarmed that such tips leave the impression with servants that there is more to it than just driving the cab or serving the meal, or whatever it is. I have spoken to Marcel about this before and he is always mortally offended at what he calls "my insinuations." Anyway, their argument quite spoiled my pleasure at seeing Marcel out of doors again, after his recent attacks. Dick breezed through for tea and just laughed about the whole thing, and said, "With Marcel, what do you expect?" He finds a way somehow to remove himself from our cares and seems to regard his family increasingly as nothing more than light entertainment. But I am unfair, he is a devoted son. They both are.

Despite the *Figaro*'s evidence, everyone is saying that Esterhazy will be acquitted, so our joy seems to have been premature.

PARIS. THURSDAY, JANUARY 13, 1898.

It is a brave thing M. Zola has done. It was all over the streets this morning and Jean could not avoid the news when he went out for the bread. He brought me the paper himself at breakfast, saying very discreetly, "I think Madame may be interested in this." The headline is inflammatory—"I Accuse"— and the letter underneath even more so. He has openly accused the army of mistakenly convicting Dreyfus of espionage, forging documents to cover the mistake, and acquitting Esterhazy of the crime on government orders. Adrien was furious when he saw *L'Aurore*, demanded to know how it got into the house—I did not tell him that Jean has been sneaking it in occasionally since it seems we can no longer count on the *Figaro* for our Dreyfusard news. Luckily, Adrien did not pursue the issue but announced the army should sue Zola for libel. "These people seem determined to undermine France," he said, and went off to the faculty in a huff. Once he was gone, I woke Marcel, knowing this to be dramatic enough that he would want to know at once. He was hugely impressed by Zola's act, and dressed hurriedly to get out to his friends to see what action was planned. In his haste he left with only one scarf, his outer one, but nothing inside his coat. It is an indication of how excited he is, since usually he bundles up so methodically. Dick was up and out before the rest of us this morning, but no doubt he heard the news in the street. It is out now, there will be no more whispering in the salons. Something must be done.

PARIS. THURSDAY, JANUARY 20, 1898.
The government has indeed charged Zola with libel. I can barely believe that President Faure will permit such an attack on a distinguished man of letters, but it is all in the morning papers. Marcel is well pleased, pointing out that a trial, while difficult for M. Zola himself, may be for the best. After all, to win a libel judgment, the government must prove that what Zola says is untrue. "Zola's trial may yet be Dreyfus's retrial," Marcel says.

I have not discussed the affair at all with Adrien. It is easy enough for him to avoid Dick, who is always off somewhere, and Marcel, who is not awake when his father breakfasts and lunches, and either out with his friends or sequestered in his room when his father returns in the evening. So, he need not discuss his sons' opinions with them, and I hold my tongue.

There are reports from the provinces of riots, mobs throwing stones through the windows of Jewish merchants.

Paris. Monday, January 24, 1898.
Adrien will not speak to the boys. This petition has unmasked his disagreement with his sons; both their names have now appeared on the lists of intellectuals published in *L'Aurore* and they can no longer hide from each other that they are Dreyfusard and he not. Marcel and Dick are still busy obtaining signatures: the committee is optimistically hoping to collect ten thousand names before Zola's trial begins the week after next. They are asking for a retrial of Alfred Dreyfus—nothing more, nothing less. Anatole France himself has signed, and Marcel is out every day meeting in the cafés with his friends to get more names.

It all exploded last night, when Marcel and Dick came home—if I were not so upset by their falling out with their father, I would be pleased to see them working on a project together; they usually spend so little time with each other. Dick was bold enough to ask his father if he would sign, and Adrien turned to me and said, "Your sons know my opinion on this matter. I will have nothing to do with this foolish nonsense." He went off to his study and asked Jean to send in a tray for dinner. I have never heard him so cruel and so pompous. I have hidden from him my suspicions that Marcel and Dick are in the right camp, and tried to believe we are a family in which there is room for real debates, that intellectual disagreements are not the same as familial discord. But we have reached our limits with this affair.

It was Georges Sand who wrote that revolutions have put one half of France in mourning for the other. We seem to have another revolution on our hands.

Paris. Wednesday, January 26, 1898.

I ate my breakfast all alone this morning and was thankful at least for that. The boys had escaped early to the streets and the doctor now avoids me too. We are in the fourth day of his great campaign of silence, and yesterday's events were so painful, I find it hard to describe them.

Dick was at home for lunch and Marcel had risen early enough to join us for once, so there we sat *en famille* with Adrien refusing to speak to either of them. He insisted on that ridiculous formula by which the persistently affronted engage in conversation with their enemies by the use of an intermediary. In this case, myself. "Jeanne, would you instruct your son Marcel that if he is going to take luncheon when he was in bed but thirty minutes before, he should certainly eat more slowly." or "My dear wife, will you kindly tell Robert that I will be unable to offer him a seat in my cab when I return to the faculty this afternoon." (Marcel blushed and put down his fork while Dick retorted directly that he is always happy to take the omnibus.)

Finally, I could bear it no longer, and tried to remonstrate with the doctor, suggesting that his campaign was unsustainable and gently expressing the hope that we were a family in which there was room for rational debate. My intervention only angered him further and he replied most unkindly that while I might consider the arguments in favour of Dreyfus rational, they were in fact emotional and failed to grasp the political peril in which they placed the French state. He went on to explain that while he understood how one of my faith might feel great sympathy for a co-religionist . . . and there he never managed to finish his sentence, for I cried out that we were speaking not of religion but of justice, while Marcel and Dick were so outraged by their father's words—or perhaps embarrassed by their mother's uncharacteristic anger—that they both sprang up from the table. Marcel stumbled from the room without speaking, while Dick shouted, "Papa, how could you?" before he followed his brother.

So, I was left alone with the doctor, staring aghast both at him and how this miserable affair was now dividing us.

"Both in the nation and in the home, loyalty is the greatest virtue," he told me, and I felt the bitter irony of his words ringing in my ears as I too withdrew from the room.

J'ACCUSE. The headline is indeed inflammatory, blazoned across the front page of the *L'Aurore*. I suppose the title was the invention of the paper's radical editor, Georges Clemenceau, "the Tiger," not Zola's own choice, but they are nonetheless the two most famous words the novelist ever wrote. The document that followed clove France in two just as it separated the Prousts.

After a long and outraged recitation of the details of the case, Zola comes to his point. Citing generals, majors, and colonels by name, he accuses the army of a judicial error compounded by a violation of human rights for convicting Dreyfus on secret evidence that was withheld from his defence. He goes on to accuse the officers of a massive cover-up that included forged documents and fraudulent reports from corrupted handwriting experts, and of then acquitting Esterhazy when they knew him to be guilty. Zola's essay fills six densely packed columns across the entire front page of *L'Aurore:* the print is small and tight, making it a challenge to read through the glass of the display case at the Hôtel de Saint-Aignan.

The Bibliothèque Nationale must have a copy of the *L'Aurore* from January 13, 1898, somewhere in its vaults, but I happen to have found it here, in the exquisite seventeenth-century mansion that houses France's Museum of Jewish Art and History. Once an aristocrat's house, then the city hall for what was then the Seventh Arrondissement, the Hôtel de Saint-Aignan was used to house workshops for local craftsmen from the mid-nineteenth century on. By the time the Dreyfus affair was raging those craftsmen were all Jews: the hotel is at the heart of the Marais, the old quarter of Paris's Right Bank and the centre for Jewish gold and silver-smithing in the city. Many of the building's tenants disappeared during the Second World War and, in 1962, the City of Paris bought the Hôtel de Saint-Aignan and eventually turned it over to this brand-new national museum.

That much I gleaned from my Michelin guidebook before I set out for the Marais, thinking that this morning I would take a break from my translations and acquaint myself further with the rich culture from which Jeanne Proust sprang.

You still pass a clutch of posh jewellery shops on your way from the Métro to the museum. To actually enter the building, you must clear an intimidatingly antiseptic security room, walking through a labyrinthine metal detector while an impassive guard watches you from behind a double wall of glass: Jewish sites in Paris are frequently vandalized and occasionally subject to terrorist attack. Inside, I wander through rooms of art and artifacts, absent-mindedly admiring Italian wedding rings and a German Torah crown, a medieval gravestone, a coffered chest from the Renaissance, and a painting by Chagall. Soon I wind up here, in front of the display about Dreyfus, gazing at the photograph of the innocuous, bespectacled middle-aged man falsely accused of spying, and painstakingly reading through the front page of *L'Aurore*. While a few saw Zionism as the solution to anti-Semitism, the Dreyfus affair was, a text panel explains, an opportunity for most French Jews to stress their status as law-abiding, assimilated republicans—or perhaps I should translate that last word more subtly as loyal citizens of the Third Republic. They were upstanding Frenchmen and Frenchwomen; they were people like Jeanne Proust.

I wander further into the museum, following history into the twentieth century and come across an exhibit, still under construction, about the fate of Parisian Jews from 1941 to 1945. In the middle of the room a few display cases stand empty; around them the walls are covered with photographs. There are pictures of individuals, families, children, school groups, solemn-faced shopkeepers posing in front of their stores, prosperous burghers smiling gently for the camera, a rabbi with a black hat twice the size of his small face, an elegant woman in a long fur coat, a nervous couple in their wedding clothes. On a panel beside each photo, the subjects are all identified and their histories traced. A tax record shows the shopkeeper has operated these premises on the Rue des Francs Bourgeois since 1923. A family file from the Police Prefect of the Seine records that he was born in 1892 in the Eleventh Arrondissement, enjoys French citizenship, married in 1925, and now lives at an address on the Rue de Malte, before it lists his wife and children. A file from Drancy notes that he arrived at the camp in August 1943, and was deported six weeks later on convoy number 27.

He is dressed in an apron and stands proudly on the threshold of his shop with his arms folded across his broad chest but, beside his fine figure, it is another image that catches my eye. It shows a row of about ten well-dressed men, some diffident, others haughty, photographed in a courtyard. It must be winter, for they are all wearing fine wool coats, some with fur collars.

One or two sport chic homburg hats while the rest expose heads of well-groomed hair to the cold. The caption explains that these are members of the Paris bar interned at Drancy in November 1942. Someone has thought to assemble them together and take their photograph on their arrival at the camp—out of misplaced pride for their professional status? out of gloating victory over their humiliation?—and there they stand, their prosperous and happier pasts still visible in their demeanour, their integrated, law-abiding republican selves not yet erased by hunger, despair, and death. Each one is identified, citing the same kind of files as those of the shopkeeper, and amongst their number I read a name I recognize: P. Bensimon.

My museum-induced languor evaporates and I turn my newly awakened attention to the text panel for this name. It notes that, although there is no record of his or his family's internment at Drancy, the P. Bensimon of the photograph is most probably Philippe Bensimon, a Paris lawyer who, according to tax records, was born in 1900 and lived at 22, Rue de Musset in the Sixteenth Arrondissement with a wife and child. Their fate is unknown.

Frantically, as though the photograph and the text might disappear before my eyes, I pull my notebook from my bag, and start to fumble desperately for a pen. I put one in here this morning, I must have a pen. Not this pocket, not here, no. Finally I locate it, hiding beneath my hairbrush. I flip open the notebook and start to scribble furiously.

S ARAH SEGAL WAS STANDING at the sink, washing up
the breakfast dishes, when Daniel came into the kitchen to
say goodbye for the day.

"What time will you be home?"

"Should be back at six."

"Don't be late."

He ignored the admonition and kissed her.

"Bye."

"You won't be late, will you?"

"See you later," he called over his shoulder.

"Daniel . . ."

The front door closed and he was gone.

An hour later Sarah set out herself, stepping into a day of sharp sunshine and newly warm air. The house in North Toronto where she
and Daniel had lived for five years now was built in the Californian
style, a large split-level with a sprawling expanse of flat roof. Daniel
had judged it best, easier for Sarah and safer perhaps for their marriage, that they live at some distance from his parents, so they had
moved east and north, settling on this well-established neighbourhood because they had fallen in love with this surprisingly modern
house. It had been squeezed onto a lot where a fire had destroyed the

previous one, back before the war, and the rest of the street was older, made up of narrow two- and three-storey red-brick houses, shaded by mature maple trees. The comforting Ontario scene that lay before Sarah as she walked the four blocks out to Yonge Street was leisurely and secure. There was a wide street of fresh, flat asphalt with neither pothole nor bump to trouble the men as they drove to and from work in their big American sedans. It was lined by equally smooth sidewalks in which each square section was stamped with the date of a recent resurfacing. Each tidy house was set back a bit from the street, leaving room for a broad lawn now showing a rich green turf. And each front yard included a large tree whose branches reached out towards its neighbour across the way, creating a canopy that by midsummer would cover the whole street in a pleasant shade, but today, as the leaves were just now exploding from their buds, cast a pleasant dappled light. Sarah felt cheerful as she walked, running through her shopping list in her head, reminding herself to stop at the pharmacy for a few other requirements.

It was as she turned onto Yonge Street that her mood quickened and changed, growing deeper and less peaceful now. It was something about the smaller trees here, the sharp shadows cast by their thin branches and the wrought-iron grilles set into the pavement at their feet . . . or perhaps it was simply the warmth of the air that reminded Sarah fleetingly of something else, something past or something future. She felt a little urgency, an anticipatory frisson that might just be called spring.

On that day early in May 1964, a small miracle had occurred: white asparagus had arrived in the city. At the little Italian greengrocer that Sarah increasingly patronized, Mr. Lombardi presented the vegetable to her with shy pride.

"Signora, I have a surprise for you." He gestured her over to a prominent display, snatched up a bundle of the pale, thick stalks, and held it high for her inspection.

"Oh." Sarah almost swooned. "Asparagus. Real asparagus."

"I thought it would make you happy."

"Mr. Lombardi." She paused, stilling a sentimentality that seemed out of place in a greengrocer's shop. "Where does it come from?"

"From France, only from France. They are flying it in now. You can buy it already in New York. Now, they try Toronto. Maybe . . . you know why it's white?"

"Because it grows underground. They pick it before it has a chance to ever see the sun and turn green. And the flavour, the flavour is . . . I remember . . ." Sarah could not speak her memories, and brushed them away with a flip of the hand and a smile. "I'll have three bunches, please."

"I knew the Signora would understand. People, they don't know, they are stupid. They have never heard of it, they complain it costs a lot of money."

Mr. Lombardi carefully selected three of the best-looking bunches and placed them on his countertop, beside the till.

"What else, today, Signora?"

Sarah selected some green beans, a head of lettuce, and a bag of oranges and waited while Mr. Lombardi did up the bill by hand with a stubby pencil on a chit of paper and then rang the total into his cash register.

Sarah could still remember the fruit and vegetables of her childhood, and the street market where her mother had bought them from vendors who also added up their bills with a stubby pencil clasped in a dirty, work-worn hand. In late April or early May, the first asparagus, harvested before it ever appeared above the ground so that its flesh would maintain a delicate pallor, made its debut in the new sunlight of a Paris spring, like some shy debutante at a glittering ball. For two brief marvellous weeks, the vegetable vendors seemed to sell nothing else, trussing a few dozen stalks into a bundle and then building pyramids of these bundles on the tabletops of their makeshift stalls as they cried out, "*Les asperges, les asperges. Regardez mes belles asperges.*" At home, the maid would bring to the table a heaping dish of the stuff bathed in a frothy yellow sauce of egg yolks and lemon juice that Maman had made herself. She always insisted on that. Papa, as he plucked a white stalk from his plate to demonstrate, would once again repeat that the only way to eat asparagus was with the fingers, before he popped it into his mouth, nibbled through the soft tip, and then dragged the more fibrous end back out through his teeth to tackle it again. As it shredded and collapsed in the mouth, each piece revealed joyfully to the tongue that undefinable flavour that one could never quite remember from one spring to the next, an exquisitely delicate bouquet enriched by the molten egg yolks and then suddenly, sharply enlivened by the lemon juice.

In Toronto, as she struggled to cook appealing meals for her new husband, Sarah found produce—that was the grim word they used at the big supermarket down the street—a trial. When she had first arrived in the city, in the midst of the war, Rachel had served potatoes, cabbage, onions, carrots, turnips, and parsnips all winter and spring. There were always apples, but all other fruit came in cans saturated in a sugar syrup that eclipsed the very flavour it sought to preserve. Briefly, in the late summer and early fall, there were pears and peaches, berries, tomatoes, and a selection of green vegetables grown in the flatlands of Niagara, south of the city, around the lake. Oranges and bananas were a special treat; green peppers were exotic, asparagus came only in cans, and nobody had ever seen an artichoke.

Well, you couldn't live on such a diet, and sure enough, after the war, the selection started very slowly to grow. Florida oranges and South American bananas could now be eaten every day. Thanks to California, there was plenty of lettuce in the winter. And today, there was white asparagus, flown in all the way from France.

Mr. Lombardi carefully lowered the fruit and vegetables into a paper grocery bag, handed it to Sarah with both hands, and then bowed ever so slightly as she left the shop. She stopped next at the fishmonger, where she settled for some rather expensive sole to accompany the asparagus, remembered her errand at the pharmacy, and then walked slowly home to unpack her few groceries and make herself a light lunch. Tonight she would cook Daniel a dinner fragrant with springtime and hope.

Daniel, meanwhile, was sitting in the reference section of the main branch of the Toronto Public Library, leafing through the *B*'s in the Paris phone book. He occasionally asked his secretary to block out an extra hour at lunch for him, or some time first thing in the morning, so that he could attend to personal business. After eight years of private practice, his business was finally growing. People might distrust a new face at first, wonder that this boy could possibly be competent even if he was the son of Dr. Segal, the surgeon, down at Mount Sinai, but some of them eventually grew to like a younger doctor. They figured that he was up on things and, at the very least, could be counted on to outlive his patients. The years when Daniel barely had enough patients to fill a day of work, let alone a week, were long gone, but it was still easy enough to find a little gap in his schedule.

He did not tell Sarah about these small absences of his. He was working on this particular project with her permission, to be sure, but not her active participation, and he thought it best not to report too regularly on his activities until he had some results to show. He would even ask Miss Beauséjour, the French girl down the hall in Dr. Whitting's office, to translate the letters he would write rather than risk building up Sarah's expectations or stirring her memories. "*Cher monsieur: Je vous écris de la part de ma femme . . ."*

He finished up at the library, returned to the office for a 2:15 patient who was suffering from asthma, and spent the rest of the afternoon with healthy babies of various ages. He left the office in time to catch a northbound subway train at 5:30 and did get home punctually that evening, at ten minutes before six.

"Oh, good, you're home. Daniel, where's your jacket?"

Sarah looked startled at the appearance of her husband in shirt sleeves. He looked down at his arms.

"Guess I left it at the office. It's warm out."

"It's not summer yet. You never know at this time of year when it's going to suddenly get chilly. And what will people think—you're a doctor, in shirt sleeves. It's not appropriate."

"They'll just think it was a warm evening."

"What are you going to do tomorrow morning? What will you wear to the office? Oh you know, I had just had it dry cleaned."

"Well, I can wear the check, and bring the other one home at the end of the day." Daniel was starting to wonder if he had not left the jacket at the library, and silently began planning how he might retrieve it in the next day or two without Sarah noticing its absence again.

"What's for supper?" he asked, thinking to distract her.

"Fish, some sole . . . And a surprise, a treat. Look at this—" Sarah held up one stalk of the white asparagus from the cutting board where she had been carefully whittling the thicker ends with a carrot peeler.

"What is it?"

"Asparagus, real asparagus. The white kind, from France. Mr. Lombardi had it in his shop this morning, and I couldn't resist. We used to eat it when I was a girl . . ."

"I'll set the table," Daniel replied, and reached for the cutlery.

"Oh, no, use the fish forks," she said with a trace of irritation, reaching across him to show him the utensils she wanted.

At the table, Sarah tried to drop the subject of the missing suit jacket from her mind while Daniel tried to appreciate the flavour of his special dinner, and they passed the evening companionably enough. But with these smaller worries to distract her, Sarah had forgotten to tell Daniel what was really on her mind. They were lying in bed that night when she remembered.

"Daniel?"

"Hmmm . . ."

"You know, I'm late this month, three days now."

After eight years of marriage, Daniel knew better than to get their hopes up.

"We'll see, darling, we'll see." He reached across for her hand, clasped it, released it, and then rolled over towards sleep.

One late-summer afternoon about four months later, Sarah was carefully cutting beefsteak tomatoes into translucent slices with the sharpest knife in her kitchen when the phone rang. It was September and Mr. Lombardi was proudly displaying wicker baskets full of big, local tomatoes. Each one was a perfect globe of deep red, its yearning flesh threatening to erupt from beneath the green button at its crown. Its flavour would perfectly combine acidity and sweetness; its texture would balance a pleasing firmness with a lush softness. Sarah had carefully picked through the baskets that morning, selecting the roundest and ripest specimens for Daniel's dinner.

Sarah and Mr. Lombardi increasingly agreed on the importance of seasonal produce. As the wonders of California, South America, even South Africa and Europe started to show up at the supermarket, Sarah had at first snatched them up and eagerly popped them into her shopping basket. But she was often disappointed: They didn't taste quite right. She would never say so to Mr. Lombardi but the asparagus of her memory tasted more fragrant than the ones he had sold her last spring. It was as though their flavour was somehow dissipated by the trans-Atlantic flight. In the supermarket, big Californian strawberries were now available by April, two months before the local ones would appear, but they were watery and bland. Tomatoes could be had at any time of the year, but they were hard and greenish, and when she tried to ripen them on the kitchen windowsill, Sarah found they only became woody in texture. No one else seemed to notice or care, but Sarah knew better. She had become a connoisseur of the seasons, Mr. Lombardi's most treasured client, and it was only now, in August and September, that the tomatoes were really worth eating, thinly sliced, with a little salt.

As she cut into the first, however, her mind was not fully on her task. She was busy imagining a phone call from the police.

"Mrs. Segal, Mrs. Daniel Segal?"

She would reply politely in the affirmative.

"I am afraid there has been an accident . . ."

She would remain calm. Afterwards, people would comment on that, praising her cool-headedness. She would remain calm as she took the news, drove to the hospital, and rushed to his bedside.

It was 6:40 and Daniel was ten minutes late for their appointed supper hour. Sarah was worried. Daniel tried hard never to be late. He knew how much it upset her, gave her opportunity for worry. She always feared the worst. And so, to combat her fears, she sometimes played this little mental game: she really and truly imagined the worst. He had been hit by a car, crossing the street on the way out of his office, and was now lying in a downtown hospital. Or perhaps his subway train had derailed and he had fallen into a tangled mess of passengers as ambulances flocked to the scene.

Sarah had discovered in life that things were never quite as you imagined they would be. She had, for example, rehearsed her wedding day in her mind for a whole year in advance yet found the actual event wholly different, a blur of light and darkness, cold and heat, pain and joy, quite unlike the serene pageant she had anticipated. Applying this lesson to the sadder or simply the more mundane days on her calendar, she reckoned that if she imagined Daniel's accident in gruesome detail, there was sure to be some other explanation for his lateness. The game was not always successful, for Sarah had a powerful imagination and sometimes only fuelled her fears by confronting them, but the alternative, an empty, placid mind that would take life as it came—and only when it came—was beyond Sarah's capability.

On this day, she was doing rather well with her game, embroidering her conversation with the police with what seemed to her a wealth of realistic detail, when the phone really did ring, arousing her so harshly from her reverie that her hand slipped and the knife sliced into the first knuckle of the middle finger of her left hand. She flinched and gasped simultaneously and instinctively raised her finger to her mouth. The taste of the blood was pleasantly metallic, but there was an alarming amount. The phone kept ringing. Sarah turned, unsure what to do, panic rising within her. The phone persisted. Sarah found her mouth filling with blood. The phone rang again. She turned, crossed the kitchen, and with her good right hand took the receiver off the hook.

"Hi. It's me . . ."

Sarah, her bleeding finger still jammed in her mouth, moaned into the mouthpiece like a wounded animal.

"Sarah?"

She moaned again, this time dripping blood onto her chin.

"Sarah? Is that you? What's wrong?"

She removed her finger from her mouth.

"I'm bleeding." Freed from the suction of her mouth, the wound now started to bleed even more profusely, the blood dripping down onto the telephone table.

"Bleeding? Well, that's . . ." Daniel paused a moment, realized he had perhaps misunderstood and backed up. "What do you mean you're bleeding?"

"Daniel, it's all over the place. You were late and I was cutting tomatoes and the knife slipped . . ." Sarah's voice rose with each complaint.

"You've cut yourself?"

"My finger. I'm bleeding. There's so much . . ."

"Sarah, try to calm down. It's only your finger. The blood can't be spurting?" Daniel was, after all, a doctor.

"No, but there's a lot of it."

"Yes, there's a lot of it, but if you had cut muscle or down to the bone, you wouldn't be talking to me."

"It's bleeding . . ."

"Put the phone down and get a dishcloth. Wrap it around your finger, wrap it good and tight. Then come back. Okay. Can you do that for me?"

"I'll try."

There was a moment's silence on the line as Sarah followed her husband's instructions.

"All right. Is that under control?"

"I don't know. I can't see it now, it's all wrapped up." Her tone was now sulky.

"Okay, well, keep it that way until I get home. I was just calling to say I was running late—Mrs. Katz showed up at six, just begging for an appointment. Her baby is still colicky. She's beside herself. Anyway, I'm leaving now. I'll be with you in twenty minutes. Just sit tight. We'll get a bandage on it as soon as I get there."

"Twenty minutes. Can't you take a cab? I'm still bleeding, it's coming through the towel now. Daniel . . ."

"Try to be calm. I will be there as quick as I can."

Daniel usually left his 1958 Ford in the garage, reserving it for weekend errands and visits, and took the subway the three short stops up and down Yonge Street from home to office. Tonight, worriedly dismissing the extra expense as necessary under the circumstances, he did flag a cab outside the door of the medical building and was back at the house ten minutes later. He hurried into the kitchen to find Sarah still sitting by the phone, cradling her hand, wrapped in the stained dishtowel, on her lap. He got the first-aid kit from the bathroom, bandaged up her finger—it was a fairly small cut and had, by then, stopped bleeding—washed some blood from around her mouth, and settled her in the living room with a cup of tea, while he heated up some leftover soup for their dinner and finished slicing the tomatoes himself.

"Daniel . . ." Sarah called from the living room. "Just put a little salt on the tomatoes, won't you? They taste better with just a little salt, not too much, just a sprinkle. The shaker's on the windowsill."

Daniel sighed, reached for the salt shaker, and followed his wife's instructions.

That night in bed, once Sarah had finally dozed off, her injured hand now resting on a pillow he had fetched for her because she complained that her finger still throbbed, Daniel reflected, as he did increasingly, that it had not been a good day.

Good days were ones where nothing happened to upset Sarah. She had not cut her finger, or stubbed her toe, or caught a cold, or merely worried that she might be catching a cold. She had found all the ingredients she needed at the supermarket. It had not been a day when a new postman, one whom she didn't recognize, had come to deliver a parcel, prompting her to call Daniel at the office to check whether or not she should open the door to him. She was in the middle of her cycle, so neither her period's worrying delay nor its disappointing arrival nor yet the cramps that sometimes accompanied it would disturb her on this day. Nor had she read an article in the paper suggesting the economy was due for a downturn, nor one that insisted there were far too many doctors in the province of Ontario for all of them to get work. She was not, today, worried about the possibility of nuclear war. Those were good days.

It was Daniel himself who had given Sarah the luxury of fear.

At thirty-three, she could barely believe now that she had once been a young woman capable of buying passage to Europe, boarding a ship without any companion, sailing to France, and spending weeks alone ferreting out information as to the fate of her parents. Outside the house, she was usually a woman of great exterior composure—indeed, her slight air of aloofness from events around her often led others to consider her something of a snob—but once she met Daniel, interior courage was no longer required. That was his department. Calmly self-confident, Daniel had been raised to help others, he believed it a duty and a joy, and in the postwar years, as immigration officials slowly began to accept the European refugees they had once kept at bay, there seemed no more appropriate person to help, no more delicately pretty girl to love, than the quiet and resolute young Sarah Simon. Her fractured history seemed to him hugely attractive and he longed to make it better just as surely as he would cure his patients of strep throats and broken bones.

The next morning, the day after Sarah cut her finger, Daniel set off from the house early, took the subway down to King Street, and joined a short queue in front of the information desk at the German Consulate. The line was moving well, an officer dispensing visa forms and tourist pamphlets with quick precision, until the young woman ahead of Daniel moved up to the counter. She was about to leave for Germany on a student visa, Daniel gathered that much from the English half of the conversation, but since she seemed intent on proving to the boyish-looking officer that she spoke German, moving haltingly through her requests in that language despite the officer's replies in impeccable English, the transaction took rather longer than it should have. She finally secured the information she needed about what inoculations and vaccinations were required—the words for typhoid and diphtheria proved elusive—and moved on, thanking the officer for his kindness and assuring him how much she looked forward to her trip, in English, before essaying a cheery *auf wiedersehen* as she left. Daniel advanced to the counter.

"I wanted information . . ."

His voice sounded too loud in the consulate's echoing front hall. He hesitated, cleared his throat, and tried again in softer but unhesitating tones.

"I was looking for information about indemnification, for war claims."

"Yes, sir. I will get you the forms. Just a minute, please."

The officer turned to a cabinet behind him, opened a drawer, and started leafing through files. He seemed unable to find what he was looking for, turned to Daniel and indicated with a gesture he would be another moment, and walked back towards a closed door, knocked, and entered. The woman behind Daniel in the queue shuffled her feet impatiently. Someone coughed. After a minute or two, the officer emerged with an older colleague, a middle-aged woman dressed in severe grey. She advanced to the counter, and bent her head to speak to Daniel.

"The person who is applying, that is . . ." Her voice, already quiet to the point of inaudibility, trailed away.

"My wife." Daniel prompted.

"Yes, your wife. Is she . . . was she? She lost property? She was interned?"

"Her parents died in the camps."

"Yes, but was she interned, herself, yes?"

"No, she escaped, here, to Canada."

"Yes, she is the child of a victim." The woman turned to the same cabinet her colleague had searched, pulled out a file, and showed it to him. "These forms here."

She came back to the counter and spoke delicately to Daniel.

"There is a form you can fill out, but I must warn you, yes, that the German government is paying indemnification to the heirs of victims in not many, um, very limited number of cases. Most money is going to survivors. You read the form, yes? And then if you want more information, you can telephone us, the number is stamped on the form here. Or, also, um, you can get advice from the Canadian Jewish Congress too. They also have these forms, yes?"

Daniel nodded, although he already knew that. The congress's offices were located uptown, well west of his house, and he would have had to drive over there. The consulate was more convenient. With a hint of defiance, he had decided there was no reason why he should avoid it.

The woman continued.

"Also, sir, you should know that the German government has announced a final deadline for all applications, next year." She seemed to want to apologize for something with her polite, slightly hesitant smile. "The program has been running more than ten years now."

"Yes, I heard about the deadline."

Indeed, that was why Daniel was here. A story in the *Canadian Jewish Chronicle* had caught his eye only the week before, a story reporting that the German government was holding firm to a final deadline of December 31, 1965, for all applications to its indemnification fund. If Sarah was to apply, it had to be now or never. Daniel couldn't remember how long he had known about the reparations—he must have heard about the German fund around the time of his marriage—and soon after they were married, he had urged Sarah to apply. She had quietly refused.

"I don't need German charity," she had said, and closed the subject with a look of cold pride that occasionally passed across her face, if she felt she was being patronized or snubbed, and that Daniel had come to hate. There was unfinished business here, but it was only in the past year that he had started to broach the issue again, convincing her that he would start investigating what had happened to her parents' property in France. It wasn't straightforward: Sarah had no birth certificate, let alone bank or insurance records, and did not know if her parents had owned or rented their Paris apartment. She had acquiesced passively—"If you think it's worth it, dear"—to his French project, but he had not had the courage to open again the subject of German reparations. He was on his own here, judging that if he found out that it was worth her while to apply, if he could name a sum to her, it might change her mind. He took the form, thanked both the German officers, and left the consulate, heading uptown to his office in time for his 9:45 patient.

Sarah, meanwhile, was trying to park the car in front of a meter on Bloor Street but had misjudged the angle and now found her rear right wheel was hitting the curb. Frustrated, she pulled back out, tried to remember what Daniel had said about watching something appearing or disappearing in her side mirror but failed to grasp the trick of it, and hit the curb once again. Flustered now, she gave up, drove on, and found a space two blocks further on with no car in front so that she could simply drive straight into it. She got out of the car, tried to decipher the instructions on the meter as to the required fee, settled on a dime, fished it out of her purse, and slipped it into the meter. She started to walk the three blocks back to her destination, still punctual for her ten o'clock hair appointment.

As she walked, she smoothed her skirt with her left hand and absent-mindedly noticed the way the slight roughness of its wool rubbed against the coating of the bandage that Daniel had wrapped around her finger the night before. It was one of these fancy new waterproof ones made of plastic rather than cloth. Everything was plastic nowadays. She breathed slowly and let the frustration of parking fall away from her so that she would enter the hair salon with the right degree of composure—it was so easy to feel oneself snubbed by a hairdresser and arriving all hot and bothered would not strike the right note. She allowed her mind to float above the street a little, and it was then she noticed that the light was back. The clear light. Yes, there was a small chill in the air. The mugginess that had hung over Toronto all summer long was gone and this new clarity seemed to invade Sarah's soul, inflating it with soft hopes, piercing it with a small, sharp pain, leading her backwards and forwards simultaneously, removing her from the present and depositing her in a place that was somehow both future and past. Sarah stopped for a moment, closed her eyes, opened them again, and mentally brushing the feeling away, took the last three steps towards the hairdresser's and pushed open the door.

These small episodes were commonplace in her life. If Sarah knew rationally that she lived in Toronto and would live here until she died, she could not really bring herself to believe that she would not some day return, if not to the place of her childhood, then to its time. She found it hard to believe that the past was actually over and this was, most of all for her, a sensory experience. When she had first come to Canada, she noticed that light and temperature were in opposite relation to each other than they were in France, where sunlight produced heat and clouds cold. In a Toronto winter, when the sun shines and the sky is a cloudless blue, locals know to wear a hat and secure a scarf tightly around the neck of their coats, for the thermometer has dropped to zero Fahrenheit. But the overcast days are warmer, as the clouds insulate the city from the arctic air that hangs high above it. In spring the air is briefly clear, but by June, as the real heat arrives, a veil descends, the atmosphere becomes muggy and unfocused, and remains that way for the rest of a sweltering summer.

Gradually, Sarah had come to recognize and even love peculiarly Canadian effects of light and temperature. She knew well those early-summer days when the sky is huge, the puffy clouds immobile, and the green of the lawns and verges so intense they look unreal. Or, sitting inside around noon on a sunny February day, she was familiar with the very particular smell and look of heat, slightly dusty in odour yet shimmering with a lucidity forcefully distinct from the atmosphere around it as it rises out of the air vents to warm the house.

But if stepping out on a barely warm May morning she were to catch sight of the shadow of a tree, sharply delineated in the new sun of spring; if walking under a spreading chestnut in October, her shoe banged against a shiny conker rolling on the ground; if she were to enter the subway to be greeted with a blast of warm air; or if she were to sense, as she did this day, a certain foreign quality to the light at the first hint of fall, then the agony of remembrance would pierce her heart and she would stop walking and stand for a moment with her eyes clenched shut until she felt strong enough to move on. Spring on the boulevards, autumn in the Bois; the sunlight of late summer, the sweet, sooty scent of the Métro—these were the sights and smells of the world she had lost.

In her Toronto present, a life of Daniel, and the house and the shopping, a few friends, visits with Clara and Lionel and Daniel's brothers and their wives, trips to the library, the hairdresser, the synagogue some Saturdays, in this life, November had become Sarah's favourite month—for perverse reasons. It was the month when the pain passed, the light could no longer injure her with its brightness, its vague familiarity, its unpleasant newness; the air could no longer fill her with nostalgia or longing. After the promise of May and the disappointment of September, it was a neutral season where Sarah no longer felt haunted by comparisons, where she could shelter indoors in a state of sensory amnesia and live unconsciously for a while.

It was one morning this November that she felt peaceable enough she could say casually to Daniel, at breakfast, as she watched him quickly tuck a few pieces of paper into his briefcase:

"Any news from France?"

"No, no news," was all that he replied.

At his office that morning he found a large package from the Conference on Jewish Material Claims against Germany, an organization based in New York. It was the Claims Conference to which the Canadian Jewish Congress had directed him, and the envelope was stuffed with information about the process of seeking redress. How to find lost birth certificates. How to produce affidavits establishing presumed death. When to engage local lawyers. How to approach banks. Who might be eligible for reparations from the German government. It included a copy of the form that Daniel had secured from the German Consulate, and that sat, still blank, in his office files.

It was not until February, three months later, that he received a personal reply from the Claims Conference, advising him on Sarah's case. It was waiting for him at his office on a Tuesday morning when he arrived at work. He would have had it the day before, but he had not been in the office on the Monday. Indeed, he was hard pressed to be there on the Tuesday, but had dragged himself in. He had spent the last three days in bed, nursing his back, which he had wrenched while shovelling out the car to drive to the synagogue Saturday morning. He and Sarah went to *shul* from time to time; his parents liked to see them there; but, in hindsight, they should have left the car at home that day. Lionel and Clara always walked, no matter how cold the weather. Of course, their house was close by. But, like many in a congregation now scattered around town, Sarah and Daniel lived at some remove, and when Rabbi Cohn had retired a few years back, his successor had quickly agreed that it was permissible to drive on the Sabbath, at least to *shul*. Many of them had been doing so already. So, Daniel had been clearing the driveway when something snapped.

Sarah was still busy upstairs in the bathroom, when he hobbled up the front steps, pushed open the front door, and called out to her.

"Sarah. Come and help me."

She had the water running and couldn't hear.

"Sarah," he yelled with some desperation. "Come down here. I've gone and put my back out."

"What? Is that you?" She stuck her head out from the bathroom and called down the stairs. "Did the car start?" It had snowed heavily the night before but the sky had cleared and the temperature plummeted, leaving the city to dig out in frigid conditions. The thermometer outside Sarah's kitchen window, which like all Canadian thermometers in those days measured temperature on the Fahrenheit scale, was showing one below.

"It's not the car, it's me. Come down here and help me. I've hurt my back."

At the word "hurt," Sarah ran down the stairs.

"Oh, my God. What's wrong? Are you all right? What happened?"

Daniel was now kneeling on the vestibule floor, collapsed over the small bench on which they would sit to change in and out of their winter boots. He had not fully closed the front door, and as Sarah hurried towards him, a nasty wind caught it and would have blown it open had not Daniel's body been there to block it.

"Daniel. You haven't shut the door properly. What's happened? What's wrong with you?" Sarah leaned across him to push the door shut, and then bent to touch at him worriedly. Her hand grazed his back and he let out a yelp of pain.

"It's my back. I had a load on the shovel, you know, and I must have twisted something as I was dumping it."

"What can I do? Can you move? You've got to get upstairs to bed. Can you stand up?"

Sarah offered Daniel her hands and he tried to stand, but as he began to move, she noticed that he was still wearing his rubber galoshes over his shoes.

"Your rubbers. You'll trek snow all over if you don't take them off."

"I can't take them off. Can you?" He sank back down.

She bent awkwardly, not wanting to go down on her knees in her skirt and stockings on the cold linoleum floor, and pulled first one rubber, then the other off the bottom of the shoes that were sticking out from underneath Daniel's kneeling body. She righted herself, tidied the galoshes away on the boot rack, and turned back to him, extending her hands towards his.

"We've got to hire that boy that the Brownings use," she complained. The neighbours were never to be seen clearing their own driveway; a man with a pickup truck came and did it for them. "This would never have happened if you didn't always insist on doing everything yourself."

As Sarah said this, Daniel's attempt to get upright failed, and he collapsed back on his knees with another moan.

"You've got to stand up. What am I going to do? We have to get you upstairs to bed. Maybe I should call the hospital. I am going to go call emergency." Sarah stepped around him and started towards the phone in the living room.

"Sarah, please. I don't need a hospital. I just need to get to bed till it clears. Can you go outside and turn off the engine? I was warming up the car."

"You mean it's being running all this time? It shouldn't be left running. Somebody could just come along and steal it."

"It will be right where I left it. Turn it off and put the shovel away. I'll stay here until you come back."

Sarah hunted for boots and a coat, pulled them on, and hurried out the door. She returned a few minutes later, cold and flustered.

"What are we going to do about the car? There's still too much snow to get out of the driveway."

"Let's worry about the driveway later. Give me a hand and I'll try again."

With some grunting and moaning and worried encouragement from Sarah, Daniel made it as far as the stairs. He lifted one foot towards the first step and cried out in agony as the motion of his leg sent reverberations through his lower back. Startled, Sarah reared up in alarm.

"Are you all right? I don't know what to do. What are we going to do? I just feel sick. This is so horrible. What am I going to do? I think I need to sit down." Sarah's voice was rising, and behind Daniel, she darted from one side of the hall to the other with each phrase, like a small animal panicked by a predator.

Daniel held onto the banisters, took a breath, and spoke firmly. "Sarah, go into the kitchen and make us both a cup of tea. I will get upstairs. By the time the pot's brewed, I'll be in the bedroom. Then you can come up with the tea and help me get into bed. I just need to get flat on my back, that's all."

"Are you sure? I think we should call the hospital. Oh, Daniel, this is so horrible."

"It's all right, it will be all right." Steadying himself with his left hand, Daniel reached out with his right and gently touched Sarah's sleeve as she hovered beside him. "There's nothing to worry about. People wrench their backs shovelling snow all the time. It's just muscular. It will clear up in a day or two."

"You shouldn't have shovelled the snow. We should have paid the boy to do it. You don't think of me. What would happen to me if you were injured?"

"Please make the tea." Daniel was beginning to realize that climbing the stairs was going to be hard. Not only did he not want Sarah's help, he did not want her watching. It would only upset her further. She finally retreated to the kitchen, and he spent five agonizing minutes getting to the bedroom, pain shooting through him with every step.

Sarah reappeared, without the tea, a few minutes later.

"Daniel . . ."

Her voice was hesitant, as though she were a small child about to request a favour. "Daniel, you know how sometimes, when I'm nervous, my period arrives a day or two early. It feels like . . ."

She hovered at the bedroom door.

"I'll be fine. You go look after yourself. Just take my shoes off for me, would you, before you go."

Breathing heavily with the approaching ache of menstruation, Sarah bent down, unlaced Daniel's good shoes, took off his socks, and pulled off his pants.

"That's fine. I can get the rest. When you get a second, there's some Aspirin in the medicine cabinet. Bring me the bottle and a glass of water."

She pulled back the covers of the bed and hurried off to the bathroom.

She spent most of that weekend in the spare room, racked with menstrual cramps that finally caused her to vomit up the dinner Daniel managed to make for them on Sunday evening. They might have called on Clara or Rachel—both women would have been hurt to know that these children had been in trouble and had not asked for help—but Daniel had his pride as much as Sarah. Instead, they limped through Monday alone, and on Tuesday morning, his back stiff but less painful, Daniel casually asked a neighbour for a hand with the last of the shovelling because he still could not face the walk to the subway. With a path now cleared behind the car, he bent himself carefully forward to slide into the driver's seat and drove down to the office.

The letter from the Claims Conference was lying on his desk, along with a circular from the provincial Ministry of Health and a few bills. He reached for it first, sliced into the envelope with a paper knife, and began to read.

"Dear Sir: With regards to your letter of November, 25, 1964, describing the case of your wife, Mrs. Sarah Segal, our advice is as follows."

There was little chance of indemnification from the German government: the first priority of the fund was survivors of the camps who were former German citizens. Reparations paid to the State of Israel recognized the loss of millions of victims who left no heirs, and that state's burden in integrating the majority of the European DPs. Living heirs of victims were the fund's lowest priority, and the few awards made thus far had been paid out in cases of extreme financial need. Should Mr. Segal still wish to pursue the case further, his wife would have to make application to the German government before December 31, 1965.

He stared at the letter for a while, reading the New York address of the Claims Conference, noting the regularly inked letters of the type, until the page began to blur in front of him. He pondered responses but knew his answer. No, there was no point arguing with Sarah about an application to the German government, no point going through all the worry and disagreements it might take to persuade her, if there was little chance of success. Daniel opened a drawer in his desk, flipped through files until he found the correct one, and put the letter into it, dropping along with it the idea of seeking compensation from the Germans. He would redouble his efforts in France, approaching the French Consulate for advice on searching title to the apartment on the Rue de Musset and renewing his requests to the Paris banks.

It was not that Daniel anticipated some huge windfall from a forgotten French savings account or from the German fund, nor thought that money would make Sarah happy. They had no particular need for more money: he knew that within a year or two he would be able to replace the car and could see a not-far-distant future when they would take annual holidays to gentler climes. Rather, he pursued these inquiries because his marriage had not proved all that he expected. What marriage ever does? He had assumed he would have children by now, and that their care and upbringing, along with the fervent, if abstract, love with which he and Sarah had first embraced each other, would prove sufficient for all their emotional needs. When he found that unfinished business haunted them, as he lived the daily grind of Sarah's seemingly inescapable domestic worries and exaggerated fears, some huge and vague, others specific and mundane, knowing full well that these present sorrows could be expressed only because the greatest sorrow of them all remained unspeakable, he wanted to take action, any action that might make their marriage as happy as he had assumed it would be the day in 1956 when he had stood beside Sarah under the *chuppah*.

He saw Sarah trying too, at first especially, cooking and loving with commitment if not passion, always hoping for a child, quickly and gamely recovering her optimism each month as her body let loose the dark, thick blood within her. But in their fifth, sixth, seventh, and now their eighth year of marriage, it seemed to him that she grew increasingly anxious as though the only way she could experience life was through fear. Perhaps, over the years, Daniel would recognize how naive was his belief that he could make another human happy, would see that he could no more end Sarah's grieving than he could stop the cancers that ate away at the dying old folks whom he consigned to the hospital wards, but if so, he did not acknowledge it in their life together, a place where he maintained the facade of contentment with the bedside manner of a true professional.

In his heart, unspoken, he felt their infertility as painfully as she did, knew a child would prove compensation, and sought to bring that about the best way he knew how. Unable to do any more in that department—they had both discretely been tested; there was no medical impediment that his colleagues could find—he had turned to the paper chase as a kind of action, not in the end wholly futile nor hugely successful, but the only thing he could think of that might help his wife enter into life.

It was the following May, a year after he had made his first inquiries, that he finally got a reply. The letter again came to the office, and filled with the joy of the news and the pleasure of the newly warm weather, he decided to walk home, pushing up Yonge Street at an energetic pace, before stepping into the pleasant side streets, cutting a street west, then heading another block or two north until he finally fetched up just a few houses away from his own. He could spot his front yard at a glance, for the previous fall Sarah, a life-long city dweller with little understanding of gardens, had for the first time planted bulbs, seeking advice from a neighbour about the correct day in October to do her digging and the right depth to position these unpromising things that, to her eye, looked only like misshapen onions. Her labours were now colourfully rewarded with white and yellow daffodils, while the closed heads of tulips were just now discernible amongst those flowers' broad leaves.

Daniel bounded up the front steps of the house and pulled open the front door with unnecessary force, anxious to give Sarah his news. After the long winter months of apologetic replies informing him only that his correspondents had no records that would be of interest to his wife, Daniel had received that morning an answer from the Banque Centrale de Paris.

"*Cher Monsieur* . . . We are privileged to inform you that the branch of the Banque Centrale de Paris that is located on the Avenue Victor Hugo has a safety deposit box in the name of Philippe Bensimon. We record no movement into or out of this box since 1942. Under the circumstances, we understand that it is difficult for your wife to produce the documentation we would usually require in order to open the box. However, in such cases, it is the bank's policy to accept legal affidavits in lieu of proper documentation. Can you please forward to the bank an affidavit provided by a lawyer and signed by your wife stating her date of birth, affirming that she is Philippe Bensimon's daughter, that to the best of her knowledge her father is dead, and that she believes herself to be his sole heir. You mention in your letter Red Cross files that would record M. Bensimon's believed date of death. Could you also provide the bank with copies of these files?

It is our experience in such cases that some of the documentation we might normally require from an applicant in order to open the box is, in its turn, located in the box itself. On receipt of your affidavit, we would propose therefore to open the safety deposit box in your wife's presence, before making our decision on the ownership of its contents. If she finds herself unable to journey to France for this purpose, we would ask that she appoint a legal representative here in Paris, in whose presence we would open the box. To avoid any hint of conflict of interest in these cases, it is the bank's policy never to recommend a lawyer. If you do not already have legal representation in France, we would suggest that you might seek help from the Canadian Embassy in finding a local lawyer.

Please accept, monsieur, my most sincere . . ."

It was to be three years, however, before Sarah and Daniel made the trip to Paris. Inside the safety deposit box, they did indeed find Sarah's birth certificate along with a few worthless stock certificates and a gold brooch that had belonged to Sophie. Daniel wondered if the Bensimons had not emptied it of other valuables, perhaps removed all Sophie's jewellery, to finance Sarah's escape, to attempt to purchase their own safety, or merely to live in the last desperate months of 1942.

At the time, it seemed worth all their trouble just to have the gold brooch, to give Sarah a second memento of her mother, but fifteen years later, Daniel was to finally abandon a torturous attempt to have a French court pronounce on the legality of the 1946 sale of the apartment at 22 Rue de Musset, a sale transacted by an owner whose deed to the property was not registered with the city hall of the Sixteenth Arrondissement. He would never manage to find any record of a bank account despite his pleas to the Banque Centrale, nor would he ever trace the contents of the apartment. So the Segals would never know that the Delisle family uses the Bensimon silver to this day, occasionally telling each other as they cut with a knife blade solidly affixed to a carefully weighted handle or stir with a teaspoon delicately etched with a tracery of vines that these beautiful things were the gift to their mother, the concierge, from a grateful Jewish family she helped during the war.

It would be three years before Sarah and Daniel made that trip to Paris and the bank on the Avenue Victor Hugo, and it would even be a whole day before Daniel remembered to tell Sarah about the letter, because he could not get his news out of his mouth that evening. As he hurried into the house, Sarah ran out from the kitchen to greet him.

"I was at the doctor's again this afternoon." She shone with pleasure, wanting him to guess, and then blurted it out herself: "I'm pregnant. I really am, this time, I'm pregnant."

For nine years now, they had struggled to make their love a physical one. Their bed had been a place of small joys and small disappointments, gentleness, frustration, and occasional delight. He would utter one single sigh as he came; she would moan quietly during the brief moments when he stroked her. Gradually, over time, affection built what passion had not: she took her pregnancy as a sign that they had sexually come of age. It was her belief that if she had not conceived before, it was because only recently had her body proved capable of the spasms that would draw his seed into her, welcoming it shuddering into her womb.

This one child, her only child produced by her only pregnancy, she would name Maxime, not because the tiny wrinkled peanut who was born less than eight months later, in December 1965, could be counted on to grow large—neither the Segals nor the Bensimons had height in their genes—but rather because he figured so large in her life.

By the next winter and spring, slowly changing his diaper or preparing him for a careful bath in tepid water, she would gaze upon the new baby in amazement, delicately touching the tiny penis that sat between his chubby legs, admiring his pink flesh, at first still wrinkled from the womb but later perfectly smooth, and repeat to herself the miracle of it all: that he belonged to her and she to him.

She sensed that miracle from the start, within a few days of this soft May evening, and knew it for a certainty by summer's end. For as this child grew inside her, she glimpsed the implications of her every pang, his every kick, her every discomfort: Sarah had at last re-established the bonds of blood.

Paris. Tuesday, February 1, 1898.

Very worried that Marcel is overdoing it with all these politics. His bowel movements are not what they should be, and I fear he will catch cold rushing about from the cold streets to the heated cafés. The doctor is speaking to his sons again—it is impossible to maintain such silence forever, it just takes too much energy to remember not to talk—but we now maintain an appearance of calm only by avoiding any mention of D.

Georges will drop by tomorrow to discuss settlement of the estate. How these things drag on. Marcel and Dick will do well by both their uncle's and grandfather's wills, but one would rather have the dear men back again than any amount of money. One is forced nonetheless to pay attention and make decisions, which inevitably makes me feel sordid, as though we were all birds of prey picking over the carrion. Still, I am glad Uncle did not live to see his lovely house ploughed underneath for the sake of the new Avenue Mozart.

Paris. Sunday, February 6, 1898.

The trial begins tomorrow. Marcel plans to attend, although it will mean rising no later than eight if he is to be there for the start of the proceedings. Hahn and the young de Flers have promised to save him a seat. Dick has a lecture and cannot attend but Marcel will come back straight away and inform us of all the details before his father gets home.

Marie-Marguerite and I visited the Louvre yesterday, ostensibly to continue our investigation of the Venetians, but instead I unburdened myself to her, telling her of our recent quarrels. I feel caught between my duties as a wife and my sympathies for Marcel and Dick's beliefs, and fear I have damaged our family by making it clear to the doctor where I stand, but Marie-Marguerite consoled me. "Well, we are in the right, and he is in the wrong, and it will do the man no harm to hear you disagree with him for once. For my part, I have told Anatole frankly that the government's refusal to revisit the case is sheer cowardice—if not something much worse."

Then, she said something that surprised me greatly: "If our homes lack peace these days, just imagine what poor Mme. Faure has to contend with."

"You can't mean she doesn't support her husband in this matter?" I asked her, and she replied that she had heard on good authority that Mme. Faure closets herself with the Dreyfusard papers every morning and is barely speaking to the President. And to think, I haven't left a card with my friend in months only because I assumed she was of the other camp!

As always, Marie-Marguerite's frankness was a bracing tonic and I returned from the Louvre in a better frame of mind, although I doubt the affair will be over soon. I fear Zola's trial will resolve nothing, despite Marcel's best hopes for it. If he is acquitted, it will mean the government must then give Dreyfus a retrial, and there will be yet more scandal. If found guilty, the whole thing will just keep simmering along as it has for months now.

Paris. Tuesday, February 8, 1898.
Marcel set out very excited yesterday, as though he were looking forward to a particularly gay party, but came home rather downcast, saying the whole day had been spent on complex preliminaries. Zola looked fabulous, he said, with his great beard and fierce look, like some biblical prophet squeezed into a black suit. The crowd cheered him when he entered, until the judge threatened to expel the lot of

them. We do not expect a verdict for several days. Adrien avoids us all.

The lawyers were expected to conclude their remarks yesterday and so we began the day in anxious anticipation of a verdict. Marcel and Dick left early for the Palais de Justice, for it is very difficult to get a seat, and I spent the morning pacing about, picking up a book but not reading it, fiddling with the ornaments on the shelves. I tried to read the papers that Jean brought me—he smuggles them into Marcel's room every morning now so the doctor will not see them—but I had time neither for the inflamed rhetoric of those predicting certain victory nor for those few calmer voices who argued that by successfully narrowing the charges to Zola's more outrageous statements, the prosecution had craftily won its case from the start. They were proven right, of course, as I was to find out.

Lunch with Adrien was difficult. He must have known my anxiety about the outcome of the trial, but we spoke of nothing but of his plans for his next book and where we might spend the summer. He was quizzing me on how well I liked Kreuznach, and had I spoken truly, I would have said that in my current state I could barely remember the place. I complained of feeling poorly—indeed, I have had a little pain in my side these past few days, so it was not altogether a falsehood—and I escaped to the bedroom to be alone.

I hid there for a while waiting for him to leave for the faculty, but after a half-hour or so I could hear him still moving about in his study and I could stand it no longer. I took up my hat and coat and, checking there was no one about, slipped across the hallway and out the front door without even bothering to tell Jean I was going out. I passed Mme. Leotard in the lobby where she was polishing the banisters. Seeing there was neither carriage nor cabman at the door, she professed some surprise, asking, "Surely, Madame is not going out on foot? The streets are hardly safe these days." But I just shook my head and brushed past her.

The day was warm enough and I had some notion that I would walk over to the Louvre, but once I had crossed the Tuileries, I thought it was not that far to reach the Palais de Justice and perhaps I might find Marcel and Dick there and discover if a verdict had come down. As I crossed the river, I realized I had been naive: a huge crowd had gathered outside the Palais and it was unlikely I would find anyone in such a mob. I could see people waving placards and hear the noise of the throng, but at first I could not make out their cries. Then, as I drew nearer, words began to emerge from the chaos and their awful slogans were now borne back to me on the breeze: "Death to Zola!" "Death to the Jews!"

Marcel had told me the crowds cheer Zola daily, but no one here was championing him. I was appalled by their spectacle and began to wonder if such demonstrations took place every day and Marcel had hidden the fact from me. I had come such a way, but I could hardly plunge myself into this mob to discover if there was any news. Instead, I turned down the quay to skirt the Palais, in hopes perhaps I would find fewer people at its back door. And indeed, as I approached the Place Dauphine, the crowd here was smaller, and jubilant now, as some news seemed to pass through them. I hurried forward as far as I could and watched as two men embraced each other while another looked on in amusement. This one smiled politely at me, so I asked him, "A verdict, monsieur?"

"*Oui, madame.* Guilty, of course." He grinned broadly as

he said the words, but when he did not see an answering smile, he looked at me with increasing puzzlement. I turned from him and hurried across the Pont Neuf, anxious only to get away from this place. But, in truth, as I reached the Right Bank again I did not know which way to turn; both the streets of Paris and the rooms of my own apartment were hostile to me now.

AFTER MY MORNING TRIP to the Jewish Museum, I bought a sandwich from a bakery, ate it sitting on a bench in front of the nearby Pompidou Centre, and walked the short way back to the *salle des manuscrits* where I have translated these few entries. I stop here, in February 1898, and flip through the remainder of the year. The entries are increasingly short and sparse that winter, and there is a long gap from the late spring well into the fall: the pain in her side proved to be a cancerous growth in the pelvis and Mme. Proust was operated on that summer. She survived but clearly lost many months to convalescence. I see little of interest in the rest of the year, and scanning my last translations, I read her restlessness on the day of the Zola verdict as a sign. It is three-thirty and I will contain myself no longer. I rise, return my box to the desk, and follow my diarist's lead—out into the streets.

Leaving the library, I begin to cross its cobblestone courtyard but hesitate there. Where am I going? I pull a Métro map out of my bag, consult it briefly, and move forward through the library's gates to the street outside. I could simply walk south down the Rue de Richelieu to the Louvre, turn left, and I would, like Mme. Proust, have breath to spare for an easy walk across the Pont Neuf to the Palais de Justice on the Ile de la Cité. Instead, I turn north and get on the Métro at the top of the Rue de Richelieu. From here, it's a direct line westwards to La Muette, at the outer reaches of the

Sixteenth Arrondissement. From their nineteenth-century head-quarters in the Eighth, the Parisian bourgeoisie has grown steadily westwards and now the neighbouring Sixteenth is also described with the same kind of scornful adjectives—staid, suburban, quiet as a tomb, bourgeois—with which Proust's biographers routinely dismiss the streets on which he lived.

Coming back above-ground, I emerge at the top of the Avenue Mozart. The avenue leads southwards, all the way to Auteuil, once the bucolic village in which Louis Weil kept his country house, now just more suburbs. I walk in that direction, glancing up at the facades as I go. Some belong to post-war modernist buildings of unadorned concrete and glass; others, more decorative, must have been built in the first decades of the century. One of these bears a black-lettered plaque of the kind you can find here and there, all over Paris. It displays the name and dates of a resister, killed on this very spot in August 1944. As the Allies marched towards Paris, the Resistance emerged from hiding to take the fight to the streets: some were shot dead by the German army before it retreated. *Mort pour la patrie.* France has always celebrated her resisters, but it seems to me that with these plaques, with the carefully worded memorial at Drancy, with the displays at the Hôtel de Saint-Aignan, that the years of the war, their courage and their betrayals, are recalled with some honesty now.

Walking down the Avenue Mozart, the Rue de Musset is the third street on your left. I find number 22, and stand across the way from it, on the edge of a small park, only a median really, created by the junction with another street that branches off at a forty-five degree angle. Surveying a flowery art nouveau facade, I wonder what it is that I am searching for. Do I really expect the ghosts of a woman I've never met to emerge from these wrought-iron front doors just to satisfy my curiosity, my longing? What right do I have to go foraging in someone else's history?

One of double doors does open, and an elderly woman in a pink pinafore steps out. She is carrying a mop, and looks briefly up and down the street before shaking the dust out onto the pavement. She steps back inside without seeing me, and the heavy door bangs shut behind her. I stand there a moment, listening to its reverberations die away in the moist but warm air of early autumn. Dissatisfied, I head back towards the Métro.

Tomorrow, I will start on the next notebook and follow Jeanne Proust as she takes up her pen again: in 1899, the affair continues apace.

PARIS. TUESDAY, FEBRUARY 21, 1899.
There were fearful demonstrations at the funeral, Adrien tells me, with Dreyfusards and anti-Dreyfusards using it as an occasion to fling insults and even rocks. As though the whole business of his death were not disgraceful enough without adding politics to it.

I have sent Mme. Faure the most straightforward letter of condolences and added how much I always enjoy our walks and would happily take them up again when her first mourning is past. It is perhaps one of the inevitable trials of marriage that husbands are not always faithful, perhaps natural that they seek some diversions as their wives age but their male appetites remain undiminished, nonetheless discretion is surely the least that is owed a loyal spouse. To have one's heart attack in one's mistress's arms is not itself a crime against marriage, but to have not established the parameters of one's domestic arrangements securely enough to avoid such a death becoming common knowledge in the salons and tea rooms, well, that is a posthumous insult to the new widow.

PARIS. FRIDAY, MARCH 10, 1899.

Marcel is hugely taken with this new friend of his, Antoine Bibesco, a prince no less, and a very handsome one from his description. They met at one of the salons recently, and Marcel is very eager to become part of his set, saying they are both great fun and truly sensitive. I can only hope their pretty manners and well-tailored suits are matched by some subtlety of intelligence. Marcel tends to confuse social nobility with spiritual nobility, but he will hear nothing against new friends, and one does not wish to become one of those parents who does not let their children choose their own acquaintances. I only fear sometimes that these boys do not take his emotions seriously, and do not realize how easily he can be hurt.

He spends more and more time with the men in the cafés—these days, it is always politics—and less and less with his hostesses. Many have not come over to Dreyfus, fearing they will lose their aristocratic visitors, I suppose, so Marcel has simply dropped them. And he says that dear Mme. Straus, the fiercest Dreyfusard of the lot, is now so twitchy in the face she dreads the entertaining she once so loved. It was a nervous complaint that drove her mother quite mad, poor thing.

There is increasing pressure on the government to reopen the case and it seems it will prove irresistible.

PARIS. FRIDAY, APRIL 21, 1899.

Geneviève has announced she is leaving us to return to her family in Nantes. Her mother is getting old and she feels she needs to be nearer them. I have persuaded her not to leave until August as it hardly seems possible to find a new cook before the summer. She would only be getting used to the household before the holidays break everything up. As it is, I do not know whether I should interview candidates in July or wait until September.

Jean has kindly suggested his cousin could come in for a few weeks in September and tide us over, which would be handy although, as I recall from the last time, her cooking is very heavy. One of those who favours a great deal more oil and salt than suits my tastes. I told Jean by all means to have her in, but to leave the cooking to Félicie during that time. What we really need is a young person who is ready to gradually take over from Félicie, someone knowledgeable but still willing to learn. I suspect Geneviève has just decided she will never be allowed to run the kitchen herself, even if she now does so much of the cooking. Félicie can be so ferocious, and it galls Geneviève to pay deference.

I also worry that her decision was hastened by having to prepare meals for Marcel at all hours. Jean has been complaining lately about his schedule and I do have to agree that the household is turned upside down by his requirements. He is always saying he will get his own breakfast but with him that just means going out to a café and incurring unnecessary expense. He insists that these hours help his writing, but I see little progress on his book and really wonder if it is not just a fantasy.

PARIS. MONDAY, JUNE 5, 1899.
The announcement came yesterday. There is to be a new trial. Already the boat has sailed that will bring poor Dreyfus back from Devil's Island. Finally, the affair will be laid to rest, M. Zola will return from his ridiculous English exile, and France will be able to hold her head high once again.

The men, meanwhile, are now all debating this question of the century. Dick says the Bureau des Longitudes insists the new century does not begin until the first minute of 1901 while Georges told us the Kaiser has decreed Germans are to celebrate at the end of this year. Certainly, all the hostesses are planning their parties for this December, not next. Dick is greatly looking forward to it, but cannot get Marcel the least bit excited. Marcel was pointing out that when you are a child waiting for father to come home and lunch to be served, time seems to drag on forever, but when you are an adult, and want to write a letter, and see a friend, and buy new gloves all in the same afternoon, it rushes by, and there is never enough of it. "How does the year or the century make any difference to how we perceive the time to pass?" he asked. His brother and his uncle did not have any answer to that, and Dick just started on about automobiles and telephones.

Evian. Monday, August 14, 1899.
Adrien and I have been dutifully taking the waters, and so the doctor grew rather annoyed with M. Cottin yesterday, who is a skeptic in these matters. M. Cottin said their medicinal properties remain largely unproven, and when I argued that I always feel better after a dose, he said that it is only the bracing effect of the conversation at the spa alongside the emotional benefits of believing one has just done something improving, a phenomenon that he argued rises in exact proportion to the taste of the water one is imbibing: the more horrible the water, the larger the benefit. He got quite ribald about the whole thing and was ready to draw us graphs on a paper showing two parallel rising lines—one denoting the optimism of the patient, the other the sulphuric content of the water. I was embarrassed least the attendants in the pump room should hear and feel their wares were being insulted! Adrien made some joke about lawyers being experts in all matters, including medicine, but he does

not like it when others question his professional knowledge.

I await with interest the news from Rennes, although I do not say so to Adrien. We have restored the peace between us through silence on certain topics. He will never say so, but I know he knows he was in the wrong about D. and the one welcome side effect of my illness last year has been his renewed solicitude.

EVIAN. WEDNESDAY, AUGUST 16, 1899.

One of the things I love about summer is the way in which one's schedules and goals are reduced to the most luxurious and leisurely pace. One does not abandon such things altogether—lunch is at eleven-thirty, dinner at seven; the post office remains open only until six if one wishes to get a letter sent off that day—but one reduces them to fit different expectations and rhythms.

Yesterday afternoon, I bought a new sunbonnet. That is all I did yesterday or at least all I remember doing beside eating meals, sleeping, and taking the waters. I had been admiring the window of the milliner's shop on the main street since I arrived and debating whether I was not in need of a replacement. I finally made a decision and accomplished this momentous task yesterday between three and four. Every day I say to myself, "I must take up my *cahier* this evening, and bring things up to date," and every day a walk that has left me particularly exhausted, a dose of fresh air that has sent me to bed early, a new book to read or perhaps a magazine proffered by a friendly neighbour across the breakfast table and set aside for later perusal eats up a whole evening and leaves one the next day saying, "Well, I have not accomplished what I said I would yesterday, but I have been most frightfully busy and there will be no luck today, for there are to be charades after dinner."

Marcel writes from Paris that he will definitely join us by the end of next week, and take advantage of their proximity to visit Antoine and the Bibesco family at Amphion. They always sound so fancy and I do hope he does not spend more money than he should to keep up with them.

EVIAN. FRIDAY, AUGUST 25, 1899.
Marcel arrived full of the stories from Rennes, bringing with him all sorts of articles he had clipped from the Paris papers. They say Dreyfus's hair has gone utterly white and his voice quavers like that of an old man although he is only forty. His lawyer Labori has launched into the most vicious attack on the army. It hardly seems necessary, for surely this time the court martial is a mere formality and his acquittal assured.

Marcel's breathing seems strong, apart from one brief attack late in July after I left Paris; he has been well, he says, and he looks stronger. Perhaps this summer, by starting from a more stable position, we will fulfil my goal of using the vacation as a leg up another rung towards good health, rather than simply a recovery period. Marcel will stay on here through September, to avoid the worst of the heat in Paris, and I have counselled him to limit his intake of Trional to the most conservative doses possible.

PARIS. MONDAY, SEPTEMBER 11, 1899.
The verdict is unimaginable. How could they? What an idiotic verdict. To suggest there are attenuating circumstances to a crime of high treason. "Guilty with attenuating circumstances."

The judges have hoped somehow to satisfy both camps. It is monstrous cowardice. To sentence the man to ten years hard labour on top of what he has suffered. The judges acknowledge his innocence by their hedging yet will not deliver the verdict that justice demands. All the papers say it will not hold but will be quashed on appeal.

Paris. Wednesday, September 20, 1899.
They have offered Dreyfus a pardon. A pardon for a crime he did not commit. The question now is, will he accept this sorry compromise?

The first possible candidate to replace Geneviève comes tomorrow. Jean and I were agreeing how silly it is to interview a cook; we should simply ask her to make a meal.

A NOTEBOOK FALLS, slapping the ground, and I remember that I was watching Max and Max was watching Susan. She is conventionally pretty and has the good fortune to be blonde.

Well, that sounds only contemptuous, and you will think that you detect envy not far beneath that description.

Let me try again. Susan has a delicate face with blue eyes that are astonishingly round. She has hair that is not only blonde but also curly, in those big looping spirals that turn to ringlets after a rainstorm or on a muggy summer day. It is not a deep beauty, but it is, in its way, a perfect one, the kind that makes men ache. Susan is not unaware of this.

She and Max and I and a few other of his friends—a new chum from medical school, and an old classmate from his undergraduate days—are sitting in a small concrete courtyard outside the library building on the McGill campus. Our respective classes are over, but we cannot bring ourselves to move on. It is spring and the still-cold air is threaded through with warmer passages that occasionally touch our faces, making us gently pine for something undefinable. We long for event or excitement, sense it approaching too, and each one of us is all ready to convince himself that he is in love with one of the others.

"What are you doing Friday night?" Max asks Susan. It's Wednesday, two days to the weekend, the day for making dates.

"I'm not sure yet."

"Come to the pub. We'll be there."

"I'm not sure. I have to check with my friend Marianne. I promised her we'd get together this weekend."

"Bring her too. She'll love it. It's a blast. You have to come. It'll be so much fun."

Max moves forward and playfully takes Susan's hand, swinging it to and fro. "Come on, say you'll come. Please."

His powerfully focused attention, so flattering at first, is taking on a hint of desperation. Perhaps Susan was about to relent; now she is sure it wouldn't do to acquiesce.

She pulls her hand away, saying, "I'll see. It depends on Marianne," and as she drops Max's hand, it knocks the notebook that was sitting on her lap. The notebook slaps the ground, making a hard sound that echoes slightly in this concrete chamber.

Max dives for it, grabs it up, and extends it towards Susan's reaching hand.

"Thanks," she says, and takes the notebook.

But as her fingers touch it, Max grabs it back, laughing. She smiles. He proffers it again, she touches it, but he again pulls back. He repeats the trick a third time.

"Max, don't be an asshole!"

Susan stands, ready to get serious about retrieving her property. She walks up to Max and reaches firmly towards the middle of his body where he holds the book. He whips it out and up, away from her hands, and holds it above his head, his face now flushed with excitement and his breath coming quicker. He is not tall, but neither is she, and he can hold it an inch or two out of her reach. She stands on tiptoes, stretching up fruitlessly, threatening to topple against him.

"Max, please . . ."

Both of them appear silly now, lacking grace. To tell you the truth, I'm surprised at Susan. I didn't think she'd play this adolescent game. She doesn't need to.

I watch Max. His eyes sparkle with anticipation; his lips part with breathlessness. I squirm in my skin.

Susan laughs now with a high-pitched sound that, as it begins, resembles the giggle of a small child, but as it prolongs itself, changes into some inhuman cry, the gulping of a tortured fish or the squeal of a trapped mouse. She chokes it off.

What does he want with her?

He leans back, still keeping her at bay. My flesh itches and I must move. I rise up.

"*Max, arrête donc!*" I yell at him in French and, surprising him with my swiftness, succeed in grabbing the notebook from his hand. I give it back to Susan, who says thanks but doesn't look especially pleased. Max is baffled by my action.

"Marie . . ."

"I have to go the library." I stalk off towards the glass doors.

In the *salle des manuscrits*, the sound of a dropped notebook echoes rudely. Heads bob up, someone angrily hushes, as though the sound were voluntary and might be repeated. I look up shamefaced and scrape back my chair, but the assistant assistant librarian is passing by and before I can reach down to retrieve my property, he picks it up. He smiles at me, a slow smile that perhaps he supposes to be flirtatious but looks to me merely mocking.

"*Toujours la Proustienne?*"

He doesn't return the notebook, but instead turns it over to find the cover. This is torture, and he knows it. He looks back at me again to check that I am watching and then he slowly opens the flyleaf as though he might read what I had written.

S ARAH JUST NEEDED a handful of pebbles, a few nice round ones, but was puzzled as to how she might find any in the midst of the snow-covered garden. She looked vaguely around her at the spreading blanket and soft lumps that in summertime would form the firmer figures of flower beds, lawn, and shrubs, and saw no obvious solution. An hour ago, this project had seemed like a grand idea, but now she felt the first little twinge of defeat as a bitter taste at the back of her mouth and a slight tightening in her stomach.

Behind her, Maxime beat his stubby legs against the porch steps and waved his little arms in the air: bundled into his powder-blue snowsuit, he had also lost all his hard edges, and his puffy figure with its rhythmic movements looked like some funnyman on the Saturday cartoons, a friendly astronaut floating in space, or a goggle-eyed diver exploring the deep. As he flapped about, he kept up a chant: "*Un oeil, deux yeux, un oeil, deux yeux...*"

A minute ago, these words had amused and delighted Sarah. Her son was proving very slow to speak, and said little more than Mama, Papa, and no. That winter, she had been encouraging him by teaching him vocabulary, pointing to her eyes, then to his, to her nose, then to his small pink button, to her lips, then to his tiny rosebud mouth, and saying the words as she went: "*Un oeil, deux yeux, le nez, la bouche.*" Now, he was finally repeating the words back, and had, miraculously it seemed to her, not only recognized the nature of their current project but also grasped the irregularity of the plural all in same moment. *Un oeil, deux yeux.* But as he kept it up, his first delicious giggle at having mastered this trick had disappeared and he started to chant listlessly. With each repetition, Sarah felt increasingly desperate. *Un oeil, deux yeux . . .* The snowman she had built for her two-year-old son lacked eyes, and she was not sure where she would get some.

She had hatched this plan that morning, when a heavy, wet snow had started to fall on the city. She had never built a snowman, but she remembered them from her childhood, or at least from the Canadian years of her childhood, and since then, from time to time, she had seen one decorating a front garden or a schoolyard on a day of fresh snow. But not just any kind of snow. She knew that too. Snow came in all sorts of different weights and consistencies, and it would take the wet stuff of late winter to build a good snowman. That was what had started falling that March morning, and as she looked out at it, gauging its properties from the way it plopped out of the sky and sat lumpishly on the street, she said to herself words she had heard Daniel utter before. "Good snow for a snowman," he would say without any intention of building one, just commenting on the weather. Why shouldn't she try building one, she wondered that morning. Could it be so difficult? It was thirty degrees or so, not really very cold, and after lunch, if the snow had stopped, she could put Maxime in his snowsuit and take him out into the garden. They would give it a try.

At first, things had gone very well. Dressed in a thick pair of wool trousers and an old car coat, with her hands secured inside Daniel's work gloves, Sarah had started by making a big snowball on the ground, encouraging Maxime, who was crawling at her side, to push more towards her. Realizing this was a limited technique, she instinctively began rolling the ball in front of her so it would pick up snow as it went. Maxime ran alongside her laughing brightly as she pushed the growing ball down the length of the garden and finally brought it to a halt near the back fence.

"This is a good spot, Maxime. We'll make him stand here. See, that's his bottom. Now, we need a second one, for his middle."

And so they began again, rolling their way back towards the porch, before realizing they now had a large snowball at the wrong end of the garden. Valiantly, Sarah lifted the ball. It was an awkward thing to carry, and heavy too, weighing her backwards like her pregnancy had done, and it was with a waddling gait that she made her way again to the base of the snowman.

Maxime was greatly pleased by his mother's unusual behaviour and toddled after her, trying to help her with her burden by flinging himself underneath the ball as she walked, which only made her progress more unsteady. Halfway down the garden, as he launched himself at her body with particular vigour, the ball slipped from her hands and fell to the ground, splitting into four pieces.

"Oh oh." Maxime bit his lip and looked up at his mother to measure her reaction. Was this a catastrophe or a big joke? Was this like the game of throwing the soft toy on the floor over and over while his laughing mother picked it up each time, or was this like the tragedy of the plastic milk cup brushed off the counter and spilling its contents all over the kitchen floor as she cried out in exasperation?

"It's all right, Maxime." Today, his mother was all smiles. "We'll fix it." She sandwiched the pieces back together and rolled the whole through the snow a few more times for good measure, winding up beside the first ball. Awkwardly again, she lifted it up and secured it on the base by blurring the seam between the two with more sticky snow.

It was when she placed the third ball on top that Maxime began to glimpse what it was they were about, and when she broke two errant twigs off the trunk of the nearby maple and stuck one on each side of the middle ball, he shrieked with delight and, in some trans-port of ecstatic recognition, ran backwards until he reached the porch. He plopped himself down on the steps and cried out for the next requirements. Eyes, eyes, the snowman would need eyes.

What did one do for the eyes and mouth? Sarah wondered. In Maxime's picture books, a snowman would always have two little black diamonds for eyes and a crescent-shaped row of the same for a mouth. They must be pieces of coal, she realized, now that she actually thought about it, but nobody used coal any more. She and Daniel had always had an oil furnace in this house, and if there had been a coal burner in the house where she had once lived with Sam and Rachel, she supposed they must have got rid of it years ago. The coal had a very particular odour when it burned, she remembered, but she had not smelled it in years.

"*Un oeil, deux yeux.*"

"Maxime, come with Maman," she said, and with no plan other than to distract the child, she led him by the hand out the garden gate and into the alleyway that ran between their house and the neighbour's. Perhaps they would find something in the street, some gravel or a stray pebble. But as they were walking down the alley, their progress slow and clumsy, for it too was covered by the fresh fall, she saw exactly what they needed. The neighbour had covered an odd patch of soil which jutted out into the alley with a pretty collection of flat, round stones, almost a little rock garden in its own right. The stones sat close enough to the house that they were protected by its generous eaves and remained largely free of snow. Sarah looked about her. It was wrong perhaps, but she would only borrow a few, the neighbour would never notice they were gone, and she could certainly return them in a few weeks, when spring arrived and the snow-man inevitably melted. Letting go of Maxime's hand, she bent down and quickly gathered a few of the smaller specimens, two for the eyes, and just three more, that would have to do for the mouth. She stuffed them in the patch pockets of the car coat and, taking Maxime's hand again, led him slowly back into the garden.

"*Un oeil!*" Exultantly, she stuck the first stone on the left side of the snowman's face, then dipped into her pocket for the second "*deux yeux.*" Then, she carefully positioned the other three in a rough crescent. "*La bouche.*" She turned grinning to Maxime and, before he could say anything, demanded his attention and his patience with a raised finger. She knew exactly what came next. "*Le nez* . . . wait there for just two seconds. Maman will only be minute. Just wait right there, Maxime."

She bolted up the porch steps, flung open the door, kicked off her boots in the back mud room, and ran in her stocking feet through the kitchen to the refrigerator. Rummaging through the vegetable bin, she pulled out an old carrot the tip of which had twisted rather artistically in growing. It was just the thing. She pulled her boots back on and, spotting an old toque of Daniel's in the mud room, seized on it too with sudden inspiration, returning to Maxime with both the carrot and the hat. He had gone back to his leg-drumming seat on the porch steps and was now simply chanting for her return.

"Mama Mama Mama."

"Come, Maxime." They went back down to the bottom of the garden and Sarah laid the toque carefully in the snow before handing the carrot to Maxime. "Hold that, carefully. No, like this, with the other end facing out." Then she bent to him and lifted him towards the snowman. "Put his nose on. That's right, right in the middle."

With a jabbing thrust, Maxime managed to get the blunt end of the carrot firmly stuck in between eyes and mouth, and his mother lowered him to the ground. "Bravo!" She picked the hat up herself and stretched it over the snowman's bald head, and mother and son now stood back to admire their work.

"*Regarde le bonhomme* . . . See the man we've made. Your papa will be so proud of you when he gets home. Just wait until he sees what we made."

The days were growing longer now, and it would still be light when Daniel got home that afternoon. She would catch him at the door before he slipped the rubber galoshes off his shoes and tell him to go out to the garden. She had triumphed.

She ushered Maxime back into the house now, thinking she would give him a bath to warm him up before it was time to start making dinner. In the mud room, she encouraged him to sit down on a low stepstool by giving his shoulders a little push, and then knelt at his feet to take off his boots, noting that one sock had got quite wet during their play. As she pushed his boots to one side and lifted him off the stool, preparing to lie him flat on the ground because that was always the easiest way to coax him in and out of the snowsuit, its peaked hood fell away and exposed his head.

Her first thought was automatic. It was the thing she had thought for several weeks now, every time she saw his hair. Daniel was right, they really must try to take the child to a barber. In his two years of life, he had never had a proper haircut and his hair, black and gently curly, was now hanging in ringlets that fell to his shoulders. She loved it and was reluctant to go after it with the scissors, while Daniel's few attempts at pruning, on a weekend while Maxime was in the bath, had been met with such howls of fear and protest, his father had abandoned the effort.

"Okay, let's hand him over to the professionals," Daniel had laughed. "He's starting to look like a girl."

To Sarah, thus far, the only thing Maxime resembled was a baby. People would say, "Doesn't he look like his father?" or "Why, he's got your eyes, Sarah," and she would agree pleasantly but saw none of it. His little features, the mouth, the nose, and the two round black eyes, were sweet things and infinitely lovable, but they were also unformed, and reminded her of nothing. The bond she felt with him lay deeper inside her; it was that mute swelling, that warm grasping that she had sensed since pregnancy and that had been irrevocably forged by feeding him at her breast. But today, something new happened as her immediate thought about the barber was gradually replaced by something else, something stirring, a memory perhaps, or a little glimpse of the future. And then, as he shook his head to be perfectly free of the hood, jostling his long hair so it settled again at his shoulders and tilting his face a little to look up at her as she reached down to him, it quite suddenly materialized. She shut her eyes for a moment, and then looked again. There, hovering in his face, only twinkling but not receding, was a face for which she had almost stopped searching. Suddenly and quite powerfully, Maxime reminded her of her own mother.

She would never again see Sophie Bensimon glimmering there in Maxime's face with the same breathtaking freshness of this first recognition amongst the clutter of the mud room, but neither would she ever lose sight of her mother again. She would always be reminded of Sophie by Maxime, especially if he shook out his hair, those curls that she was loath to see cut, that she would encourage him to wear long, for many years to come.

Now, she just smiled at his two-year-old self, and said his name: "Maxime."

He smiled back and replied, "*Bonhomme,*" before holding out his arms towards her.

And as mother hugged son in the midst of the garden tools, old bottles, and discarded boots of the mud room, she thought that perhaps this summer it was time to finally return to Paris and finish up that business with the bank on the Avenue Victor Hugo.

Suzanne is really working out quite nicely. Jean and I were agreeing this morning that she has settled in very quickly and is most amiable. We are so used to Félicie, I suppose we think it quite normal for a servant to shrug or grimace when a dinner party is proposed, but it is pleasant to work with someone who seems to view special meals as an occasion to show her talents. I can only hope Félicie does not drive her away as she did Geneviève, although at least she does seem agreed that the new one is to do most of the cooking.

Marie-Marguerite and Anatole came for dinner last night, and Suzanne really did a fine job. The *blanquette de veau* was absolutely velvety, and she is clever enough not to need to be told one cannot have a creamy pudding after a rich sauce like that, and served a good crisp apple tart with the first of the new apples.

We fell to discussing Dreyfus over dinner. It has been so long since Adrien and I have had an honest conversation on such a difficult topic, but Marie-Marguerite is never one to shy away from a subject simply because it is controversial and has taken to telling the men quite frankly they were wrong. I was saying how sad it was Dreyfus had accepted the pardon, but that I did feel those who criticized him were being very hard. They can stand on principle, but no one has asked them to serve five years on Devil's Island. Anatole has his official position to remember and now remains tactfully silent on the issue, but Adrien and I agreed Dreyfus had no choice but to take the pardon and end the whole affair. Marie-Marguerite was arguing a purer position and still wants to see a proper trial. "He had a proper trial," Adrien exploded, to which she retorted, "But not a proper verdict."

Emboldened perhaps by the amicable atmosphere of our

family dinner, she went further still and said to Adrien he should show more regard for my feelings when discussing this matter. I tried to hush her but she persisted: "You would not want to put distance between yourself and your loyal spouse by allowing her to believe you have sided with those who show nothing but blind prejudice towards the Jews."

Adrien replied, as he has before, that he believed the affair does not turn on issues of race or religion, but Marie-Marguerite retorted that if this were the case, he should make clearer to all his disapproval of the anti-Semitic faction. Now, Anatole really did intervene and asked to her stop. She shrugged off his remonstrations and replied, "Well, I was just standing up for Jeanne," and we left it at that, moving on to other subjects. It was an awkward moment, but still, it did not ruin dinner. It seems perhaps that finally we can agree that our opinions differ. That is what all France must do, and put the thing behind her.

Marcel writes from Evian requesting my copy of de La Sizeranne's book on Ruskin by the next post, but I cannot lay my hands on it anywhere. By the time I send it off, he will be home anyway.

Paris. Friday, October 6, 1899.
I have told Adrien I really do not know how much longer I can put up with this apartment. My bones seem to ache every day this autumn. I try not to bother him with my complaints, but really there is no reason why we should not move soon. After all these years, he could certainly be said to have grown a bit beyond the Boulevard Malesherbes. I have never tried to push us up the social ladder, nor wanted to frequent the Faubourg, but one should surely take what one has earned in life. The doctor

insists he must make a trip to the Mediterranean ports before negotiations on the *cordon* can be completed—it really does look as though the English will finally sign—but he still hopes his own book will be finished by the spring. Perhaps there will be an interval in between when we could look for a change of address.

Marcel seems utterly discouraged about his novel, and compares himself to Eliot's Casaubon, collecting intellectual trivia that really has no use. Such a sad image for a young man to consider. I tried to reassure him, and urged him to continue the work now that he is back from holiday. I suggested we come up with a schedule for daily amounts he might complete, but he dismissed the idea out of hand, and said the only thing that interests him now is Ruskin. Reynaldo's cousin knows his work well. Being English and an artist, I suppose she would have to, and Marcel says he has written asking her for her advice and for a record of all the Ruskin books she has read. We still can find no French translations, but Robert de Billy also promises to help Marcel with his reading should the English prove impenetrable.

PARIS. FRIDAY, OCTOBER 13, 1899.
Marcel is spending every moment over at the library buried in Ruskin, only occasionally emerging to meet up with Antoine's set in the cafés. He proposes a trip to Amiens to view the cathedral through new, Ruskinian eyes, and to Bourges too. I have never visited the latter and have not been to Amiens since I was a girl, I do not think. Of course, I have seen Chartres many, many times since it is so close to Illiers. You could even seen the towers of the cathedral from the train window every time we made our trips to and fro. I thought Chartres was the

finer monument, more beautifully decorated than Amiens, but Marcel says that is simplistic of me. I cannot remember when he last went to mass, but he will find himself back in church to admire the line of a sculpture or colours of the stained glass. It was always that way: the *curé* at Illiers used to have to bribe him to do his catechism class by promising to tell him all about the windows afterwards. Marcel's religious fervour is all for art, but then, Ruskin himself is a Protestant, when you think of it.

I must ask the doctor for some little remedy, for my bones seem to ache horribly this autumn. Fifty! When I was a girl I could hardly imagine such an age existed.

Paris. Thursday, October 19, 1899.

Marcel's trip to Amiens was a great success. He came home quite inspired by what he had seen, and by the act of comparing his own reactions to those of Ruskin. I had roughed out a version of Ruskin's text in French, since the book on Amiens has never been translated, and it seems to have served him well, though goodness knows my English is rusty. He is greatly enlivened by this new intellectual passion, and managed the train journey without mishap. Jean packed two large flasks of coffee for him, in case he could not find any when he needed it, and he bundled himself in that horrible old overcoat. An infected thing, but warm, I suppose. He looks old sometimes, when he is all bundled up like that—and other times so young, a pale little child dressing up in his father's old clothes.

Adrien will be at home for dinner and requests a beefsteak, for a change—"a good bloody beefsteak cooked in butter." I can still see Papa wrinkling up his nose in disgust at the offer of such a meal.

PARIS. TUESDAY, OCTOBER 24, 1899.

We read in the *Figaro* the news of Ruskin's death. Sad, but he was an old man and had been going a bit mad in his last years, one hears, although, of course, the *Figaro* would not mention that in the obituary. Marcel is seized with the idea that he will write an appreciation. One does not like to rejoice at other's misfortunes, but I was actually delighted by the idea. It seems like just the small, realizable project he needs, and gives him a good reason to be writing about Ruskin. Perhaps the man's death will create a revival of interest here in France and Marcel could do more about him. It seems his only passion these days.

Georges for dinner tonight. He is becoming a great admirer of Suzanne's cooking!

PARIS. MONDAY, OCTOBER 30, 1899.

Marcel's essay has appeared in the *Figaro.* It really is a lovely piece, describing his trips to Amiens and Bourges, and he now thinks that he might fill in the gap and provide France with the translations that are only Ruskin's due. I am buoyed up by the prospect of his commitment to such a project and have promised him that I would help all I can. Marie Nordlinger is also ready to support him—via the post for the moment, but she says she plans a Paris visit to Reynaldo and his family soon. She has lent Marcel her copy of *The Queen of the Air,* filled with her own notes in the margin. She must be a highly intelligent girl, that goes without saying. I counselled Marcel to wait a while before he tells his father of his plan. We must pick the right moment.

"No."

He shakes his head, and in doing so loosens a single curl that now falls across his forehead. It sits there like a black punctuation mark on his brow, making him look vulnerable somehow, more accessible than before. But he is adamant in his refusal.

"No. It is not here."

"But why not? It was here yesterday."

"That was yesterday. Today is October 5."

"October 5?" He doesn't answer. He seems angered by my ignorance, and remains silent.

"So, it's October 5 . . ." I persist but the North African clerk only glares at me.

I wouldn't be cowed and stare right back. He unbends slightly.

"Your reserve is for eight working days. It expired at five o'clock yesterday."

"Oh, well I didn't realize."

"Eight days. That is the system."

"But you could have told me . . ."

"It's not my job to go around the library reminding all the patrons how the system works."

It occurs to me that if the clerk did not bother to point out that my reserve was about to expire, he is probably withholding other helpful information.

"Can I renew?"

He pauses a long moment, then sighs and pulls a piece of paper out from under the counter. Apparently I have won.

"Fill this out."

I do, and pass it back to him. He sighs again.

"It will take an hour or two. The file has been returned to storage and we don't have time to get it right now. If you had told us that you would be renewing, we could have kept the file on the reserve shelf, but now I have to go back into storage . . ."

I lose patience.

"How was I supposed to tell you that I would be renewing if you didn't warn me the reserve was about to expire?"

"Well, mademoiselle, it's not my job to count the days of the week for you. The date is stamped clearly on the ticket—September 23."

"Yes, it says September, but it doesn't say the hold only lasts eight days."

"Well, mademoiselle, I have to follow the system . . ."

I give up.

"Please, when you have time, if you could just retrieve the file."

There is about forty minutes' delay—I suspect the clerk is not the least bit busy but feels he must keep me waiting to prove his point—but then File 263 reappears on the reserve shelf and one of the other clerks wheels it up to my desk. I am reunited with the notebook covering the years 1899, 1900, and the early months of 1901. These are the years of Proust's Ruskin translations. His mother would help him immeasurably with this project, but he also relied heavily on Marie Nordlinger, who was to become his constant visitor. Proust's biographers tell us she was a cousin of Reynaldo Hahn's, an artist and a jewellery designer, but I am looking for something more.

PARIS. THURSDAY, NOVEMBER 2, 1899.
An annoying piece of news. An inspector has apparently been snooping around the library and noticed Marcel's almost permanent absence. The librarian came by this morning to see Marcel and tell him that he must regularize his position before the end of the year. I had to take a message as he was not yet awake. I feel sad thinking back to our enthusiasm for the idea of a job at the Mazarine, even if he

was only shelving and cataloguing books. Little did we know it was unrealistic to believe Marcel would ever pursue a career. It is just like his health—each time you hope you are making a permanent step forward, it turns out to be a passing fancy or an illusory change.

Dick is full of stories from the hospital. He is wonderfully happy to be working on real patients. I was saying he must find them rather unsavoury, since only those who cannot afford their own doctor turn up there, but he just laughed and said any living soul was more savoury than a cadaver. It is surely true: when we were first married, Adrien used to tell me that the cadavers at the faculty were the bodies of old tramps they had found dead under the bridges, with rotting teeth and decaying innards. I do not imagine the source of bodies has changed, it is just that as I have grown older both the doctor and Dick seem to feel I must be spared these details. Unnecessary, really, it is not as though anyone were asking me to actually look at the cadavers. When Papa died he just looked like he was sleeping, and Maman looked quite beautiful, I recall, so peaceful, and healthy again somehow.

PARIS. MONDAY, NOVEMBER 6, 1899.
I do not like to complain to Adrien, but I do hope we can make a move before the winter. We looked at two apartments this week. Neither will do, unfortunately. The Rue de Longchamp is just too small and really too far out for Adrien, although I would appreciate being nearer the Bois. On the other hand, the Rue de la Boétie is a lovely apartment but the street not quiet enough, I fear. There is no point going to all the trouble of a move to improve one's conditions only by a small percentage. We really need a place that is airier and where the heating is more

modern. This rheumatism wears me horribly. Perhaps one cannot expect one's good health to continue much beyond fifty, and I have certainly slowed up since my birthday last year and the change of life, although the doctor is fifteen years older than me and continues as vigorous as ever. We have both grown stout, of course, but his age never stops him from working. I, on the other hand, have barely been out of bed all weekend.

Paris. Thursday, November 16, 1899.
Adrien is very pleased with himself because he made an inquiry of Dr. Pozzi and discovered there is an apartment on the Boulevard Haussmann that might just do, owned by the Marquis des Réaulx. From the descriptions, it is large enough. Adrien and I will go and take a look at it tomorrow.

Marcel has resigned from the library, which seemed the only sensible solution to the question. I suppose there is not much to regret; he never set foot in the place after his interview. He continues his Ruskinian correspondence with Marie in Manchester, but we have yet to settle on a text for our proposed translation.

Georges and Emilie came for lunch yesterday. He was telling us all about an engineer he met who is working on the new Métropolitan line, and is very enthusiastic about the thing, although I must say they seem to have been building it forever, and I wonder if it will ever open. But from all accounts, the one in London is most useful, so we must have one too.

Marcel has been writing to one of the Marquis's associates whom he knows, patiently explaining that Adrien really does not receive patients at home very often. Apparently, the Marquis thinks a professional person will create too many comings and goings in the building. We have tried explaining to his agent that it simply is not the case; the doctor's work is almost entirely his research and teaching at the Faculty. It has been years since he has regularly taken private patients. I am certain we are simply being snubbed, and that the Marquis does not really understand who Adrien is nor his position at the university. These aristocrats who do no work themselves will fail to recognize the value of a tireless worker who has, along with his colleagues, surely saved half of Europe from cholera. If Adrien had been elected to the Academy, we would not have been treated this way. I suggested writing to the man directly, but Adrien will not hear of it and says we are better to wait until his return from abroad and look again in the new year. So disappointing, as it seemed like a swift solution to our housing woes.

A great row erupted in the kitchen yesterday because Suzanne had bought a tin of peas, insisting we might at least try them. Félicie would have none of it, and Jean called me in to mediate. I said we might each have a spoonful to taste, but could not coax Félicie into trying them at all. I thought the flavour was poor, but Jean pronounced them rather good and said he likes his peas a bit mushy. After all that, Suzanne was unimpressed and told Félicie she would use tinned goods only if they could match the flavour of fresh, which mollified her somewhat. However, Suzanne has also been researching these new stoves and dreams of the day we will buy one. I would be firmer with her if I did not believe that she has real talent and knows how to combine the new with the old. While Félicie decries the death of gastronomy, I notice that Suzanne not only studies the new machines but has carefully observed how Félicie lets her *boeuf en daube* cook overnight.

PARIS. FRIDAY, DECEMBER 8, 1899.
We have signed the lease on the Rue de Courcelles and will move in February. The task ahead is intimidating, but the relief at having found the right place is huge. So glad we never reached an agreement with the Marquis in the end, because really this apartment is the pleasanter, spacious and bright, with the electricity very tidily installed throughout since it was designed with that in mind, none of the odd bits of wire that we have here. They really do a wonderful job of that now, compared to how messy it all was when they first brought it in. The only gas left is in the kitchen, for the stove! Indeed, there has never been gas in the place, so the walls are beautifully bright and clean, with none of those marks that Jean is always scrubbing at to no avail. The elevator is a marvel, smooth and quiet, one is barely aware it is moving, and Adrien says we might even have the telephone installed before we move in.

He and I are to have connecting rooms. This seemed like a good opportunity to come to a sensible arrangement. I toss and turn so much with my rheumatism that I keep him awake. The two rooms will work better, though it will be sad, after so many years, not sharing our bed. I have missed its fierce joys for some time but shall now be deprived of its gentler comforts too, the simple reassurance of a sleeping man at my side. Thus, we give things up to age, without protest but not without regret.

Marcel is uneasy and worries about the disruption of the move, but the doctor is well pleased that he has settled the issue and can now return to his work.

PARIS. MONDAY, JANUARY 1, 1900.
All that fuss—what noise last night!—and to tell the truth the world does not look much different this morning. Not that it should, but it is just like waking up on one's birthday as a child and somehow feeling that being ten should be different from being nine, as if one's eyes should have changed colour or one should have grown an extra finger in the night. But no, one is the same. When change comes, it is imperceptible at first and, once it can be perceived, irreversible, like my grey hairs.

Dick is still arguing the government's position, that the century does not actually begin until next January 1, this debate about zeros that I can never quite grasp. No more can most Parisians, for they were celebrating in the streets, zeros and government ordinances notwithstanding.

Hugo said if the nineteenth century was great, the twentieth would be happy. The doctor believes it, that we will cure our ills and speak on the telephone every day. Yet it seems to me our hearts remain the same, as capable of joy, love, altruism, and grace as they are of hatred, envy, contempt, and bitterness, as prone to smallness and to greatness as they have ever been.

AT SOME POINT IN their lives of particular optimism and wealth—New Year's Eve, 1989? No, it must have been earlier, a Christmas in the boom years of '87 or '88, perhaps—my parents throw a large party. The door of our house in Westmount is opened to receive old friends, new connections, valued clients, and reliable family members, who burst into our spacious hallway, bringing with them little gusts of cold wind and the particular wintertime energy produced by joyful anticipation and frigid air. They retire to the vestibule to remove their outdoor things, awkwardly bending over to slip off rubbers or unzip boots, slowed by their layers of heavy clothing, hurried by their desire to join the party. They greet my parents with cries of cheer and delight, presenting little gifts of food and wine, boxes of shortbread, homemade jellies, a special vintage, a scented candle.

Standing in the hallway, my mother looks overwhelmed—by the grand occasion, by the ostentatious red evening dress that she is wearing, by my father's much larger presence at her side. She smiles tightly; he beams. I am in my twenties now, old enough to know that I'm not fair to her. She has never been permitted to live in her own country. She never really knows where she is.

"Danzer. How are ya?" My father is in his element. "Darling, you remember Michael . . . *Bonsoir, bonsoir . . . Cherie, enfin . . . Marie, viens ici.*"

He draws me towards the most recent arrivals. He hopes some day I will take over his business and wants to introduce me to his professional circle. Or perhaps, on this expansive night, he just wants to share his good fortune, display family to friends and vice versa. *Grand-mère* is also in attendance, presiding graciously over the evening from a wingback chair by the fire in the living room, regally greeting those who approach her to chat, smiling so benignly when she is alone that she removes all awkwardness from such moments. Max is about somewhere, hovering at my elbow—"Can I do anything?"—then disappearing into the crowd to find our McGill friends.

The evening is glowing, candlelit, Dickensian in its warmth.

Towards the end of it all, I am standing in the vestibule, part of a laughing party that is helping a very pregnant woman look for her boots amongst a chaotic collection of gear. My mother has forgotten to remove the family's own things so that the narrow little space is full to bursting with both our guests' coats, furs, and winter boots and our own macintoshes, umbrellas, running shoes, and tennis rackets.

"They were black, high ones, like almost knee-high . . ." She cannot really bend over herself, so she stands above us issuing instructions as we grovel about at her feet.

"These, honey?" Her rambunctious husband holds up a pair of men's rubber galoshes and we all laugh.

Just when the moment has lasted too long to still be funny, just when I am starting to organize all the shoes and boots into rows in an attempt to fend off true desperation, the pregnant woman, momentarily forgetting her girth, pounces: "Oh, I forgot. I wore my brown ones."

We have all been looking for the wrong pair of boots. We laugh and laugh, and as the couple take their leave with the brown boots firmly in place, we remain in the vestibule, as though to stay a little longer in this amusing place.

There is an umbrella stand in one corner of the room, one of those great china cylinders with an orange dragon curling itself around the side. Max spies it and, on some whim, with some desire to find a reason to prolong our presence here, pulls out a bamboo cane, brandishing it aloft in the narrow room. It is my father's, an object that has been in our house as long as I can remember, in the apartment in Paris before that, so little used and yet so ever present that I have always taken it for granted and never much considered its worth. But as Max pretends to fence with it, crying *"En garde!"* it occurs to me that it might actually be, knowing both my father's trade and his passions, a rather valuable antique.

"Max. Careful. That's my dad's."

But Max isn't listening much, and continues to fence, backing me towards the end of the room. He lowers the cane now, dodging it about my feet, as though fending off a snapping dog. Then he tries to manoeuvre it between my ankles, as if to lift my long skirt with it, and each time I dart away, giggling, he persists, insisting that he will place the stick between my legs. The atmosphere has gone queer now; the hilarity evaporated. The meaning of his gesture is too apparent to be ignored. As my giggles choke me and a gasping sound comes from my throat, I am suddenly and completely aware that there is embarrassment rippling through the few observers left in the room and also, simultaneously, I remind myself of Susan, she of the astonishingly round eyes.

I realize what Max is doing, and the word, in the context of our earnest friendship, takes me by surprise. Max is flirting. With me.

I push past him, back into the hall.

"Let's get something to drink."

PARIS. FRIDAY, APRIL 20, 1900.

The household is in an uproar as we prepare our valises for Venice; it is all rushed but actually great fun. Marcel suddenly decided that the trip must be this spring with Reynaldo in Rome, ready to join us there, and Marie already visiting with her aunt.

Adrien is ignoring it all, and has retired to his study to do his last revisions, so neglected with the move and his negotiations this winter. He says the manuscript should be off to the publisher next month by the latest and is well pleased with his progress. I suppose I should try and read his book when it comes out, even though it will be incomprehensible to me. I skimmed the last one, as I recall. He always just laughs and says it does not matter that I do not read his research, he would not expect a layperson to follow it, but nonetheless wifely duty would seem to demand one at least have some idea of what the work entailed.

Dick promises me that he will take me to the Exposition when we get back. There have been the most intriguing pictures in the papers, and all sorts of dignitaries including the Prince of Wales himself.

VENICE. HOTEL DE L'EURÔPE. SATURDAY, MAY 5, 1900.

I rose unusually early this morning, long before the hour Marcel would show his face, put on stout shoes, and slipped out into the streets. My walks at home have become severely curtailed this past year, but Venice, for all that one might expect the sea air to be damp, seems to have invigorated me. I managed a good walk from the hotel into the small back streets on the other side of the Piazza San Marco, keeping very careful tally of how many bridges I had crossed for fear I would lose my way. In one quiet square, I came across the most unusual sight, which I looked down on from the bridge above, half in delight, half in horror. The square was filled with cats, perhaps twenty or thirty of them. I tried to count but kept losing track. There were certainly more than I have ever seen in one place. They appeared to be alley cats, not domestic ones, half wild almost, and terribly scrawny looking. It was the oddest moment, gazing down at them all, as they sunned themselves in the square like bathers at a beach.

Marcel is utterly captivated by the architecture and spends every afternoon out with Marie and Hahn admiring the buildings, with Ruskin for their guide. Meanwhile, I keep to my room at that hour, as do the Italians, whose ability to stay up late eating and drinking but still rise early is explained by their lengthy disappearances in the afternoon. The hotel is absolutely ghostlike by two o'clock and does not come to life again until tea time. I take tea in the lobby; it is absolutely charming with an exquisite view onto the canal.

"All great art is the work of the whole living creature, body and soul, and chiefly of the soul," writes our Ruskin in *The Stones of Venice.*

Venice. Hotel de l'Eurôpe. Thursday, May 10, 1900.

Marie really is a charming girl, full of intelligence and literary knowledge without ever being pretentious. She discusses art and architecture with such confidence, and with all her enthusiasm for her topic, manages to impart a great deal of information without becoming professorial. She and Marcel are well matched in that regard, sharing the same interests, but her lively spirit balancing his tendency to become obsessive when a subject has captured him. She teases him about his passions, and he always takes it in good part, knowing that she is as erudite on the subject at hand as he. Reynaldo, who arrived the day before yesterday, laughs to see them together, just happy to have introduced Marcel to such a companion.

She is not perhaps what men would call beautiful, but is a striking-looking woman nonetheless. She has those round, protruding eyes, like red currants about to pop their skins, that look quite awful on some people, but on her, for some reason, are enchanting. Their irises are a mahogany colour, as is her abundant hair, yet her skin is ivory. Her nose is slightly Semitic, yet delicate enough, giving her face strength but not aggression. Indeed, her physiognomy is truly in keeping with her character.

We took tea with her aunt yesterday, a cultivated German Jewess who speaks no French but good English. I struggled away in English—always harder to speak than it is to read—

while Marie translated to and fro for Marcel. It was in the end a lively conversation with everyone nodding back and forth before they had really grasped the other's words. She was telling Marie and Marcel about a small church in the streets behind the Salute that they should go and examine.

Venice. Hotel de l'Europe. Friday, May 18, 1900.
I spent yesterday afternoon re-examining San Marco, stone by stone, inside and out, but could not keep Ruskin's analysis in my head. Instead, I keep rehearsing retorts to Marcel or trying to justify myself, and finally I gave up on tourism, retreated to the coolness of my hotel room, and ordered a restoring ice. I have never wished to be an overprotective mother, nor to restrain or hamper my sons in their pursuits. On the contrary, I have, within reason, tried to encourage them. I have never complained about Dick's bicycles nor that canoe. Have I not spent hours translating sections of *The Bible of Amiens* and *The Stones of Venice* so that Marcel might be prepared for his travels? Did I not organize our trip here? Still, it is clear that Marcel feels I am a burden, and would prefer to be travelling alone so that he might explore the nightlife of the city. He stalked off after our argument yesterday and did not come back to the hotel for dinner. He has yet to appear this morning, but through discreet inquiries at the desk I have ascertained that he returned late and is still in his room. I will perhaps slip a small note under his door.

Venice. Hotel de l'Europe. Monday, May 21, 1900.
So, we end our Venice sojourn on a happier note, having reconciled on Friday and spent a pleasant end of week making

sure there was not a single Ruskinian site we had overlooked. I shall miss Marie, who left for England early this morning. For all her great enthusiasm for life, she is a tender soul and I know Marcel values her highly.

We had agreed to indulge ourselves in a farewell tea in the lobby yesterday as she would be occupied later, dining with her aunt on her final evening in Venice. I was perhaps a few moments late descending from my room, for when I arrived in the tea salon, Marcel and Marie were already deep in conversation and did not see me approaching the table. As I drew nearer I could hear that Marcel was reciting poetry to her—some piece of romantic suffering courtesy of de Musset, I gathered from the little phrase I heard. I barely had time to wonder to myself how it is that men always know their dissection of their own pain will enthral women when I realized I truly was trespassing, for Marcel had raised Marie's hand to his lips. Just as I was thinking I might retreat a bit and attempt to make my entrance again, they saw me and looked up. I did not want there to be any awkwardness, so I bustled up to the table, made myself comfortable, and launched into the tale of sighting the cats, for I had been up early yesterday morning to visit them again for a last time. So, we fell to discussing the oddities of daily life in this watery city, before taking our last farewells.

IT SEEMS TO ME that Max had a cat in those years in Montreal. Or at least sometimes there was a cat in his apartment when I visited. Maybe he was just looking after a friend's pet for a while. Anyway, I remember standing in that tiny apartment with the animal rubbing against my legs, purring, demanding attention. I think she was orange, orange and white, with long fur. I suppose she was a she;

maybe not. Somehow one always assumes cats are female although I don't actually know in this case.

I lean down to pick her up, and the second my arms are open to her, she jumps up into them. A friendly creature. So I am standing there, with an armful of cat, stroking her coat, when Max comes up behind me and simply puts his arms around me. I can feel his body touching mine, his embrace gently containing me. Neither of us says anything. Perhaps speech is unnecessary in this moment; perhaps I just don't know what to say. I don't remember which it was. I just remember that we stand there for quite a while, me with the cat, him with me, taking some comfort in our closeness. Well, more than comfort perhaps. I lean back into him, simultaneously excited and reassured by his embrace. He tightens his hold on me just a fraction. Still, we stand there, neither of us making a move.

And then, I suppose, the cat must have leapt out of my arms.

PARIS. FRIDAY, JUNE 8, 1900.
Setting aside the doubts of Mme. de Sévigné, who compared translations to bad servants delivering the very opposite of the message with which they are charged, I am working my way through chapters one to three of *The Bible of Amiens*. (Chapter four I had already done for Marcel last autumn when he made his trip there.) His progress is rapid, and he seizes up each notebook as quickly as I can finish it. I am often sent scurrying to my dictionary—my English does seem slow from lack of use—but still I get through. Marcel is always urging me on, reminding me there need be nothing literary about my translation. I have done my best to render Ruskin's English, complex, authoritative, but always elegant, but it will take Marcel's beautiful ear to turn it into comparable French. For all that his topic is the cathedral at Amiens, his approach is

spiritual rather than religious, his sense that the soaring arches and translucent windows speak to some yearning within man rather than define some creed of the Church.

With the exception of the sympathetic M. de Billy, his friends have expressed amazement Marcel would undertake such a project, and Georges de Lauris said, "Why, Marcel can't even read a menu in English." But I do not see why it should not work, with him polishing up my rough work into his own beautiful French. He is consulting Marie by post on some of the more tricky expressions, as she has now returned to her family in Manchester.

The doctor is much encouraged by his latest conversations with Dr. de Fleury, and now really has the full support of the ministry in these last, difficult negotiations. He leaves for London on Monday, and expects to be gone all week.

PARIS. TUESDAY, JUNE 19, 1900.
Marcel has finally told his father of our plans to translate Ruskin, and Adrien has lent cautious support, although he told me afterwards that he is skeptical anyone would really buy such a book. I was trying to explain our enthusiasm for the great British critic—how he makes you not only examine the line of a Gothic arch but also think of the anonymous hand that once fashioned it, inspired by a simple, awestruck love of the Almighty that our more advanced age, with all its technological improvements, might find difficult to comprehend—but I cannot say he was really listening.

Dick is exhausted by his work at the hospital. He was so enthusiastic when it started but the hours they expect him to keep are quite ridiculous. The students have small rooms they can retire to so they can nap when they have to work at night, and he might as well move his clothes and his books over there, for all that we see of him. Adrien is unsympathetic, and says he worked just as hard in his final years. He is a horse when it comes to work and can never believe everyone else does not have his energies. Indeed, I worry that he continues to expend so much energy on his various projects, embarking on his Mediterranean and London trips even though we will celebrate his sixty-sixth birthday this spring. Certainly, some of his colleagues keep lecturing at the Faculty after seventy if they have the health, but I do feel that he may be spending the last years we have together on his work. Not that he has ever done anything else, his profession has always taken first place, as it should, but when the *cordon* is finally established, I hope that we can rest.

With Marcel joining his father's and brother's side, I have finally relented on the subject of the telephone. Marcel says Antoine is known to his friends as Telephas, he so loves using the instrument, and my little wolf now so wants us to be on the line that I could not refuse him.

PARIS. THURSDAY, SEPTEMBER 13, 1900.
Marie N. is in town and came to visit yesterday. After three nights out in a row, Marcel has taken to his bed with repeated attacks of breathlessness and was not about when she called at three. We took tea together and had a lovely chat about her work in London—she has convinced a new gallery to show some of her sculptures—before I ventured to see if Marcel was fit to receive her. He urged me to show her into his room. I was not sure if this was appropriate, especially for a young lady from Britain, for the English are often more punctilious about these things than we French, but it is true that with his torso dressed in two

sweaters despite the warm weather and the rest of him well hidden under the bedclothes, Marcel could hardly be called indecent. I showed Marie in and she stayed a good two hours. She had brought various books and Marcel was very eager to have the advantage of her instantaneous replies to his many questions. I wonder what she makes of him, lying in bed at four o'clock with papers strewn all over the covers, the drapes drawn against the sun, but a fire in the grate, while the thermometer still reads twenty-seven.

He has also been consulting Robert de Billy regularly, whose English is certainly better than mine and who does know his Gothic architecture. He is especially useful on all those parts of the arches and doorways that I am always confusing, much to Marcel's chagrin.

The widow Faure came to call yesterday. I have been remiss in not inviting her sooner, since it is surely several months now since she emerged from mourning. She looks very well and, it seems horrible to say, liberated, I sense, by her husband's death. I took much delight in showing her our lovely new accommodation, and she duly admired all its wonders!

PARIS. FRIDAY, OCTOBER 19, 1900.
Summer is truly over but we can console ourselves in the colder weather with the telephone! It took the men most of last week to install all the wires—metres and metres of the stuff—and most of yesterday to put the instrument in place in the hall. I cannot say that it is an elegant machine, but I suppose we will find it useful in the end. I dialled up the Catusses' number late yesterday just to announce to Marie-Marguerite that the Proust family was now officially ready for the twentieth century.

Marcel is quite taken with the idea that he might place a

telephone call to his friends on the day of a soirée to check what time they intend to appear or dial up a hostess to thank her for last night's ball, and has already tried calling Antoine. I pointed out to him he could perfectly adequately accomplish all these missions with the usual *petit bleu*—he is always sending Jean off to the post office with messages for someone or other. Dick, who has been supervising things, defended him stoutly and said, "Just wait, Maman, soon there will be no more pneumatic tubes, just telephone wires!" I warned Adrien last night at dinner that he had better watch or the instrument will never be available for his business calls.

Jean was quite intrigued by the whole installation and said, "Well, madame, any machine that saves us from running errands will make the ménage more efficient," but I believe he may find he spends an inordinate amount of time answering the thing and copying down messages. Félicie swears she will not touch it. I had Marie-Marguerite ring us back just to try it out, but it took her some time to get through, so when the bell finally went off we had moved back into the salon and there was great scurrying out to the hall to answer it. Marcel reached it first, but could not hear a thing she was saying for all the crackling on the line. Finally, he gave up and rang off, but Dick was so anxious to get his turn, we had to ring her back and try the experiment all over again, thankfully with better luck this time.

Paris. Saturday, November 10, 1900.
No sooner is Marcel recovered from this cold than he is off dining with his grand friends. I sometimes wonder these days if he would even raise his hat to a man without a de or du in his name. He is very taken with the de Brancovan set—Mme.

de Noailles's brother Constantin and that crowd. I am always slightly suspicious, perhaps it is uncharitable of me, but I wonder if they do not regard Marcel as an object of curiosity more than anything else. They mock our work on Ruskin since they have no such projects themselves. Well, they are not a group with any scholarly pretensions—except Mme. de Noailles with her poetry, of course, and Constantin to some degree. But his friends are all without vocation, well-educated men frittering away their brains since their wealth never requires them to establish careers. Antoine is supposed to be joining the Romanian diplomatic corps, but his life thus far appears to be one rather long vacation.

They all seem to dine out every night, and Marcel is always rousing the servants to do his bidding when he comes home. I tried to tell him yesterday that we are not running a château here with domestics to sleep at the foot of our beds. One must have some consideration. The racket he made last night when he came in woke me from a good deep sleep. I am glad to see him well again, but wish only that he would settle down to some more sensible hours. Georges says I worry too much, and if I do not like the hours he keeps, Adrien and I should simply give him a proper allowance and tell him to establish his own household elsewhere. It is preposterous. He said it at dinner yesterday just to cut short my complaints.

Lovely letter from Marie who should be back with us for New Year's Day—or at least back with her Hahn cousins, and to visit here as soon as possible without making dear Mme. Hahn feel that she is only a boarding house for the friends of the Prousts! We are eagerly full of Ruskinian questions.

PARIS. TUESDAY, JANUARY 8, 1901.

Marie came to visit yesterday afternoon with some notes for
Marcel, answers to his latest queries and, as he was not yet up,
sat with me for a while. She was speaking of her delight in the
gargoyles on the cathedrals, and noting that they really are not
Christian images at all, but rather little pagan beasts that harken
back to the folk beliefs that preceded the religion of the priests.
So, we fell to discussing how one might as a Jew or free thinker,
as Marie describes herself, view Amiens—she believes Ruskin's
Protestantism made him more sensitive to the beauty of Catholic
art because his eye was sharper as an outsider to the faith. I
agreed with her that our position of aesthetic appreciation and
respect was preferable to one of blind faith, which perhaps
cannot distinguish between the grace and honour of a Gothic
Virgin, with her densely pleated gown and carefully folded
hands so exquisitely rendered from the stone, and the excesses
of some ghastly Pietà painted all slapdash in a Paris studio last
week. Yet, I had to point out that Marcel's Catholicism—perhaps
more sentimental than fervent, but an adherence of sorts—
did not interfere with his appreciation. On the contrary, his
familiarity with the Church has always fuelled his love of its
art. Summarized all this in a little note for Marcel, as I was off
to dine with Georges and Emilie, and he was still not about
when I went out. I have not seen him this morning, but he left
me a response, saying he had slept poorly because of a draft
under the door and wanted an extra comforter for his room.

PARIS. SUNDAY, JANUARY 20, 1901.

I lose myself these days in Ruskin, his spiralling sentences
twisting out of my grasp as a description of a gargoyle on the
east porch or the buttressing on the transept gives way to other

discourses. Before I know it, a discussion on the nature of man is underway while I, bewildered, stand still gawking at a stone Virgin in the cathedral at Amiens.

Of course, my English is not as good as it should be, so that his text is slightly vague for me, fluid and removed. Yet here, in this other language, one might dare other things, the way on holiday one tries a new dish or dispenses with a corset.

And too, I have a sense of promise as I persevere. Marcel is but a few pages behind me, panting to catch up with my translation. I work diligently by day; he feverishly by night. I have quite abandoned all other reading, and the weather continues cold, so the great outdoors does not tempt me. The project will be realized.

RÉALISER. We say sometimes realize—this project cannot be realized without a firm commitment, etc.—but, even as I write the word, I know fulfil or achieve would be better, the meaning more quickly seized by the anglophone ear. The francophone will occasionally borrow the English meaning and offer *réaliser* for understand, recognize, or grasp, but the usage is sloppy and would have been unknown to Mme. Proust. "The project will be achieved," or "We will complete the project."

I pick at these words, plucking them out for you, rejecting the bruised ones, amassing them together like berries in a basket. What will I make of this rich bounty? What project is fulfilled here?

Language is a veil that separates me from experience. I possess both my English and my French self-consciously, flourishing my mastery of an extravagant colloquialism in the one or a labyrinthine construction in the other like a child parading about in her mother's high heels. I always speak with firm fluency yet words are an achievement rather than a home.

English has at least double the vocabulary of French, always offering the speaker the choice between the Anglo-Saxon and Latinate. Will you begin or shall I commence? To speak English is to pick words carefully, cleverly, methodically, slowly, for meaning is found in its vocabulary, imparted through the choice of cheap over inexpensive, push over shove, love over like. In French, the choices are limited, the field more restricted but the play swifter and more subtle. Meaning lies in syntax, in what order one places the lovely Latinate syllables. The decisions must be made with both lightning swiftness and sharp foresight: once embarked on a sentence, a route and a message have been chosen, there is no turning back, no halting to seek for a different word, for there is only the one right word, and the very hunt betrays the speaker as a foreigner to this tongue.

To speak English is to carve figures, mighty yet hugely detailed, from solid rock; to speak French is to compose poetic symphonies of cascading sounds. To speak either is to live in a mansion; to speak both is to know that language is only a game. The bilingual are philanderers; having taken two lovers they are always and inevitably cheating.

Instinctively, Max knows this, and slips into the gap. When he can, he plays between language, speaking one one minute, the other the next. We have a bilingual friendship, which in my experience is unusual. Normally, people decide: you are one of my English friends or you are one of my French friends, and we will stick with our chosen language unless forced to change by the presence of others. I cannot bear speaking French with my mother, it feels so artificial. But I would never speak English with my father unless my mother was also present. There's a powerful sense that each relationship has its natural tongue, its first language, no matter how bilingual its membership. Shall I know you in French or shall I know you in English? Decide.

Max and I, however, ignore this rule. We switch back and forth erratically, with him using the changes to delight and destabilize. If it is late and we are lazily discussing philosophy, he will suddenly force my attention on a fine point by swiftly moving the conversation into English. On a cold afternoon, if I am belabouring some domestic detail before we can leave for a film or a gallery, he will drop out of English to coax and cajole in French.

And perhaps it is because I am friends with Max, because I am ensnared in this game, that I choose my career. My father would like me to finish up my much-prolonged art history degree and start working in his shop on Crescent Street, that I might learn the business of antiques. I try for a while, but it doesn't suit. I cannot see what a minor nineteenth-century landscape sitting in the front window, its clouds hesitant, its grass the most lurid shade of green, has to do with Vermeer or Caravaggio. I cannot understand why a pigheaded customer in a badly fitting suit does not see the exquisite beauty in a piece of Venetian glass that is my favourite item in the shop. Most of all, I cannot understand money. In the end, my father knows better than to force me into trade against my will. He lets me move to Ottawa to study translation and earn my diploma as a conference interpreter, to embrace my confusion and live forever between language and meaning.

PARIS. TUESDAY, SEPTEMBER 10, 1901.
We return from holiday to find no word from Ollendorff. I fear we shall never publish our Ruskin, although Marcel assures me these things always progress slowly.

Meanwhile, he distracts himself by chasing after Antoine and his friends. They have added Bertrand de Fénelon to their set. Marcel is quite smitten and says that I must meet him. A count, of course. But when I raise an eyebrow, Marcel defends them all, and points out they are

Dreyfusard, and have been since the beginning.

Adrien says he must visit London at least twice this autumn now that they are actually setting out the parameters for an office of public hygiene. He is pleasantly surprised that the English have agreed to the Paris headquarters. Only fair since it is a French idea.

PARIS. THURSDAY, OCTOBER 3, 1901.
Joyous news from London. All is agreed upon. We are to have our *cordon* at last! Adrien will be back with us for Sunday dinner.

Meanwhile, I am looking forward to seeing *Pelléas et Mélisande* tomorrow night. For all his skepticism about Debussy's music, Hahn has invited me, and promises that he will not prejudice my enjoyment beforehand, but insists on a frank musical discussion afterwards.

Marcel will not be in attendance. He waits upon the Bibesco brothers and especially Comte de Fénelon, and will not agree to a date for the opera, lest they should want him to dine. In pursuing his new friends, he risks forgetting the faithfulness of the old.

PARIS. FRIDAY, OCTOBER 18, 1901.
Marie-Marguerite and I finally took our promised trip on the Métropolitan, riding from the Place de la Concorde out to the Porte Maillot where we walked for a little in the Bois before returning home. Dick was very amused we had yet to try it—he and his friends all behave as though the thing had been there for centuries—but I have not seen the need for it and, truth to tell, have been a little apprehensive about the idea of going

underground to travel, so I have stuck with old habits. Still, I abandoned my prejudices once inside. I was expecting something rather cave-like but the whole affair is lovely and clean and new, with the most modern banquettes and railings throughout, and very bold signs announcing the stops. The second-class carriages are green and the first-class a bright, bright red, and both are filled with all sorts of proper people. I was quite converted.

The opening of the International Office of Public Hygiene is set for December 12 now. They are already at work setting up files and hiring clerks and the like, but there will be some ceremony on the day—a ribbon-cutting at the office door, Adrien says. He is so pleased, and I hope now he can rest. Really, if the English had not been so stupid about the whole thing, it would not have taken all these years. It is such a delight to see Adrien recognized for what he has done and I am sure the Academy appointment will come in the new year.

Paris. Wednesday, November 13, 1901.
The cold weather is torturing Marcel—as is Antoine Bibesco, who came yesterday to tell him that Bertrand is off for the rest of the week on a country jaunt and will not see him until Monday at the earliest. I do believe Antoine delights in these little intrigues while Bertrand is too joyous a character to be really aware of the games his friend plays, nor yet the serious pain they cause Marcel with their thoughtless boasting and cheerful galavanting where he cannot follow. His attack on Sunday was ferocious. I spent much of the night at his side, and do not expect him to rise from his bed before the end of the week. If only his character were less prone to excess, we might overcome his sickness yet.

Paris. Friday, December 13, 1901.

"To conquer without peril is to triumph without glory,"
Corneille so rightly wrote.

It was magnificent. One of those occasions where the
ceremony is simple because the sentiment is real. Just a few
words from the various doctors and a little glass of champagne,
and there we were, feeling all buoyed up, as though some truly
mighty peak had been scaled, which indeed it had. Just that
little brass sign on the door—the International Office of
Public Hygiene—made our hearts pound.

I felt so proud of the doctor, who was glowing yesterday
although he had been very tired Wednesday and is not yet up
this morning. Hearing Dr. Thompson actually acknowledge
his initial reluctance, and de Fleury praise Adrien's ceaseless
efforts, made such a difference to him. Adrien does not need
all the accolades they heap on the Curies or institutes named
for him like Pasteur, just some recognition of what he has
achieved not merely for France but for the human race.

I was wearing my blue suit, Eugénie having done a very
tidy job fixing the sleeve. Dick was very happy to be there, not
quite a full-fledged member of the fraternity yet, but soon.
Marcel is still recovering from his jaunt with Antoine, and
was too ill to attend. It had looked on Wednesday afternoon
as if he might have been rested enough to rise yesterday, but
he had an attack of breathlessness during the night and left
me a note saying not to disturb him. Perhaps it was for the
best, since I know it pains him to witness his father's success,
not for any reason of jealousy but only because he knows how
it disappoints his loving parents that he will never achieve
such prominence in a chosen career.

Absolutely no response from M. Ollendorff about our Ruskin. I despair, but Marcel says he will approach Mercure de France.

PARIS. SATURDAY, MARCH 29, 1902.

A quiet Easter. Dick has a country-house invitation, and Marcel was off all day yesterday motoring to Senlis and several other churches in the area, and has now taken to his bed with a head cold. He seems to have instilled a Ruskinian appreciation for the Gothic in all his friends, for Antoine and Bertrand de Fénelon went with him, along with Robert de Billy and Georges de Lauris. Robert would be very useful—he is so knowledgeable and can keep Antoine and Bertrand from excessive behaviour. Marcel says they get quite silly when together, and all wind up giggling, which is not the right manner in a cathedral on Easter Friday after all. De Lauris apparently has no interest in architecture or religion whatsoever, but they dragged him along because he has fallen in love with a married woman, and needs the distraction!

Certainly, it is not piety that sends them to the churches. Marcel has no plans to attend mass tomorrow, nor does Adrien. He has fallen away increasingly, since he no longer feels that he needs to take the boys, nor set an example for them, I suppose. It is not my place to remind them of their religion and I cannot claim any great loyalty to my own. Nonetheless, believers or not, Adrien and I will have a good piece of lamb for dinner tomorrow. Suzanne has promised as much.

PARIS. FRIDAY, APRIL 11, 1902.

We can now say Dr. Robert Proust. We were planning dinner at
the Ritz to celebrate last night, but Marcel had a horrible attack
yesterday afternoon, so I thought it best to stay home with him
while Dick and his father went out to dinner. He insisted I leave
him be, but when I awoke this morning he had left me a most
piteous note describing his symptoms and suggesting his father
at least prescribe him something for his earache, which he says
has worsened considerably since Tuesday. Dick came into
breakfast to describe dinner to me. The gentlemen had oysters,
lobster, and partridge, so our absence did not hold them back,
and unable to resolve a debate as to whether they should start
with a Sauternes or champagne, decided to have both! Dick was
looking a bit grey for overindulging, but is wonderfully happy.

We should plan a dinner for Dick to solidify his contacts
and launch him professionally. He has the support of Dr. Pozzi,
which is crucial, but Adrien and I agreed it would do him very
well if we were to show off that support in a social setting.

PARIS. WEDNESDAY, APRIL 16, 1902.

Adrien is most alarmed about the measures against the clergy
that the government is proposing, and got quite angry at dinner
last night with the Cruppis, since Monsieur was defending
them. Adrien says it is simply vindictiveness on the part of the
Dreyfusards, but M. Cruppi argued that it really was time to
separate Church and State for once and for all. Indeed, he said
the government is not going far enough. They got very heated
on the subject, and I could see that Louise was embarrassed by
it, feeling that one should not be arguing like this when one is
amongst family. I suppose they had not realized Adrien had
been against Dreyfus, since Marcel and Dick were so active in

the cause and have thus labelled the whole Proust family Dreyfusard. My cousin cares little enough for politics, but her husband was rabid on the subject of the army a few years ago and was in full form last night. This time, however, I have to agree with Adrien, as I know the boys do. It is mean-spirited and dangerous to punish the whole institution for the opinions of certain clergy, who are not truly worthy of their Church. Nonetheless, Adrien should not insist so much on his Catholicism in these arguments: it insinuates that members of my family cannot understand because of our grandparents' race.

Louise served us the most luscious rabbit with a mustard sauce and an excellent piece of Brie, so in the end food and wine covered over our differences.

PARIS. SATURDAY, MAY 10, 1902.
I went yesterday afternoon with Dick to see the apartment he is considering. The room at the front that he may use to receive patients is small, but nicely appointed, and the other rooms, particularly the salon, light and pleasant. It seems highly satisfactory for a young doctor, suggesting comfort without extravagance, which should set the right tone with his new clientele. It is only right for him to set up shop, but still it is hard to see one of my little wolves all grown up and heartbreaking to think he will soon leave the house.

Marcel, who can be so dismissive of his younger brother, urges me now to pay closer attention to his advice for my rheumatism, and has consulted Dick himself about the possibilities of hypnosis for his attacks, which Dick and his father call experimental but potentially useful. They say the Germans report some good results using hypnotic treatment for what they consider nervous diseases—and increasingly believe that illnesses involving a hypersensitivity and inability to conform with the requirements of daily life fall into that category. Certainly, we have always believed Marcel needs to exercise more self-control in all areas of his life.

Dick is now off to the country again this weekend, visiting the Dubois clan to whom his father has recently introduced him, but joined us last night for dinner with his uncle. Suzanne made a pork roast in George's honour, all stuffed with apples and prunes, just as he likes it. We were laughing about what Papa might have thought. He dined in Catholic homes often enough and permitted me to marry Adrien, but still he used to joke that the reason Jews ate different food was so that we would never be tempted to socialize with the Gentiles. He and Maman were not great ones for religion, but they would never have eaten pork at home and certainly our grandparents and great-grandparents observed the dietary laws. Well, I don't have a kosher kitchen and my grandchildren will be Christians. It makes me a little sad sometimes to think that Marcel and Dick have lost a heritage they might have passed on in their turn.

Paris. Monday, June 16, 1902.
Marcel's bad habits really must be controlled so I have told Jean we are to burn no more wood until October. Last night, he came in at three and rang for a fire to be lit since he found his room cold. I have left him a little note remarking on his behaviour, for really he is so selfish. He did not leave for Mme. Lemaire's until very late, which I thought was unfair to Bertrand who had arrived here at nine and waited patiently while Marcel dressed. A young man wants to make the right impression, and no doubt Bertrand would have liked to arrive at the soirée while the other

guests were still about, especially since he was being introduced to his hostess for the first time. I remonstrated with Marcel to hurry up and apologized to Bertrand, whose manners are always impeccable and demeanour energetic and cheerful, but all to no avail, since they did not leave before eleven. And then this morning Jean comes to me with the story about the fire.

Dick informs me he plans to spend three weeks chez Dubois next month. I expect it is the cousin who is the attraction.

PARIS. SATURDAY, JUNE 21, 1902.
Marcel has quite given up on M. Ollendorff and after making some initial inquiries has written a letter to Mercure. He still has corrections to do on the manuscript, but they need see only a page or two to recognize the quality of his French. I am so anxious for Marcel's sake that he succeed at least in this small thing. He will be thirty-one next month and must watch his brother establish a practice and a career while he accomplishes little.

MAX IS ON THE PHONE, talking to his mother. He hasn't told me that it is her and I can't hear her voice properly, but I can tell from the way in which the faint squawking emanating from the receiver rises and falls that his interlocutor is subjecting him to a fusillade of syllables in Parisian French. And I can tell from his air of resigned annoyance that the speaker is his mother. He replies for a while in her language, then switches over to English.

"I haven't decided yet . . ."

There is a furious response.

"Yeah, well, I am going to think about it . . ."

These phone calls have been going on for several weeks now. I know because sometimes I have overheard Max's end of the conversation while visiting his apartment on the weekend, and other times I have heard the messages on his answering machine when we come back here after an outing.

"*Maxime, c'est Maman. Appelle moi donc. Il faut qu'on discute de ça, quand même.*"

He is slow to call her back, and right now he is hanging up.

"I'm hanging up now . . ."

Another burst of sound.

"No, really, we have talked about it. I am hanging up now. Goodbye."

He hangs up and sits still for a moment, seemingly defeated by the conversation.

Max is threatening to quit medical school. Well, he has been threatening to quit medical school all the years I have known him, before he even enrolled there. Max does not seem to have any better ideas about what he might do for a living. He got a job one summer working in the information kiosk at the Royal Ontario Museum, and talks about studying art history full-time, but he has only vague and romantic notions of what might follow.

"I'd become a curator or something," he will say.

"Max, you have to do a Ph.D. to be a curator. That's another five years, at least, after a master's, and you don't even have the right credits to get into a master's art history program. And there are no jobs in the museums anyway."

"You sound like my mother—there are never any jobs, we are all going to starve. I could work in a museum without a Ph.D."

"Doing what?

"Well, in the information booth or something . . . I could be one of the guards."

"Max, there is no way you want to spend your life doing the drudge work in a museum."

"You'd get to look at the paintings all the time . . ."

"Oh yeah. I can just see you as a guard, looking at the paintings all day, until they fired you because some kid put his fingers on the Van Gogh and you failed to notice it."

"Yeah," he laughs. "I'd be too busy back with the Caravaggios and El Grecos."

Max is going through a baroque phase in his artistic tastes.

"But no, Marie, I am serious about this."

"All right, quit medical school then. If you aren't happy, you shouldn't be there. I'm dropping by McGill on Monday before I go back to Ottawa. I can go into the art department and get you a copy of the graduate calendar."

"I don't have to be a curator. I could run a shop, like your dad, or a gallery."

"Well, you can talk to him about it any time, you know that."

I am jealous of Max's company and like to keep him to myself. My parents have met him only a handful of times—introduced at their Christmas party or perhaps it was the medical school open house, chatting briefly on one of the rare occasions when I let him pick me up at our house—but they have pronounced him charming nonetheless.

"My parents are always asking after you. My dad would be happy to tell you about the business . . ."

But Max doesn't pursue the issue further, never investigates careers in art and keeps attending his classes as usual, until a few months later he will announce, yet again, that he is disgusted by his ambitious classmates and lacklustre professors and will not continue at med school next year.

I am not sure why he plays this game—except perhaps to torture his mother. He says he enrolled at medical school in the first place only because of family pressure, and seems to have hit on a strategy of graceless compliance as a way of punishing his mother without disobeying her. It is as though he wanted to test the limits of his conformity with her plans, yet doesn't have the courage to make different ones.

But this time Max is serious. He is quitting medical school for good, hence the recent phone calls. Next September, he must begin his internship. Three years of classes and exams are over; he is almost finished clerking. He will graduate and the hospital work will begin in earnest. It would be pointless to suffer through the long hours in the wards and the nights on call only to quit the profession. This time he is determined, he will not seek an internship—or at least that is what he is telling his mother when she catches him at home.

I have never met the woman, but I feel sorry for that fretful voice at the other end of the line from Toronto, desperately trying to control him long distance. I picture her, her face pressed against the receiver, and for some reason I see a fragile beauty, a young woman with hair as black as Max's. Of course, she would be as old as my own mother is, and probably age is turning her hair grey. What does she looks like, Mrs. Segal, and what is it that makes her so anxious?

"She worries about you. I guess that's natural." Visiting Montreal for the weekend, I have been puttering around his small apartment, trying not to eavesdrop, but as he sits sadly silent for a long while after putting down the phone, I give up pretending I don't know who the caller is.

He doesn't reply.

I try looking on the bright side: "You can do good as a doctor, you can help people."

"Oh, Marie," he says with exasperation, "It's only about money, that's why everyone is there. There's no way I want to be part of that bourgeois thing."

"You have to make a living, at least."

"Yeah, you have to be normal, you have to make a living, you have to fit in . . ." His voice grows sarcastic. I was only trying to help and am injured by his tone.

"Okay, then go ahead and quit, for God's sake," I answer with some anger.

"Yeah, well, I don't know, maybe I will."

Max flirts with rebellion.

PARIS. WEDNESDAY, SEPTEMBER 24, 1902.

And so, it is as I expected. The big news. Dick came in all beaming and proud for dinner last night, drew himself up—he looks so much like his father when he wants to be important— and announced he has secured a promise of marriage from Mlle. Dubois-Amiot. I had assumed that was in the wind and that he had sought his father's advice although Adrien had not told me directly. Apparently, this last visit really confirmed their mutual affection, and Dick had already this summer been calculating how soon he could afford to take on domestic responsibilities. Not that the bride will not do her share—the family is already being generous about the dowry, Dick assures me. We are to meet her next Sunday. It seems ridiculous I do not yet know the young lady, but I do not go out into society as much as I should so have not become acquainted with the family. I will call on her mother next week as well.

I have just completed a small letter to Bertrand and shall send Jean to post it right away; having decided to do the thing, let it be done. Just a very short note, urging him to visit Marcel soon, as he values his friendship so highly. I will not tell Marcel that I have written him and am, perhaps, as bad as the boys themselves, forever indulging in intrigues, but did think that a mother's urgings would count for something. Marcel has been so upset that he has not seen Bertrand since their return from Trouville.

He has been in bed ever since, and had Félicie fussing away over him yesterday, although I have told him before she is far too old to be fetching and carrying for him.

Paris. Tuesday, September 30, 1902.
We heard today with deep regret of the passing of Emile Zola. France will never forget his bravery in bringing a gross miscarriage of justice out into public debate, at a time when it was only whispered in corridors. It is sad that the great man died without having seen Dreyfus's innocence proclaimed—one is told that he still strives to prove his case, even though he accepted the pardon, and that the affair still moves through the Department of Justice. These things are so impossibly slow: the bureaucracy has no sympathy for the human misery its interminable machinery can cause. Marcel will participate in the official cortège, and is out at Sandford and Merton, as Dick will always call them, buying a new black coat, for his old one is a fright and would certainly dishonour the man were he to wear that in the procession. They say he was killed by gas in his room because the fireplace was not drawing properly. Adrien is always warning Marcel about the dangers of such things, and advises an open window even in winter. I hope now Marcel will listen.

Marie plans to stay in France until after the new year, so we will be blessed with her visits all autumn. She stopped into the salon yesterday afternoon to offer me congratulations on Dick.

Paris. Wednesday, October 1, 1902.
She is very pretty and very polite, but rather distant. Perhaps intimidated. An illustrious medical family may seem particularly

elevated, by nature of its vocation, to the daughter of a stockbroker, even if the Amiots are certainly wealthy people, and the Dubois side of the family wealthier still. She was quiet at dinner, but not ungracious. I am reminded of what Mme. de Sévigné said of her new daughter-in-law—that she is in no hurry to please us, but will do so in time.

Marcel did not help, by chatting very intensely and paying her some very silly compliments in the first half of the evening, and then getting up from the table, complaining of a headache, before we had reached dessert, and retiring, looking quite pale. There is no doubt she found him odd. Well, in years to come she will be our Marthe and all this awkwardness will seem very far away.

Bertrand has returned to our midst and Marcel now wants to travel to the Low Countries with him, on an artistic pilgrimage, and has asked his father for the money. Meanwhile, he is discussing his translation with Anna de Noailles's brother, the de Brancovan boy, seeking some advice on publication.

PARIS. TUESDAY, OCTOBER 7, 1902.
Another letter from Marcel this morning, more informative. He and Bertrand are delighted with Bruges and with the art. A little Venice, he says, with all its wonderful miniature canals, and laments that Ruskin so disliked Flemish art that he never visited the city. (I am not sure he did not, and must check. I had thought his grand tour with that poor wife of his would have included Bruges and Brussels, although Marcel seems to think not.) He says the damp is still leaving him a little breathless, but thankfully he is without attacks. Bertrand has been forcing him to get up at

a reasonable hour. Bravo! By this time, they will be in Amsterdam.

I have been thinking of the red tapestry for Marthe and Dick.

PARIS. THURSDAY, OCTOBER 9, 1902.
The letter arrived this morning, following last night's telegram.
Adrien is very angry, and was not mollified by Marcel's account,
which I do not think he believes. I suspect he thinks Marcel has
simply spent a lot more than was planned, and has invented the
theft. Nonetheless, he did go out to the post office on his way to
the Faculty just now, to wire Marcel the money. It is a large sum
to lose. I really do not know what to think.

PARIS. FRIDAY, NOVEMBER 7, 1902.
Adrien says the only thing for it is to put Marcel back on a
fixed allowance and when that is spent, even if it is long before
the end of the month, there will no more. I agree it is probably
the one way to discipline him and teach him the value of
money. There is Dick, running a business and planning a
household, entering into discussions with Marthe's father
man to man, and Marcel, in his thirties now, cannot be
trusted not to overtip the tailor's assistant so extravagantly
that one is embarrassed to be seen in his premises again, least
the wrong motives be ascribed to his actions.

The doctor will speak to him this evening.

PARIS. TUESDAY, NOVEMBER 11, 1902.
I had thought Marcel had taken the suggestion of the allowance
well, and we had agreed we would start on December 1, but I
should have known better, and realized he would take it out on

me, not on his father. When he woke yesterday, I came into his room to remonstrate with him for waking Marc again last night to relight the fire, when he got very angry with me, and said the doctor and I do not treat him as an adult, and always prefer Dick—which is nonsense, it is just that planning the wedding is distracting at the moment.

Marcel accused me of having no sympathy for his sentiments and not recognizing how delicate he was feeling because he had lost Antoine's company and was now to lose Bertrand's too. It is true that Bertrand's decision to take the post at the embassy in Constantinople has laid Marcel low, but really one cannot expect one's friends to change their career plans for the sake of comradeship. I said as much to Marcel, which remark he took very bitterly and said I did not understand how precious their trip to the Low Countries had been, and how disappointed he was that Bertrand could go away after that. I made the mistake of responding that perhaps Marcel would be more sympathetic to Bertrand's choice if he understood the value of a career, at which point he said something horribly vindictive and cruel. I have ordered the servants to stop answering his bell.

Paris. Saturday, November 15, 1902.
Georges says the President cares nothing for the measures against the Church, but feels he cannot count on his supporters unless he pushes ahead on these issues and is seen to be punishing the anti-Dreyfusards even if innocents get caught in the process. Well, we are all thoroughly tired of politics, so it comes as no surprise that the government is acting out of expediency rather than conviction. Adrien just shakes his head over the stupidity of the whole thing. Some compassion in

victory would go a lot further to heal France's wounds.

Emilie was looking much better, and we had a lovely hare thanks to Suzanne. They are delighted with Dick's news, and anxious to meet their future niece.

I stand firm on the issue of Marcel's bell.

PARIS. TUESDAY, NOVEMBER 25, 1902.

I am so angry with Marcel I took away that little lap desk that belonged to Maman and on which he so likes to work. Perhaps it was vindictive of me, but his attitude is insupportable. I had spent all day yesterday going through things for Dick and sat down with Marcel when he awoke to discuss with him what might be appropriate. At first he started to quibble, and say Marthe would surely not appreciate the red tapestry, and should not have this thing, nor that. I tried to gently point out she will be family now and that Dick is setting up a proper home, and cannot be simply surrounded by the furnishings the Dubois-Amiots have picked. Marcel then became quite resigned, and said it was all the same to him, which was not very helpful either, since I really wanted his opinion on matters of taste.

I went off to finish the job on my own, and thought I would consult Dick today anyway, although he is never much judge of these things and just says anything will do. Like his father that way. While I was putting things away, with Jean and Marc helping me, Marcel rang for Marc and wanted him to stoke the fire and bring in the lap desk, which was in my room because I was using it last week when my rheumatism was bad and I had stayed in bed. Marc went off, but I got more and more angry thinking about it, the way he is always ringing for the servants, as though I had no need of them, so I marched into his room and reclaimed the desk and said he could not have it, I was thinking of giving it to Marthe, at which he wept. Of course, I would not give away Maman's desk, but will keep it in my own room for a bit.

PARIS. SUNDAY, DECEMBER 7, 1902.

Marcel left me a little note this morning describing a tantrum that he blames entirely on me. Yesterday evening, after I had retired, Bertrand came to take his leave—he is off to Constantinople now and we certainly shall miss him. Marcel says that his room was freezing since the servants had not relit the fire because of my interdiction. He got so angry that he could not entertain his friend properly, and in his frustration he seized on Bertrand's top hat and ripped the lining out. The poor man—he was on his way to a soirée and it was a new hat. Marcel says we must replace it, and that the cost must be added to his allowance, but I have slipped a note under his door with my reply. He can pay for a new hat himself—although he had better hurry since Bertrand leaves this week.

Dick and I have almost finished our discussions on the furniture and linens. He suggested we should consult Marthe—he really has little tastes of his own in this regard, and generously wants to let her make the decisions. But I pointed out to him that we do not wish to put the girl in the awkward position of having to choose her own gifts, and that she would only accept all we showed her for fear of hurting sensibilities by declining anything. Dick is also so progressive in these matters, but really it is customary to present the bride with the basket, and the custom serves well.

PARIS. TUESDAY, DECEMBER 9, 1902.

Marcel's note yesterday said he has stopped his work on his
Ruskin, and will not start again until his father and I relent
on the subject of paying for the hat. It is absolutely silly,
since Constantin de Brancovan has now agreed to publish the
introduction in the *Renaissance Latine*, which might surely
spur Mercure de France to finally make an offer. Marcel's
translation is the one thing he is doing with his life; it would be
tragic were he to abandon it now. It would prove his father
right, that his literary aspirations are mere dreams.

Marie came to call in the evening, so I stopped her on the
way in and told her this news. She said she would remonstrate
with him and send me a note to let me know how she fared.
She suggested I come out with her to visit Reynaldo at Versailles
before the end of the year, which was so thoughtful of her.

PARIS. SATURDAY, DECEMBER 13, 1902.

Bertrand called yesterday for his final visit, and was particularly
anxious to see Marcel immediately since he had a number of
errands ahead of him. Marcel was not up, of course, but
Bertrand was insistent so I offered at least to go and see if he
was stirring.

When I entered the room, he was in a deep sleep, his chest
rising and falling with that heavy, regular breath that has always
sounded so sweet to my ears. To think that to the healthy,
breathing is an affair so banal they do not notice it.

As I turned to leave the room, I caught sight of something
on the divan, partly hidden by that Chinese screen. I realized
it was Marie, also deeply asleep, spread out on the divan. She
had removed her jacket and her shoes, and—I could tell by the
lumps beneath her skirt—loosened her stays. I withdrew hastily,

and told Bertrand, truthfully enough, that Marcel was still asleep. He said he would try again in the afternoon, but was not free later, having made arrangements to dine with his parents before his departure.

After he left, I retreated to the drawing room and closed the doors, thinking Maire would wake soon enough and would be able to slip out of the house unnoticed and thus be spared any embarrassment. Luckily, Jean was out on errands. She must have managed it, for when Marcel rose at three there was no sign of her.

I wonder if I need to speak to her. She must surely understand that Marcel will never make any girl a husband. He is far too ill and the hours he keeps are impossible for me and the servants, let alone a wife.

I AM NOT ASLEEP. I am lying on the narrow pull-out bed in Max's studio apartment, staring wide-eyed into the dark. I can hear his even breathing, just across the room from me—the place is so small I could almost reach across the gap between the couch where I lie and his bed, and touch him with my hand. I long for him to be awake, for him to reach out and touch me.

This night, we have attended a party in a small street on the Plateau Mont Royal, Montreal's neighbourhood of intellectuals and immigrants. I am flattered to have been included, pleased Max would want to share his friends with me, and my joy has made me talkative all evening. When we emerge after midnight, part of a laughing group that plans to move downtown to a bar, an early snow is falling, with small flakes sparkling in the light of the street lamps. It must have been snowing for some time, for the world that was bare and brown when we entered the party has disappeared. Max stops me as we step off the stairs that run up the outside of the house and, to quieten my movement towards the others who are now several steps ahead out on the street, takes my mittened hand.

"Look at the railing," he says, indicating the wrought-iron banisters that follow the outdoor staircase up to the second-floor flat that we have just left. "Two hours ago, it was just metal, but look at it now." Indeed, there is a growing, vertical coat of snow perched all the way up it, so that its hard, narrow, and reliable diagonal line is transformed into a soft yet perilous object of quiet impossible dimensions.

He looks expansively up at the sky, and smiles.

"Snow, it's like falling in love," he says. "Makes you see the whole world differently."

We pull each other forward to catch up with our companions, and the moment passes, but I clasp this little pearl of poetry to me, treasuring its beauty, admiring its sheen, and trying to read an announcement into its metaphor.

I have waited, anticipating, longing, ever since the day when, following Max off the bus that leads down from the Plateau as it stops at the Place des Arts, I admire the hair on the back of his head and realize with a sudden, piercing emotion that I no longer love Max with the adolescent tremors and twinklings that have marked our friendship from the start, but with some newer, larger, less-sparkling feeling that seems to take hold of my soul.

During the previous school year, while, lonely and uncertain, I work away at my translation certificate during the week in Ottawa, and visit my comrades in Montreal every weekend, my friend Max has made me the gift of several other pearls. On an October day, playfully pursuing me through a park near his apartment, for we are late and I have urged him not to dawdle, he grabs a handful of the dried, fallen leaves that sit in piles where the gardeners have raked them up, and stuffs them down the back of my coat, as though needing some excuse to put his arms about me, just as he did on the day

I held the cat. Again, I delight in the moment, but cannot help noticing, four months later, when he repeats the identical game in the same place with a lump of crystalline snow balled up in his gloved hand, that nothing has changed in our friendship.

One morning, sitting in a deli eating bagels and scrambled eggs washed down with thin coffee, we talk to a child, a boy of three or four, who pops his head over the booth, ignoring his parents' pleas to sit down. Max warms to him, speaks to him rationally, asking what he is eating for breakfast and whether he prefers syrup or jam on his pancakes. The boy holds his attention fully, and while the child occasionally glances up to make sure he has secured my affection as well, Max ignores me, entering into this conversation with a gravity that might suggest this was a rare opportunity to consult a true philosopher as to the existence of God. When the child leaves, waving cheerfully at his new friend, Max turns to me and asks, "Do you want children?"

A chasm seems to open beneath my feet. No answer seems possible or right. I mumble something uncertain, noncommittal.

And now, lying on the pull-out bed in Max's apartment—for it is my second year in Ottawa; I often do not tell my parents that I am in Montreal for the weekend, and go directly to stay with him—I cannot sleep. I have lain here often, a few feet away from his bed, and slept fully, but tonight my thoughts keep me awake, and grow increasingly dark as the dawn approaches. And here, in this particular moment of the small hours, I am given new vision, an adult perception of the matter, and know he does not love me nor will he ever. Gripped by my sense of both hopelessness and truth, I become determined, and think I will rise, dress, leave him a brief note—or perhaps not—and be gone, forever, never calling, ignoring his messages, until I am free of his image in my mind's eye and the sound of his voice in my ear.

But instead a fitful slumber finally overtakes me on the spare bed, and I think that I hear his mother calling me to save her. She is trapped in a hole and her voice comes from faraway over the telephone line and yet she is also in the room with me.

I fall into a deeper, dreamless sleep and by the time I rise late the next morning I have forgotten my resolve. Our desultory friendship continues in this way until the following summer.

PARIS. THURSDAY, JANUARY 15, 1903.

Marcel is impossible. We have spread the wedding goods in the library, so that Dick and I can make our last decisions before we present everything to Marthe, and I have lace and tapestries sitting out uncovered. I had told Marcel he must do his fumigations elsewhere for the duration, but yesterday afternoon found him in the library polluting the fine cloths with those foul powders. He insists the smoking of them helps but I wonder they are not just like the Trional, and become a crutch rather than a cure. I remonstrated with him, and he argued he could not possibly use his own room because Jean was seeing to the chimney, which has been smoking of late, and had wanted to get into the room as soon as he rose. I went and spoke to Jean who, of course, was perfectly happy to wait until after dinner—I do hope it is just some soot caught in the damper, for the last thing I need in the house at the moment is a chimney sweep.

I conducted Marcel back to his room but he was sulking horribly by this time, and when I tried to speak to him, he hissed at me that he did not wish to be embarrassed in front of the servants once again—the once again being his modifier, not mine. I just gave up and tried to air the library a bit.

We have decided to have the dinner for the men on the twenty-ninth, two weeks from now, on the night before the day before the civil marriage. I thought the Friday night might be more appropriate, just the night before and Dick's last as a bachelor, but Adrien gently pointed out to me that if the boys all overindulge it would be difficult for Dick the next day. And for Marthe too.

PARIS. MONDAY, JANUARY 19, 1903.
Nice family dinner last night with just Georges and Emilie. He was singing the joys of conjugal life to Dick, which was sweet although not altogether accurate in his case. I had forgotten how we tried always to keep from the boys any word of his mistresses—that actress especially, who was not discreet. He handles it all with much more delicacy these days, which is what one requires of a husband. And I suppose after all these years Emilie does not care as much as she used to, although we have never shared our feelings on this matter. But I am sure Dick will be a loyal husband, and I am so happy to have one of them married at least. A grandchild is perhaps not too much to hope for before Adrien and I are that much older.

We finally have positive word from Mercure, but Marcel must now try and get the manuscript back from Ollendorff, who has been really infuriating with his slowness and indecision. It serves him right to find the project stolen out from underneath him. Publishers should be business people after all.

PARIS. FRIDAY, JANUARY 23, 1903.
Marcel has now delivered the second part of his introduction to Constantin, who ensures him that it will be published in February, but he is glum about the whole thing, says translation is not real work at all, and angry at the disruptions of his brother's wedding. I do not have the energy to remonstrate

with him, although now that Mercure has agreed he must push ahead and finish. I only wish Bertrand or Antoine were here to comfort him a bit, but I have written to the loyal Hahn asking that he might come from his Versailles retreat and see Marcel soon.

PARIS. THURSDAY, JANUARY 29, 1903.
Only now risen from my bed to oversee Jean's preparations for this evening. Thank heavens I do not need to be present. I feel exhausted when I should be joyful. I spent most of the week in bed with a cold, as did Marcel who is preparing for this evening with care. He believes that if he has all day tomorrow to rest and then Sunday again in bed, he should be able to assist at both the city hall on Saturday and the church on Monday. He tires so easily, but I fear all the time he spends supine only allows fluid to gather in his lungs and worsens his constipation. On the other hand, when he rises, he so quickly exhausts his capacity for breathing it is frightening. I plead with him to achieve some kind of normalcy, a regular schedule and more hygienic habits, but it seems all in vain.

PARIS. WEDNESDAY, FEBRUARY 4, 1903.
At last, some peace. Marthe looked lovely although very nervous. I would have thought that the civil ceremony rather prepared one for the mass a few days later, but she looked quite white with fear on Monday. Dick was very good and grown-up, and clearly his presence helped her, which is a good sign already.

The church was splendid. Marie-Marguerite was altogether right about the flowers, and I was so glad Madame took her tactful advice. It does not do to exaggerate things—overwhelm your guests with blossoms and they only think you are ostentatious. Better to spend the money on the wine, as Adrien always says. Besides, what the original proposal might have done to Marcel I hate to think. As it was, he wore two overcoats to the church to prevent against chills. If he had pollen into the bargain, he would never have survived.

He was supposed to take Valentine in, but she was quite aghast by his appearance and balked—silly girl, Henriette does need to teach her a little more seriousness. It is all very well to be spritely when one is young, but giddy is not right at all. It is something I very much like about Marthe who is always gracious, and when she gets the nerves, she does not giggle but simply retreats into silence. Anyway, in the end Georges got Valentine under control—she was all for crying about it, which was ridiculous, but he put a stop to that right away and saw her into the church himself, while Marcel in his two overcoats gave his arm to his aunt. Marcel can be quite the gentleman with his grand hostesses, but I do think the younger ones just make him nervous in the end.

Dick and Marthe got safely away. Her going-away dress was the most lovely pale blue and she was looking much cheerier by that point, and thanked me most prettily for everything. So, we are starting off on the right foot, I believe.

AT THE WEDDING, I wear a pink dress with bright flowers spattered across its full skirt. Afterwards, I wish I had worn any other colour, a deep blue or lush green, some colour that would make me look gracious and distant, but instead I am dressed with immediacy in shades of need. Max stands beside me in a suit.

I have just finished my certificate in Ottawa and will now return permanently to Montreal, free to push our friendship in some clearer direction. But I am too late. Max has completed an internship here and returns home in a month's time. After much pleading from his parents, he has agreed to begin his residency in Toronto. He has found a place in internal medicine at Toronto General. It is downtown; he likes the look of the work, thinks he will see interesting patients. He is leaving for good then, this summer. Time is running out and I am desperate that something should finally happen. And, I suppose, in a way, it does.

At the end of the night, when I thank the bride's mother and compliment her on the day's events, she says airily, "The kids just wanted something small but I wanted for it to be nice." So, while everything is small, it exists in huge profusion as mother and daughter have fought to reconcile their conflicting notions of display. The guests are thin and carefully sheathed in tight little cocktail dresses or smooth dark suits, but they number in the hundreds, milling about before dinner eating dainty pieces of black bread coated in smoked salmon and sipping French champagne. A single, glossy white lily sits at the centre of every table, and all three bridesmaids are dressed in white, in minor versions of the wedding gown itself.

We arrive late at the ceremony, as the bridal party is entering the low-ceilinged salon that will stand in for the synagogue, with rows of padded chairs, made to accommodate overfed executives dozing through training sessions and sales meetings, taking the place of pews. I mistake the first bridesmaid, with her white lace gown and small bouquet, for the bride herself, but she is then followed by a second and a third, until the mightiest dress of all trails into the room. We follow in its wake and cautiously settle into our chairs, but not quietly enough to avoid sidelong glances from the other guests.

As the ceremony begins, I scan the room and realize every man is wearing a small satin yarmulke carefully pinned to his scalp. I wonder momentarily that there are no Gentiles amongst the guests but quickly realize my mistake. The yarmulkes have been distributed at the outset and Max alone has not got one, having arrived too late. He appears bare-headed in the sight of God, if God is present somewhere beneath this stucco ceiling with its bronze domed lamps. He sits with his hands folded, a hint of slightly superior amusement animating his features. He notices that I have my arms crossed, and silently mimics me, mocking what he perceives as my discomfort with his culture, but I suspect he is more ill at ease here than I am.

Under the *chuppah*, the bride stands gloriously tall in a dress that buttons all the way down her back, with a row of a hundred little pearls disappearing into the folds of its great skirt somewhere below her waist. The groom crushes the wedding cup under his foot with conviction, and the guests applaud the splintering sound.

The meal that follows is long and slow, with course upon course of fine meats and creamy sauces presented on big white dinner plates that are decorated with the petals of the pansy and the nasturtium. We seem only to have paused for a moment, after eating the three or four little mouthfuls of chocolate mousse secreted inside the fold of a golden biscuit shaped like a cornucopia, when the young and eager master of ceremonies approaches a microphone and announces that the dessert table is ready.

Max takes my arm and propels me towards a new room, at the back of the dining hall, where the doors have been flung open to reveal a table that runs the whole length of this long, narrow space. The table is so full I cannot at first comprehend it, but gradually my eyes seize upon individual shapes in this great profusion. There is a dark-chocolate torte with serpentine lines of black icing drizzled across its surface. There is a lemon meringue pie with a glorious white crown flecked with gold where the heat of the oven has toasted it. There is a light, flat cake iced with a pale-green paste that can be counted on to offer the soft, sweet flavours of marzipan. There is a long strudel, its hundreds of papery layers concealing apples and raisins within, and dusted with powdered sugar without. There is a giant layer cake covered with a chocolate icing whipped into peaks that look like little waves on the sea. There are massive glass bowls of fruit salad in which perfect little pastel melon balls of pink, green, and orange nestle beside each other like candies in the jars on a confectioner's countertop. Beside them, there are plates of petits fours, flat little circles and diamonds with pristine surfaces of pink or white icing, and biscuits, golden discs studded with slivers of almond or tapering tongues softly shining where the dough has been brushed with egg white. There are numerous cheesecakes, bathed in fruit sauces or simply plain, a cracked surface exposed to view with the full confidence that this simple one will be the best, the one that melts in the mouth, delighting the tongue with the kiss of the sugar and the bite of the cheese. There are three big silverware barques, filled to the brim with candies, each one wrapped in a twist of coloured foil. At the centre of this vast array, mounted on a china pedestal so that it towers over the rest of the table, stands the crowning ornament, the pièce de resistance, the concoction that the French call a *croquembouche*, a stack of cream puffs held together by strands of spun sugar to create a pyramid of soft clouds encircled by a web of gold filaments.

I am usually a greedy eater, forever sampling, loath to forgo any flavour lest the next mouthful prove yet more satisfying than the last. But in front of this laden wedding table I seem frozen, unable to pick anything at all. I stand at the very beginning of the table, in the middle of a queue that is forming both ahead and behind me, holding a white plate onto which I have managed only to place a single ladyfinger.

Max stands ahead of me, reaching across the table to cut into the chocolate torte. He has lost me and does not notice that I stand behind him while others are stepping around me to help themselves. Across from Max, on the other side of the table and just down a few feet, a tall, blond-haired man with a muscular form that looks unaccustomed to its well-tailored suit is standing surveying the scene. As I watch, Max glances up from the knife he is holding and meets the man's gaze. For a long moment they hold eyes as if they recognize each other.

I look down. My dress is crumpled now, with wide horizontal ridges disfiguring the skirt where it stretches across my belly and thighs. My shoes pinch. I move to the table in front of me and start to pile cakes and sweetmeats onto my plate.

PARIS. TUESDAY, MARCH 3, 1903.
Cheered by the final delivery of our Ruskin to Mercure, Marcel and I have agreed to a triple reform of his schedule, eating habits, and drug use. He is to take three meals a day at regular hours; he is to make sure he is asleep well before dawn and is to rise no later than ten in the morning at which point he will eat a light lunch, followed by afternoon tea, dinner at six, and whatever refreshments he chooses to eat with friends, should he be going out, or if needed, a snack here in the late evening. He will gradually curb his use of Trional, attempting at first to use it only every other day, with a goal of only once a week or in case of very bad attacks. He is to drink no more than three cups of coffee a day. He will begin Friday, after his big dinner at the Pierrebourgs on Thursday night. I have said he can have the dinner party for which he has been pestering me, once he undertakes this reform.

Mme. de Noailles dropped in to see me yesterday on her way to visit Marcel in his room, and said the most complimentary things about what her brother has published so far in the *Renaissance Latine*. Said she cannot wait for the second bit this month, and was also, with a wink, praising the anonymous

Horatio whose society articles are so enlivening the *Figaro* these days. Such a pretty girl, even if she does talk far too much. I suppose it is a sign of her intelligence, but it is unladylike to never let one's interlocutor get a word in.

Paris. Thursday, March 5, 1903.
Marie N. came to visit yesterday afternoon, and sat with me while we waited for Marcel to wake. She has decided to settle in Paris for a while, much to our delight, for she has apprenticed herself to a silversmith—a M. Bing, whom she says is very respected in his field. I find it so odd that a girl should work for her living. Marcel says Marie's parents are perfectly able to support her and settle a good sum on her at marriage, but she seems determined to pursue an artistic career with a diligence and regularity I only wish Marcel would exhibit. English girls are so lively and Marie always radiates energy. Perhaps domestic duties would not be sufficient to occupy her, although were she to have children she would discover soon enough they require every drop of energy a mother can muster.

I told her of Marcel's plans for reforming his schedule and habits, and she kindly offered to lend whatever support she can.

Paris. Sunday, March 8, 1903.
Disastrous beginning to our triple reform. I pointed out to Marcel yesterday, when he rose at three in the afternoon, that he was already more than twenty-four hours into his new life and had yet to mend his ways. He took it ill, and said now that I had bothered him about it, he was too upset to start that day.

Still, we must persevere, even if the road is difficult and the sacrifices painful. Vice is a false comfort, virtue a true joy. The habits that Marcel must abandon, the behaviours that pervert and seduce, will be trifling things, barely remembered, let alone regretted, once he has established a healthy life.

PARIS. MONDAY, MARCH 23, 1903.
Adrien and I have agreed to July in Evian, and perhaps a trip to Montreux in August.

The ever-scheming Antoine is visiting practically every day. He is seemingly unchanged by his mother's death and his time in Romania. He confided in me that Marcel does not see our Ruskin as real writing, an opinion he has expressed to me himself. I urged Antoine to encourage my little wolf, and he promised he would do that and drop me a note to report his progress in that regard.

PARIS. THURSDAY, APRIL 2, 1903.
Marcel tells me he has abandoned our reforms to prod me in this matter of the dinner, so I have relented and said there will be dinner if there is, immediately after, reform. I know he hates it when I call his friends *cocottes,* but really they are nothing better. None of these young aristocrats work and his latest acquaintance, the Marquis d'Albufera, even keeps a mistress in high style. The idea that the editor of the *Figaro* is going to be impressed by such company is nonsense. It will only affirm Marcel's reputation as a literary dilettante if M. Calmette meets such people at our table. Marcel can never believe that not everyone in the world is dying to meet a duke or a count, the way he is, and that many hard-working people like his father

actually are not the least bit interested in the talk of the beau monde. Still, since I like nothing less than people who agree to a plan but then carry it out grudgingly, I have kept my thoughts to myself and we are going ahead with a dinner party in cheerful spirits.

Dick will bring Marthe for lunch on Sunday. We must get into the habit.

PARIS. SATURDAY, APRIL 18, 1903.
Apparently I under—or perhaps over—estimated M. Calmette, for he was bowing and scraping Thursday night as though his own achievements were for nothing in the face of a great family name. I expected the editor of the *Figaro* to be a bit more serious in temperament even if it is the society paper, and a little more aloof from the high and mighty since he is always ready to dig up scandal at their expense. But he turns out to be a veritable social climber. One of those who wants to be both the principled outsider and the charmed insider too. After I greeted Marcel's guests, I retired, but Marcel left me a little note yesterday morning saying it had gone well, he thought, and that the mousseline sauce was in the end the right decision.

PARIS. MONDAY, APRIL 27, 1903.
Adrien says I must not upset myself so, but what am I to do when Marcel sets out to spite me. We have made no progress on our reform. He has so little strength he must spend every other day in bed, yet when he rises it is to dine with d'Albufera and his lady in some restaurant. Or last week, Marcel insisted that he must go all the way out to Passy to see the Comte de Montesquiou. He

ignores *Sesame and Lilies,* which he promised he would consider as a second Ruskin project while we wait for the proofs on *Amiens,* but will spend a whole day fretting because his new friend, the Duc de Guiche, has not responded to a little letter he sent him last week. This morning he left me a note asking for the little divan in the hall to be moved back into his room this afternoon, but I have told Jean he is not to have it, and I will not respond to any more demands.

Joyous news from Marthe. I must get Marie-Marguerite on the telephone to tell her.

PARIS. THURSDAY, MAY 14, 1903.
Marcel regaled me with tales of Tuesday's ball. Although he had ignored the theme—Athens in the time of Pericles, demanding for those who are not classicist—and just went in his regular black tie, the other guests had outdone themselves with robes and wreaths and sandals. Marie was looking exquisite, he said, and had done her hair in the Greek style, all piled up at the crown of her head with ringlets coming down the side. She sat out the dances to keep him company, which I thought was unfair of him, since it is all very well being artistic but the girl must eventually find herself a husband.

He spent yesterday in bed and I do not suppose he will rise today.

PARIS. TUESDAY, MAY 19, 1903.
The proofs of *Amiens* arrived from Mercure de France yesterday morning and Marcel started in on them as soon as he woke. Within an hour, he had Marie on the telephone with queries. She will call in person today. I am overjoyed to see him so

committed to this work. Indeed, we are both greatly cheered by it, and quoted Baudelaire to each other: "Art is long and time is short."

Adrien tells us that he and his colleagues have been consulted about the Panama Canal, for the yellow fever amongst the workers is so ferocious that the authorities fear it will never get built, and after all those scandals about the money, they can hardly afford more delays. I can see the old doctor straining at the bit, wishing he were still young enough to go running off to South America to investigate, but he must be content to spend these years resting on his well-deserved laurels. I am sure it is only a matter of time before we are informed of his election to the Academy.

PARIS. THURSDAY, MAY 28, 1903.
Marie is our daily visitor as she and Marcel work their way through the proofs. He has also consulted Robert d'Humières, who did the Kipling and has promised any help he can give. So kind, since he might consider Marcel a competitor of sorts.

Marthe is progressing well now that her bouts of morning sickness are past. She is starting to show just slightly, not so that anyone but a mother would recognize it, but I could not help but notice on Tuesday that she has surely relaxed her corsets somewhat.

PARIS. FRIDAY, MAY 29, 1903.
A disaster. Marcel close enough to tears it was embarrassing, according to his father, and Adrien himself was so angry I was afraid he would burst a blood vessel just telling me about it this morning. We have Antoine to thank for this. I have never really

trusted his taste for intrigue—such things so easily become malicious. Adrien says Marcel started it when they had not even finished their dessert by telling some story about Antoine singing an off-colour song—the trouble with these tales is that the men will never tell you exactly what transpired for fear of offending—and Antoine decided to take revenge by telling Adrien that last week Marcel tipped the waiter at the Café Wéber sixty francs. Adrien lost his temper—he still has not entirely recovered it this morning—and was made only angrier by Marcel's evident distress. In the end Adrien abandoned the dinner, leaving the boys to themselves. If only I had been there I might have been able to keep the warring factions apart. Certainly, there would have been no mention of the song in the first place if I had been presiding at the table, although on the whole I think the men are better left to their own devices on these occasions.

I imagine there will be no further friendship between the two of them. These young noblemen, with their mistresses and motor cars, they may all laugh at Marcel's passionate approach to friendships, but isolated as he is by his disease, it is no wonder his friends matter so much to him. I have calmed Adrien, who decided to go into the Faculty for distraction, and will try to soothe Marcel as soon as he wakes.

Just when I had thought we had achieved some peace. As Bossuet wrote: "It takes so many pieces to make human happiness, there's always one missing."

PARIS. FRIDAY, JUNE 12, 1903.
It was borne in on me yesterday what has happened. Marie has not had the heart to tell me—although I had noticed her visits were less frequent of late—and Marcel has hidden his decision from me. However, when he went out for dinner

with d'Albufera last night, I took the opportunity to look over the proofs and realized he has made no progress at all since the scene with his father. I suspect he has abandoned the translation, and I plan to confront him with my discovery as soon as possible.

Dick says Marthe hopes for a girl, as she feels a boy would be too much trouble.

PARIS. SUNDAY, JUNE 14, 1903.

Marcel will not listen to reason. It was as I suspected, and I pleaded with him to take up the task once more. I sympathize that the correcting is the most tedious part, but we are within sight of publication, and cannot abandon now. He is quite depressed about the whole thing, half guilty for hiding it from me, half angry that I discovered it myself, but says there are just too many mistakes to make it possible, and that every session Marie delicately corrects yet more, while he starts to feel that his own French eludes him. "At the end of three years' work, I speak no language, know nothing about art, and even less about Ruskin or Amiens," he told me. I had to quote his master back to him: "To know anything well involves a profound sense of ignorance."

PARIS. THURSDAY, JUNE 18, 1903.

Marie and I have hatched a plan to get Marcel back to work: she will compare the proofs to the English and mark with a red star any phrase she feels needs further attention from Marcel the translator, while I will read the French alone, and mark with a blue star any phrase I feel is less than felicitous and might want some work from Marcel the writer. This way, we hope to present the problem to Marcel in a more manageable way, simply as a list of decisions that need to be made.

She is such a large-hearted girl, and without meaning any disloyalty to Marthe who is displaying every patience at this difficult time, although she is somewhat prone to fragility, I often think what a delight of a daughter-in-law the "bluestocking" would make. (She rides a bicycle, no less. I do not remember that Marcel had told me that.)

EVIAN. FRIDAY, JULY 3, 1903.

After Marcel's letter yesterday, I spent the whole afternoon debating with the doctor what I should do. My immediate reaction was that I should book this morning's train back to Paris, help him locate the missing proofs—they must be in the apartment after all, he has not taken them out anywhere—and then he could accompany me back here, arriving around the time we had planned anyway. The de Noailles are in residence at Amphion now and have a dance planned for the eleventh, so he will want to be down here next week at the latest. Adrien would not hear of such a plan, and said I could not be rushing off to Paris to help him find his socks—the proofs are surely not trivial things, I countered—and must stay put. He even said he may have done it on purpose—or at least that these doctors of the mind whom he and Dick find so fascinating would argue that Marcel had misplaced the proofs because he really wishes to abandon the translation. Such nonsense, my doctors talk sometimes. I am sure the proofs will turn up under a pile of papers soon enough and have agreed I will not return to Paris just yet, but I feel for my little wolf, and sent a telegram this morning before breakfast.

Weather continues fine.

Evian. Saturday, July 4, 1903.

Telegram (a very expensive one!) from Marcel saying the heroic Marie saved the day, finding the proofs bundled up with the day's newspapers that Marcel had been reading, and hidden away in a corner of the room. He will be with us Monday evening, and will secrete his papers in a document case he has borrowed from his uncle Georges. I hope the journey does not overly tire him, and have consulted the hotel about the room in the far wing. Invitations from the de Noailles have arrived.

Paris. Wednesday, July 29, 1903.

Adrien returned late last night, quite disheartened by his trip to Illiers for the prize-giving. The old *curé* is no longer invited to the school under any circumstances, as if religion itself would pollute the boys, while Jules, all puffed up with his mayoralty, delivered a speech to these future citizens about the necessity of separating Church and State. Adrien was revolted but could not bring himself to remind his brother-in-law that the same *curé* saw Elisabeth through her long illness with devotion and patience. It is all very well for Jules Amiot to decide he has no immortal soul worth worrying about, but to deny others things of the spirit is unconscionable. Well, we have Emile Combes and his ghastly attacks on the Church to thank for this monstrosity. Adrien is just sick about it, for in his heart he now knows that Dreyfus is innocent, although he will never say it, yet he sees the triumphant Dreyfusards punishing the Church for a crime she never committed.

He was angry with Dick and Marcel last night, and told me,

"You see where their bloody Dreyfusism has brought us," but I begged him not to repeat the story to Marcel especially, who would be so upset. He always loved the old *curé*, who taught him his catechism, and Adrien knows the boys are as opposed as he is to Combes.

If these Philistines are victorious, there will be no more Chartres, no more Amiens. By the time they are finished separating Church from State, they will have ripped down the Crucifixions and Nativities from the walls of the Louvre, arguing no doubt that it is a state museum.

Marcel says all that is higher and larger in France resides in the Church, and surely believer and non-believer can agree. I think with such admiration of our Ruskin at these times. If a Jewess can transmit a Protestant's understanding of a Gothic arch or rose window, that these great achievements are an expression of our yearning for the spiritual, then surely the Catholic church can be kept safe from overzealous Dreyfusards.

PARIS. FRIDAY, SEPTEMBER 11, 1903.
I can barely put pen to paper my hand shakes so as I recall yesterday's events. I tremble, but not in fear nor sorrow. It is still anger that moves me. Regret may come, perhaps forgiveness too, but it will have to be later. Today, I am on fire. I am betrayed by his selfishness, his thoughtlessness, his single-minded pursuit of his own desires without care for what grief they may cause me. Yet even as I write these words I know that I love him, more than I should.

As always, I thought only of him. I began with his best interests at heart, I began with love to translate *Sesame and Lilies,* that he should have the rough draft available as soon as he was ready, that when critics heaped praise on our *Bible of*

Amiens he might reply easily, in the manner of a much-published author, that *Sesame* was now forthcoming. With all the quietness of August leaving me time at my disposal since our return from Evian, I had managed to finish a good twenty pages or so when I thought yesterday to offer him my efforts as a gift. I asked Eugénie to fetch me some nice piece of ribbon from her sewing basket, and she proffered a lovely pink one, which I used to tie the pages into a tidy bundle that I left on Marcel's desk so he would find it when he awoke.

He rose after lunch, and I was sitting here in the salon as I heard his footsteps approaching and anticipated his reaction with delight. But it was not with gratitude nor joy that he came to me. Furious instead, he accused me of meddling, of machinations, of setting him against work by thoughtless urging on. I have tired of this argument, which he has used against me before, especially in the matter of our triple reform, maintaining that my slightest encouragement towards an agreed-upon plan acts instead as new impediment to his resolve. So, I rejected it forcefully this time, said what nonsense it was to blame his tragic lack of will on others, that if he wasted time, it was his own fault, that I had done everything in my power to help him towards achievement. That I had watched as he indulged his sickness and dallied with his *cocottes,* that I had watched as he failed in his studies, abandoned the law, absented himself from the library, and now refused to finish the only task he had ever managed to push at least halfway to completion, that I had watched in sadness but had never given in to despair, that I had always found new remedies, new schedules, new strategies, new plans, and new hope, and this was how he treated me in return, with callousness and ingratitude. But my anger served only to inflame his and he yelled at me: "Now, I will never, ever touch *Sesame*. I abandon it," he cried before he rushed from the salon.

I was so impassioned now I could not leave it there and ran out after him, pursuing him to his room, where I found him with his back to me standing at the window, his body shaking, his head turned to look down towards the street, although I doubt he can have seen anything that passed before his eyes.

"How can you be so ungrateful?" I demanded, but he would not reply nor turn to face me. So, desperate somehow to capture his attention, to impress my sense of betrayal on him, I did as he once had, and thoughtlessly grabbed the first object that came to hand. It was that little wooden long-necked Virgin that Fénelon once gave him, surely thinking more to please Marcel's eye than his soul. And so, I raised my hand and flung it to the floor, hurling it some distance as though I knew it would take force to break the wood. Sure enough, its dainty head splintered from its graceful body with a sound that may have only been small but that seemed deafeningly loud in the midst of our silence. And then, I turned and ran from the room.

I wonder now whether we will ever be able to say that little figure was our wedding cup, its shattering the symbol of our unity.

CHRIST SUFFERS. His twisted body groans. His face collapses as though the very flesh were giving way. His eyelids flutter for he is now half unconscious from the pain. A strand of blood, deep red, almost black, trickles down his plaster cheek. Vicious nails skewer his sculpted flesh, pinning him to this gilt cross.

I come here often on my lunch break. I eat a sandwich in the library courtyard and then walk down the Rue de Richelieu, past the Palais Royal and turn the corner onto the Faubourg Saint-Honoré to the Eglise Saint-Roch and its gory Crucifixion. But today, I have wandered in here in the middle of the afternoon, seeking distraction—or even comfort, I suppose. I am somehow dispirited by what I have written. What I have translated, that is. I don't want you to think Mme. Proust did not love her son, that their life together was some kind of purgatory. As Marcel stalks out of a room crying "*J'abandonne!*" I don't want you to accuse me of overdramatizing their disagreements. Of course, I have built to a climax here, intentionally, dropping all those irrelevant diary entries through the month of August and hiding her work on *Sesame* from you until, in September, I have brought mother and son face to face. This is my doing.

But they did fight, however much they loved each other. The battles over the shattered Venetian vase, grandmother's lap desk, and Fénelon's top hat are a matter of historical fact. And Proust did abandon his translation of *Sesame and Lilies* for some months in 1903. It's only the truth that I am translating, and I sit here in one of the pews at Saint-Roch thinking a bit about the truth and our duty to it.

This is not the most beautiful church in Paris, nor even in the neighbourhood, but it feels familiar to me. Saint-Roch was established by Louis XIV in 1653 but it was fifty years before the money was raised to build the church, so it is designed in the baroque style of the eighteenth-century and packed with the cloying art of the Counter-Reformation. The crucifix is by Lemoyne. It reminds me of home, I guess. The churches of Quebec are not medieval cathedrals, after all, but eighteenth- and nineteenth-century buildings erected by the same aggressive Jesuit faith that drove Saint-Roch, and filled with extravagant religious art in the French style. Indeed, the Christ at Saint-Roch is the same one who presided over my teenage years.

Childhood belonged to the tender figure of *Bébé Jésus*, the little bean in the manger in the Christmastime crèche, but adolescence was the territory of the bleeding Christ. He is made of white plaster that the artist has not coloured but rather covered in a translucent glaze, giving his skin a deathly glow. His body is cruelly emaciated as though his Roman captors had starved him before the Jewish crowd pronounced his sentence and the centurions nailed him up. His eyes are almost shut, his cheeks are sunken, his face is gaunt. A dribble of blood flows down his forehead from beneath his crown of thorns. Under his hallucinatory gaze, Father Ambrose preached a doctrine of suffering and guilt, sacrifice and debt, original sin and perpetual repayment, from the pulpit of Notre-Dame-des-Douleurs on Dorchester Boulevard in Montreal.

In the midst of my university years, I suddenly saw him one day with an art student's eye, noted the exaggeration of proportions, the hysteria in the colouring, the sentimentality in the sculpting of the face. He is too manipulative a figure to be considered great art, yet his suffering holds sway. He looks like a corpse in a death camp, a starving Ethiopian, an addict on the street. I still long to reach up and touch his face, to make it better, to heal the son and comfort the mother, to stop history in its tracks. If only I had been there, if only I could help . . .

I remember the creed, can still say it now. I believe in God Almighty, maker of heaven and earth . . . and in his only begotten son Jesus Christ, who was born of the Virgin Mary, suffered under Pontius Pilate, was crucified, died and was buried . . . On the third day, he rose again to ascend to heaven where He sits on the right hand of God and will come to judge the quick and the dead.

But how will He judge us, collectively or individually? I remember once when I was only seven or eight years old, our ferocious French teacher finally lost his temper with our chattering and set us the task of writing lines—*Je ne parlerai pas en classe;* I will not talk in class—hundreds and hundreds of times. Three of my classmates were off in the school library working on a project and, returning to the room to find it silently and sullenly engaged in line writing, were forgiven the task because they had not been present for the talking. "I wasn't talking, either," I grumbled under my breath as this purgatory dragged on and on, the task unfinished at the end of the hour and taken home to be completed that evening. Does God know who was in the room when they loaded people into cattle cars? If He can be counted on to understand that you and I were not yet born when they fired up the ovens, will He forgive us for standing by as flickering images on the television screen showed us Ethiopia, Bosnia, or Rwanda? I wanted to mend one life, to save one soul.

At Saint-Roch, I walk back down the nave. I pass a small side chapel dedicated to victims of Nazism. It lists each camp by name and reports the numbers who died there—Auschwitz 140,000 martyrs, Buchenwald 150,000 martyrs, Dachau 100,000 martyrs . . . These seem large numbers, too large to merely represent the French priests and nuns who resisted. Perhaps they measure all the European clergy who were killed. Or perhaps all the French citizens, including Jews and Christians, believers and atheists, Catholics and Communists, resisters and deportees. What distinction is being made here? Who is being remembered and who not?

The confessional booths stand near the entrance, dark little wooden bipartite houses that are so discreet they almost disappear into the panelling behind them. In a delicate slot at about waist-level, a small white sign bearing the priest's name has been slid out from behind its wooden cover, indicating that confessions will be heard. I hesitate here.

Forgive me father for I have sinned. It has been five years since my last confession.

But what am I to confess? The sin of patience? of blindness? of having loved too much? The sin of being chaste when I should have been lustful, of lusting when I should have simply loved, of waiting when I should have spoken, of speaking when I should have touched, of betraying when I was betrayed.

You cannot approach the communion rail unless you have made confession, yet sometimes, on a Sunday in Montreal, I still go to mass with my mother. We attend Notre-Dame-des-Douleurs, a gracious remanent of the nineteenth century left amongst the modern office blocks on that boulevard my mother persists in calling Dorchester although it was renamed René Lévesque several years ago. I don't think my mother actually believes in God; she belongs to the hedge-your-bets school of churchgoers. This is the downtown francophone parish my father first brought us to when we moved to Montreal. He rarely bothers to join us any more except at Easter and Christmas, but we have stuck with Notre-Dame and keep worshipping in his language. Nervously, my mother attends the mass, just in case there is life after death and divine retribution, although on the whole she finds it hard to think there is.

I believe. I eye the bleeding Christ above the altar and make my prayers to God. At least, I must have believed, for on the night of the wedding reception and in the long months afterwards I often found myself speaking to him, invoking his name the same way I still wish on stars.

"First star I see tonight, wish I may, wish I might . . . Please, God, please . . ."

Please, do the impossible, make rivers run upstream, turn the world on its head.

But I knew my prayers wouldn't be answered, for if there is a God, He has surely created two kinds of people, those who love what is different and those who love what is the same. And He will not change the divine scheme of things for a tearful girl in a crumpled pink party dress.

At Saint-Roch, I make my decision. I turn towards the confessional booth and quietly open its little door, preparing myself to tell a story.

S ARAH SEGAL TURNED from the pot she was stirring on the stove and greeted the sound of Maxime coming through the front door. She called out to him but got no reply, only the thud and scuffle of his running shoes on the stairs and the muffled bang of his bedroom door. A few minutes later, excruciatingly loud rock music sounded through the house.

She waited for a while to see if he would turn the volume down, but nothing happened. After enduring a few minutes, she climbed the stairs with deliberation and knocked quietly on his door. There was no answer. Refusing to be reduced to pounding and yelling, she turned the handle and pushed the door away from her. There was some frantic movement from the corner of the room, and by the time she was inside, Maxime was lying there on his bed with the blankets gathered around his midriff, looking flustered.

She pointed at the stereo. He reached across without shifting his lower body and snapped the music off altogether.

"Did you have a good day?" She spoke to him in French, but he replied in English, as he increasingly tended to do.

"Yeah, fine."

"You can listen to it, we just do not need to blast the whole neighbourhood. Why do you not use the headphones your father gave you?"

"Yeah, well, no."

"Yeah, well, no," she mimicked his mumbled English, and continued with dignity in her own language. "What does that mean? Is there something wrong with headphones? With a little courtesy for the neighbours, if not for one's old mother?"

"Sorry, I'll keep it down," he replied.

"*En français, s'il-te-plaît,*" she spoke sharply, letting her annoyance get the better of her.

"*Okay. Je diminuerai la volume.*"

Maxime silently willed her to leave, so he could get back to the matter at hand, but his concentration seemed to have the reverse effect, for she walked further into the room, sat down on the end of the bed, and smiled at him as if to begin again on a more amiable note.

Then, noticing the cover of what looked like a book or a magazine poking above the crumbled covers, she reached laughingly towards him: "What have you got under there?"

"Go away and leave me alone." The words exploded from him in anger and exasperation.

"You're always bugging me," he added sulkily as if to justify his tone, yet this addendum only served to further wound his mother. Sarah rose, turned, reminded him over her shoulder that dinner would be at seven, and left the room without looking back.

In the kitchen, moving with delicate dignity as her anger made her acutely aware of her own presence, she started to prepare the evening meal. She had already made a crème caramel for dessert: the small porcelain pots holding the velvet custard drenched in a syrup of burnt sugar had come out of the smaller oven an hour ago and were sitting cooling on a metal rack on the countertop. She gave the vegetable soup, slowly simmering at the back of the stove, another stir, and turned to the massive refrigerator to take out a dish of whitefish left over from the night before. She skinned and boned the fish, and then began to feed the flesh into the food processor.

Daniel and Maxime both liked dessert—cheesecake, puddings, custards, pastries—but father and son were locked in a permanent debate about whether or not it was worth forgoing meat as their main course and suffering fish, cheese, or vegetables, so that they could eat dairy at the end of the meal.

It was Daniel who had insisted that Sarah keep kosher. In the world she left before her twelfth birthday, the dietary laws had been reduced to a mere heirloom or two—a rich egg bread baked on special occasions, a long-simmered stew served on a winter Saturday—and a reluctance to cook with pork. On Gladstone Avenue, Rachel had taught her the names of these dishes, the challah and the cholent. She had fed her bagels, lox, kugel, and kreplach, and at Passover, both introduced her to the symbolic foods like the matzo and the charoseth and taught her the recipes for the gefilte fish and the chicken soup that would grace their table on the first night, the day after Sam had gleefully paraded through the house with his candle and his feather searching for the last crumbs of leavened bread that would have to be swept away before the holiday could begin.

But it was not until Sarah met Daniel, and entered Clara's large kitchen, that she first began to understand that cooking was some greater obligation than the preparation of food. Daniel had been raised with a host of prescriptions and prohibitions, and if he had fallen away from observance during his medical school days, struggling to find anything eatable let alone kosher from the sparse offerings at the hospital cafeterias, on marriage he wanted only to return to the patterns of his childhood. As they began their life together in a small apartment near his office, Sarah had struggled to understand and observe in her tiny kitchen. But once safely installed in the split-level house in North Toronto to which she and

Daniel moved as soon as his practice was well enough established, she turned her attention more resolutely to the task.

In the big cupboards that still smelt of sawdust, she carefully stored the two separate sets of dishes that had been their wedding gift from his parents, one the unadorned white porcelain that was the smartest, most modern china any newlywed could wish for, the other a more classic pattern, its ivory surface speckled with delicate flowers and its rim lined in gold. She had separate sections in the big new refrigerator for milk and meat, two sets of tea towels and dish-clothes, one blue, the other red, to remind her never to wipe the chicken pot with a cloth that had washed the butter dish, never to rub the pan she used for cheese sauces with the towel that had polished the steak knives.

As Daniel's practice flourished, as lungs were sounded, blood pressure measured, boils lanced, and babies born, their increasing affluence was reflected in the kitchen. A plumber was brought in to install a second sink and a dishwasher for the meat dishes. A few years later, Daniel decreed the room itself should be enlarged, extending the house out into the backyard. By the time Maxime was a teenager, there were two dishwashers and two sets of double sinks, while the cupboards were carefully categorized as *milchik, flayshig* and *pareveh*, the neutral foods, neither milk nor meat. The rabbis argued that the impenetrable surface of glass was exempt from these distinctions, but Sarah carefully categorized these vessels too, hanging the stemware upside down in a wooden rack suspended from the kitchen ceiling to which she could happily turn to reach a wineglass for a weekend aperitif while placing the tumblers for Maxime's daily milk in the small cupboard over one sink.

At first, Sarah had dutifully copied the cooking that Rachel taught her, and which reflected Daniel's tastes: long-stewed meats, heavy soups, pickled vegetables, smoked fish, fruit compotes, latkes, and blintzes. She attempted to improve on these recipes, priding herself on a gefilte fish that was more tender and flavourful than the dry, overly sweet version in which Clara specialized, or carefully reducing the fat in her soups so that the surface did not glisten with the disgusting sheen that made Sam smack his lips and declare, "Good soup." Soon, she began to experiment, inspired by the Gentile housewives and their recipe swaps, by the richly illustrated cookbooks she found at the library and by the smooth-talking hosts on the television cooking shows who sipped wine while they tossed together such outrageously *trayf* combinations as a chicken Kiev bursting with butter or a meat-sauce lasagna topped with melting cheese.

Somewhere on her tongue, in the centre but towards the back, Sarah retained the memory of a good bloody beefsteak, and as Toronto abandoned the overcooked cuisine of its colonial past and French restaurants sprouted along the uptown avenues, she increasingly recalled the delights of her childhood. Meat quickly seared and doused in wine, endives wrapped in ham and smothered in a cheese sauce, a mullet bought at the fishmonger's that very morning and poached to a perfect softness, a sharp goat cheese smeared on crisp bread: these were the dishes that her father had sighed over as they came to his table for a long Sunday lunch. And so it was that Sarah set out to recreate classic French cuisine within the confines of the kosher kitchen.

To some, the project might have seemed counterintuitive—what is the glory of French cooking if not meat served in a cream sauce?—but Sarah did not dwell on the whys but rather the hows of the task. If she were to eliminate the cream and butter, relying instead on a roux made of flour, egg yolks, and fat trimmed from the meat, it was possible to make a *blanquette de veau* that would have brought a smile to the lips of the most demanding bourgeois housekeeper of the Sixteenth Arrondissement. She already knew how to render chicken fat to an intensely flavoured schmaltz. If she were to cook the steak from the kosher butcher and the potatoes in the schmaltz, she could create a *bifteck-frites* as rich as that fried up in butter in the galley of a Paris bistro. The recipe was perfected yet further when, overhearing a conversation between her sisters-in-law, she realized that if she bought a cut she could broil, allowing the juices to run freely as it cooked, she was permitted to eliminate the soaking in salt water, the required *kashering* that, she always suspected, killed all flavour as it drained the blood. She made many experiments developing a vegetable stock, for she had come to realize that if she were to avoid a chicken broth when cooking leaks and potatoes, sorrel, Brussels sprouts, fennel or carrots, it was possible to make soups into which she could stir the thickest cream. On the other hand, if she were to eliminate the cream from the recipes for pâté and venture down to Spadina to pick up some chopped liver and spicy kosher salami, she could put a full plate of charcuterie on her table. If she were to encourage Mr. Lombardi to stock a few more exotic mushrooms than the bland white buttons on offer at the supermarket, she could, with the addition of some dried specimens that came in expensive little packages, collect enough varieties to fry up a garlic-soaked appetizer that might compensate for the forbidden snails and mussels so lovingly described in the oversized encyclopedia of French cuisine that sat beside the kosher cookbooks on her kitchen shelf.

She was also a favourite customer at the fish shop a few doors down from the greengrocer, and if the fishmonger did not understand why she politely refused all his beautiful shellfish, he worked to find for her fresher and finer catches than the slabs of cod and bluefish that might satisfy most of his clientele.

Fish was crucial to Sarah's project, for as long as she could coax Daniel and Maxime to eat it, cooking up the flour-dredged sole *meunière* in sparkling butter while ignoring their demands for meat, she could serve not only an orange crème or chocolate éclair for dessert but also cheese at the end of the meal, picking up a melting piece of the increasingly acceptable Bries available at a new gourmet shop that had opened over on Mount Pleasant. She came to recognize that quenelles, with their delicate flavour and airy texture, were a kind of gefilte fish: you blend together the fish with eggs into a smooth paste that is formed into little sausage-like shapes and poached in boiling water. In France, the dish is served in a lobster sauce, but Sarah discovered that a creamy tomato sauce or one made with smoked salmon was equally acceptable. And the day she realized that a mousse made with pure bitter chocolate and egg whites contained no milk, and so was the perfect dessert to follow a roast, steak, or stew, marked a little victory.

Other women might wonder at her; they might, seeing her popping into the corner store on Saturday morning or passing Daniel raking the leaves the same afternoon, point out that the Segals were not particularly observant in other areas of life. Rachel might consider the expanding kitchen in North Toronto as an unnecessary fuss created under the influence of Sarah's ostentatious in-laws; Clara might suspect that her own cooking was being upstaged by her daughter-in-law. Daniel might scratch his head sometimes, only to conclude that anything that kept his wife happily occupied was a gift. But Sarah did not care what others might think and pursued her project further. Assiduously working butter into the flour, she spent Fridays making croissants that dissolved in the mouth on Saturday morning before *shul*. The kosher kitchen became for Sarah a place of reconciliation.

At six-thirty, hunger winning out over injured feelings, Maxime appeared and asked, in French, "What's for dinner?"

"I'm making quenelles. And there's crème caramel for dessert."

"What's that?"

"You remember, those little fish things, in sauce."

"Fish, again." Maxime lapsed querulously back into English.

It was increasingly this way between them. She sensed that he resented her very presence, not only in the outside world but even within the house. He chafed against any of the more pronounced manifestations of her character, her history, her religion, her cooking, and most of all her language, the phrases she had so lovingly imparted to him since babyhood. They had spoken French together as though it were their own private dialect so that he was amazed, on entering high school and encountering for the first time a teacher for whom this was also a mother tongue, that these precious syllables could be spoken with fluency anywhere outside his own home. Yet now he refused them: once introduced to the larger world, Maxime could not return to the microcosm of his mother's culture with the same ease, and adolescence sat awkwardly upon him.

Whether it embarrassed her son or not, Sarah made no apologies for who she was, indeed she made few efforts to fit into the larger Anglo-Saxon environment in which she lived. As she grew into middle age, her accent, barely perceptible as a young woman, seemed to strengthen rather than diminish, so that she could see Maxime shrinking when she spoke to strangers, pestering a repairman about his muddy boots or questioning the department-store attendant as to the location of boys' underwear, in tones that increasingly hinted at the outrageous Parisians, the Mimis and Maurices, from the old movies his father so loved. And to Maxime himself, she spoke in French all the time as she had always done: no matter how much he might mumble or reply in English, he could not impart to her, when it came to their conversations, any sense of awkwardness in her own language nor ease in the other. He had heard his father speak Sarah's language only on one or two uncomfortable occasions, but Daniel understood it perfectly well, for she often extended her French conversation with Maxime out towards her husband, so that much of the talk in their home was in her language and under her control.

No more did Sarah hide her history. To Daniel's earnest yet abstract lectures on the events of the war, she added her own story, delivered with less emotion because it contained more pain, uncovered cautiously lest it explode yet resolutely that it never be a secret from her son. And here too, he seemed ashamed to accept the heritage she tried to offer him without shame, and if he was willing to define himself within the rich and cultivated circles of North American Jews, he did not see himself as a grandchild of the Shoah.

To him, growing up without privation of any kind, Rachel and Sam and all the smells of the house on Gladstone Avenue offered a pleasant exoticism easier to grasp and to cherish than the confused image in his mind's eye, inspired by old photographs and movies, of a glamorous young Parisian wife boarding a train that eventually led to Auschwitz, with her small black hat on a cocky angle and the seams on her stockings running in two perfectly straight lines down the backs of her legs. The memory of his grandfather, the food exploding his shrunken belly, he put from his mind.

"More?" Sarah picked up the serving spoon and reached into the dish of quenelles as she turned to Daniel, speaking in English. He was still finishing the last mouthful of his first helping, and indicated with a hand that he was satisfied.

"Maxime?" She turned to her son.

"No thanks."

"Oh, you are not going to leave me with leftovers, are you? Maxime, there are just two left." She had switched to French.

"No. Can we have dessert now."

"Maxime!"

Daniel then interrupted in English, maintaining the bilingual rally that often marked their dinner-table conversation: "Well, maybe I'll change my mind. Just one more. They are so good."

Sarah spooned a single quenelle onto her husband's plate before scrapping the very end of the dish onto her own, leaving the casserole empty but for a few creamy pink smears of tomato sauce.

"I went over to the building on Yonge today . . ." The landlord in Daniel's medical building was raising the rent, and he was investigating alternatives. "You know, it's nice. There's a big office and good reception area, and they've proper soundproofing between the reception and the surgery. But he wants over a thousand . . ."

"Can we have dessert now?"

Daniel stopped speaking, and looked across at his son with some annoyance: "What is eating you? Can't we have a normal family dinner any more?"

"It's all right, dear. We'll talk about it with coffee." Sarah rose and cleared their plates. "I'll get the salad." She considered a green salad a poor excuse for an appetizer and always served it at the end of the meal, in the French fashion. But in a concession to Maxime's impatience, she also picked up a tray on which she had placed the three little pots containing their dessert and held it in one hand while clutching the wooden salad bowl in the other and pushing back through the swinging door that separated kitchen from dining room with the weight of her body. She put the dessert on the sideboard, so when they had finished the salad she had barely to rise from her chair to reach it.

Now that she thought of it, the crème caramel was too rich a dessert to follow the quenelles, both saucy in texture. She would have been better to serve a fruit salad or apple compote, with a little whipped cream since it was permitted after the fish, or perhaps the featherweight anise cake, rich in eggs and butter, delicately flavoured with licorice, which was a speciality of hers she had not made in months. At least the green salad had provided an acidic break between creamy courses, but she resolved to consider these issues more carefully in the future. Perhaps she overestimated her audience's powers of discrimination, for Daniel and Maxime now dug their spoons into the crème caramel without hesitation, but these niceties did matter to the cook herself.

Maxime had hurriedly eaten about three mouthfuls of the custard, barely registering its velvet smoothness and soft vanilla flavour, when his mother leaned towards him and inquired coyly, "Find anything?"

Just as she said the words, he spied in the pale-yellow cream the minuscule red veins of colour, like threads of saffron in a dish of rice. Prodding with his spoon, he unearthed a maraschino cherry.

"A surprise," he said, in a dull voice in which sarcasm hovered just underneath his evident boredom.

"A surprise," laughed Sarah and, leaning forward, ruffled Maxime's long black curls with her hand.

This was a treat she had prepared for him since childhood, when he had giggled with fresh delight every time his spoon found the colourful cherry. She had discovered the tall bottle of maraschino cherries on one of the lengthy trips to the supermarket during which she scrutinized the labels on any number of cans and jars. She wondered to what use she could put this permissible treat, and perhaps unconsciously recalling from her prolonged reading of cookbooks the English habit of telling guests' fortunes with silver charms secreted in the Christmas pudding or the French custom of hiding a bean in the flat almond cake served at Epiphany to determine which child shall be king for the day, she placed a single red cherry at the bottom of Maxime's custard.

"A surprise, a surprise!" Sarah felt her great love for her son running in her veins, rising up towards her heart and her head, and she smiled at this sulky seventeen-year-old with such affection that he could no longer maintain his disdainful pose and he grinned back at her happy face.

When they had finished the meal, Maxime ran upstairs while his parents retreated to the kitchen where Daniel loaded the dishwasher and Sarah prepared coffee. This was her favourite time with her husband, the moment at the end of the day when they would sit in the living room together, carefully sip their coffee, and weigh their joys and their cares; measure their achievements and make their decisions—should Daniel move his office?; would they finally visit Israel next year?—or, if lacking topics for conversation, turn to books or a favourite television program for entertainment. They were emerging from the kitchen, both carrying mugs of coffee, when Maxime bounded back down the stairs and headed for the front door. Sarah carefully placed her mug on a side table and darted towards the front hall.

"Where are you going?"

"Out."

"What do you mean 'out'?"

"Just going out for a bit. I won't be late."

"What about your homework."

"I did it."

"All of it?"

"Yes, all of it. I only had a chemistry lab. I worked on it with Roger at lunch and then I wrote up the results before dinner."

"That school. Your teachers do not give you enough homework. Exams are next month and you should be working hard now, at this time of year. How will be ready for university if you do not learn to work? On a Tuesday night, you should have studying to do. I should speak to Mr. Saunders."

"Okay. I am off now. Bye."

"No. You are not going until you tell me where."

"Ma . . ."

"We still have a right to know where you are going. You could be out doing drugs or . . ."

"Ma, I am not doing drugs." Maxime's tone was one of infinite patience finally worn down by persistent stupidity. "I am just going down to the park to meet Roger for a bit."

"The park! You know there are all those druggies now in the park, and the police patrol there all the time. They might stop you, you never know with the police, they always distrust young men, and then who knows . . ."

"Yeah, yeah, I am going to get arrested by the Gestapo."

She did not reply. In the silence, mother and son savoured their respective hurts. Daniel, who had been sitting in the living room listening to this exchange in French but not intervening, now quickly rose from his chair to join them.

"Max. Home at ten. No later. Say hi to Roger for us."

"Thanks." Max hurried out, banging the door in his haste to be gone.

"I don't know what we are going to do." As they returned to their chairs, Sarah was grudgingly acknowledging defeat by grumbling about it first. "You know, he is not going to get into U of T if he keeps this up. He doesn't have proper study habits. It may not make any difference now, but next year is Grade 13. He has to get good marks next year. He is going to wind up at Western or Windsor or somewhere, and from there he will be lucky to get into any medical school, let alone U of T. I know they favour students from their own science programs. It makes sense. And if he doesn't go to med school here, we will never see him. He will be off for years, miles away . . ." Sarah, who had been gesticulating with increasing fervour as she built her complaint into real fear, now let her hands fall to her sides in hopelessness as her words trailed off.

"Sarah." Daniel's tone was gentle. "You worry too much."

It was true; she knew it. As Maxime became a Toronto teenager, making friendships with the English-speaking Jews and Gentiles who peopled his school life, she often felt annoyed at him for being someone different and apart from her, so distant from the cherished baby who had seemed to share her soul. His integration was inevitable, but she felt it as a betrayal nonetheless. There was, however, one fault that she acknowledged as her own: Yes, she worried too much.

When Maxime was a baby, these were common enough fears—that his temperature was too high one day or his weight too low for a month, that his acceptance of solid food seemed belated, that it was past time for him to speak, that his winter cold was dragging on, or that his tiny feet were not warm enough. But as Maxime grew from babyhood to childhood, and from childhood to adolescence, the source of Sarah's anxieties was not some external inadequacy over which she could exercise, at the very least, vigilance if not outright control. As he took a public bus to high school, ventured downtown on a weekday after classes, insisted that he be allowed to attend a party on a Saturday night, and eagerly anticipated the fast-approaching day when he would learn to drive, her worries were his actual creations, new hurts he forced upon her. She knew she should not rise to the bait, and yet, inevitably, she did. She would watch him, on a February morning, getting ready to go out the door to school without a hat on his head and only thin gloves on his hands. She would be unable to bite her tongue, knowing full well what annoyance and petulance would greet her remarks, and she would persist: "It's twenty below this morning. You must wear a hat."

"*Non, maman. Ça va.* It's okay."

She would pull a wool cap down from the coat rack, and reaching up to him—for she had always been a small woman and he, although short, was already several inches taller than her—try to secure it over his head. He would rip it off with a vengeance, fling it at her, and run out the door.

"Maxime, you will freeze," she would call after him, and on some occasions would even run outside, still wearing her dressing gown, in an attempt to make him, at very least, carry the hat in his pocket. Two days later, when he was fighting a head cold but refusing to stay home in bed, she could not remain silent, and would nag and pester on the subject.

"If you would dress properly for the cold, this would never have happened."

Well, this was the way with many mothers, indeed every shivering teenager in a scant jacket and blue jeans has been told on his way out the door to dress more warmly, and if he hasn't, the world should pity him that no one cares enough to tell him how to live his life. Yet Sarah's anxieties, her nagging, her mothering, went far beyond the usual. Her fears were legion, ranging wildly and unpredictably from the insignificant to the cataclysmic: what if Daniel was killed flying home from a conference?; what if Maxime failed his exams?; what if the gas leaked?; what if the pipes froze?; what if the neighbour's dog, who could be seen digging up bones in his own backyard, burrowed under the fence and disturbed Sarah's newly planted tulip bulbs?; what if that car speeding towards them had failed to see the red light, did not brake in time, and struck Maxime, leaving him crippled for life?; what if Daniel cut his finger with that newly sharpened knife?; what if that tea towel brushed against the stove and caught fire?; what if that cheque had got lost in the mail?; what if Daniel put on the freshly ironed shirt before its newly smoothed surface had been given proper time to set?; what if dinner burnt?; what if they all died?

The worst of it was, Sarah could not keep silent. She knew that her fears were often ungrounded, and that their articulation was no great form of social intercourse, that she annoyed her husband and embarrassed her son, putting them from her as much as she tried to bind them to her, the very existence of the only two people she truly loved paining her day after day. Yet still she spoke, as if to speak was to arm against.

Patient, calm, and reassuring, Daniel was accepting of this aspect of his wife's character—accepting, or perhaps quietly resigned after twenty-seven years of marriage. He had done what he could to make her happy, provided a good home and removed any possible source of anxiety that he could imagine. He had believed first that the resolution of her business affairs in France would somehow close her grief and then later assumed that the birth of a child would bring her placidity, but he slowly gave up those expectations, daily letting another little fragment of hope slip away as he watched her mothering become as fearful and all-consuming as her domestic cares had proved before Maxime's birth. If this continually heightened state was not a particularly happy way of being, it no longer seemed to him that it was a particularly unhappy one either. This was how they lived, that was all.

He was not a man who often discussed his emotions, nor those of others, but he was not stupid nor unobservant. He sensed that Sarah continually rehearsed the potential hurts and disasters of the future, as though she might guard against them, because she could do nothing to rectify the catastrophe of the past. But he could not understand how exactly history gnawed at Sarah, for Sarah herself would have been hard put to describe it. It was not, as a woman of 35, of 40, or now of 52, that her grief sat fresh upon her. Her parents were faint memories now, with little place in the forefront of her consciousness, compared to the shopping list that she was working her way through as pushed her cart along the aisles of the grocery store, the tempting pictures in the travel brochure featuring the location of Daniel's next medical conference, the difficult fact of Sam's failing health, or the necessity of attending Maxime's school play the following week. It was just that, even as she fulfilled her role as wife, mother, and adopted daughter, she maintained a certain distance from them, as though displaced from the very reality of her own life. It was only through frantic worry that these things became real for her. Indeed she secretly wondered to herself at times if her anxiety was only an act, a facade she adopted to convince those around her that she felt, belonged, and cared.

She struggled continually to inhabit the present, the place where Maxime, still a child, dwelt effortlessly. He knew that his very existence as anything more than a carefully cossetted baby could pain his mother beyond bearing, but was too young to understand why. Forty years seems to a teenager an unimaginable eternity, more than twice his own lifespan, and the notion that the truncated lives of his unseen grandparents shaped his mother's current existence did not occur to Maxime. To him, his mother appeared only alarmist and ineffectual, and where his father had learned to live quietly with Sarah, the son raged and chafed, uncomprehending and unsympathetic. In the house in North Toronto, Daniel would attempt to fix and rationalize while Maxime would sulk and hide.

One year and one summer after the spring night on which his mother had served quenelles and crème caramel, he managed to escape. On a baking hot Tuesday in early September 1984, he waved goodbye to his parents and watched them climb into their car and drive away. He mentally brushed aside a clinging tendril of emotion, climbed back up the steps on which he was standing, and returned to the small room in which he and Daniel had, just the day before, deposited two overstuffed suitcases, a few cardboard boxes of books, and one full of the coffee mugs, cutlery, and tea towels that Sarah had carefully packed for him. It was time to unpack and settle into the first home of his own, these sparsely furnished quarters in a students' residence with space only for a bed, a desk, a bookcase, and an armchair.

Aside from his immediate, mundane needs to buy a few posters for his walls, rent a bar fridge for the room, and register for classes, the way ahead looked hazy but exciting. If, for Sarah, the future was a place that could be imagined with alarming acuity and required strict planning if it were to prove any better than the past and the present, then for the teenage Maxime, unburdened by the past and alternately overjoyed and deeply frustrated by the present, the future had always seemed a vague but deeply desirable place. He still sensed that it posed as-yet-undefinable problems that would require solutions, but since he could not yet foresee what they were, he remained largely unworried and saw instead bright visions of independence and belonging, achievement, and respite. Here he was then, catapulted into his own adulthood by means of the family sedan. He let the air out of his lungs with an audible whoosh, turned to the first box, and ripped open the lid.

His plan had been a clever one, almost devious, and suggested that, if he did not sympathize with his mother, he certainly understood her well enough to see his way around her. In his Grade 13 year, he had applied not only to the University of Toronto but also here, to McGill, in Montreal, five hundred kilometres east of his parents' home. When he was accepted, there was no arguing with it. McGill's undergraduate programs were as respected as Toronto's; its medical school was particularly venerable, historic home to doctors Osler, Penfield, and Bethune. And if the university itself were anglophone, the city was bilingual: in Montreal, Maxime would speak French. It was to his mother's linguistic pride that he ultimately made his appeal for freedom.

Sarah was torn. At first, she was frantic about the idea of his departure, secretly afraid that geographic distance would make permanent the widening gap between them, openly expressing one objection after another, citing the expense, the risk of loneliness, the dangers of bad companionship, the shortage of clean laundry, and most of all, the certainty of bad cooking.

But in the end, he went with her blessing. She recognized that if her son was to find an enduring place for her language in his head and in his heart, he must discover for himself a francophone world beyond their home. He had grown reluctant to speak French, shrugging off the language with a few mumbled words before he switched to English, and when she did force more lengthy conversation upon him, she noticed that his grammar was slipping. He no longer used the subjunctive in which she had so carefully coached him, enlarging on his high school French lessons with the help of a thin red-covered book of verb conjugations that provided her with concrete evidence of the spellings and usages that she knew by instinct alone but with complete accuracy, despite the long distance that separated her from those who had taught her a mother tongue. On occasion, Maxime could also be heard to attribute a masculine article to a feminine noun or vice versa, a mistake that surprised and appalled her, for she had believed that whatever agonies it might cause an anglophone, the correct gender of a word would always remain second nature to the native speaker. His mistakes convinced her that he might abandon her language altogether if it proved so difficult to maintain. In Montreal, he would find adult uses for the words of childhood, and she hoped that once he had completed his studies and returned home, the joy they might share in talking together could repair their weakened bond.

So, she was willing to view Montreal as a useful place for her son, although in her heart she disliked the city. It had failed her. On her first visit, pushing the eighteen-month-old Maxime around Expo 67 in a sturdy red stroller provided at the entrance gate, she felt herself an outsider not only in the cheery hubbub and colourful optimism of the world fair held on an island specially constructed in the St. Lawrence for the occasion, but also on the original island, the real city beyond the carnival. With its ebullient French speakers growing more confident by the day, its broad modern avenues and picturesque old churches, its three-storey limestone apartment buildings and their curving exterior staircases of brightly painted wrought iron, Montreal was the city they called the Paris of North America. Friends in Toronto were surprised that Sarah had yet to visit and were convinced she would love the place.

Perhaps if she had delayed suggesting such a trip to Daniel until the summer in which the entire world descended on Montreal and it seemed impossible not to go, it was because she secretly wanted something from the city, yet simultaneously knew she could not have it. With a longing so suppressed it was almost unconscious, she hoped Montreal would satisfy her by containing within its streets both her losses and her present, that it would be precisely that for her, a Paris of North America. Yet such comfort also seemed improbable, so she postponed the moment when reality must surely disappoint her.

As she and Daniel bundled themselves and the baby into a cab at the end of a long day's sightseeing; as they parked Maxime with the hotel daycare; as they picked over the fish and vegetable dishes on the menu of a French restaurant that came highly recommended, she spoke eagerly to the driver, the babysitter, and the waiter in her own language. But she found their colourful vocabulary difficult to parse and their thick accents impenetrable in places. And in the cab driver's eyes reflected back at her in his rear-view mirror, in the babysitter's little laugh, or the waiter's raised brow, she thought she detected a note of disdain, as though she somehow insulted them with her speech. In the end, they all just seemed happier to speak to Daniel in English. Perhaps they had sensed that she willed them to be something they were not and would have none of it. Here, she saw the streets, the architecture, and the language itself as one sees one's own face reflected in the bulbous surface of the bathtub taps, experiencing the city as a horrible distortion of the familiar.

Looking back with a twisted smile, Montreal refused her longings.

Well, it was only right. Why should Montreal be other than itself? This game of comparisons was one they played in Toronto. This restaurant was better than New York, that play as good as any you might see in London. The Windy City seemed just like home; Montreal recalled the City of Lights. If you ever visited Hong Kong, why, you'd think you were in Vancouver. Normally, Sarah knew better than to enter into these parallelisms. Like the alcoholic who will never appear to be drunk, she knew that for her to make comparisons was to betray dissatisfaction, even to feed it. No, Montreal was not Paris, and she found it best, on the whole, not to visit there, but to await Maxime's return to Toronto.

That was what she was doing one Sunday afternoon in early May at the end of his first year in medical school when she realized that she had run out of milk. She turned from the fridge, opened the door that led to the basement, and called down the stairs.

"I'm just going out for a minute. There's no milk left."

Daniel raised his head from an as-yet-unsuccessful attempt to repair the coffee grinder, which had emitted a painful squeaking sound when asked to perform its job that morning and then halted altogether.

"Take the car. Max will be home any minute."

"Oh, no. I can't be bothered. It's nice out."

So, she walked, happily covering the few blocks between the house and Yonge Street, where she turned northwards. There, she passed the new Thai restaurant that had opened last fall—God only knew how they had made it through the winter—and the shoe repair shop where the faded advertisements for Cat's Paw soles had remained unchanged in all the years she and Daniel had lived in the neighbourhood. The next building housed a small florist's shop, and the sidewalk outside was covered with red buckets full of pink tulips and blue hyacinths, forced in greenhouses so they would appear a few weeks before their natural time, seducing the impatient with a ready-made spring. There were small bunches of miniature irises too, each dainty dipping blue petal licked with a tongue of brilliant yellow from its centre to its edge. Here, Sarah slowed her step, mentally hesitating. She might actually buy a bouquet, compensating for an anticipated lack: the ones in her garden had not flowered last June. The rhizomes were old, probably exhausted, but she was giving them this one last season before she gave up and replaced them. So far, there was no sign of flowers on the fine spiky green leaves in her back flower bed, and it was the bucket with a black-on-white label marked "Dwarf Irises $2.99 a bunch" that tempted her most of all.

She looked back up, towards the plate-glass window, barely taking in the unremarkable sampling of humanity inside the shop. A woman about her own age, but rather stooped, was waiting impatiently behind a young man whose black curly hair contrasted sharply with an electric-orange T-shirt. The shop assistant wore a baby-blue smock and had bleach-blonde hair that fell across her face as she packaged up the young man's flowers. Sarah shook off the notion of irises and moved on, covering the last steps to the grocery store with a skipping little step. It was the kind of place that could be counted on for milk, baking soda, or a light bulb until eleven o'clock at night and on Sundays too, and Sarah went to the back of the store, took a carton from the refrigerated display case, paid for her purchase, and hurried home.

Daniel was standing in the kitchen, beaming.

"Fixed it." He pressed a button and the coffee grinder dutifully reproduced its regular whirring noise without protesting squeaks.

"You're so clever. What did you do?"

"Well, at first I thought it might be the motor had burned out. And if the motor is gone, you might as well throw the thing away. A small appliance like this, there's no point replacing a motor. But then I thought it might be worth looking at the ball bearings . . ."

Sarah was not especially interested in the inner workings of the coffee grinder, and turned to put the milk away.

The doorbell rang.

"There he is."

They both hurried towards the front hall where Daniel, arriving slightly before Sarah, stepped aside to let her open the door. Maxime stood on the front porch, dressed in blue jeans and a bright-orange T-shirt, and carrying a bouquet of three massive yellow-and-brown sunflowers on giant stems.

"Hi."

Sarah stood there for a moment, unsure how to approach him, the bouquet blocking her path towards his body. He held the flowers out to her and she took them, only to find that with her hands now full she was still unable to reach him. Daniel stepped out from behind her, grabbed at Maxime's arm, and tugged him into the house. Once inside, it became apparent where his luggage was: he was wearing a large backpack that propelled him forward and there was no room for the three of them in the small vestibule. Sarah found herself backing away, into the house.

"Was the train busy?"

Maxime had convinced his parents it would be easier and quicker for him to take the subway north rather than have them meet him downtown at Union Station.

"Yeah, tons of people got on at Kingston. Everybody gets out of school the same week."

"Do you want tea?" Sarah did not wait for an answer but turned and headed back towards the kitchen, carrying the sunflowers in both hands. Where on God's earth were they growing sunflowers in May, she wondered, as she left them on the countertop and plugged in the kettle. Turning to the cupboard, she took out both the teapot and a plate, leaving one sitting beside the bouquet while she took biscuits from a tin to place on the other. Reaching for the sugar bowl, she started to arrange everything on a tray as though preparing for a party. But once the tea had steeped, she wound up pouring it into mugs and placing them directly on the counter in front of Daniel and Maxime, who were standing there still talking about his train ride. She picked up the sugar and made as though to spoon some into Maxime's tea, but he stopped her.

"No, thanks."

"But you take sugar."

"No, thanks, just plain."

She doled out sugar for Daniel and herself, but left her mug on the counter.

"I should put the flowers in water. They are gorgeous, so large . . ." She reached for a glass vase, unsure how to arrange huge blooms of late summer that, it always seemed to her, belonged more in the open fields than in any garden or drawing room.

"I wasn't sure what to buy you, but I liked the sunflowers." Maxime looked quizzically at his bouquet which now threatened to overturn the delicate vase in which Sarah was attempting to balance it. "They remind me of Van Gogh," he explained.

"Van Gogh?"

"Yeah, you know. He painted sunflowers."

"Oh, yes, painting." Sarah, judging that the vase was balanced, gently removed her hand. It toppled, spilling water all over the countertop.

Art was a sore point that spring, for Maxime had come home from Montreal to take a summer job working at the information desk in the museum, pointing visitors towards the dinosaurs and the Chinese porcelain. It was a good wage for a student but the position had nothing to do with becoming a doctor, as Sarah had pointed out several times. It was all very well in his undergraduate years to take odd jobs serving in restaurants and shops, but surely now that he was in medical school, these mundane occupations were beneath his status as a soon-to-be-doctor. She was no great lover of art, secretly suspecting that all cultural interests were frivolous even if she knew better than to voice this opinion to her many friends and acquaintances who saw fit to visit galleries or concert halls. And whatever their social merits, she could state openly and with certainty that these fields did not provide steady employment, so she did not regard the museum's information desk as any improvement over waiting tables. She had urged Daniel to find some colleague who would take Maxime on as an assistant for the summer, despite her husband's protests that this kind of work would have to wait for his internship. Brushing aside her urgency, Daniel argued there was no particular rush, and when Maxime accepted the museum job, she felt that her men were in collusion against her, neither trying hard enough to find the correct alternative. She fretted that Maxime would not be properly prepared for his last years of medical school, would fail to secure a good position for his internship, and would thus delay the day when he could take over his father's practice, the day when she could breathe easily as she contemplated his future.

As her cherished baby had grown to manhood, the first of his mother's many anxieties in his regard remained the issue of his career. From childhood, it was understood by his parents that Maxime was to follow his father into medicine; for Daniel, the son of a doctor and the grandson of a rag merchant, this was the choice demanded by family history. For Sarah, it was the choice demanded by fear, because she saw in it a profession that offered the surest route to middle-class security. Anything else seemed to open up gaping vistas of uncertainty: paltry salaries or no salary at all, unpaid rents on cramped apartments, soiled clothes, and unwashed dishes. She had never known poverty, but it too loomed up as yet another danger that might yet destroy her son. Maxime himself had few other ideas about professions with which to counter his parents' plan; he knew how high marks in science and math led to medical school and how medical school led to internship, residency, and private practice, but had little sense of how one might become a museum curator, an English professor, or a stockbroker. He knew that the sharpest tool with which to torture his mother, the surest way to blackmail her, was to express doubts about this agreed-upon future, but since he also sensed from adolescence that he would inevitably disappoint his parents, that in some unspoken, almost incomprehensible way his soul was not that of the son they wanted, he chose mainly to acquiesce on the subject of his profession. Through his university days at McGill, he was to dance a fraught little tango with his mother—advancing with "I think I'll quit and go to Europe," and "You know, Ma, I really enjoyed that art history course I took last year," but then retreating in the face of "Once you have started something, you finish it, Maxime," or "There are no jobs in the universities these days, especially not in the humanities." For all that Maxime flirted with rebellion, he had the personality of a conformist. Sarah wanted her son to be a doctor and that, at least, he did. In 1994, four years after the day he appeared with the sunflowers, almost ten years after he first left for Montreal, he returned to Toronto with a B.Sc., an M.D. and a year's internship to his credit.

Up at the top of Bathurst Street, isolated at the northern edge of the city where a string of gas stations, low apartment blocks, and kosher delis is sliced in half by the twelve traffic-choked lanes of the 401, the Villa Nova Retirement Home exudes false cheeriness. It is a squat steel-and-glass box with ostentatiously clean and open lines, decorated with pots of pansies and low pine trees on the outside, checkerboard linoleum and bright-red curtains on the inside. Its name is Italian, its decor Milanese modernist, but there is no hiding the truth that its exclusively Jewish clientele is waiting to die. Shrivelled souls confined to wheelchairs or shuffling about with the help of canes, they look as out of place here as kindergarten children on a day trip to the glass towers of the stock exchange, so disproportionate is their shrunken scale to that of their bold surroundings. Sarah, who loathed her weekly visits here for Sunday dinners full of lengthening silences, wondered that its inhabitants did not find their surroundings bizarre. Surely these men and women, who had grown up in the dark drawing rooms of Europe or in the claustrophobic apartments over their parents' shops down on Spadina Avenue or on Montreal's Boulevard Saint-Laurent, would have preferred crown mouldings, mahogany, and red velvet, or at least some chintz.

Rachel, however, professed to like this place—several of her old friends lived here, and besides, "It's clean," she had told Sarah when they inspected it together. Or at least she had professed to like it back then, when she had first moved here after Sam's death, four years ago now. Today, she was eighty-eight and Sarah, who had sometimes heard her snap back at the overly friendly staff with uncharacteristic sharpness and saw that she was slipping, losing some of her hold on life both mental and physical, did not ask the old woman if she still liked it here. There were no other options. At least Rachel was largely uncomplaining and still chatted to the other ladies and the few men who were left too. She was talking about Maxime now, boasting about him to a neighbour: Sarah and Daniel could hear her small, quavering voice echoing in the big, empty lounge as they made their way to her side.

"My grandson. At Toronto General . . ."

"Eh?" Mrs. Lieberman either hadn't heard or was feigning deafness to avoid giving Rachel the satisfaction of impressing her.

"He's starting at Toronto General. You know, downtown.

He's a doctor and he's going to work downtown."

"Oh, downtown, eh?"

"Rachel. Look at you. Is that a new sweater?" Daniel called out deep and loud as they reached her chair, and as she clasped his hand, set to admiring the soft-pink fluffy cardigan she was wearing. Behind him, Sarah bit her lip and sighed.

"Hi." Rachel extended her free hand around Daniel to Sarah, and clasped the fingers in hers, not letting go of either of them until they broke away to settle in the chairs across from her.

"I saw Max last night."

"You mean a dream?" Sarah was puzzled.

"He came to visit."

"Yes, Maxime often comes to visit, when he's in Toronto," Sarah agreed.

Rachel's voice was more hesitant now, but she persisted: "He came yesterday."

"He's still in Montreal, Rachel. He gets back Wednesday, this week. He'll come and visit soon, I'm sure. He has to move all his things back, you know, and get started at the hospital. It will take a bit of time, but I'll tell him that you were asking to see him."

"No hair. He's got no hair."

Sarah and Daniel caught each other's eye. Daniel shrugged.

"Yes, dear." Sarah agreed. "What do you think they are serving for dinner tonight?"

"No hair." Rachel looked over at Daniel. "I'm getting old. I don't understand these things."

Daniel instantly demurred. "No Rachel, you aren't even ninety yet. You'll live to see the year 2000, I bet you will, only a few more years."

"Six more years," Rachel corrected, and in the firmness of her voice and brightness of her eye, she seemed herself once more.

Dinner that night was boiled beef. It was usually that, or macaroni coated in a heavy sauce of ground meat and tomatoes. Afterwards, there would be stewed prunes or applesauce. Sarah sighed and thought fondly of the soufflé she was planning for tomorrow's dinner. When Rachel had first moved here, Sarah had dropped by to visit on the occasional weekday afternoon, and every other Sunday Daniel had picked Rachel up and brought her back down to their house for a meal, but now Rachel was always asleep if Sarah called during the day and it was getting more and more difficult to manoeuvre her into a car. This past winter she had refused to go outside altogether and Sarah and Daniel's biweekly visits were now weekly events, the only contact they had with Rachel. Sarah wondered guiltily if she was only finding excuses not to visit, and sighed again.

"Where's that girl? They are also so slow, those *shvartzes*." Mrs. Lieberman looked querulously up from her empty plate while Sarah and Daniel winced. Rachel, meanwhile, looked placidly around her, apparently unaware of their discomfort.

"I am here, Mrs. Lieberman."

The waitress, a large woman of Jamaican extraction, forty-five if not older, was within earshot and moved over to the table, bearing two plates of food. Daniel tried to catch her eye with a rueful smile to distance himself from Mrs. Lieberman's remark, while the waitress plopped the food down with unnecessary vigour, if no particular anger, in front of Mrs. Lieberman and Rachel.

"There you go, dears." She stepped back a bit from the table and laughed. "There you go. I'm not kosher but the food sure is." She laughed again and, reaching back towards Mrs. Lieberman, patted her on the head.

Sarah felt her sympathies shift and her embarrassment grow. She looked down at her lap, then noticed with horror out of the corner of one eye that the man at the next table was drooling, and lifted her gaze again to the table, staring at the place setting in front of her until the waitress reappeared with two more plates for her and Daniel. Sarah thanked her quietly.

Rachel seemed oblivious to all the movement around her, taking notice only of the beef in front of her, poking it experimentally with a fork but not conveying any to her mouth. As if from some distance, she spoke.

"Sam says it doesn't matter, you don't have to keep kosher." She paused. "But he'll eat this too." Sarah and Daniel looked at each other, re-entering into an ongoing debate without needing to speak. Daniel felt it was permissible to humour her; Sarah felt the elderly must be pressed to keep in touch.

"Sam is dead, Rachel," she said firmly.

"Of course, dear." Rachel sounded surprised. "Several years ago now, dear."

She smiled as though she had won an argument and lifted her fork to her mouth.

On Wednesday, Sarah was reading the newspaper in the living room when Maxime arrived home. She had only just finished breakfast and seen Daniel out the door when the bell rang. Fearing some solicitation for a charity, she stepped into the hall with hesitation. As she opened the door and saw it was her son, she did not have time to wonder how Maxime could have caught a train from Montreal that arrived that early in the morning, but could only cry out: "What happened to your hair?"

"I cut it." He smiled a bright and brittle smile.

He had not simply cut it, he had all but shaved his head, leaving only a dark fuzz that showed where bare flesh would normally stop and hair begin. Gone were the curly locks his mother had once twisted around her fingers. He walked into the hall with the same shy defiance with which he had refused to take a bath as a child or to stay home Friday night as a teenager.

"Your hair." She said the words in French again, now more in sorrow than surprise. "What has happened?"

"Time for a change," he replied in French. She had been right at least about that, he had regained his comfort in her language during his years in Montreal. He then switched into English, with a degree of archness, as though parroting someone else: "A change is as good as a rest. My friend Marie always says that. A change is as good as a rest."

Marie, Marie. She tried to remember which of Maxime's unseen friends she was.

There was an issue that Sarah had largely ignored in her quest to establish Maxime's career. Certainly, she assumed he would marry. She had always listened with a sharp ear to the names of the Montreal girls he would drop casually like this, weighing the competing demands of language and religion, aware she was unlikely to be satisfied on both fronts simultaneously. Leah, Ruth, Esther: these would be daughters-in-law. Cendrine, Marie-Claire, Marie: her grandchildren would eat bacon but at least they would speak her language in Maxime's home. But Sarah did not think to question why none of these girls were ever invited back to Toronto. If the preparations for her son's professional future were concrete issues continually discussed and debated in the house in North Toronto, then the possibility of his eventual marriage and fatherhood was an abstract thing that shimmered on Sarah's horizon too distant and too vague in its outlines to be easily brought forward for conversation. It seemed possible to worry out loud about marks and exams; almost impossible to ask about dates and girlfriends. She presumed that Daniel had discussed sex with Maxime when he was a teenager—her husband was a doctor, after all—but she never raised the subject herself. Perhaps she sensed she could only fight successfully on one front, that Maxime would only tolerate so much intervention in his life, so she left the affairs of her son's heart to take care of themselves. Beyond the requisite little talks in which he had indeed engaged his adolescent son, Daniel was also silent, but he glimpsed the future more clearly than his wife. He had seen the signs, wondered at Maxime's occasional awkwardness, and would, that evening, quietly recognize this new haircut for the statement that it was. He said nothing to Sarah and she was to remain naive, or perhaps blind because she did not wish to see. So, as Maxime kissed a hospital nurse whom he had dutifully invited out on a date, felt his lips like rubber and his loins quiet, as he buried himself in work and avoided old friends, as he prolonged his residency year after year, as he politely declined his father's increasingly infrequent offers of a partnership in the family practice from which Dr. Segal would soon retire, as he introduced himself to colleagues across town and became increasingly engrossed in their research project, as he made new friends, as he took his first tentative steps towards a man at a party, as he lived these years, his mother did not know him.

During that time, Sarah had been investigating the idea of a stew. She had often considered it a mediocre supper, a bland solution for tough meat that hours of boiling would reduce from indigestible hunks to stringy shreds. The vegetables were sodden and the beef caught in your teeth, leaving you surreptitiously picking at them long after the meal was over. And yet, the authors of every French cookbook on her ample shelf considered the *pot-au-feu* a staple of the bourgeois home and the *boeuf bourguignon* a test of a good restaurant. Like many failed dishes, the fault of a bad stew lay surely with the cook, not the recipe. Sarah began to experiment, varying the cut of meat, the length of cooking, the heat of the oven, the quantity of wine in the sauce. She produced good stews full of flavourful vegetables and meat that was succulent rather than stringy. Yet still her tongue was not satisfied. A certain fragrance, a particular softness eluded her.

The breakthrough occurred in her doctor's office as she was waiting for her checkup. She had visited the same colleague of Daniel's for years now—that was the proper way to proceed, to seek an opinion independent from her husband's—and anticipated with neither delight nor trepidation their annual conversation about a few nagging varicose veins, the importance of breast self-examination, and the merits of hormone replacement therapy. (Daniel favoured it; her doctor was against.) As she waited for him, she idly flipped the pages of a decorating magazine and, amongst a clutter of short items towards the beginning, found a few para-graphs about the *pot-au-feu*. In isolated French villages, the anony-mous magazine writer maintained, housewives still took their meat and vegetables at night to the baker who, at the end of his shift in the hours just before dawn, banked the wood fires of his brick oven and placed their stewpots to cook. By noon, the women could return to buy a fresh loaf and pick up a meal that had long sim-mered in an oven only now slowly cooling.

Sarah had read this story before, in her kosher cookbooks. In the *shtetls* of Eastern Europe, the cholent was cooked in the com-munal bread oven, a feature of village life dating back to the Middle Ages. Before dusk on Friday night, the women prepared their pots and took them to the oven. On Saturday morning, when the long services were finally over, the men then came to fetch them on their way home from the synagogue, and so the family could eat a cholent that had been cooked to perfection without the housewife ever working on the Sabbath. Here was the secret wisdom of her ancestors: a good stew should be cooked overnight in the dying heat of a bread oven.

Adapting this practice in a contemporary kitchen for an evening dinner hour took some juggling. Sarah briefly debated a brick oven, but rejected it as impractical. Over on Eglinton Avenue, the neighbourhood Italian restaurant cooked its gourmet pizzas in the real thing, but she was unsure how one might manage stoking a wood-cooking fire in a private home even if she were to convince Daniel the kitchen needed to be expanded yet again. Nonetheless, she did have the benefit of a large gas range. In the eighties, she had become convinced of the merits of gas over electricity—everyone said it produced a moister heat, better for both roasts and baking—and Daniel had paid to have the pipes that now fuelled their furnace extended into the kitchen. Their first gas stove was a straightforward affair in white enamel, with four burners on top and an oven big enough for a significant piece of meat underneath. Sarah was an instant and happy convert, and soon pined for one of the giant, spanking new restaurant-style ranges in shining stainless steel. It appeared magically in the kitchen on the morning of her sixtieth birthday. Normally, Sarah cooked bread and pastries in the electrical convection oven that she had used for years, its fan circulating the air inside to plump up her baking, but she now began to experiment with the gas range.

And so, more than an hour before the late and feeble dawn of a damp November morning in 1997, Sarah was standing in her kitchen punching dough. It was six o'clock. She had prepared the dough the night before and placed it in the refrigerator where it had slowly risen to double its bulk, pushing the clean dishtowel with which she had covered it up into a comforting fat mound. Pulling the dough out of its bowl onto a floured board, she punched it down again, kneading the overblown lump back to a more reasonable size and putting it to one side. She bent down to open a cupboard and pulled out a deep, round baking tin with high-fluted sides. She was making brioche. She greased the interior of the tin with a little knob of butter and then carefully placed her ball of dough in it, covered it with the same dishtowel, and gently lowered it onto a heating grate in the kitchen floor before she went back upstairs to bed. While she dozed lightly, awake enough to luxuriate in the delightful sensation of being asleep, the dough would rise again.

At eight, she heard Daniel stirring beside her—it was Sunday, and he was sleeping late—and she got up and went back to her kitchen. She lit the gas, set the thermostat to 375 degrees Fahrenheit, and turned to the fridge. She got out a single egg out of the carton, broke it into a bowl, mixed it up with a fork, and then took a pastry brush from a drawer. Retrieving the pan from the floor, she delicately brushed its newly risen surface with the egg so that it would shine with a tempting sheen once baked. She had placed her favourite enamelware stewpot on the counter and was beginning to get out the meat and vegetables, when a small beep indicated the oven had reached the required temperature. She opened the door and slipped the bread onto the lower rack, noting with satisfaction the rows of red bricks she had placed there the night before. They created an inner wall around all three sides of the oven's box; for their roof, she lay another layer on the upper rack. It was her secret weapon, her own invention: the thirty-six clay bricks, coaxed from the owner of a building yard who was accustomed to sell them by the truckload, would hold heat in the oven long after the metal surfaces had cooled.

She could hear water running upstairs—Daniel was showering—and she set to washing, peeling, and chopping her vegetables with energy before turning to the meat. She cut it into small chunks, removing any particularly large streaks of fat and setting them to one side. She dusted the pieces in flour, heated a few spoonfuls of oil in the bottom of her stewpot, tossed in the fat she had removed from the meat, and when it was all liquid, she quickly seared the beef before tumbling all the vegetables on top and dousing it all in wine. At nine o'clock, the bread would be ready to come out of the oven and she would replace it with the stew before turning off the gas. At nine-fifteen, they would sit down to a leisurely Sunday breakfast of coffee and fresh brioche; that evening, Maxime would come to dinner and they would eat a *pot-au-feu* that belonged to another century.

"Nice stew, Ma." Maxime chewed slowly, concentrating on the food.

"Your mother lines the oven with bricks, that's her secret. She talked the man over at Dominion Coal into giving her some. They don't usually sell such small loads, but when he heard what it was for . . ."

Maxime nodded. His father had told him this story on at least two previous occasions. He suppressed his annoyance and then wondered guiltily if his parents could not keep track of which piece of domestic news they had told him, and which was as yet untold, because he seemed to come home for dinner so infrequently these days. He stayed away too much. Tonight, he would say something. He was thirty-one.

He drew a deep breath, but his parents were speaking. His father was discussing the likelihood of a doctors' strike.

"You know, the government talks big but . . ."

Maxime skewered a piece of vegetable with his fork and tried hard to savour the mingling flavours of onion, wine, and beef as it collapsed on his tongue.

"It's all very well for the specialists, but what they don't realize is that the family doctors carry the system." That was his mother, outraged on his father's behalf. The political debate continued throughout the main course, and then Sarah went to fetch the salad. Daniel topped up his son's wineglass.

"Wine doesn't really go with salad but . . ."

"It's the dressing actually," Sarah added as she placed the wooden bowl on the table. Maxime had heard this many times before: don't drink wine with salad, the vinegar in the dressing obscures its flavour. He offered his family's customary response— "But it can't hurt . . ."—and reached for his replenished glass. His parents had always drawn the line at kosher wine, and were drinking that night a hearty Bordeaux. Now, they were talking about a neighbour's trip to Europe.

"Great fares at this time of year, but it rained every day they were there."

Maxime stabbed at a leaf of radicchio—"It's almost tasteless, even a bit bitter, but it does look so pretty in the salad," his mother would say—and conveyed it to his mouth. She had put mustard in the dressing, and it stung his tongue.

There was an apple tart for dessert, glazed with apricot jam. Maxime ate one mouthful but found the flavour only papery now. He spoke.

"I am helping with some research over at the Don Hospital . . ."

"The Don Hospital?" His father seemed to greet this with delighted surprise. "You know I clerked there when I was in med school. It was a foul place then. We used to call it the Contagion, you know, because it had been Contagious Diseases, back in the old days. We thought they'd close it down any day. Sarah, do you remember . . ."

"I guess they've done some renovations," Maxime offered, frustrated that he had only woken memories for his father.

"That was the place they put me when I had measles, do you remember?" Sarah turned to her husband.

"That's right." Daniel looked across at Maxime. "We probably never told you about it. It was just before your mother and I were married. She somehow got measles. It must have been going around. You know, they didn't have the vaccine in those days and . . ."

"Yeah, so, I am doing some drug research, you know, providing clinical information . . . um, my patients . . . well, research, as well as my work at the hospital."

Daniel suddenly fell serious and silent, his smile faded.

"It seems so silly now, nothing more than measles, but I was really quite ill with it. I fainted one day in the street and . . ."

Daniel reached over and touched Sarah's arm, stopping the flow of her memories. Maxime continued.

"You know they have the immunodeficiency clinic there, but there's also this lab . . ."

"Well, that's interesting." Sarah was puzzled. "I thought . . ."

"What kind of research, Max?" His father prompted him firmly.

"Vaccine research for HIV . . . HIV research. That's what I'm doing."

"But, Maxime." Sarah, her attention suddenly focused, switched to French and stared at her son. "Those . . . they . . . You might catch . . ."

"No, it is perfectly safe. We are very careful with the blood."

"But, those men . . ."

"Yes, those men."

Sarah laughed nervously and then choked on her laugh.

"It's a surprise. A surprise . . ." Her voice trailed off.

Mother and son stared at each other for a while in belated recognition, and then in the silence there was a sound, the harsh rasp of Sarah's chair scraping back.

Daniel, who had been waiting for several years for some kind of announcement or explanation, the suspicions he had never dared voice to Sarah now confirmed, his bedside manner firmly in place, promptly said the right thing: "We love you, Max."

But Sarah, a thousand new fears, hurts, and anxieties churning up from the pit of her stomach and clogging her throat, found tears in her eyes, and tears were something that pride had seldom let her shed. She rose and left the room without speaking.

"YOUR PAPERS, PLEASE."

The request is routine but there's a threat somewhere behind it. One must follow the regulations, carry the right identification. The official does not smile as I rifle nervously through my briefcase.

I have been summoned into the head librarian's private office by the North African clerk. The unctuous assistant assistant librarian has watched me go with amusement, as I pass into the mysterious world beyond the glass door at the end of the manuscript room. The anxious M. Richaud has bustled after me and now hovers in his boss's presence, finally sure that he has made a mistake in permitting me to keep working in the library. It is the third week of October, and I have been here for almost a month.

"*Je pensais, M. Valéry . . .*"

M. Valéry, a patrician Frenchman with a large head covered in salt-and-pepper hair and an air of easy authority, dismisses the anxious M. Richaud with a wave of his hand and concentrates on me. I have made a mistake. I have applied for a second renewal on the permitted eight-day reserve on File 263 of the Marcel Proust papers (miscellaneous letters and notebooks belonging to the author's mother, Jeanne Proust). Once was permissible, but twice? More than sixteen working days with the minor Proust documents in File 263? Well . . . I have drawn attention to myself. I am to explain.

I show M. Valéry the letter, a crumbled piece of fax paper, with which I originally obtained my library card.

"You work at this institution?" He raises an eyebrow as he reads, seeing right through Justine's carefully worded letter of introduction.

My heart pounds as though I have been caught in a grotesque lie, but I swallow and, estimating that truth is the best hope here, reply honestly, "No. I am a translator, an interpreter."

He dismisses the profession with a shake of the head.

"What is your interest in Proust?" he asks.

What is my interest in Proust? I hesitate.

Do you have time for a story? I was fifteen when I first encountered . . . well, I have told you that already. But I returned to Proust, in the years after the night of the wedding reception.

It was five years ago now, when I was launching my career as an interpreter in Montreal and Max had just moved back to Toronto to start his residency, that I remembered my girlhood love of Proust. Looking for some diversion from my own affairs, I recalled that I had always promised myself that I would finish the whole novel, and so I began reading, returning to the story started years before in school.

I start in French at the beginning, rereading the first book quickly and then turning, more slowly, to the remaining six. I savour the description, linger over the satire, longing to dwell in this world of dove-grey gloves and white orchids. Finishing *A la Recherche du Temps Perdu*, I pick up a paperback edition of the English translation, entitled *Remembrance of Things Past,* and begin the voyage again, comparing the vocabularies, testing my own knowledge of the two languages. I am not a fast reader: as though compensating for the swift decisions required by my profession, I approach the written word with hesitant leisure, never quite sure in either language that I have fully grasped the true value of a phrase and may proceed to the next. The novel measures more than three thousand pages, and, with work, household chores, the occasional family obligation or mass on Sundays, dinner with Justine and her husband, or a visit from an old school friend, this doubled reading project fills my life for a whole three years. Perhaps I purposefully prolong it, for Proust has become my favourite companion, my solace in an empty place. He consoles me and advises me too.

Knowing the stabbing pain of separation from a lover and the gnawing guilt he felt at the worry he caused his mother, Proust believed every love was filled with agonies. Great invalid that he was, he concluded romantic love was a fatal illness, a passage from pain to defeat. In the second part of the first volume of *A la Recherche*, entitled in English *Swann in Love*, Proust told the story of the erudite and cultured Swann's obsession with his mistress, the vulgar, demimondaine Odette. After years of jealous pursuit, Swann finally awakes from his fever with a cry:

"Dire que j'ai gaché des années de ma vie, que j'ai voulu mourir, que j'ai eu mon plus grand amour pour une femme que ne me plaisait pas, qui n'etait pas mon genre!"

In my Penguin edition, the passage is rendered thus: "To think that I've wasted years of my life, that I've longed to die, that I have experienced my greatest love, for a woman who didn't appeal to me, who wasn't even my type!"

Once finished my reading, I feel bereft and buy yet another copy, the most recent revision of the English translation in hard cover. I admire the silvery dust jackets that surround six compact little volumes and weigh each satisfying book in my hand. Their title is now *In Search of Lost Time*. Proust himself considered the Shakespearean title chosen by his first translator, C. K. Scott Moncrieff, to be inaccurate and would perhaps be pleased to find the English translation of his novel finally, in the 1990s, more sensitively named.

I turn next to the biographies. They are also in English—George D. Painter's 1959 classic *Marcel Proust;* Ronald Hayman's more recent *Proust*—and in French—*Proust* by Ghislain de Diesbach.

Here, I discover the Proust never taught in school, the lover of men and boys who fantasized about living with his friend Reynaldo Hahn and who would later turn an obsession for his chauffeur Alfred into the narrator's passion for Albertine. A sensual man who knew the inside of male brothels well enough he could easily create an aging sado-masochist called Baron Charlus, based on the real Comte de Montesquiou. A flirtatious and flattering man who had some kind of misunderstanding with his dear friend Marie Nordlinger, the English artist who helped him with his Ruskin translations.

I dig out my old school reader and flip through the excerpts it offered a girl, passages in which cakes were nibbled, seasons savoured, women loved. Its brief biographical note makes no mention of Proust's own great loves, other than his mother. On the same page, the author's pale portrait in the guise of fragile dandy stares out at me. I can just make out the faint pencil markings where Justine once darkened the circles under his eyes.

And so, I began a quest for the adult Proust, the hunt that eventually brought me here.

"What is your interest in Proust?" M. Valéry repeats the question.

"My interest is not in Proust himself. Well, of course, I am interested, I have read . . . but I have become a student of the work of his mother."

"His mother?"

"Jeanne Proust. That's what is in File 263—Mme. Proust's papers. Her notebooks.

"Yes, yes, it has all been published."

In fact, this is not true. It is precisely because these papers have not been published that I convinced M. Richaud to sign my request form in the first place. The Bibliothèque Nationale directs readers towards printed books or microfilm whenever possible, to avoid unnecessary wear and tear on the manuscripts. M. Richaud explained that at our initial meeting as we ran through the library's catalogue of Proust holdings. Each file has a full call number—the Proust archive covers dozens of numbers in the sixteen thousands—but is usually known by the Roman numeral assigned to it, from I to CCLXIII, or File 263. We eventually go through the whole list, file by file.

Files 1–19 contain small notebooks in which Proust composed his first drafts of *A la Recherche*.

Files 20–71 contain the actual handwritten manuscripts for all the books of the novel with Proust's many additions and revisions, including his famous *paperoles*, the long strips of paper he would glue onto existing pages. It was File 20, which contains the first pages of *A la Recherche*, that I originally requested. M. Richaud is so appalled by my gall in this regard that he has asked to see me so that he may personally dismiss me. Files 1 through 71 are available only to an exclusive list of well-recognized Proust scholars. There's a copy of the microfilm downstairs, in the audiovisual department. End of discussion.

"What about Files 72 to 135?" I ask, gently urging him down the list.

Files 72–135 contain the original printer's galleys with more revisions in the author's hand. They are also available only to Proust scholars; they are also on microfilm downstairs. Warming to his subject, M. Richaud relents a little and confides in me that the library is planning to build an electronic version of the archive. Hypertext will be particularly useful in rendering the effect of the *paperoles* accessible to the public. Not for several years, of course, but it will be a magnificent thing when it is accomplished. I smile wanly. I had wanted to see the actual ink Proust had penned, to see his hand in the flesh. I encourage M. Richaud onwards.

Files 135–139, the manuscripts of Proust's two translations of Ruskin, *The Bible of Amiens* and *Sesame and Lilies*. The translations, dating to 1903 and 1906, are now out of print, but are widely held in library collections. They can be had downstairs, on the ground floor, in the *salle des imprimés*, the room where printed books are kept. The introduction to *Sesame and Lilies* has itself been translated into English. M. Richaud eyes me carefully: he believes that slim volume is still in print. So, the answer on Files 135–139 is no.

File 140, the draft of *Jean Santeuil*, an early unfinished autobiographical novel dating to the late 1890s. Published posthumously and still in print. An English translation is also in print. The microfilm of the manuscript is downstairs. No again.

File 141, the manuscript for *Les Plaisirs et les Jours,* a collection of juvenilia with original illustrations by Madeleine Lemaire published in 1896. Out of print, but the library itself has two copies of the book. Downstairs.

File 142, two drafts and a final manuscript for a short story, "La Mort de Baldassare Silvande," published in the *Revue Hebdomadaire* in 1895. M. Richaud concedes that collections of the *Revue Hebdomadaire* are scarce, and that the Bibliothèque Nationale's own copies have been packed for the move to the new building and so are currently not available. "Perhaps, mademoiselle could be allowed . . ." By all accounts, the story may have been beautifully written but was improbably romantic. I could look at it, but I had hoped for more, and push M. Richaud on down the list.

Files 142–258, the correspondence, from a childhood note to a cousin dating to 1880 up to the author's last letters to friends before his own death in 1922, all of it collected up from his many correspondents by the assiduous staff of the Bibliothèque Nationale who have matched the blandishments of American universities with calls to national pride and the occasional cheque. A popular three-volume edition of selected letters is widely available in both French and English; the complete twenty-one-volume scholarly edition in the original French can be had in many university libraries, even in North America. The microfilm of the original letters can also be viewed here at the Bibliothèque Nationale. M. Richaud gives me another piercing look.

And so we come to the miscellaneous files:

File 259 (oversized), newspapers found in the author's bedroom at the time of his death.

File 260, household notes found in the author's apartment at the time of his death.

Files 261–262, rough translations of Ruskin's *The Bible of Amiens* and *Sesame and Lilies* executed by the author's mother, Jeanne Proust.

File 263, the contents of a small desk found in the author's apartment at the time of his death and containing papers belonging to his mother, Jeanne Proust, including letters from the period 1878 to 1904 and notebooks from 1890 to 1904. (I am to learn that the cataloguer has made two mistakes here. There are no letters in the file; perhaps they have been moved over to the boxes containing the collected correspondence. And the sixteen leather-bound journals that are here do not stop in 1904, but continue until Jeanne Proust's death in 1905.) Pausing here at File 263, M. Richaud raises his head from the paper quizzically. Mme. Proust's original versions of the Ruskin translations have not been microfilmed, neither have her notebooks. Yes, I will take the ill-catalogued and much-neglected File 263.

So, I found Mme. Proust's diary partly by design but mainly by chance.

"Yes, yes, it has all been published."

If M. Valéry thinks that the contents of File 263 have been published, he knows the collection less well than M. Richaud. I go carefully here.

"The letters, yes, the letters have been published," I reply. "But there are her diaries . . ."

"Oh, Madame's diaries . . ." M. Valéry rolls his eyes heavenwards.

"The natterings of a housewife—day after day of them, year after year—there's nothing there."

Apparently, M. Valéry has made only the most cursory reading of the material. I begin to lie.

"No, there does not seem to be much. That is to say, I have not found anything yet, but if you would permit me another renewal . . . I am approaching the end of the diaries. I would only need a few more days."

"Ah." M. Valéry thinks he understands now and smiles indulgently. "*Féministe* . . . a feminist."

He has catalogued me and so dismisses me: a mystery is often more interesting than its solution. He draws towards him the form that I proffer and duly signs.

"Thank you."

He steps out from his desk, opens the door of his office, and calls out, "Ahmed!"

The North African clerk reappears.

"Mademoiselle can renew as often as she wants. Fetch the box."

Ahmed sighs as though he had been asked to fetch Sisyphus's stone and carry it over to my desk in the library. He leaves the office with emphatic slowness.

"*Il a des soucis* . . . He has troubles," M. Valéry explains, showing more kindness now that our transaction is over. "Immigration troubles. His visa has expired."

Paris. Friday, February 26, 1904.
Today, I held baby Suzy in my arms in the morning, went home, ate lunch alone, and in the afternoon, opened the package that had come with the first post, so that I could admire *The Bible of Amiens.* Perhaps twenty years from now Suzy will

read her uncle's translation and so Dick's child will meet Marcel's. A happy thought at least.

PARIS. SATURDAY, MARCH 5, 1904.
I suppose I should pity her. I have his sons, my little wolves, even if one of them has grown up and left me. I have the apartment filled with his books, his papers, his photograph in every room. I have his honours, I have his name, I have my widow's weeds. What does she have? A few memories, a bunch of Parma violets thrown on top of a coffin as it passes.

The boys supposed that I did not notice her at the funeral, or that in pretending not to notice, I somehow achieve a state in which she makes no difference to me. I cannot say I did not know, but no more can I pretend it does not hurt.

PARIS. MONDAY, APRIL 11, 1904.
Finally a good talk with Marie-Marguerite, in the tea pavilion in the Bois where we took refreshment after our walk. We agreed it is not that one is particularly surprised, nor that one minds that much, as long as he continues to be courteous and attentive at home and diligent in all financial matters. I had always been aware of Adrien's lapses; they never greatly interfered in our life. It was being forced to remember their existence on the very day of his funeral that wounded me, as though his discretion, so assured while he was living, had collapsed with his death.

Marie-Marguerite was philosophical as usual: "Some have their mistresses, others have their boys, they are men, after all. In the end, it is often much easier for the wife if they exercise their tastes outside the home rather than in the conjugal bed."

For all her bluntness, she comforts me. She urged me not to let the perfect be the enemy of the good in the realm of my memories, to cherish what I had, which was much. And we agreed that Adrien went as he would have wished, planting his cabbages, in Montaigne's phrase, struck down by his stroke while at the Faculty.

Marie gave Marcel the most lovely gift this week—a handful of Japanese paper pellets that once submersed in water blossom into delicate little aquatic flowers. And so, a safe and kindly spring blooms in his dark room.

PARIS. THURSDAY, MAY 12, 1904.
We have hit on an excellent idea, Marcel and me. We will ask Marie to sculpt a medallion for Adrien's grave bearing his profile. I can think of no better way to honour him, nor a finer artist to execute the task.

Marcel says he will ask her today. She and Ruskin are his constant companions these last months, since, for the sake of his father's memory, he took up his work again and moves ahead with *Sesame and Lilies*. She is always a comfort, both to Marcel and to me, so delicate in her little entrées into my salon on her way in to visit him.

PARIS. TUESDAY, MAY 17, 1904.
I read in the paper this morning that the Americans have hired Dr. Gorgas and are sending him to Panama to try and stop the yellow fever with a new vaccine. They have made slow progress in recent months, fighting against the heat, the mosquitoes, dysentery, and an outbreak of cholera, and have now been forced to halt work altogether because the fever is decimating

their workers. Perhaps they are discovering for themselves why the French had such difficulty completing the canal. If Adrien were here this morning, he would be reading me a lecture on hygiene, which might have prevented the diseases in the first place. It was always medicine that took his attention. The cholera. Well, the cholera and a fine lady or two.

Marie has agreed to the medallion.

PARIS. TUESDAY, JULY 19, 1904.

Dick and Marthe insist that I go with them to Etretat next month. We have never holidayed there, which is, I suppose, why they have picked it—no memories at all. I will acquiesce, although I am not sure I can bear a whole three weeks in a hotel with Marthe. She means well but she does fuss an awful lot, both about her own health and the baby's. Of course, one cannot help but feel for her, what she went through with the confinement—that day we went to visit her after Suzy was born, Marcel and I changing out of our mourning clothes in Dick's study, so as not to give her any hint of what had transpired, we were all so worried about her fever. Being cheerful was almost more than I could bear. And her own poor mother on the day of the funeral was at a loss for words when Marthe saw the procession from her bedroom window, making its way to Saint-Philippe du Roule, and speculated that it must have been someone particularly august who had died. The subterfuge, for all that it was necessary, made me feel faint from grief, the gap between the normal cheerfulness of daily life and one's true emotions so overwhelming it appeared as farce rather than tragedy.

PARIS. MONDAY, SEPTEMBER 5, 1904.
Etretat was tedious and Dieppe damp. I am glad Marcel did not join me there. He would have found the rooms uncomfortable and his mother poor company. My bones ache horribly and I seem unable to get through a day without lying down several times for a nap.

For Marcel's sake, I must not give in to despair and lassitude but I feel, like Malherbe, that "I am vanquished by time and cede to its outrages."

PARIS. SATURDAY, SEPTEMBER 24, 1904.
I managed a trip to the Louvre yesterday, with the Comtesse de Martel for my companion and encouragement. We spent some time admiring the Italians. Ruskin has certainly sharpened my eye and we pursued a careful examination of light and colour in the Venetians. On leaving we passed the Caravaggios, and I remembered how I used to think that Marcel resembled the *Fortune Teller's* gay client. Yet now he is so sallow and pale, with none of the pink-cheeked ebullience of the figure in the painting. He looks like an old man these days, although he is only thirty-two. At times, his illness angers me, for I feel he throws away all hope of a normal life in his pursuit of an extravagant invalidism. And then I chastise myself for not sympathizing with what he cannot help.

PARIS. FRIDAY, OCTOBER 21, 1904.
Marthe says Suzy can now pull herself up onto her own feet and will surely walk by Christmas. I wish I could find more solace in her small presence, so cheerfully greeting life, as I sadly take my leave of it.

Marcel is determined to reform his schedule by the new year. I doubt he will do it.

Sesame and Lilies is going well and Marie has been a faithful editor and visitor. The medallion is magnificent—she has followed our instructions so accurately, and created a strong likeness from all the photographs I lent her. Marcel says we must install it at Père Lachaise on the first anniversary next month. Marie does not look happy, however, and I only hope she has not misunderstood Marcel's need for her.

PARIS. FRIDAY, OCTOBER 28, 1904.
Marcel has been giving much solace to the beautiful Mlle. de Mornand these days. She visits regularly to cry on his shoulder, for d'Albufera's engagement to the Princess was finally announced last week. I suppose every mistress believes she is so cherished that she will surely be the exception, the one who successfully makes the move from demimonde to beau monde. Well, we all believe our own loves are unique and are loath to see they are simply repeating predictable patterns.

Marie worked all afternoon with Marcel yesterday, and just as I was seeing her out, she crossed Mlle. de Mornand in the hallway. Dear Marie looked stricken. I can hardly take her aside and tell her there is no reason to be jealous.

No more can I tell Mlle. de Mornand that if she waits until six months after the society wedding, she will find that her lover will probably take her back, albeit under circumstances that will require more discretion. They say d'Albufera paid for her carriage and pair, although perhaps today the greatest proof of love would be the gift of an automobile.

I BELIEVE THIS IS as close as I will come to an answer: Mme. Proust knew much, but did not speak. There is only one more notebook in the document box, the journal for 1905, and skimming it, I find that the entries are sparse. I will be finished soon, and should go to the Air Canada office to book a flight home. It's just past three o'clock: if I pack up now, I will make it there before closing.

I take File 263 back up to the reserve desk, and pass the box across the counter to Ahmed. I am still tempted to study his face, to look for comparisons, and I must be staring, for he snaps at me: "What?" I look shamefacedly away.

It is an old habit this, sometimes conscious, sometimes not, to find the one who is missing in the throng, to read a beloved face in the profile of a total stranger. Max and I lost touch after he moved back to Toronto. At first, he phoned from time to time; I didn't answer or didn't return the messages and soon enough he stopped. But I still would see him often, a few rows ahead at a concert or play, rounding the next bend in the subway corridor, or crossing the street and hurrying away from me before I have time to really examine his face. Most of all, I see him in the lecture halls, hearing rooms, and conference centres where I work. I will slip into the translator's booth, hang my purse over the back of my chair, put on the headphones, and ready my microphone, preparing to speak into it my version, in the other language, of the day's speeches, papers, and disputations. And then I will look out at the room and catch sight of a head amongst those busying themselves with notepads, pencils, and briefcases as they wait for talk to begin. It is his head, I am sure of it. I recognize the curly hair, the way it follows the back of the scalp tightly but then bursts into a tangle of ringlets that sit thickly an inch or two above the collar.

My stomach tightens. It is always fear I feel now when I see Max. The hurt is done, if not forgotten, an encounter would at worst be uncomfortable, yet I flinch at the thought of it the way an animal once kicked will forever cower. He is the past but I think only of how to run. I shrink in my chair, desperate that he should not look up and back, yet staring so hard at him to ascertain that it is actually him, that he will surely feel my eyes on him with that sixth sense one has in public places. Indeed, he turns in his chair to adjust the coat he has been sitting up against and so doing glances upwards. I cannot always recall Max's features in my mind's eye, sometimes they are far from me, but these are not his. This is some other dark-haired man, and relief eases into me.

Often my mistake is ludicrous. This man is far too tall, that one much lighter complexioned. Why would Max, a Toronto doctor, be sitting in the crowd at a Montreal colloquium for urban planners? Why would Max, a Jew, be bent over a hymn book at the Christmas carol service at Notre-Dame-des-Douleurs? What would Max be doing here, shelving boxes in the Bibliothèque Nationale?

Once recognizing my mistake, I take to comparing the difference, to see if I can still remember Max's face readily enough to know why this is not his, using what is absent to conjure something into the present, attempting to turn what is not into what is. This face is larger, the nose longer, the cheeks flatter. This hair is thinner, the brow higher. This face is more conventionally handsome and the wearer knows it, his eyes are shallower, self-conscious of his body rather than his soul. He is more present yet less alive.

Sometimes, it is simply a single feature that I recognize in others. I am sitting on a train, travelling to Ottawa to visit old friends from school who now work as parliamentary translators there, and I see Max's nose. The bearer is utterly different, but it's the same nose, a delicate little isosceles triangle inserted high on the face. Or I notice that the aerobics instructor in the gym I sometimes visit blushes in exactly the same way, involuntarily flustered at the least excitement, so that you quickly forgive him his evident self-absorption.

I have never, however, seen Max's lips on any other man. I remember them best of all, for they seem slightly deformed, a quiet blemish on his beauty that you would notice only if you observed him for a very long time. They are full lips, but not even—the upper lip, towards the left-hand side, is somehow slightly inflamed, dropping down in a little bump towards the lower lip so that, when closed, the line between the two is irregular. Indeed, the first time I ever noticed this I wondered momentarily if someone had punched Max several weeks before and a larger bruise was just now fading to an almost imperceptible swelling. Or if he had inadvertently bit himself, stumbling when running perhaps as a child does, mouth dangerously open, teeth suddenly clamping down and catching flesh. But almost instantaneously I also realized that this was not a temporary disfiguration but rather the permanent outline of his mouth, as though he always carried with him a small wound visible only to those who looked long and hard.

Why do we love those that we do? How do we choose the objects of our desire? I saw something in those lips that I thought could heal me, something in those eyes that would make me whole. And, detecting need and hurt in a sigh or a silence, I longed to return the favour, to nurture and mend. I lusted for his otherness, to share his language, to fix his history. At the restaurant and café tables, by my side on the park benches, in the seat next to me at the movie theatres, I thought I had glimpsed the weight that would perfectly balance mine, the other half of my soul. What did he see looking back at him? Stability, normality, heterosexuality? What was it that he wanted? Belonging, affection, a mother's love, or just me?

I don't suppose I will ever know, but I did actually seem him again, no chimera, but the real thing. It was last fall, after a gap of four years. It was 1998 and I was thirty-three, soon to turn thirty-four. In French we call that *l'age du Christ*, the age Christ had reached when he was crucified. A watershed year, if you will excuse a bit of ironic understatement in the translation.

It is at a medical conference in Montreal where I am working. There are interpreters who specialize in medicine, but I usually avoid it, a little peculiarity of mine. I do everything else. The demand is mainly for politics and economics; occasionally there's stuff on agriculture or the environment. Recently, I have been pursuing a strong line in intergovernmental relations. I translate deficit for *déficit*; negotiate for *négocier*; separation for *séparation*; nation for *nation*. But this time, a colleague has fallen ill, and I get a last-minute call. The night before the conference I read through recently published papers, write up vocabulary lists, and run a mental check list; antibodies is *anticorps*, obviously. *Dépistage* is . . . quick, one of those self-sufficient little Anglo-Saxon gerunds . . . screening, mucus membranes, *les muqueuses*; needle exchange, *aiguillage*. There's a pun there: *aiguille* is needle and *aiguillage* the term for switching on a railway track. A drug cocktail can be called a *cocktail des médicaments*; *toxicomanie* is drug addiction. *Récepteurs*, receptors. *Inhibiteurs*, inhibitors.

I enter the translator's booth as the conference participants are settling in their chairs, and agree with my two colleagues inside that I'll begin, covering the first half-hour before handing over the job to the next in line and taking a break. A half-hour on, an hour off is our standard professional relay for a full day's work. Then I take a look at the day's agenda, which I had forgotten to pull out the previous night. The opening address is to be delivered by Dr. M. B. Segal. Deep inside me a fluttering lightness seems to animate my organs. I feel sick. Far below me, at the front of the room, a man with very short hair wearing a dark suit is shuffling his papers in preparation. He speaks and I remember it is him.

"Ladies and gentlemen . . ."

"Mesdames et messieurs . . ."

"Colleagues . . ."

"Collègues . . ."

"I am not here to speak about good hygiene."

"Je ne vous parlerai pas d'hygiène."

"I am not here to speak of condoms and precautions."

"Je ne vous parlerai pas des préservatives et des précautions."

"I am not here to speak of pie in the sky."

"Je ne vous parle pas des fantasies."

"I am here to speak about the realistic hope for a vaccine in 2000 . . ."

"VIRUS"

"virus"

"antibodies"

"anticorps"

"cure"

"remède"

time

temps

desire

le désir

love

l'amour

loss

la perte

shock, heartbreak, anger. . .

And then? Acceptance? Forgiveness? Or merely forgetfulness?

No one notices the conference interpreter. No one says, "Good job"; "Like the way you cleaned up his ending for him"; "Glad to hear someone still knows how to use a plus-perfect subjunctive." Unless she "ums" and "ers" to the point of distraction, gets her expert terminology all twisted up, or expires in mid-sentence, the translator is invisible. At the end of Max's speech, while the delegates break for coffee, I take off my headphones and prepare to slip unobserved from the auditorium. I've worked half an hour and then spent the last twenty minutes of his speech listening inside the booth, trying to calm myself and take a proper professional interest in the proceedings. I still have forty minutes to clear my head before I return to work. Later, on my next hour off, I'll take a long lunch break alone, try to find a quiet corner where I can eat my sandwich, maybe finish reading the last chapter of the Hayman biography before returning to the afternoon sessions. The exit doors are placed towards the front of the hall, and as I pass near the podium, the speaker disengages himself from a little cluster of people and a voice calls to me.

"Marie, Marie." This is Max. He is grinning widely, with an expression of delighted surprise.

"What are you doing here?"

"Working."

"You're translating?"

"Yes. I just did your speech."

"That's great. So, what did you think?"

"I'm just the translator. It was fine."

"How are you? It's been a long time . . ."

"Yeah. A long time. I'm good."

"So, uh, how's work?"

"It's good. Busy, there's lots of it. I don't usually do medical stuff but one of my colleagues got sick."

"How are your parents?"

"They're good. My dad's retired now. He sold the business. It took my mother some time to adjust but he loves it."

"Are they still here?"

"Yeah, they still live in Montreal."

This kind of exchange continues for several minutes as we catch up on four years of family and career.

Then he says, "So, what are you doing for lunch?"

I feel anger rising inside me and fight back tears.

He has not changed physically—except for his hair. He now wears it cropped close to the head, a spray of curls across his forehead the only reminder of the shoulder-length locks he has cut off. Sitting at a table in the conference centre cafeteria, I want to reach out and push those last curls back with my hand to see where the hairline now falls. It is not a malicious desire, a jealous urge to see if he too has aged. On the contrary, I seek reassurance that he remains the same. It is the same hand with which I almost daily, delicately touch the skin under my chin, absent-mindedly, riding on a bus, sitting in the booth, checking that the flesh is still taut, frightened that it seems infinitesimally softer than it did a week or a month before. Lines have yet to appear on his face; my first showed up in my twenties, cracks around my eyes where I have smiled too much or squinted in the light. Now, in my thirties, two furrows are slowly tracing a path between my nose and the corners of my mouth. I will age like my mother, my face collapsing quickly into sagging and folded flesh.

A young man hails Max from across the room and beckons him over. He excuses himself and walks away from me, his narrow form moving carefully amongst the tightly spaced tables and chairs, his head, small now that it has so little hair, held erect with a quiet confidence, his face animated by an expression that is lively but slightly aloof. I watch him and wonder how I could have ever mistaken him for other than who he is.

He greets his friend, consults with him a while, and then brings him back to the table. I do not need to hear the proprietary tone with which Max introduces him to know. They look remarkably alike; small men, olive-skinned, dark-haired, brown-eyed, straight-nosed, thin-limbed, beautiful boys. Theirs is belonging.

He doesn't stay long, sensing perhaps my resentment, and when he goes, I ask Max the conventional questions: where they met, what he does for a living.

"He's very beautiful," I say, hoping to hide any hint of jealousy or reservation.

"Yes. I always think he looks Italian, like someone Caravaggio would have painted. I told him that once, that he looked like a Caravaggio. Know what he said?"

"What?"

"What's a Caravaggio?"

We laugh together, catching each other's glance, delighting for one forgetful moment in our sameness.

"Have your parents met him?" I ask.

"No, I take that slowly. My mother"—he hesitates—"Well, you know my mother . . ."

We say goodbye after lunch, agree to stay in touch, and as I watch him go I find myself thinking, again, of his mother, of her anxiety that he establish himself in medicine, in middle-class life. What does she feel now, I wonder, she who has come so far for safety, about her gay son, the AIDS doctor. In my mind, I find images floating and words forming, a story composing itself.

A BISCUIT? SOME OF your own rugelach?"

Sarah held out the plate of cookies towards Clara, who helped herself to a rugelach and perched it on the saucer of her teacup.

"A good woman. So good to you, Sarah." Sarah nodded and sipped her own tea.

"Yes, she was always generous to Sarah," Daniel agreed and smiled at his own mother, who had been firmly installed in their living room for the past three hours.

The purpose was to air one's grief, give it room to breathe so that it would lead a natural life and fade quietly and properly in its own time rather than reappear angry and unwanted at inappropriate moments long after it should have past. Sarah knew the rationale and the protocol, but sitting shivah for Rachel was wearing her down. She felt guilty, she supposed, that she had not ever succeeded in being the daughter that Rachel had wanted, and now it was irrevocably too late.

Sarah had always done her duty towards Rachel, had let her serve as Maxime's grandmother, taken him regularly to see her, invited her for the holidays, finally eaten dinner every week at the Villa Nova. For years, she had visited and chatted, but without the depth of affection that would have given these actions joy. It was Daniel who brought joy into the house on Gladstone Avenue, and later to the old age home, always flirting, cajoling, complimenting. "Your cheesecake, Rachel, like no other . . ." "That dress, such a becoming colour . . ." "Rachel, your health . . ." Sarah had repressed her annoyance at these attentions, just as now she bit back her anger as Daniel supplied the words of agreement with Clara's platitude. She felt that he shamed her and she secretly suspected that was his intent, and also, in the way of long-married couples, that he knew she thought that. Nonetheless, he had continued, covering for her, supplying what she could not, so that if Rachel never had children, she had at least a son-in-law who could say the Kaddish.

She had made it to 2000, but whether or not she could claim to have seen the new millennium was another matter. Her first stroke, a few weeks before the new year, had left her partly paralyzed and increasingly senile. The second followed with merciful swiftness and they had held the funeral service on a cold, sunny day in late February. Several days later they were almost finished their shivah, and a whole parade of old ladies as well as many of their own friends and all their relations had already visited their living room, bearing with them a wide array of cookies, sandwiches, and casseroles that each evening left Sarah annoyedly laying a table with all these mismatched contributions while Daniel and his brothers said prayers in the other room. Mrs. Field, a long-ago neighbour from Gladstone Avenue, perhaps ten years Rachel's junior, had quietly come to pay her respects and sweetly stayed, delicately offering memories where there was need for conversation, remaining silent when there was none. Sarah, remembering that Mrs. Field had first appeared on the street at some point during the war, realized to her surprise that she must have known this woman longer than any other living soul, and kissed her warmly when she took her leave. Doddering old Mr. Seeger from Villa Nova appeared, with a young Filipino woman for his nursemaid, and laughed and cried in a way that left Daniel amusedly speculating on his relationship with Rachel. Lisa came, all the way from Calgary where she and Michael now lived, but they had reason to be in town for his business anyway. Sarah saw her irregularly since her move, and they spent the time catching up with each other's lives as much as they did mourning Rachel. Lisa asked after Maxime, and Sarah did not know what to say.

"He's working very hard. He wants to stick with research."

"No daughter-in-law yet?"

"No, not yet."

The new rabbi came. Really, Sarah should be able to remember his name. He was the one who had replaced Rabbi Vine, who had replaced Rabbi Cohn, now long dead. Sarah thought it was good of this young man to bother since he had never met Rachel. She had never joined their congregation, even if she had kept in touch with Rabbi Cohn over the years. Daniel's colleague from the new medical building, a dermatologist named Dr. Ritz, dropped by, bringing his wife too. Sarah liked them. She and Daniel had invited them over to dinner a few times and now Laura Ritz suggested an outing some afternoon.

"Soon. When you feel up to it. This time of year, it's so easy to get stuck indoors."

Rachel's cousin Leah from Montreal was there. She had split up with her husband, years ago, and moved to Toronto to get away from her family, or so she said. She must be at least eighty-five, Sarah reckoned, but she still lived on her own, and was fully mobile, for she boasted to Daniel about her regular gambling sprees, at the casino in Niagara Falls. She took the bus there.

"It's a hoot, and I never even see the water. Don't go anywhere near those Falls. Too busy with my chips."

Sarah looked out over them all, as they came and went, and wondered at them. These were her friends, her family, her community. She supposed, at seventy, that she belonged.

And Clara came daily, settling her large frame into the good leather armchair, while Daniel and Sarah perched on the sofa from which they had, following the tradition, removed all the cushions so that they would sit lower, diminished by their loss. Holding her matronly head of thick white hair high and proud, Clara regarded them and their guests with an appraising look. Lionel had died fifteen years ago, back when Maxime was still in high school, but his ninety-two-year-old widow was utterly undiminished, indeed somewhat enlivened by a recent operation that had successfully removed a cataract from her right eye.

"I brought some cookies, Sarah," she had announced on the first day as she opened a tin packed with rugelach and brownies. "I wanted to do my share." Actually, Sarah had baked herself. She had foreseen the eventuality of shivah since the December day when the doctor had said Rachel wouldn't last, and although she had predicted many contributions from family and friends, she had wanted her own cooking to be served in her home. She had concentrated on sweets, they were comforting, after all, and spent January baking batch after batch of vanilla wafers, thin little almond cookies, and Rachel's own recipe for sponge cake, all of which she had carefully packaged up in plastic and stored in the freezer. She had avoided all richer cakes, considered rugelach and rejected it, eschewed anything with chocolate, because she reasoned that only the most delicate, the most tactful of pastries would be acceptable in a house of mourning.

In the living room, as Clara conveyed the rugelach to her mouth, the doorbell rang. Maxime, who was sitting with them, rose.

"I'll get it," he said and left the room for the vestibule where he could be heard quietly greeting and helping with coats.

He had been there all week, opening the door, talking with their guests, making the tea and coffee, passing the food. Sarah looked at him in wonder too, and, aside from the odd thank you, did not speak to him.

At first, Sarah had behaved as though the night she made the *pot-au-feu* had never happened. She ignored Maxime's announcement about his research and all its implications. Some Fridays, he would come to his parents' house for dinner. He and his father would talk medicine, without ever really discussing Maxime's work. He would still name friends, male and female, without ever really explaining to his parents what kind of friendships these might be. Sarah, who had spent so much of life anxiously anticipating things that never did happen, now tried to block out something that really had happened, as though her son's unspoken sexuality was a phase she could wait out. Maxime made no attempt to penetrate this atmosphere of silence and illusion, and as it lengthened he increasingly stayed away. By the time they were sitting shivah, three years after the evening on which he had first spoken, Maxime had not set foot in the house in North Toronto for months and had last seen Sarah and Daniel in December at the hospital when Rachel first had her stroke.

Now, he reappeared in the living room with some long-time neighbours from down the street, a portly man in a bright-red sweater with a painfully thin little wife hovering silently behind him, her arms full of a large, foil-covered dish.

"Sarah. How are you? Our condolences. A sad occasion, but good to see you all the same. Good to see Max, too," the man gestured back behind him. "Never see you these days, Max. You should come round more. Neglecting your parents in their dotage, eh?"

"No, no, not all," Maxime said, attempting to laugh, while accepting the dish from the woman's outstretched arms.

And so it went for the rest of the afternoon and into the evening until Sarah thankfully shut the door on the last of the friends and relations while Daniel set off in the car to drive Clara home.

Sarah cleared up some teacups and cake plates in the living room and came back into the kitchen to find Maxime stacking the dishes in the wrong dishwasher.

"*Laisse-les, laisse-les.* Leave it," she instructed him. "I'll do it."

"I can do it."

"No, no. Leave it." She closed in on the dishwasher, making shooing motions with her hands until he moved aside, and then began taking the dishes back out.

"What are you doing?"

"This is meat, this one."

"Oh, right. I wasn't thinking. Sorry."

"It doesn't matter. I'll just run it through empty to clean it out."

"Right, well. I should get going then . . ."

"You're not going to stay for some dinner?"

"No, no. I'm stuffed. All those cookies . . ."

"It's late, but I was going to make a proper dinner."

"No, really. I still have some work I should do tonight."

"Okay. You'll come Thursday."

"Yes, Ma. I'll be there."

On Thursday, after their shivah was over, all three of them had agreed to visit the Villa Nova, where the manager, a high-energy woman who looked young enough to be Sarah's daughter and rejoiced in a personality that was part social worker and part hostess, had insisted on some gathering to mark Rachel's passing.

"This was her home, Mrs. Segal. We are in mourning too, and most of the residents can't get over to your place. Besides, it's good for the old people. They need to acknowledge that somebody has left. There is no point hiding death from the elderly." The manager smiled a powerful smile and Sarah, made to feel she was somehow being selfish and that if she refused it would be all too obvious she was deeply relieved to be free of her weekly obligation to visit the Villa Nova, had been forced to agree. But it was, as she had anticipated, a painful affair filled with awkward pauses as she tried to make conversation with the deaf and the confused, unsure whether they had actually known Rachel at all. Daniel fared better, of course, talking or not talking, smiling or serious, with Maxime at his side to occasionally enliven, prompt, or merely give him some respite. But Sarah felt increasingly distant from her surroundings and, by the time they left at four o'clock, deeply weary.

The weather, which had turned warmer in the days they sat shivah, had changed again and was now sharply cold. The sky was blue and cloudless, still light in the afternoon as the short, dark days were now, with March approaching, suddenly and swiftly replaced by longer, lighter ones. That afternoon the kitchen in the house in North Toronto was frigid but filled with sun. Sarah stood there now with Daniel and Maxime waiting for the kettle to boil for tea, her annoyance that her ever-charitable husband had once again shown her up still fresh upon her, and her estrangement from her son rippling through the chilly air. And it was in this atmosphere of exhaustion and irritation that Daniel made the mistake, prompted by a sigh from Sarah, of offering some thoughtless consolation: "Well, we all have to die some time. She had a good life."

Sarah turned on him and replied angrily: "Some time, some time. She had her time, ninety-four years of it." She switched now into sharp and bitter French. "Some were not so lucky, some did not have their time. Some did not live to see their grandchildren grow up, grow up to be what, what . . ." She gestured contemptuously towards Maxime. He and Daniel stared at her, uncomprehending, as she started to confuse her grievances and sorrows, jumbling them all together, anger flooding into her heart and filling every little cranny of discontentment or disappointment, until she was a shaking mass who could not distinguish between her genuine grief at losing Rachel and her jealousy that this woman had been given the long life her own mother had not, between her incomprehension of her son and her frustration that the kettle seemed to be taking forever to boil. She jerked its cord furiously from the outlet—"Oh, this stupid thing, we might as well give up"—and as she did so, knocked with her sleeve the china cups sitting on the countertop waiting for the tea.

The sound of the china shattering on the floor seemed to break the last of her reserve: she turned on the shards lying at her feet and hurled the milk jug down to join them. As it fell, its contents spilled all over the trim black wool suit that she wore with Sophie Bensimon's pearls sitting tidily at the neck. Then she tugged at the cutlery drawer nearest to her and, holding up one end while the other simply fell away, dumped its contents onto the pile. Seized now by a sudden inspiration, she crossed the kitchen to the second cutlery drawer, where the knives and forks for cutting and eating meat were kept, and pulled it out, this time having to fling the cutlery a good distance, to join the stuff already there.

"Is this why they died? So we can live here, in this house, with two sets of dishes?" She turned to the meat cupboard and flung several plates out, before purposely striding across to the milk cupboard and grabbing a bowl that came to hand, hurling it down to join the rest. The little pots in ribbed white porcelain into which she had so often poured crème caramel crashed down to join the dinner plates on which she had served a *boeuf bourguignon* made with oyster mushrooms, pearl onions, and a solid red wine. Shards of the bowls in which Maxime and Daniel had eaten breakfast cereals covered in milk now mixed with chips off the big enamel casserole in which Sarah liked to simmer her famous stews. *Milchik* and *flayshig*, the two sets of dishes came pouring from their cupboards, breaking, shattering, smashing until Sarah stood weeping in a pile of fragments.

Daniel backed away, horrified by an anger he had never seen before, refusing to know that this was the emotion that lay underneath Sarah's gracious melancholy and fierce anxieties.

It was Maxime who moved gingerly forward, picking his way through the bits of glass and china until he reached his mother.

"*Maman.*"

He gave her the name of his childhood, and took her in his arms the way he had held patients as they, shaking and crying, faced the results of blood tests.

And as he too began to weep, they stood there together, holding each other in the ruins of the kosher kitchen, finally mourning his grandparents and her grandchildren.

THEY SAY WE MONTREALERS are insular. It isn't true. We may live on an island, but we know the world. We seek the Florida sun in winter and, French and English alike, we are fascinated by New York. Sometimes, I'll fly down there for a weekend, treating myself to the museums and shops, pretending the price tags are in Canadian dollars, ignoring reality for a day or two. Wouldn't it be glorious to be a New Yorker, to speak their hard American English, to know that you ruled the world and lived at its epicentre?

We crave Paris too. I save up for the visit here every few years. My parents have friends who own a studio off the Canal Saint-Martin, and I'll rent it out when I can afford a longer stay. How luscious to live in French, to speak only one language, and that the most beautiful in the world, to speak it fast, smart, and proud. How glorious to pretend, for a moment, for a week or two, that one is Parisian, that there is only one metropolis, and beyond it merely the provinces.

No, we Montrealers are not insular. When they say that, what they mean is that we never visit Toronto. That's true. We don't visit Toronto. Why would we want to? It's unilingual and monolithic, not in New York's brash, exciting manner, but in some duller, less colourful way. It doesn't tempt, as we say in French. Well, in truth, we don't know much about the place, and perhaps we are a little afraid. It's a confusing city, hard to pin down, so resolutely anglophone yet so visibly polyglot. On one of the few occasions that I have visited Toronto, I rode a bus downtown from Bloor Street and found myself suddenly in Hong Kong surrounded by Chinese faces, food shops selling bok choy, and restaurants with slabs of meat all plastered in a brilliant-red sauce hanging in the window. That same evening I was taken to dinner in a neighbourhood where the street signs were in Greek.

It's not that we don't have our immigrant communities in Montreal, we are francophones, anglophones, and *allophones*. It is our little joke that has become a label. Through a polychrome archway recently erected across a southern section of the Boulevard Saint-Laurent, you'll find two blocks of Chinatown. In May, there's a huge Portuguese festival that stops traffic up on the Plateau Mont Royal. But these are contained demonstrations that do not disturb our original dance of English and French. We are surprised and puzzled by Toronto's reality. What if we were to speak not merely English and French, but Cantonese and Mandarin, Greek, Farsi, and Italian? To a Montrealer the prospect is alarming. In Toronto, they barely seem to care, as if, there, language itself could be taken lightly.

So, one day last winter, I am resentfully picking my way through the slushy streets of Toronto, visiting the city for perhaps the third or fourth time in my life. Since we bumped into each other at the medical conference, Max has called occasionally to chat over the phone. He seems to want to draw me back into his orbit. He urges me to visit.

"Come and see Toronto. The city has really improved, Marie. You'll have fun. You can stay at my place, there's a guest room."

I debate a visit, feel myself pulled, resist, offer excuses.

"I'm kind of busy at the moment . . ."

"You Montrealers are always so insular."

I hesitate. Perhaps. No harm in a visit. There's hope inside me. That's dangerous.

And then the issue is resolved by work: Toronto is playing host to an environmental summit and lacks the interpreters it will need to keep the proceedings running simultaneously in two languages. I have travelled across Canada translating at conferences; I do a lot of work in Nova Scotia and New Brunswick, have often visited Vancouver and Calgary, but I never go to Toronto. They have lots of their own translators there, and if they need extras, they just phone Ottawa, national capital of conference interpreters. But this time, there are several other conferences going on in Ottawa and an organizer phones, seeking my services. Would I come for the week, stay at the downtown hotel where the summit is taking place? It feels like a solution, a good reason to visit and provides the safety of a hotel. I agree to the job and, the week before my trip, phone Max. He suggests we meet Wednesday evening at the museum, the Royal Ontario Museum.

"They have a really good restaurant now, upstairs on the roof."

Toronto is always boasting of improvements, as though perhaps the past had not been much good at all.

"And then after dinner we can go back into the galleries. They've redone the Chinese collection."—more improvements— "I've been meaning to see it. I'll leave the lab at six pronto. Dinner at six-thirty, okay?"

Over dinner we talk about work.

"So, are they going to get a deal on these emission standards, or what? I mean, the Europeans have stolen the last of our fish and now the Americans want to maintain their God-given right to pollute our air. Canada is going to hang tough, right?"

"I don't know. I have no idea."

"But you're there, it's great, you can hear what they're saying, follow all the politics. What's happening with it?"

"I don't really know. I don't think about the issues while I'm translating, Max. If you do that, you can get totally distracted. I do words, not meaning."

We talk about his practice, his lab, about the drug cocktails, and the vaccine.

"It's nuts, you know. My patients have stopped dying, but I've never been more afraid. The governments just want a magic pill, and they think they've got one—or thirty-five magic pills. The mortality rates have dropped; the drug companies are making heaps of money. So who needs to fund vaccine research? I'm scared our grant won't be renewed this time around. They'll just pull the plug on us, even when the end is in sight. We're pushing, still pushing, but we aren't quite there yet. We are doing some work with the guys at the Institut Pasteur in Paris, and with the Americans. They'll probably get there first. That's fine with me. I hope they do, the sooner the better. I'm not looking to win any contest."

After dinner, we wander through the Chinese galleries, clean and quiet modern spaces full of ancient bronze and porcelain but empty of people on a weekday night. Max stops to examine a vase closely, giving it the same rapt attention he must apply to the blood cells magnified on their glass slides.

"*Viens voir ça* . . ." He speaks in French as leans towards the display case. His fine, straight body bends forward from the waist, his dark head moves closer, and one long finger extended, he indicates through the glass the curving dragon whose orange body wraps itself around the vessel.

"*Regarde, Marie* . . ."

In a museum in The Hague, Marcel Proust is examining a view of Delft painted by Vermeer, a canvas that he will, a decade later, champion in literature. I can see him in the gallery as he admires the fine brushwork that has conjured up the brick houses with their red-tile roofs under a large sky of monumental clouds that cast a shadow over the buildings in the middle ground. He leans gently forward to notice one area on the right-hand side where a little corner of wall emerges from the darker forms around it and shines bright yellow in its own patch of sunlight. He smiles to himself and turns to Bertrand Fénelon: "*Regarde* . . ."

There was a certain similarity, in my mind at least, a boyishness that was also an exoticism, a sensitivity that some might call precious, a beauty and a love of the beautiful, that I valued, that I misunderstood. The attraction lay somewhere in aestheticism, his or mine, I'm not quite sure, but I saw us as two fragile flowers in the same bilingual hothouse, failing to note the differences between the plants. Ruskin perceived morality in beauty and so could picture our human longings as a yearning for the divine. My need for God is a faint thing, but certainly I desired Max as I desired the author of *A la Recherche,* animated by the same force that binds my father to his antiques, that sent Mme. Proust to the Louvre, that attracted Ruskin to his cathedrals, and that propelled Marcel Proust not only towards *The Bible of Amiens* but also to his aristocrats. We all confuse having and being, and think that by possessing what is better than us, we will better ourselves.

But those are insights I have gleaned only here, in the Bibliothèque Nationale. In the ROM that day, I had but some faint sense of a link between Max and Proust, a hunch that sent me scurrying back to Montreal determined to pursue the French novelist yet further, that in understanding him I might somehow be free of Max. By the spring, I had found both the collected correspondence and the *Encyclopedia of the Holocaust* in the library at UQAM and I spent the summer poring over those volumes. In August, I booked a plane ticket for Paris, a plane ticket with an open return, ready now to confront my desires.

Ahmed has gone missing. Or at least, there has been no sign of him in the library all day. I only hope that he is off somewhere helping with the removal to the new building. They have been packing up all week. I should be finishing too.

PARIS. TUESDAY, JANUARY 10, 1905.
Marie came to take her leave yesterday. M. Bing is setting up an exhibition devoted to the Art Nouveau, as they call it, and wants to show it to the Americans. Marie is to travel with it, starting in New York, and then move it to Detroit. She had delayed telling me of her decision to leave us, partly out of

embarrassment, I suppose, that I might read a humiliation into it. She was trying very hard not to cry, and said how much she hoped Marcel would soon complete *Sesame and Lilies* and that she hoped she had been of some help. She was being modest: I said I did not know how we could have managed the last year without her, not only for her practical advice on the English language but also for her ability to reawaken Marcel's interest in Ruskin and her gentle, humane wisdom too. I would have told her that I loved her as any mother would love a daughter, had I not thought this might hurt her tender soul.

She sails for New York on Saturday.

PARIS. SATURDAY, MARCH 18, 1905.

I spoke with Marcel last night. I asked him if he would he miss me terribly were I ever to leave him. Perhaps it was a pointless question. Perhaps honest communication is impossible on such a subject. He hesitated at first, and then pointed out what a creature of habit he has always been. "You know, Maman, if someone I were terribly close to, say Reynaldo or Albu, were to die, I should feel bereft at first, unable to cope without their visits or their services as ready messengers, telling a friend he was wanted, or fetching a book from Calmann, but the humdrum nature of my solitary life would reassert itself, the surface of habit would close over the loss, like skin heals over a wound, and in the end I would manage without." I know to others his answer might sound callous, but he means only to reassure me that he will survive, to spare me anxiety. And like some long-married couple, we both know that I know that is his strategem. We do not speak of my departure, but thus, I have his permission.

PARIS. MONDAY, MAY 29, 1905.

A postcard has arrived from Canada. Marie has visited the great falls at Niagara, not that far from Detroit, she writes. She says the sight both delighted and appalled her, such was the grand rushing spectacle of the water but so large and heartless did nature seem in comparison to our own small sorrows. The picture reveals little of that—it is quite banal and shows some prim tourists peering over a railing at a mighty blur that could as easily be stone as water. The Bing exhibition is a huge success, she adds. I am cheered by the idea of Marie poised on the brink of a great artistic endeavour in the new world.

PARIS. TUESDAY, JUNE 6, 1905.

Marcel is almost finished *Sesame,* which should appear next year. He ventured out last night for the first time in weeks, and left me with his wonderful introduction to read. He writes so exquisitely, is so convinced of the rightness of the artistic life, and falsely modest about his own talents—or at least, so his dear mother thinks.

" . . . the critic should then go further. He should try to reconstruct what the unique spiritual life of a writer haunted by such special realities could have been, his inspiration being the measure of his vision of those realities, his talent the measure of his ability to recreate them in his work, his ethics, finally, the instinct which, making him consider them from a viewpoint of eternity (however particular these realities appear to us), impelled him to sacrifice to the need of perceiving them and to the necessity of reproducing them, in order to ensure their lasting and clear image, all his pleasures, all his duties, and even his own life, which has no raison d'être except as the only possible way of entering into contact with those realities and has no value except that which an instrument indispensable to his experiments may have for a physicist. I need not say that I have not attempted to fulfil this second part of the critic's duty here with regard to Ruskin. That can be the object of subsequent studies. This is only a translation . . ."

So writes Marcel Proust.

THOSE ARE THE FINAL entries in Mme. Proust's diary, except for an illegible scrawl on a subsequent page that is otherwise blank. In 1905, her handwriting has become increasingly difficult to read, and I cannot make out these few last words. I pack up my document box and walk up to the reserve counter. There is still no sign of Ahmed, and I regret that I did not speak to him yesterday, ask him whether he had solved his visa problem. In his place, the assistant assistant librarian is ready to take back File 263, and I feel obliged to announce myself.

"I am finished, monsieur. I am going home to Canada. I wanted to thank you, and then, well, to say goodbye." I use the usual word, *au revoir*.

The assistant assistant librarian smiles with a trace of superiority and corrects me: "Back to Canada? *Alors, ce n'est pas au revoir, c'est adieu.*" To God. Until God? I'm not sure how to translate the phrase.

I walk away from the desk, but the librarian has an afterthought, and calls me back.

"If you really are finished, make sure you return your library card when you sign out."

"Yes. Goodbye then. *Adieu.*"

There is one last place, however, where I have yet to look for Proust. The next morning, on my last day in Paris, I visit Père Lachaise, carrying a bouquet of pink roses that I have bought at the fruit-and-vegetable shop near the studio. This is the city's most famous cemetery, home to Oscar Wilde, Sarah Bernhardt, Anna de Noailles, and Marcel Proust. It covers several acres of rising land in the northeast corner of the city. The graves are densely scattered under spreading trees, between winding paths. Proust's is uphill from the main entrance, on a plateau at the northern edge of the cemetery. The writer's gravemarker is a big, flat slab of black marble, very fresh looking as though perhaps it had been recently replaced or repolished. On its largest expanse, the broad flat top, his name and dates are inscribed. On the narrow sides beneath him are written the names of his father, mother, brother and sister-in-law. I think perhaps I should leave my roses down here, nearer the ground, beside Jeanne Proust's name.

However, my study of the grave is hindered by two American backpackers who are parked in front of it. One is sitting, with an air of resigned boredom, on a stone across from it while his eager companion bobs about snapping pictures of it with an impressive-looking camera and introducing his friend to the wonders of *A la Recherche*. "The description is amazing," he explains, as he fiddles with f-stops and squints through his lens.

I turn away, unsure how long I can wait for a moment of communion with my dead. My plane leaves for Montreal this afternoon, and I should get back to the studio to retrieve my bags and lock up. I hover uncertainly in the narrow alley between gravestones that leads to the Proust family monument, and then, taking a step backwards, I find that I am stumbling on uneven ground. I almost fall but recover myself, and I realize I have been standing on a low wall, almost invisible here where it measures less than a few inches but rising to perhaps a foot or two in height as it progresses towards the edge of the cemetery. A Star of David catches my eye. Apparently, I am standing on the edge of the old Jewish sector—once it must have been walled off from the rest of Père Lachaise—for there is a row of graves bearing the six-pointed star and names like Bloch, Becker, Dreyfus, Haas, Klein, and Weil. And here too, in large letters on a upright marker, is the family name BENSIMON. Underneath are a list of several people buried around the turn of the century. They are of an age to be my great-grandparents. Who knows who they might be? It is not, after all, a rare surname. Today, there are dozens of them in the Paris phone book. I looked them up once, in an idle moment. So, I place my pink roses on the grave of a family I do not know, and leave the backpackers to contemplate history and literature.

I walk back down the shady dirt paths of Père Lachaise, to the Métro stop on the avenue outside the cemetery, and travel back to the studio. At five o'clock I board a plane at Charles de Gaulle and fly home.

ON THE SOUTHERN EDGE of the island of Montreal, along the bank of the St. Lawrence River, there stand a few remains of New France. These narrow eighteenth-century streets are lined with low stone houses, their hard facades now softened by a fresh paint job on the front door or a window box full of pansies. Nearby there are the warehouses that once stored the pelts destined for Europe: their upper storeys have been converted to offices while antique shops are tucked into their ground floors. Horse-drawn carriages carry American tourists over the cobblestones.

I live on a forgotten street in the northeast corner of Old Montreal. My building was made from red brick in the nineteenth century and looks neglected rather than picturesque; the tourists never venture down the butt end of the Rue du Champs-de-Mars.

This neighbourhood suits me. I like its history: these streets might be mistaken for the Norman towns that my father's ancestors left three hundred years ago. The location is convenient: the conference centre where I often work is a short walk northwards, towards the new city. And the neighbours, singles or childless couples, keep to themselves. When we do speak, we converse in French.

My parents, on the other hand, chat in English with their neighbours. They live uptown, in Westmount, with its ample brick houses and, above them, the mansions of the truly rich perched on the side of the big hill that Montrealers call the Mountain. Politics may have chiselled away at this enclave of Anglo entitlement, but it remains a place where my mother can still call out, "Lovely day, Mrs. McIntosh," to a lady who is pruning her roses.

Montreal is a rarity, the truly bilingual city. There are these pockets—Notre-Dame-de-Grâce and Westmount are English; Outremont, Saint-Henri, and the east end are French—and there is a tapestry, of signs and billboards, announcements and conversations, orders given in a downtown café; homeowners lamenting as they shovel snow. You can live exclusively in one language, in splendid isolation in the other; you can resentfully speak a foreign tongue, you can instinctively embrace a dual heritage. French and English are everywhere, so are pride and humiliation, joy and frustration, choice and obligation, reality and desire. Where shall I begin with the taxi driver, the waiter, the bilingual colleagues, the English-speaking friend and her francophone husband? How can we assure that the children will learn proper English, will speak good French, will become bilingual? Things are getting better. No, clearly, there's been a turn for the worse. We are complacent. We are insecure. We are never comfortable. We love it here.

Since my return from Paris last week, I have realized that I feel at home not only amongst the historic streets of Old Montreal but in the whole jostling city north of it. Its edginess suits me, its instability matches mine. Here, half of us are outsiders and none of us fit.

I got back Thursday to find a message on my answering machine. I have not heard from Max in several months, not really much at all since last winter's trip to the museum. He says he will be visiting Montreal on business the following week, staying for the weekend. Can we get together?

Yes, we can get together one last time. We are now five years late for a final showdown. He can find my apartment at 6 Rue du Champs-de-Mars.

So, Max pays me a visit and sits awkwardly on the edge of a chair in my apartment. He smokes now—I suppose if you have seen a lot of people die, you worry less about these things—and I have to search about for a saucer that he can use as an ashtray. Sensing that no talking will get done in this way, I suggest we move to the roof.

Behind my living room, there's a galley kitchen that runs across the back of the apartment, with a window that opens onto an iron fire escape. Climb these stairs and you discover my garden—a tar-papered rooftop dotted with battered lawn chairs. The building is a full six storeys, just high enough that from this perch you can see over the rooftops to the St. Lawrence, a few streets away. Directly beneath us lies the Old Port where pleasure craft now tool about the marina. Look eastward, towards the giant silos of the Molson brewery and the Ferris wheel that still operates on the site of Expo 67, and you can see the modern port, where the heavy freighters await the cargo they will carry across the Atlantic.

It's a fine day in late October, almost warm enough to sun ourselves outside. We settle on the lawn chairs, and leaning forward but with my eyes cast down, I start to talk. Slowly, I recount the progress of an affair, crafting from each little episode a single perfect pearl of pain.

Do you remember the time you stuffed leaves down my back? I thought you wanted to hold me.

Do you remember the time, in the deli, when you asked me if I wanted children? I thought you meant you wanted children.

Do you remember the time you said that fresh snow was like falling in love because it made you see the whole world differently? I thought you meant you were in love.

I string my pearls together for him, finding a thread of narrative on which each bead can hang. I hold them out towards him as though if he were just to see my pearls, to admire them for a moment, then I could finally take off this necklace.

Sometimes in this recital a smile crosses his face, sometimes a frown suggests he is puzzled or disagrees; sometimes he nods. When at last I finish, he says nothing, puckering his uneven lips forward as though to speak and then dropping them back in place with only an "Mmm . . ."

I tell him that I forgive him, for that is what he has come to this place to hear. I forgive you my mistake.

Yet if he is forgiven, it is I who have confessed. And who is to say that tomorrow I will not sin again. The sin of anger, the sin of pity, the sin of lust, the sin of chastity, the sin of patience, the sin of haste, the sin of speaking, the sin of silence, the sin of lies, the sin of honesty, the sin of remembrance, the sin of forgetfulness, the sin of having loved too little, the sin of having loved too much.

This night, after he has left, I cannot sleep. As dawn approaches, I give up trying, pull on jeans and a warm sweater, and climb back upstairs to the rooftop where we sat.

The slow October dawn is gently rising over Old Montreal, and the St. Lawrence is awakening, the first light catching the water on one edge of one bank, and the river joyfully beginning its dance towards the ocean. It is only morning here, but in Paris it is already afternoon, and on the Champs-Elysées Marcel Proust is playing Prisoner's Base with Marie de Benardaky, while in the subterranean corridors that one day soon will be tunnelled beneath their feet, David is chasing me around a corner of the Métro station and calling my name. At No. 9 Boulevard Malesherbes, the narrator is longing for little Gilberte Swann while over on the Rue de Courcelles, Marie Nordlinger lies trapped on the divan in an overheated bedroom. On a frigid Polish morning, an officer of the Red Army unwraps his most precious belonging, a hoarded bar of chocolate, and offers it to an emaciated man in striped pyjamas while a military photographer snaps pictures that will one day shimmer in the darkened classroom where M. Delvaux teaches history. Across the Atlantic, in a lab in New York, an AIDS researcher sighs in frustration and wonders whether she will not simply test the vaccine on herself. Miles north in Toronto, you are safely back in your apartment near the Don Hospital, asleep in the arms of a boy who looks as if he were painted by Caravaggio. But I am sitting here, on this rooftop, alone.

And at this moment, at dawn in Montreal and midday in Paris, as the waters of the St. Lawrence meet the waters of the Seine and the Loire somewhere in the middle of the Atlantic, at this particular moment, I do not long for our games on the Champs-Elysées. I am finally resolved to replace nostalgia with forgetfulness. I will wear bright colours again.

I shiver and, as the day begins, I go downstairs and settle at my desk. Because I lost Max, I went looking for Marcel but instead I found his mother in the Bibliothèque Nationale, and in the pages of her diary, it was often the voice of Mrs. Segal, my mother-in-law who wasn't, that I thought I heard calling to me across the century. I read in the paper the other day that they are testing a vaccine, just in time for the millennium, which, if you accept the popular notion about zeros, begins in two months' time. Maybe I too should phone the journalists: I have found the cure for heartbreak. It is literature. But then I have not discovered anything that the son of Dr. Proust did not know a century ago.

Perhaps it is time for me, like the great man himself, to stop translating and begin a work of fiction. Perhaps the moment of my maturity is at hand. But first, I will publish my translations. They are not without interest. I will make inquiries of the appropriate journals and prepare a proper introduction. Here is my first draft.

Mme. Proust was born Jeanne-Clémence Weil on March 21, 1849, the daughter of a prosperous Paris stockbroker and a loving and cultivated mother who passed on to her an enthusiasm for the writers of the *grand siècle*, the seventeenth century, most especially for the letters of Mme. de Sévigné. Comfortably raised in a wealthy and well-established Jewish household, Jeanne was gentle, pretty, refined, a lover of music and painting who was well read in French and English literature. She was twenty-one when she married Adrien Proust, a Catholic and an ambitious young doctor who had risen well above his family's origins as shopkeepers in the small town of Illiers, near Chartres. He was thirty-six but already had won the Légion d'Honneur for his tireless work fighting infectious diseases. He was a lecturer in medicine at the Sorbonne and the principal proponent in Europe of the *cordon sanitaire*, a barricade of health officials at ports of entry that would stop the spread of cholera from the Orient.

The Prousts had two sons. Robert, the younger, known to his family as Dick, was a robust man who followed his father into medicine, specializing in the study of the female genitalia. He married in 1903 and had one daughter, Suzy, Mme. Proust's only grandchild, born the same day Dr. Proust died.

Robert's elder brother was Marcel, Mme. Proust's first-born, delivered in 1871 when Paris was under seige during the Franco-Prussian War. For her confinement, Mme. Proust escaped Paris to her uncle's house in suburban Auteuil, but the anxiety of the times led to a difficult delivery. Sickly at birth, Marcel remained so throughout his life, prone to crippling asthma attacks from the age of nine. He was a continual source of worry to his loving mother, who agonized over his every symptom, while his gruffer father, although sympathetic, accused her of spoiling him. Albeit very different in character, the outgoing Dr. Proust and his more retiring wife were always agreed that their son Marcel needed most of all to exercise willpower in regards to his health, his studies, his career, and his life.

Despite continual encouragement from his parents and some abortive attempts to study and practise law, Marcel never chose a conventional career and remained under his parents' roof until their death, always supported by family money. In his twenties, he was an exuberant socialite whose romantic looks and poetic speeches won him a place in Paris's most fashionable salons—a development that made his mother worry he was wasting time that would have been better spent preparing for a profession. By his thirties, his poor health and literary ambitions kept him increasingly indoors, writing at night and sleeping during the day, a schedule around which Mme. Proust organized her household.

Despite his bad health, odd hours, and the presence of his ever-anxious mother, Marcel took many lovers, all of them men. Youthful sexual relationships with the composer Reynaldo Hahn and Lucien Daudet, son of the writer Alphonse Daudet, gave way to unrequited crushes and passionate friendships with handsome young aristocrats like Antoine Bibesco, Bertrand Fénelon, the Marquis d'Albufera, and the Duc de Guiche, as well as paid encounters with waiters and chauffeurs. Neither Mme. Proust's diaries nor their copious correspondence, including holiday letters and everyday household notes, directly record whether or not she acknowledged Marcel's sexuality, but they do give firm evidence of a large understanding and deep love for her son.

Similarly, we can guess that she must have glimpsed his genius, but can say for certain only that she would never know the great success that would eventually crown his literary efforts. In the last years of her life, he was translating into French, with her help, works by the English art critic John Ruskin, having already published a handful of essays and abandoned a young attempt at an autobiographical novel. It was in 1913 that he published *Swann's Way*, the first volume of what had become, by the time of his death in 1922, the million-word masterpiece, *In Search of Lost Time*. His loving mother had left him long since: Jeanne Proust was ailing throughout 1904 and succumbed to kidney failure at the age of fifty-six in September 1905. It was then, closeted with her memory yet liberated from her presence, that Marcel Proust began to write.

I save the file, close it, and shut off the computer. I reach towards the printer, and from the stack of white paper sitting in its tray, I take a single sheet. I pluck a pen from the nearby jam jar, and in a small corner of the desktop not taken up by the machines, I bend my arm to the paper. Hesitant now, I begin to pen a phrase that has echoed in my head since my return from Paris.

"There will not be any more letters . . ."

I pause, wondering. What saviour is here? Is this kindness or cruelty? Who speaks? I write again.

Ruth Silver said the words softly as she took the mail from Sarah's hand: "There will not be any more letters."

Here then is my beginning.

ACKNOWLEDGEMENTS

OF COURSE, JEANNE PROUST and her son Marcel were real people. In imagining Mme. Proust's diary, I have drawn my inspiration from the actual events and personalities that filled their lives. Marcel did break his mother's Venetian glass in anger and had a misunderstanding with the English artist Marie Nordlinger. Still, literature makes different demands from those of scholarship. Not only have I invented conversations, arguments, holidays, meals, and weather conditions, I have also tinkered with chronology, repeated some tales that may be apocryphal, and embroidered fictional details into the factual. For example, not all Proust biographers would give credence to the story of his encounter with Oscar Wilde, which I, meanwhile, have moved from 1894 to 1892. And it is only literary speculation to suggest the young Marcel discussed memory with the great philosopher who married his cousin.

Readers who want true biography can turn to either of the standard English texts: George D. Painter's *Marcel Proust* (Chatto and Windus, 1959, 1965, 1989) and Ronald Hayman's *Proust: A Biography* (HarperCollins, 1990.) Also, Jean-Yves Tadié's exhaustive *Marcel Proust: A Life* is now available in English, translated by Euan Cameron (Penguin 2000.) The English translation of Proust's novel by C. K. Scott Moncrieff and Terence Kilmartin with further revisions by D. J. Enright is published by Random House/Chatto and Windus (1981, 1992) and now appears under the title *In Search of Lost Time*.

In her diary entry for June 6, 1905, Mme. Proust is reading from her son's actual introduction to his translation of *The Bible of Amiens*. The English translation of that introduction appears in *On Reading Ruskin: Prefaces to* La Bible d'Amiens *and* Sésame et les Lys *with Selections from the Notes to the Translated Texts* by Jean Autret, William Burford, and Phillip J. Wolfe and is quoted with permission from the Yale University Press.

~ 412 ~

The rest of this novel is pure fiction, and often makes free with historic and geographic fact. In describing the Marcel Proust archive in France's Bibliothèque Nationale, I have simplified the holdings and the cataloguing system, moved the microfilm out of the manuscript room, given the readers fictional white gloves, and turned perfectly helpful librarians into impediments. Meanwhile, there are no plans to move the manuscript collection to the new Bibliothèque François Mitterrand. The remains of the transit camp at Drancy, the Museum of Jewish Art and History in the Marais, and the church of Saint-Roch are largely as I describe them, although I have relocated the confessional booths of the latter just as I have moved the Rue de Musset more than a kilometre north of its actual location in the Sixteenth. The Proust family is buried in Père Lachaise but the old Jewish section is at the opposite end of the cemetery from those graves, while Henri Bergson is buried elsewhere.

In Canada, both Notre-Dame-des-Douleurs and the Don Hospital are fabrications, although the latter does share its location and its history as an isolation cottage with Toronto's Riverdale Hospital. The Workers' Benevolent Association is also an invention based on the sick-benefit societies that did exist in Toronto before the war. It was the real Jewish Immigrant Aid Society that helped the few who did make it to Canada, but Sarah Bensimon would indeed have been unusually lucky to reach Toronto: Canada accepted less than five thousand Jewish refugees between 1933 and 1945. Readers who want to know more about that sad historical reality can turn to *None is Too Many*, by Irving Abella and Harold Troper (Lester and Orpen Dennys, 1982).

Many individuals have helped me in the preparation of this novel by providing historical information or literary advice. Thanks to Katherine Ashenburg, Kateri Lanthier, and Mary Taylor for their thoughts on publishing; Sabrina Mathews reflected on bilingualism and remembered French nursery rhymes while Marie Boti described her job as a conference interpreter; Bill Seidelman and Edward Shorter spoke with me about medical education and research in Toronto; Anthony R. Pugh discussed Proust's manuscripts, and Raymond Corley, retired superintendent of vehicle development with the Toronto Transit Commission, explained to me how you build a subway. Thanks also to J. H. Taylor, Doreen Sears, and Henry Sears for many historical titbits, to the Toronto Public Libraries, where I did much of my research, and to the Toronto Arts Council, which provided me with a writer's grant.

I am specially grateful to Louis D. Levine who read sections of the manuscript with an eye on Jewish custom and Rena Isenberg who did not only that but also lent me her family wedding videos. My agent, Dean Cooke, provided crucial advice about the structure and pace of the novel and showed unwavering faith that it would find an audience. My ever-enthusiastic and always discerning editor, Martha Kanya-Forstner, believed in the characters and understood their stories, working tirelessly to ensure that their creator did not stand in their way. Always alert to error or inconsistency, copy editor Bernice Eisenstein ruled on questions of style in English, French, and Yiddish, while debating with me fiction's obligations to history.

Finally, I owe my largest debt to my first three readers, Andrew Taylor, Teresa Mazzitelli, and Joel Sears, whose criticism and encouragement have propelled me forward.

A NOTE ABOUT THE TYPES

Mme Proust and the Kosher Kitchen is set in two distinct yet complementary faces, each reflecting the timeframes and voices of the novel. The diaries of Madame Proust are set in a digitized form of *Fournier*, originally designed and cut in the mid-sixteenth century in Paris by Simon Pierre Fournier, one of Europe's most influential type artists. By the turn of the twentieth century, *Fournier*, along with its contemporary *Garamond*, were considered the pre-eminent serif faces for book text throughout France. The original matrices were re-cut by the Monotype Corporation in 1925.

Marie's voice, along with Sophie's story are set in *Mrs. Eaves*, a modern face designed by Zuzana Licko of the American digital type foundry Emigre. It draws its influences both from classic European types of the sixteenth century (including *Fournier*), and mid-twentieth century versions of the classic French text face *Baskerville*.

ABOUT THE AUTHOR

KATE TAYLOR is a Toronto writer and cultural journalist, born in France and raised in Ottawa. Since 1995, she has served as theatre critic at *The Globe and Mail*, winning two Nathan Cohen Awards for her reviews. She has also contributed to *Canadian Art*, *Applied Arts* and "The Arts Today" on CBC Radio. In 1989, she published *Painters*, a biography of Canadian artists written for children.